W9-BLE-282

DAYS OF RAGE

Kris Nelscott

St. Martin's Minotaur ✳ New York

www.minotaurbooks.com

Library of Congress Cataloging-in-Publication Data
Nelscott, Kris.
    Days of rage / Kris Nelscott.—1st St. Martin's Minotaur ed.
       p. cm.
    ISBN 0-312-32529-0
    EAN 978-0-312-32529-9
    1. Dalton, Smokey (Fictitious character)—Fiction.   2. Private investigators—
Illinois—Chicago—Fiction.   3. African American men—Crimes against—Fiction.
4. African American men—Fiction.   5. Chicago (Ill.)—Fiction.   I. Title.

PS3568.U7D39 2006
813'.6—dc22

                                                                2005054791

First Edition: March 2006

10   9   8   7   6   5   4   3   2   1

For Dean,

because he understands

ACKNOWLEDGMENTS

As always, these books come together due to a variety of people. My husband, Dean Wesley Smith, used his architectural training to draw the floor plans of the important buildings in this book, as well as helped me put a large amount of information into a coherent story. Steve Braunginn and Paul Higginbotham acted as my trusty first readers. Kelley Ragland has given me incredible advice and support on all of these books. Matt Bialer has taken them on with great enthusiasm, and Merrilee Heifetz continues to support them in all ways possible. Thanks, everyone. I appreciate all that you've done.

Revolution is no motherfucking game with us. The black
community has enough martyrs already.

—FRED HAMPTON, *October 1969*

ONE

I parked the police car in the trees, along the dirt access road. I shut off the headlights and let out a small breath.

My eyes took a moment to adjust to the darkness.

A few blocks away, I could hear the rumble and clangs from the Ford Motor Plant. The air smelled of rotten eggs and sewage, the stink so thick it made my eyes water.

My heart was pounding. I had to force myself to take deep, even breaths despite the smell. For five long minutes, I sat in the car, staring out the windows, checking the rearview, hoping no one followed me.

When it became clear that no one had, I got out, closing the door carefully so that it didn't slam. I could see my breath. My back ached, and blood still trickled down the side of my face. I swiped at it with my arm, staining the sleeve of my coat.

At least I had the presence of mind to bring my gloves.

I walked down the dirt road to the construction site. Spindly trees rose up around me, their leaves scattered on the road. The noise from the Ford Plant covered the crunch of my feet along the path.

Equipment sat along the edge of the canal, ghostly shapes against the darkness. I stopped short of the edge.

They had finished dredging this section last year when someone had deemed the canal deep enough.

The water glinted, black and filthy, its depth impossible to see.

Some lights from the nearby industrial plants reflected thinly on the water's surface, revealing a gasoline slick and bits of wadded up paper.

I let out a small breath, hating this moment, seeing no other choice.

Then I went back to the cop car. I pushed on the trunk, making sure the latch held. Then I opened the back passenger door, rolled down the window, and went to the front passenger door, doing the same. I saved the driver's window for last.

I crawled back inside the car just as the radio crackled, startling me. The thin voice coming across the static talked about a fight at the Kinetic Playground, which had nothing to do with me.

Still, my heart pounded harder.

I started the car. It rumbled to life, the powerful engine ready to go. I was shaking.

I kept the car in park, then I pushed the emergency brake. I reached across the seat and picked up my gloves and the blood-covered nightstick.

I released the emergency brake, got out of the car, and leaned inside the door. Carefully, I wedged the nightstick against the accelerator, making sure that thing flattened against the floor.

The car's engine revved, echoing in that grove of too-thin trees.

I braced my left hand on the car seat, grabbed the automatic gearshift, and shoved the car into drive. Then I leapt back, sprawling in the cold dirt as the car zoomed down the road.

The car disappeared over the bank, and I braced myself for a crash of metal against concrete—a crash that meant I had failed.

A half-second later, I heard a large splash. I ran to the edge of the road and stared down the embankment.

The car tipped, front end already lost to the canal. The brackish water flowed into the open windows, sinking it even faster.

The trunk went under last, disappearing in a riot of bubbles. I could almost imagine it popping open at the last moment, the bodies emerging, floating along the surface like the gasoline slick, revealing themselves much too soon.

But the bubbles eventually stopped, and the car vanished into the canal's depths.

I took off the bloody gloves and tossed them on top of the filthy water. No one would connect them to the car.

No one would ever know.

Except me.

TWO

Three months earlier, I parked my panel van about seventy blocks north of the Ford Plant.

The building I'd parked near dominated one of Chicago's oldest neighborhoods. Once the house had been one of the nicest in the area. Built in the Queen Anne style, the turrets remained, tall and imposing, but the rest of the house had succumbed to time and weather. The lot had been taken apart bit by bit, and now the old house was uncomfortably sandwiched between a six-flat on the right, and a U-shaped apartment complex on the left.

The street, which had once been large and wide, had narrowed too, until it became little more than an alley between rental properties, a place for tenants to drop their garbage, park their battered cars, and leave moving boxes to rot in the humid air.

Usually, standing in front of neglected buildings made me sad, but this one made me uneasy. It wasn't the shuttered windows or the cockeyed front door, and it certainly wasn't the overcrowding that greedy developers had forced on a once-peaceful neighborhood.

Something about the house itself seemed sinister.

I shook off the feeling and unlocked the front door. I had a wad of keys, most of them unlabeled. They came from the building's manager, who had also been the building's very last tenant. He had died alone in his apartment, found only two weeks ago by the mailman.

By then the manager had been dead more than a week.

Knowing that history probably led to my unease. I would be the first person to enter this place since the body had been removed.

I braced myself as I stepped inside the wide entry.

The heat was incredible. I was instantly covered with sweat. We were having a late September heatwave, which made every unair-conditioned building in the city hot. But this felt worse. It seemed like no one had turned off the building's heat last spring.

The smell, however, wasn't as bad as I had expected. Just a hint of rot, not bad enough to even make me sneeze.

I expected it to be worse on the other side of the building, where the manager's apartment was.

I shoved my clipboard under my arm, and wiped my forehead with the back of my hand. The entry was dark, probably because the conversion to apartments had walled off the wide windows in the front parlor and the library. I flicked on my flashlight, and ran it across the wall until I found the light switch beside the door. The switch was old—a punch switch put in when the building was electrified, somewhere near the turn of the century.

I was here in my capacity as an off-the-books building inspector for Sturdy Investments. I was off the books for a variety of reasons. The main one had to do with the corruption that flowed through Chicago like water. Sturdy had a long history of illegal business practices. Laura Hathaway, the company's new CEO and the daughter of its original owner, had decided to clean up all the problems she found.

She hired me because I was one of the few people she trusted. Laura and I had an on-again, off-again relationship that had been mostly off since I returned from a trip back east, but she knew that I was honest and would tell her exactly what I found.

So far, all I'd found was unbearable heat.

I pushed the top part of the button, hoping that the lights still worked and that the act of turning them on didn't start a short somewhere. I knew, because I had checked, that this building hadn't had an inspection or a repair call in more than a decade. I could only hope that the newly deceased manager had handled all of the repairs himself.

A dim bulb hidden in a dirt-encrusted chandelier added a little light to the front. It was barely enough to see by. To my left was a door with a large 1 painted across its wood frame. The only lock, so far as I could tell, was on the doorknob itself.

To my right, another door, this one marked with a large 2. And in front of me, the wide oak staircase that had once been the entry's most important feature.

I wiped my face again. I was losing most of my weight in sweat. My first mission was to shut off the heat. Then I could turn my attention to the apartments themselves.

After a little more inspection, I realized there was no easy way to get from the front entry to the back of the building where the heating system had to be. I let myself out, pulling the front door closed behind me, but not bothering to lock it. Any determined burglar could push his way inside the building. The door, which was obviously original, was in such a rotten state of repair that it barely clung to its hinges.

I paused on the top of the stairs, took my clipboard, and made a note about the door in the appropriate place on the form Laura and I had developed. Then I went around the side of the building.

I'd already examined the foundation, and taken the necessary measurements. I had hope. The foundation looked sturdy enough for a seventy-year-old, neglected house. There were few cracks and only a little water damage.

The water damage might be a problem, since the tiny basement windows lining the building's sides and back had, for the most part, been bricked closed. But that was a problem I'd worry about once I got inside.

The back faced yet another set of apartments, which were about twenty years old. Sturdy owned most of this neighborhood and had converted it to student housing for the nearby University of Chicago.

It was a smart move: students didn't care what kind of apartment they lived in so long as it was cheap and provided a place to sleep, eat, and study. The turnover was great, and the need for apartments was even greater. Sturdy, in the bad old days, was one of Chicago's largest slumlords, and student housing was one of the easiest areas in rentals to ignore repairs.

The manager's apartment was on the first floor in the back. That was how the mailman managed to see inside just enough to get worried. I expected the back door to open directly into the apartment, but it didn't. The door, which wasn't even locked, opened into what had once been a mudroom. The entrance to the apartment was to my right, and a door, closed and locked, was to my left.

Like I expected, the rot smell was stronger here. I shuddered and wiped at my nose this time, even though I knew that wouldn't make the smell of death go away. I propped the back door open, hoping for a breeze, something—anything—that would make both the heat and the stench go away.

The door to my left had to be the door to the basement. I grabbed the bundle of keys and started working through them one by one, trying to find a key that fit into the deadbolt on the unmarked door. That door was the only one that I had seen so far with a deadbolt, which helped me a little in looking for the correct key. There had to be a hundred different keys on a variety of interlocking rings, many of the keys so old that they looked like they hadn't been used in decades.

Obviously, the manager had been the kind of man who kept everything. I wondered what his apartment looked like, and realized I would find out soon enough.

Halfway through the ring, I finally found the key that opened the deadbolt. Then I tried the knob. It was also locked, but it didn't latch tightly enough to provide any protection. I pushed the door open.

It creaked, the sound loud in the house's silence. I switched on the flashlight. Its wide beam revealed dust and cobwebs and old wooden stairs that disappeared into the darkness.

I sighed. This was one of those times that I wished I was working in a team. If the stairs collapsed under my weight, no one would find me for hours. I was supposed to pick up my son, Jimmy, from his after-school program around five. No one would notice I was missing until then.

I propped the basement door open, and tested the top step with my right foot. The step seemed sturdier than I expected. They had been re-inforced against the wall. I looked between the steps and saw that someone had added extra wood underneath so that the steps could hold more weight.

On the second step, I turned and set my clipboard near the door. I'd make my notes from memory. I wanted both hands free as I descended into that darkness.

I hadn't seen any light switch near the top of the stairs, so the flashlight had to serve. Still, I braced the side of my left hand, the hand in which I held the light, on the rough concrete that formed the narrow tunnel that housed the stairs. Even if the stairs fell out from underneath me, I could hold myself in place with the railing and the wall.

That worked until the wall stopped halfway down. By then, I had a sense of the basement. It was narrow and musty. It smelled of damp, old clothes, and that persistent odor of rot.

When I reached the bottom of the steps, something brushed against my hair. I cringed, thinking more cobwebs, then looked up. It was the dangling cord attached to a bare light bulb. I pulled, having no faith that the bulb still worked.

But it did. This bulb was stronger than the one in the main entry. The light reached all parts of this side of the basement room. Ahead of me, wooden storage units had been built against the wall. Each unit had a number painted on it, one which presumably matched an apartment number above. The units were closed, and some of them had very old padlocks attached to them. The latches were rusted and covered with dirt. No one had touched this area in years.

The basement should have extended to my left, but it didn't. Someone had built a wall across that area. The wall looked old, but well made, clearly dating from the days when this building had been a single-family home.

I'd found a few large liquor-storage units in previous buildings in this part of town. Chicago's reputation as the center of sin during Prohibition was well deserved. In one old building, I'd even discovered some unopened bottles. They had disappeared into Laura's custody. She promised to destroy them, saying that a lot of the old homemade liquor from that period was deadly.

Behind the stairs, I encountered another wall, and a door that had been padlocked shut. Someone had scrawled *Boiler* with a pen along what had once been white paint, but which had turned yellow-gray with time.

I wasn't surprised to find the lock. Most public basements in apartment buildings locked off the furnace and the water heater so that tenants couldn't adjust them to their own particular needs. Sometimes that meant—at least in the case of Sturdy's bad old days—that the heat wouldn't come on until someone complained to the rental agency or the police, but often it was just a precaution to keep the temperature in the building uniform.

The bulb's light didn't reach here. I had to hold the flashlight while I searched for the right key. Fortunately, it didn't take too long. I undid

7

the padlock, found the key to the knob, and let myself in the boiler room.

A wave of steam heat nearly pushed me backwards. I stopped, caught my breath, and went inside. This room was neat and clean, clearly used a lot. To my left, a small metal shelf held a variety of tools. The boiler itself was ahead of me, a large metal thing that looked like it could play the villain in a horror movie.

It only took a minute to find the overhead bulb in this room. That bulb was relatively new, and so was the cord. I clicked it on, and clicked the flashlight off.

The boiler was pretty standard. I found the wrench that allowed me to switch the entire system off. Since no one lived in the building, the heat could remain off until the first serious freeze.

I set the wrench back onto its shelf and sighed. The boiler clanked as the water settled in the pipes. The building would talk to me for the rest of the day as the heat dissipated, the water cooled, and the radiators gradually shut down.

This room would be easy to inspect. I had to check the connections on the boiler, but I was no professional on that level. This thing was old enough that I'd have Laura bring in a repairman to flush the system, and then see if it was working properly.

There was nothing behind the boiler except open space, and the only other item in the room was a large metal cabinet on that mysterious wall. The cabinet was padlocked closed.

This padlock was tiny, so the key had to be as well. That made my search through the rings an easy one. I unlocked the lock, removed it, and pulled the double metal doors open.

They squealed as they moved. They'd been closed a long time. A cloud of dust came toward me, and I sneezed. Then I wiped my face for a third time in the past half hour, and frowned.

There were no shelves in the cabinet. In fact, there was nothing in the cabinet at all—no supplies, no treasures, no records. The cabinet had been placed against the wall to cover a door that looked as old as the wall itself.

My heart started to pound. When I'd found the booze storage in one of the other apartment buildings, the door had been hidden as well. I tried this door's knob. The knob turned, but the door didn't open. It had a lock beneath the knob, an old-fashioned lock that took an old-fashioned skeleton key.

There was only one such key on the entire ring.

I inserted it, and it turned easily, as if the door had been opened just the day before. The door pushed inward. The damp musty smell that seemed like this building's signature eased out of the back.

I sneezed again, then flicked the flashlight back on and looked.

Ahead of me, I saw a small open area, surrounded by more brick. I frowned. I had expected brick all along the far walls so that no one could see inside the windows, but I hadn't expected a tiny room. Instead, I had thought I'd find a wide-open space filled with old boxes, broken furniture, or nothing at all.

I stepped inside. Piles of brick and mortar filled the room to my left. Tools were scattered along the concrete floor. The expected brick covered the far wall, hiding the window. But that brick wasn't the same color or shape as the brick wall in front of me.

That wall seemed to have been built later than the far wall. As the flashlight played along the newer wall, I noticed that it was uneven. Some of the work seemed professional, but some of it was slapdash, as if the person who put the bricks on the mortar had never done that before.

That wall ran the width of the building, with no visible door. That didn't make any sense to me. Or maybe it did, judging by the knot that was growing in my stomach.

To my right there was an alcove, with more brick in the back, where the window probably was. That brick wall formed a U that ended against the wall I had just come through.

I let the flashlight play on the ceiling, looking for one more light bulb, and finding it. Only this one had burned out and the cord looked frayed enough that I didn't want to take one of the bulbs from the janitor's shelves and replace it.

Instead, I relied on my flashlight. I turned it into the alcove, noting that the brick was uneven here too. Then there was the section to my right. It was part of the uniform wall, but it had been bumped over the years. Mortar was crumbling out of it and falling onto the concrete floor. Near the bottom, some of the bricks had fallen inward.

I crouched and played the light inside. The space was open, more or less, like a little cubby hole. I eased the light along the crumbled dust, until it caught something yellowed.

Bone.

Long bones, like those found in the human leg.

I stumbled backwards so fast that I nearly fell against the bags of mortar.

My heart was racing.

I'd been thinking of horror movies, that was all. I was in a dank, smelly basement with unexpected walls, and I was making things up.

I had probably seen a dead rat or a pile of trapped mice. Maybe an old pipe, covered with dust.

I made myself swallow, then took several deep breaths, hoping to slow down my heart rate and make the shock die away. I'd been on edge a lot lately, and it was simply showing because I was alone in a creepy house where a man had died just two weeks ago, alone and neglected.

After a few minutes, I felt calmer. I went back and played the light slowly.

The bricks, the crumbled mortar, the long yellow thing (like a bone or a pipe), and then next to it, a curved shape—a pelvis?—and an unmistakable skeletal hand. A rib cage leaned against the wall, and a spinal column that led all the way up to a recognizable human skull.

I started to pull out more bricks, then stopped myself. I had to leave this as intact as possible, at least until I figured out exactly what I was going to do.

Still, I crouched even lower and ran the light over every visible inch of that space. I saw a lot more bone crammed next to that first body, and saw at least two more skulls.

Three bodies.

What had I stumbled into?

I shuddered, afraid I already knew the answer.

THREE

I made myself leave the Queen Anne slowly, careful to turn off lights, close doors, and replace all the locks. I didn't want anyone else stumbling onto my discovery, not before I talked to Laura.

I had parked my van in front of the house, and as I walked around the building, I brushed cobwebs, dust, and dirt from my clothes. Halfway down the narrow chasm between the house and the six-flat, I realized I had left my clipboard inside near the top of the stairs.

I decided not to go back for it.

The van was old and had a lot of miles on it. I'd been planning to trade it in on something else before winter came, but I hadn't yet, and for the first time in a long time, I was relieved to see it. It looked so normal on that tree-lined street, familiar rust along the bottom of the frame, the windows half open against the early autumn heat.

Inside, papers from previous inspections were scattered along the bench seat, and even that mess looked welcome. I opened the driver's door, and climbed in, making myself breathe.

Bodies, hidden. At least three, in the basement long enough to decay, to become remains.

I had no idea how Laura was going to take this. Her father had left a life of petty theft in Atlanta shortly after she was born. He had brought her and her mother to Chicago, where he made a career of classier crime, using the corrupt building trade to make himself one of the richest men in the city.

He had sheltered Laura from his business dealings, sending her into the heart of Chicago's upper class. She had been a staple of the society pages, especially after her marriage to the younger son of one of Chicago's big department-store families. Her divorce had taken away some of her luster; by then her father was dead, and her mother was dying.

It wasn't until Laura met me in Memphis that she learned about her father's criminal past. Laura claimed she had come to terms with her father's illegal activities, but I knew she hadn't. She was now spending her life repaying all the debts he had accumulated, trying to reverse the damage he had done, one mistake at a time.

I had no idea what she would think of this, but I knew she would harbor the same fear that I had—that somehow her father was connected to those bodies in the basement.

I sighed, started the van, and made myself drive slowly to my neighborhood, which was south of Hyde Park, not too far away from the Queen Anne. Yet it seemed to belong to a different city altogether. I lived in the South Side proper, the part of Chicago that Mayor Daley referred to as the ghetto—or, when he was feeling charitable, the slums.

He, like so many other whites here, ignored the fact that Chicago had a thriving black community, one that had been here for as long as that horrible Queen Anne house. Daley used that community when he needed it for re-election, or political propaganda, but otherwise he considered us an urban blight to be eradicated, and he'd been doing a pretty good job—putting the Dan Ryan Expressway between us and his Bridgeport neighborhood, building housing "projects" where homes used to be, and refusing to spend federal monies to clean up the streets and the parks nearest to us.

Still, we managed to have a solid community here, and it was the one I had come back to during the summer after an abortive attempt to find a new home in another town. Jimmy and I had a nice apartment in a building full of nice apartments. We had good friends and people that we considered to be family not too far from us. Jimmy went to church every Sunday, staying in touch with that community, and he reveled in his after-school study program, which taught him the things the Chicago Public School system was supposed to teach but didn't.

In the middle of the day, my street was pretty deserted. The sun beat down here, turning the grass a shade of brown and baking the ground hard. I had to be careful where I parked—street gangs repeatedly knocked out the street lights, and the residents of the street promptly replaced them instead of waiting for the city crews that would never come.

I parked in front of the building. It was a turn-of-the-century apartment building, made of white brick. The tenants in this building kept it up, unlike some of the neighboring six-flats. This entire neighborhood had been built as rental housing way back when, and most of the places hadn't been fixed up since.

After some of the apartments I'd seen in New York last July, I was happy to be here, in a three-bedroom that I could afford, with neighbors I could trust.

I went inside, and hurried up the worn wood steps to my apartment. The breakfast dishes still sat in the sink—it had been my turn to do them, but Jim and I had been running late, so I'd left them—and as a result the entire place smelled of spoiled milk.

The apartment's main room had a half-kitchen, a small dining area, and a living-room section. We had separated them with the couch we had inherited from the Grimshaw family, who had had the apartment before us.

I leaned on the couch, picked up the phone, and dialed Laura's office number from memory. Her secretary picked up and told me that Miss Hathaway was in a meeting and couldn't be disturbed.

"Tell her to call me as soon as she gets out," I said. "Tell her it's important."

When I hung up, I realized that I couldn't tell her what I had found over the phone. I debated calling back and asking for a meeting of my own, then changed my mind.

Sturdy Investments had offices in the Loop. I wasn't about to go up there right now. It had become one of the craziest parts of the city. For the past two days, white Chicago construction workers were staging demonstrations, protesting a federal plan to allow black construction workers into the labor unions. I'd been in riots that started over racial issues; this felt like it could be another.

And that wasn't all. The Loop also had become host to the entire national press corps. The Trial of the Century, as they were calling it, had begun on Wednesday—eight people had been charged with conspiracy under a new federal statute. The government claimed that the eight had come to Chicago in the summer of 1968 with the intent to incite a riot.

The defendants, all famous and none of them from Chicago, represented such diverse groups as the Yippies, the Students for a Democratic Society and the Black Panthers. Those groups were out in full force as well, holding rallies all over the city, protesting the unfairness of the charges, and the violence of the Chicago police.

I had vowed to stay out of the Loop until this media circus was over, but I wasn't sure I could manage it. The current estimates were that the trial would last for several months.

I could at least stay away until the construction workers stopped looking for blacks to beat up.

Laura wouldn't call back for a while, so I stripped out of my filth-covered work clothes and took a shower. Even though I'd only been in that house an hour or so, I was covered in dirt. It swirled down the drain and disappeared, making me shudder as I watched it go.

I'd gone through a lot of buildings for Sturdy, but none of them left me feeling as grimy as this one did.

By the time I got out of the shower, I still hadn't heard the phone ring. I called Laura's secretary back and asked Laura to come to dinner around six, stressing that our meeting was important.

Laura knew I wanted to see her, maybe rekindle the relationship that I had torn apart in the summer. If she didn't come for me, maybe she would come for Jimmy, whom she loved.

The secretary took my message. I did the dishes, straightened the apartment, and got it ready for company. Jimmy would be happy when he learned that Laura was coming over.

A few minutes later, the phone rang. Laura said, without preamble, "Smokey, I can't come tonight. I'm swamped. We have investigators here from the Model Cities program, and this whole construction worker thing is causing some problems within our ranks. The whole city's up in arms."

"I know," I said. "That's why I don't want to come down there."

"Can you just tell me? I'm sure we can find some kind of solution to whatever you've got for me without some kind of meeting."

So different from how she'd been just six months ago. Then she, like me, looked for any excuse to get together.

"No," I said. "I need to see you. You'll understand why once I tell you what's going on."

She sighed theatrically. "It can't be tonight. I'm supposed to take these bureaucrats to dinner and drinks and you know how it is."

I didn't, really. My jobs had never included wining and dining anyone. But hers did. It was just one of the many ways in which our lives differed.

"How about tomorrow, then?" I asked. "I'll make us lunch."

"Why don't I meet you somewhere?" she asked. "Maybe—"

"Laura, we're not talking about any of this at a restaurant. You need to come here."

Something in my voice must have finally gotten through to her.

"This is serious," she said.

"Yes," I said.

"Life-and-death serious?"

"I don't know," I said. "Maybe. Possibly."

"You're not leaving again, are you?" she asked.

"Laura," I said, trying to keep the aggravation from my voice. "This is about work I'm doing for you."

"All right then." She sounded so businesslike. "How does one o'clock sound?"

Like the heat of the day. But I'd make it work.

"Perfect," I said, and hung up before she could change her mind.

I wiped my hands on my pants and leaned against the back of my couch. I was as nervous as a boy, and not just because of those skeletons in the basement of that Queen Anne.

I wanted to patch things up with Laura, and I wasn't sure I knew how.

FOUR

Saturday dawned clear and warm, with just enough of a lake breeze to keep the heat from becoming unbearable. Jimmy slept in, which surprised me. He'd been thrilled to learn that Laura was coming for lunch, and in the past that would have gotten him out of bed before sunrise, cleaning and planning and bursting with excitement.

But he was moving into adolescence. When I got up at nine, he was sprawled across his bed, lying on the covers, his toes brushing against the floor. He was beginning to look more and more like the brother who had abandoned him, lanky and thin, and I was going to have a heck of a time keeping him in clothes.

I'd made potato salad the night before, and after I mixed up a green salad, there wasn't a lot more for me to do until Laura arrived. I went into the backyard, moved the picnic table under the complex's one shade tree—not that it would do much good at midday—and staked our claim with a tattered plastic tablecloth held in place with Jimmy's battered American history textbook.

I woke Jimmy and then I paced, trying to figure out what the next steps were.

If this were a normal investment company in a normal city, I would have already called in the authorities and let them handle the investigation. But Sturdy's shady past and Laura's precarious hold on the company's future didn't allow me to follow the rules.

There was a good chance that the people who had put those bodies in the basement were still alive; there was an even better chance that some of them still worked at Sturdy.

If Laura's father was connected to these deaths in any way, a lot of Chicagoans would believe that Laura knew about the deaths as well. The press would have a field day with it. They already felt that a woman heading one of the city's major corporations was wrong; this would only compound the matter.

And then there were the police. The Chicago Police Department was one of the most corrupt in the nation, and in the past, Sturdy had bought its share of policemen. Laura had stopped a lot of those payments. If this came out, the police wouldn't hesitate in arresting her in a very public manner. Or they might give her another choice: resume the bribes and any potential charges would simply disappear.

Laura wouldn't like either option. I was worried about all of this, and uncertain about how to present it to her, even though I knew she would understand the implications once I told her what I'd found.

I also didn't want Jimmy to know that anything was wrong.

I already had the grill going by the time Laura arrived. Jimmy'd been nurturing the bratwurst I'd splurged on, soaking it in beer and butter—something he'd devised after eating Althea Grimshaw's hamburgers that way.

The afternoon already felt a little surreal to me: it had been a long time since Laura had come to my apartment for a meal. One of the last times had been just before I left for the East Coast. I'd grilled hamburgers and told her that we were leaving to work on an out-of-state case. She'd figured out, almost immediately, that in addition to the case, I was looking for somewhere new to live.

The coals looked just about perfect when I heard a car door slam. A few minutes later, Jimmy came around back, holding the bowl with the bratwurst in it. Laura followed closely behind him.

She wore a pair of cut-off blue jeans, a white blouse covered with applique flowers, and flip-flops. She had pulled her blond hair away from her face, and she wasn't wearing any makeup. She had a light tan, which the white of her blouse accented.

She looked beautiful.

I set my tongs on the TV tray I'd set out beside the grill, and walked over to greet her. She smiled when she saw me, but her expression was cool.

"Smokey," she said.

"It's good to see you," I said. "I've missed you."

"Really?"

Jimmy looked back and forth between us. When she dismissed my comment, he rolled his eyes, then shook his head. He was siding with Laura—he had all summer—and he said I had to do something "really spectacular" to make things up to her.

I wasn't sure anything would make things up to her, and I wasn't sure how much I wanted to try. My trip to the East Coast had been the right decision for Jimmy and me, even if it hadn't worked out.

I took the bowl of brats from Jimmy and carried it to the grill. "One or two?" I asked Laura.

"Two," she said with a smile. "You know I can't resist those things."

I put six brats on the grill. They sizzled as the wet meat touched the metal. Smoke rose. From this moment on, cooking became an art form, and I was wedded to the grill until the brats were done.

I sent Jimmy back upstairs for the plates, buns, silverware, and potato salad. Laura offered to help, but Jimmy turned her down. He was trying to give us time alone, thinking this lunch was about our relationship, not about business.

I would let him continue to think that. I really didn't want him to hear about my discovery.

"What had to be discussed in person?" Laura stood next to me, out of the smoke, watching me turn the brats.

"The last house you assigned me," I said. "The one near Jackson Park where the manager died."

Jimmy marched toward us, plates in hand. He held the package of buns as well, and set them all on the TV tray beside me. Then, without asking, he took the bowl which had held the brats and took it back upstairs.

"He's becoming quite responsible," Laura said.

"When he wants to be." I turned the brats again. They were turning brown. They had grill lines on their plump sides.

"What about the house?" she asked.

I looked at her. She was still staring at the grill as if it provided all the answers.

I sighed. There was no easy way to tell her this.

"I found three bodies in the basement," I said.

18

"Jesus!" She jumped backwards, as if I had put the bodies there. "Did you call the police?"

"Not until I talked to you."

Jimmy came back around the building, hugging catsup, mayonnaise, mustard, and relish to his chest. He set those items on the picnic table, which was several yards from us.

"Does Jim know?" Laura asked quietly.

I shook my head.

"Bodies," she whispered.

Jimmy came over to us. He looked from me to Laura, sensing something wrong, and blaming me for it.

"Smoke tell you that we're staying?" he asked Laura.

She blinked at Jimmy, then frowned. Obviously the change of subject confused her. "Staying?"

"In Chicago," Jimmy said. "He says we got a community here. We got to stay for it. It'll help me grow up."

Laura, bless her, made the transition. She smiled at Jim as if nothing was wrong. "Smokey says that, does he?"

Jimmy smiled back at her, as if they shared a secret. "I know, I told him before we went that we got friends here, but sometimes Smoke's got to see stuff for himself."

Laura nodded, then looked at me sideways. "He hadn't told me that."

"Figures." Jimmy grabbed the bag of buns, opened it, and pulled one out. Then he carefully split the bun and set it on a plate.

"You forgot the potato salad," I said. "And the green salad."

"Yuck," Jimmy said, and set his plate on top of the pile. He headed back toward the apartment.

"You've got quite a defender," Laura said.

"Actually, you do," I said. "He's been calling me stupid and dumb and a real jerk ever since last summer."

Laura was silent for a moment. "You were just protecting him."

I couldn't tell if she believed that or if she was just parroting my own words back to me. "I didn't do a very good job of it. There's no place safe, at least for him and me."

She put a hand on my arm, startling me. I looked down at her. Her gaze met mine for the first time since she arrived.

"You do better than most," she said.

Yeah. With my dangerous job that the entire community I'd come back to wanted me to quit, and my devil's bargain with the local gangs, and my struggle to stay away from law enforcement. Jim and I were a unit, but my side of it was iffy at best.

Laura walked to the TV tray, spread the plates out on it, and then took the rest of the buns from the package. She split them, just like Jimmy had been doing.

"How long have they been dead?" she asked.

Now it was my turn to feel confused. Then I realized she had gone back to the original conversation, the one about the bodies.

"I have no idea," I said. "They're skeletons, Laura. And that's not the worst of it—"

"We don't got nothing but Thousand Island," Jimmy announced as he came around the building. He carried the covered bowls of potato salad and regular salad. A nearly empty bottle of Thousand Island dressing rested precariously on top of the pile.

"I almost forgot," Laura said. "I brought root beer."

She headed around the building as Jimmy placed the last items on the table. One of my neighbors peered out her back window, saw me, and waved. I waved back.

"She forgive you?" Jimmy grabbed the grilling fork and poked at the brats.

I took the fork from him. "It's not that simple."

"Yeah, you always say that." He picked up a plate. "These look done."

They were. I stabbed two and put them on Jim's plate. Laura brought a jug of A&W Root Beer, ice cold from one of the nearby restaurants, and set it on the table. Jim exclaimed his pleasure, and if she hadn't already had his heart, she would have captured it right there.

I served up the remaining brats, then I put the lid halfway on the grill, hoping that none of the neighborhood kids would come and play near here while the thing cooled off. Jimmy came over and got his plate. I carried mine to the table, which sat in the middle of a pool of sunshine. Laura had already found the tiny sliver of shade.

She gave me a glance, and I understood it. We agreed, with just one look, to pretend we were having a normal picnic. Neither of us wanted to discuss bodies in front of Jim. When the meal was over I'd ask him to leave, and then I'd talk to Laura.

For the most part, she and Jimmy carried the conversation. They talked about his schooling, particularly the after-school program. Laura had helped me and Franklin Grimshaw find another teacher for the after-school program after Grace Kirkland decided she needed the year off. Jimmy didn't like his new teacher—she wasn't Mrs. Kirkland, he'd say, as if that explained it—but he had a newfound seriousness, one that he'd acquired over the summer, when he walked through the gates at Yale.

I listened and ate my two brats smothered in relish. Jimmy kept looking at me as if he expected me to jump into the conversation at any point, but I didn't. He and Laura didn't get enough time together; I wasn't going to get in the way.

Finally, Jimmy finished his brats, most of his potato salad, and enough of the green salad to impress me. He wiped his mouth with a paper napkin, then said, "Should I clean up?"

I raised my eyebrows. He never volunteered for kitchen duty. "Laura's not finished yet. And didn't you want some dessert?"

He looked tempted for a moment, even though he knew we only had store-bought cookies. Then he shook his head. "I'm gonna go. Is that okay?"

I had to work at suppressing my smile. He really did want me and Laura to talk.

"Yeah," I said. "I'll clean up."

"Thanks." He slipped away from the table so fast that it almost seemed like something was chasing him.

"Be back by five," I called after him. He waved a hand to show that he'd heard me and understood, then he disappeared around the front of the apartment building.

"He's not very subtle," Laura said, scraping the remaining potato salad onto her fork.

"But he means well." I smiled at her. She smiled back. For a moment, we had a connection.

Then she looked away. The mood changed, from the lighthearted, almost family-like conversation, back to something ugly.

"So," she said with a sigh, "tell me about these bodies."

I did. I told her how I found them, and the fact that the entire basement looked built-up. I suspected there were more than three skeletons down there.

"Bricked into the wall?" she asked, her voice low. Even though we were the only people in the apartment building's backyard, we were being careful. We didn't want anyone to overhear through an open window.

"The work down there is shoddy," I said. "And it differs from section to section."

"You saw all that in one glance?"

"It's hard to miss," I said. "Then there's the remaining bricks and mortar. Someone planned to continue the work."

"But they stopped."

I nodded. "I don't know if they stopped because they sold the building, or because they died, or because they moved out."

Laura pushed her plate away. The last part of her second brat would go forever unfinished. She did take her glass of root beer and cup it between her hands.

"You said that manager had a key to this room." She rubbed the sides of the glass so that it moved back and forth.

"Yeah, but I don't know if he got the key as part of a key ring that opened everything in the building or if he was in charge down there. I didn't have enough time to investigate that."

She stopped moving her glass. She took a final sip, then set it aside too. "What're you afraid of, Smokey?"

"Your father," I said softly.

She leaned her head back. "You think he was behind this?"

"I don't know, but he owned the building."

"He's been dead almost ten years. There's no proof—"

"These three bodies have been down there for a long time," I said. "I'm no expert. I don't know if it takes five years or ten years for a body to completely decay, particularly in a bricked-off part of an old basement. But I think there's a good chance that those bodies were placed there before your father died."

She bit her lower lip, clearly thinking. "If my dad knew about it—"

I thought it was interesting that she didn't think he was involved, just that he knew. My understanding of the old man was that he had an incredible ruthless streak. We had no proof of murder yet in the things he'd done, but I wouldn't put it past him.

"—then his partners knew about it too."

His partners. The men Laura had bested in her takeover of the company. They had hated her, underestimated her, and fought her all the way. She had fired them, but she hadn't fired all their minions.

Too many layoffs in the beginning of her tenure as CEO would have scared the shareholders.

"If the old partners do know and get wind of this," I said, "then they'll fight to protect themselves. They'll fight dirty. They'll blame you. Even if it comes out that you had no ties to those bodies, the damage will have been done."

A crease had formed on her forehead. She was thinking hard, going through the same implications that had disturbed me since the day before.

I continued, "You might lose your position, and all the good that you're doing with it. Or worse."

"Worse?" she asked.

"People who commit murder aren't afraid to commit another to cover the first."

She let out a small breath. "You think we're in that kind of danger?"

"I have no idea," I said. "I'm just looking at worst case. Best case, these bodies came from some Prohibition murder, and we call the police to deal with them."

"But you don't think so," she said.

"I have no idea," I said. "I really don't. Not yet."

"What about the manager?" she asked. "Could he have placed the bodies there?"

I wiped the sweat from my forehead. Even in the shade, it was too hot for me.

"It's possible," I said. "But we can't turn the investigation over to the police until we have some idea what we're dealing with. Does anyone know that I was at the building?"

I had always worked directly for Laura, not for Sturdy and not with anyone else's approval. She wasn't supposed to tell anyone in the company what buildings I was inspecting, but we hadn't confirmed that in a long time.

She shook her head. "I didn't tell anyone you were going there. I didn't even mention that someone was going to inspect it."

"Good," I said. "We're going to have to keep this between the two of us, at least for the time being."

She looked at me, her blue eyes troubled. "What're you going to do? See the extent of what we have?"

"I'm not qualified for that," I said. "If we mess with it too much and then turn it over to the police, we're tampering with evidence in a possible murder investigation."

"I thought we weren't going to the police," she said.

"Not yet," I said. "We have to find some things out first."

She frowned, not quite with me.

"You're going to have to go into the company records, find out when your father bought the place, whether he spent any time there—"

"That'll be in the file?" she asked.

"I don't know," I said.

"Can't you get the land history at the courthouse?" she asked.

"The less I'm involved at this stage, the better," I said. "We don't want anyone to know that we're looking into this. If someone still connected with Sturdy does know about this, then they might do something if they think we've found the bodies."

She nodded.

"So find out how long this building has been owned by Sturdy. For all we know, the company might have bought it in 1965, which takes your father off the hook."

"But not the company itself," she said.

"We don't know that," I said. "You're new management. If the building is a recent acquisition, then you can report what you find without tainting. If your father was involved, that's different. That'll taint you automatically. Everyone'll assume you knew because you're his daughter."

She rubbed her eyes with her thumb and forefinger. She looked tired. "Sometimes I wish I could go back to the days when I thought he was just a rich, reclusive man."

I understood that. I'd learned a lot of things over the years that I wished I hadn't.

She nodded. "What else should I look for in those files?"

"How long the manager lived there," I said.

"Anything else?" she asked.

"Look to see who owned the place during Prohibition," I said. "We've found enough old stills and liquor-storage places to make this less unusual than I would like."

"God," she said, shuddering. "You think this is a planned burial site."

"I know it is," I said. "I just don't know the extent. And if it's planned, then it's got to be tied to some kind of criminal activity."

"Or one crazy guy," she said, obviously thinking of the manager.

"Or one crazy guy," I agreed. Only I wasn't sure the manager was our suspect. I had already voiced my doubts about Laura's father. If I had to place money on who put the bodies in that basement, I'd bet on him.

"If I order up the files," she said, "everyone's going to know what I'm doing. I'm going to have to do this work on my own."

"And leave no fingerprints," I said. "Don't move anything in the files, don't even take the files out of their storage area. Try not to disturb anything near them."

"What if I find something unusual?"

"Like what?" I asked.

She shrugged. "I don't know. Something implicating someone."

"We'll worry about it if you find it," I said. "I just want to know what the possibilities are."

She studied her hands for a long moment. "What are we going to do if this predates my father's death?"

"I don't know," I said. "But while you're looking up the building's background, I'll try to figure something out."

FIVE

I had made it sound like I knew what to do next, but I really didn't. I hoped that Laura would find that the previous management team had bought the building a few years ago, and we wouldn't have to consider her father as a suspect at all. More than anything, I wanted to leave those bodies in the hands of the police.

But I had a hunch that wouldn't happen. So I spent the next few days getting my other cases in order.

I worked for a number of different organizations, doing investigations, most of them routine. I charged less than the leading black detective agency, but I also made it clear to my clients that they would get less too.

I wasn't licensed—I didn't want any arm of local government to investigate me, even with my excellent fake identification. My real name is Smokey Dalton, but everyone in Chicago, with the exceptions of Laura, Franklin and Althea Grimshaw, and Jimmy, thought I was Bill Grimshaw, Franklin's cousin. I'd been using that identity for more than a year now. Jimmy was registered in school as James Grimshaw, and he had adopted that name as his own. I think sometimes he forgot that his real last name was Bailey, which was fine with me.

Most of my cases dealt with insurance fraud, or building inspections, or petty theft. Occasionally I took on individual cases as well, although I didn't have one at the moment. I was grateful for that.

It meant I could concentrate on the Queen Anne if I had to.

In the meantime, I wrote reports, mailed invoices, and closed every pending case that I had. If this case for Laura came to nothing, I would have to scramble for work in October, but that was all right.

My financial situation was a lot less precarious than it had been the year before, when Jimmy and I fled Memphis for Chicago. I had a savings account in Memphis, one that my friend Henry Davis put money from the rental of my house into, but I hoped to use that as Jimmy's college fund. With Jim's recent talk of Yale, I was beginning to think I would need that fund more than ever.

By late Tuesday, I still hadn't heard from Laura. I knew she'd been busy with the construction demonstrations and the Model Cities representatives. I had a hunch she hadn't found a private moment to visit Sturdy's files.

I didn't want to call her, though. I didn't want to draw any more attention to this than I had to.

I also wanted to continue avoiding the Loop. If anything, the city had gotten crazier in the last few days. Even though Mayor Daley ordered an end to the construction demonstrations—he brokered a meeting over the weekend between the white construction workers' union and the black coalition members—the Conspiracy Trial kept the Loop too active for me.

Laura's call finally came early Wednesday morning. We decided to meet at a student hangout we liked near the University of Chicago. She was curt and businesslike, and I couldn't shake the underlying feeling that she was upset.

The hangout was on Fifty-seventh, near some bookstores and funky student shops. The food wasn't stellar, but the ever-changing mix of students and professors that went through the restaurant guaranteed that no one would notice me or Laura.

It was the perfect place for a quiet conversation.

She was already sitting at a table beside the pie counter, as far from the pinball machines as she could get. A dingy, half-full water glass sat near the battered menu that she was staring at. She wore a short blue sheath that showed her legs to great advantage. Her blond hair was pulled back and her makeup was heavier than I liked.

Her business attire made her look, here in this place, like an eager young professor who hadn't learned the university's laid-back dress code.

"Hi," I said, slipping into the chair across from her. "Order yet?"

She shook her head, then smiled at me. The smile was wan. "Not that hungry."

"You'll have to have apple pie or Jimmy'll never forgive you," I said, sliding that battered menu toward me.

She laughed, reluctantly, it seemed. But she understood my reference. Jimmy loved this place, for the pinball mostly, but also for the pie. And apple was fresh today. Soon they'd move into pumpkin season, and I wouldn't be able to keep him away.

"Maybe you should take a piece home for him," she said.

"Maybe I should," I said in a tone that meant I wouldn't. The waitress came by. She was an older woman whom I'd seen before. She looked like she had worked in this place since the university opened its doors in the nineteenth century.

I ordered a meatball sub, then nodded to Laura. She ordered chicken noodle soup and half a turkey sandwich, then waited until the waitress left before looking at me again.

"I hate this," Laura said. "I lived for nearly thirty years before I found out that my father was a son of a bitch, and now I can't seem to get away from it."

I was the one who had initially helped her find out how much of a son of a bitch her father had been, and I still felt guilty about it. Sometimes I think it might have been better for her to never have come to Memphis, to have stayed in Chicago and done the charitable good works society expected of her.

"What did you find?" I asked.

"Oh, God." She rested the knuckles of her right hand over her mouth. I wasn't even sure she realized she was doing it. Then she moved them away, grabbed her napkin and dabbed at what was left of her lipstick.

I wanted to tell her we could stop right here, that we could ignore the problem. But we couldn't. Not with three bodies in that basement. Someone else would find them. Or worse, no one would ever find them again.

"It was the first property my father bought," she said.

I let out a small breath. I had hoped, for her sake, that the property had been newly purchased.

"He bought it in 1940," she said.

A long time ago. Maybe even before the bodies went into the basement.

She said, "He got some help with the financing."

"Who helped him?"

She shook her head. "That'll take more digging."

"I thought you told me that you lived in an apartment—a walk-up, if I remember right—during the war."

"We did," she said.

The waitress came back with water and a cup of coffee for me. Then she moved on to a group of freshmen who were trying to study for their first exam. Economics 101. The matching textbooks littered the table, as did notebooks and piles of folders.

No one else sat close enough to us to overhear anything.

"I don't understand all of it," Laura said as the waitress took the students' orders. "But let me tell you what I found out."

I nodded.

"The house was built after the Great Fire and the same family lived in the place until the late thirties."

"That's a long time," I said.

"Sixty years," she said. "First the parents, and then a son who apparently inherited. He remained single, died in 1938, and then I don't know what happened. I'm guessing he died without a will and there was probate, and everything went through the state courts. But that's just a guess. It wasn't in the files I saw, and I didn't have time to look elsewhere."

"I can check that out later," I said. "I wouldn't have to go by property address. I can go by his name—"

"Gavin Baird," she said, as if he didn't matter. "My father bought the house in late 1940. His name is the only one on title, but there're forms in the file that suggest he paid cash. I know that my folks didn't have the money to pay cash for a house, and if they did, why did they rent an apartment then?"

The waitress passed us with a laden tray of pies, shakes, and coffee. I didn't have to look to know she was taking it to the students.

"We know that your memory of the walk-up is correct because I spoke to the building's owner," I said, not waiting for the waitress to get out of earshot.

"You did?" Laura seemed surprised.

"In Memphis, when I was working for you." I gave her a rueful smile.

Someone cleared their throat. I looked up, startled. The waitress set down Laura's soup and sandwich, sloshing some of the chicken noodle on the side of the plate. Then she slid the sub in front of me. Its spicy tomatoey smell made my stomach rumble.

The waitress slapped the ticket on the table, then left. The moment left with her. Laura was focused on her soup.

"You spoke to the building's owner, and he remembered us?" she asked.

I nodded, trying to recall all of the details of a conversation that had taken place nearly two years before. "He said he remembered because your dad ended up owning most of the city."

"Not most." Laura crushed saltines into her soup. "But a lot."

"If I remember right," I said, "that apartment was downtown."

Laura shook her head. "Bridgeport. Back of the yards. Daley country."

Every area of Chicago had its own name and its own history. Bridgeport wasn't very far from our location in Hyde Park, and yet it could have been in another state.

"Was the neighborhood still predominately Irish?" I asked. It was now, but not as much as it had been. I had even looked for an apartment in Bridgeport when I had first come to Chicago, not realizing, of course, that Jimmy and I were about as far from ideal Bridgeport neighbors as two people could get.

"Yeah," Laura said. "Mostly, though, I remember the stink."

Most of the yards were gone now, but Union Stock Yards remained. On a bad day, the odor of butchered animals could combine with the smoke from the steel mills to the south into one of the foulest odors I'd ever encountered.

"So," I said, lifting my messy sub, "your father had an apartment and a house."

She nodded. "That house was his until 1952, when he incorporated Sturdy. Then he listed it as one of the assets of the corporation."

"He sold it to the corporation?" I asked.

She stirred her soup. "I couldn't find any record of that. But we both know he ran separate books. The records might be destroyed, they might be somewhere else, they might be right under my nose. I didn't have a lot of time, Smokey."

"I know." I took a bite of the sub. It was greasy and drippy and excellent. I had discovered during the summer that this place had the best subs in Chicago's South Side, which was good, because the other sandwiches here weren't that great.

"But the records are pretty clear. Sturdy rented the house from 1952 on." She finally ate some of her soup. Then she sighed, as if she hadn't realized how hungry she had been.

I frowned, set down the sub, and wiped my mouth with the napkin. A lot about Laura's discoveries bothered me. I couldn't piece all the information together.

"When did the house get converted into apartments?" I asked.

"I don't know," Laura said. "I don't think my father did it, although they were upgraded in the fifties—new appliances, some paint, things like that."

"What did you see? Invoices?"

She nodded.

"Any bricks and mortar?"

"I looked," she said, after taking another bite of soup. "I didn't see any brick or mortar on anything in that file. That stuff's a mystery."

"How extensive is the file?" I asked.

"The one in our offices is pretty scanty. It only refers to the buying and selling. I had to go down to the rental agent's office for the rest of the records."

"How'd you sell that?" I asked.

She smiled. "I have a key to everything. I didn't tell anyone. I just went."

I nodded, then ate more of my sub. It probably hadn't been the best choice for a meal that involved a conversation. I managed to use the few bites I'd taken to contemplate what she'd told me so far.

"What about after your father died?" I asked when I could finally speak.

"Everything stayed the same. Tenants in, tenants out. A few evictions, some notices, but no repairs, even though there were some complaints. Most of the time the manager took care of it."

"When was the manager hired?" I asked.

"Late forties," Laura said. "My father owned a lot of properties by then, and he needed help managing them. He hired a rental agent for most of them, but he put Mortimer Hanley on-site."

"Was there an application in the flies?" I asked.

She shook her head. "I can't tell where Hanley came from or who he replaced, if he replaced anyone. I got a sense, from some of the earlier documentation, that my dad posed as the live-in manager, but that's not possible. He lived with us."

I ate the last of my sub. The students were arguing over whether Adam Smith's laissez-faire doctrine led to the economic excesses of the late nineteenth century. No one at that table was listening to us, and the rest of the restaurant remained empty. Even the waitress had disappeared.

"It might be possible," I said after a moment. "I mean, who keeps track of the people in nearby apartments? Your father could have used the Queen Anne to run his fledgling business. Did he have another office?"

She frowned. She had finished the soup and moved to the tiny half sandwich.

"I don't know," she said. "I never thought to ask."

"Maybe we should find out," I said.

"You think it's important?" she asked.

"I don't know what's important right now," I said. "But your father was pretty involved with this building, more than I would have liked. Which means that we're going to have to be careful. We can't call the police to investigate."

I lowered my voice for this last. Even though the students weren't listening, sometimes phrases like that caught people's ears.

Laura sighed and pushed her half-finished sandwich away. "I know. I keep hoping that all this stuff happened before my dad bought the place."

"Maybe it did," I said. "We don't know what happened after—Baird?—died."

"Gavin Baird," Laura said absently.

"And we don't know anything about him, either," I said. "So there's a lot of unknowns before your father got the building."

"You really think those bodies—" and now she *was* whispering "—predate the 1940s?"

"I don't know anything," I said. "I do think it's interesting that in one of Chicago's highest crime periods, you can't easily track what happened with the ownership of that house."

A hand reached down and took my plate away. The waitress had reappeared. She took Laura's plate as well.

"Dessert?" she asked, as if she really didn't want us to have any.

"Three pieces of apple pie," Laura said. "Put one in a to-go box."

"Laura," I said.

She grinned at me. It was the first time all day that she looked relaxed. "You can tell Jim it's from me."

"You're going to spoil him," I said.

"I'm trying," she said.

She had always spoiled him, buying him things I couldn't afford, taking him expensive places that made me uncomfortable, pushing to finance things from his schooling to his wardrobe. Usually I turned her down before Jimmy even heard what she planned, but this time I was going to let it slip. I wasn't domestic by any stretch, and dessert was usually something out of a box.

The waitress scooped up the ticket as if redoing it would ruin her day, and left us. I watched her go.

"The way I see it," I said, not quite whispering, "is that it's too much of a risk to bring in the authorities."

"Yeah," she said. "I want to, though."

I opened my mouth, but before I could say anything, she waved a hand at me.

"I know the arguments," she said. "I thought about everything we discussed on Saturday, and I agree. I signed on for all the problems. I'm the one who thought she could change the world."

"You are changing it," I said. "Just by being who you are."

"The daughter of a one-time petty thief who didn't even acknowledge her presence?"

"A University of Chicago graduate who actually understands how to balance a bottom line and her ethics."

"The balancing act isn't working well," she said. "And now there's this. If I were truly ethical, I would go to the police."

"The Chicago PD?" I said. "The Gestapo wing of the Daley administration? The ones who held a 'police riot' a year ago, and beat college students into unconsciousness? The ones who are shooting teenagers in my neighborhood because they could be gang members? Those people?"

"They're not all bad," Laura said, "and you know it. Your friend Sinkovich—"

"I'm still not sure I'd call him a friend," I said.

"He's a friend," she said. "He's a good man at heart."

"With no power." And I almost added that the other good man I'd known on the force had been murdered because he'd been following his own heart.

"What are our options?" Laura asked. "If we don't go to the authorities—"

I noted that she didn't say "can't," which was the word I would have used.

"—then what can we do? Sturdy owns this building, and I can't just let it rot. People would notice."

"Would they?" I asked. "The company's done that in the past."

"Always with a plan," she said. "Usually one to turn the property around when the building finally got torn down. Usually that was a way to avoid city regulations or zoning or something like that."

"Make up a plan," I said. "Who would know that you didn't intend to go through with it?"

She glared at me. "And leave those unknown people in the basement?"

I shrugged.

"Smokey, even if I wanted to—and I don't—they'd get discovered when we tore the building down."

"Years from now," I said. "The building's well made. It'll last a while. And you'll have solidified your position at Sturdy then. There'll be a scandal, but by then you'd be able to weather it."

She shook her head. "I wouldn't be able to sleep at night. I'd wonder who those people were and what they did to deserve such a horrible fate."

Her hand was clenched into a fist beside her water glass. I put my hand on top of her thumb.

"That's what I'm talking about," I said. "Ethics. I just gave you the chance to pretend you didn't know any of this. I gave you a solution that a lot of CEOs would have taken, and you won't do it."

"I'll probably pay for it," she said.

"At least financially," I said. "Because this isn't something I can do alone."

The waitress came back with our pies. One piece was already in a little cardboard pie-shaped box, just waiting for Jimmy. Laura slid it toward me as she also grabbed the check from the waitress.

"Smooth," I said.

"It's a business lunch," she said. "My business."

One of the students looked our way then. Apparently he had overheard that, and hadn't been thinking we were having a business lunch.

"You guys should really factor in John Maynard Keynes," I said, letting the student know that I could hear his conversation too. "Or haven't you gotten to him yet?"

"It's 101," the student muttered, and blushed. Obviously, he had no idea who Keynes was.

They all looked at us, then turned their chairs slightly, making it clear they were shutting us out.

Laura grinned. "How do you do that?"

"What?" I asked.

"Say the right thing to get people off your back?"

I shrugged. "It's a gift."

The waitress had watched the interaction too. "Now is there anything else?" she asked me.

I shook my head.

"I'm going on break," she announced as if she thought we cared, and left us.

Laura ate a bite of pie. I slid my plate closer.

"Is there any way to tell how long those bodies have been there?" she asked quietly.

"I don't know," I said. "I suppose a specialist like a coroner or medical examiner can guess within a range of years or decades. I didn't get a good enough look down there. Things in the basement might point us to a date as well."

"Things?" Laura asked.

"Clothing, items in the pockets, or even the type of brick used, or mortar."

She nodded. "But we're going to need an official eventually."

"It depends on what you want to do," I said. "If you want to clear them out and give them a decent burial, no, we don't need anyone other than a funeral home."

"Smokey," she said loudly. Then she took a deep breath and lowered her voice so much that I had to lean forward to hear her. "These people were most likely murdered. Someone did something bad in that place. Isn't it our responsibility to find out who?"

"Why is it our responsibility?" I asked, more to hear how her thoughts went than to challenge her. My natural inclination would be to find out what happened as well, but I also knew there were times you just let things fade into the past.

"We found them," she said.

"I found them," I said.

"And you don't feel responsible for them?"

I shook my head. "I do feel curious, however."

Her lips thinned and she leaned even closer to me. Our faces were practically touching. "What if the person responsible is still alive?"

I leaned back. I felt as if our very posture was calling attention to us. A lot of people in Chicago didn't like blacks and whites at the same table, let alone sitting so close.

"I think it's possible, but not likely, that the person responsible is still alive," I said. "Those bodies are so well hidden that only a handful of people could have even known about them. Baird, Hanley, your father maybe, or—"

"Someone else at Sturdy," Laura said. "My father's been gone a long time now."

"You're thinking Cronk and the bastards," I said.

"Cronk and the bastards" was Laura's term for the team her father had appointed to run Sturdy Investments after his death.

She opened her hands, a simple gesture that meant the implications were obvious.

"That would solve some problems for you, wouldn't it?" I said. "If you can show criminal activities under their watch, activities that occurred after your father died with no benefit to the corporation."

"I can get rid of all their cronies," Laura said. "I can do a clean sweep of Sturdy without getting in trouble with the stockholders or any of our clients."

I took a bite of pie. It was sweet, with just the right amount of cinnamon. "And here I thought you were being altruistic."

"I am." She spoke loudly again.

The students stopped their arguments over which chapters to study and looked at us again. When we glanced at them, they looked away.

Laura sighed as if she were exasperated at me. "I wouldn't be able to sleep, knowing we just left them there. And I'd want to know what happened, not just because of my family connection, but also because they were people. Someone loved them once. Someone cared. Someone probably still wants to know what happened to them."

I followed my second bite of pie with a sip of coffee. I was stalling before I answered her. She really wasn't aware of all that this entailed.

"If we discover that this happened after your dad, and we bring it to the proper authorities, then we could get into trouble," I said.

"Why?" she asked.

"Tampering with a crime scene," I said.

"An old one."

"Not that old," I said. "Not in this kind of case."

She bit her lower lip.

"If it predates your father, then the authorities might not care that we've been digging around down there. But they might, particularly if they want to go after you for some reason."

"Shit," Laura said.

I raised my eyebrows at her. She rarely swore.

Her cheeks flushed slightly. "It's damned if we do, damned if we don't."

"Yes, it is," I said.

"But you said you'd think about it," she said. "You said you'd have a plan."

"It's risky," I said. "But here's what I think we should do."

Laura listened while I laid out my plan. It was based on things I'd seen in the South before the Civil Rights Movement had gotten national attention.

Often murders of blacks, particularly in rural counties, got covered up or were committed by the law enforcement agencies in the area. Sometimes the families and friends of the victims were able to do some investigating themselves. They soon learned that no one would pay attention to the investigation if it wasn't conducted properly—with documentation, correct evidence-handling procedures, and accurate autopsies.

Soon white law enforcement learned to restrict access to those crime scenes, but for a brief window, a number of higher-profile cases had gotten northern newspaper coverage because the victims' families had photographic or physical evidence that contradicted the stories the authorities told.

"Emmett Till," Laura said, citing a famous case from 1955. Till, a fourteen-year-old Chicago boy, had been visiting relatives in Mississippi when he supposedly whistled at a white woman. I never believed that part of the story. I always figured he had just looked at her and smiled, with that directness most Northern children had and all black Southern boys had learned to avoid.

For his crime—whatever it was, smiling or whistling or just plain being in the wrong place at the wrong time—Till had been kidnapped and brutally murdered. His mother, outraged that Mississippi law enforcement had done nothing, got her son's body back for the funeral and, contrary to all advice, held an open-casket funeral so that the world could see what had happened to her son.

Emmett Till became a cause célèbre, part of the budding Civil Rights Movement. When his funeral was held here in Chicago, Laura would have been sixteen—only two years older than Till had been. No wonder she remembered it.

"Yeah," I said. "Like Emmett Till. Only a lot of cases got more evidence. Enough to attempt bringing those cases to trial. We wouldn't be going for a trial. We'd just document everything in case we needed to bring this to someone's attention."

"I have no idea how to go about that," Laura said.

"I know the kind of people we need," I said, "and if we were in Memphis, I even know who I'd hire to help. But I don't have those contacts here yet, so I'm going to have to bring Franklin into this."

She nodded. "I suspected as much."

"It would be better," I said, "to hire some of these experts from out of state. Just in case."

She bit her lower lip again. The lipstick was completely gone now. "This is going to get expensive, isn't it?"

"Probably," I said. "And we have another problem."

"What's that?" she asked.

"I'm going to have to oversee everything. I'm the only person with the time and the ability. But if we do take the case to the authorities, we'll have to leave me out of it. Anyone we hire is going to have to swear they won't mention my involvement."

"If they go to court, that can be a problem," Laura said.

I nodded. "We might be worrying about something that'll never happen."

"Then again," she said, "this could be a bigger problem than we think."

SIX

Franklin knew a local funeral home director who occasionally did autopsy work and some forensic investigation, mostly of corpses. Franklin swore that the man was trustworthy. I took the name and decided to do a little investigating of my own. I wanted someone so incorruptible that I didn't have to worry about him at all.

When it came to actual forensic investigation, however, the kind that police departments did in actual murder investigations, Franklin knew no one.

I couldn't use my own past contacts, because they all knew me as Smokey Dalton, and even if they were trustworthy, they would know where I was. I had long ago decided that no one outside of Jimmy, Laura, Franklin, and Althea would know that I had moved to Chicago. Even Henry Davis, who managed my Memphis home for me and was one of my closest friends, had no idea exactly where I lived.

So I used the only other contact I could think of. I called Laura's attorney, Drew McMillan. McMillan was based in New York. He promised to have some names for me in the next few days.

We were proceeding slowly, and while I knew there was a need for caution, I still worried that something might happen while we were planning. I was afraid kids would break into the house or squatters would notice that no one was there and make it their own.

I had locked up the basement, but I still didn't want anyone else inside. I worried about that clipboard, sitting at the top of the stairs, and I hoped no one from Sturdy's rental agency would go in to check on the place.

Even though I was worried, I resisted the urge to drive by the house. I had to stay as far from it as possible until we started work in the basement. Even then, I had to figure out a way to be inconspicuous while doing what was needed.

By the time the weekend came, I had spoken to Laura a few times, played phone tag with McMillan, and had barely had time to start my research on the funeral director. I tried to save my weekends for Jimmy, and that Saturday we'd lounged around the house, watching the Mets soundly beat the Braves.

Jimmy had chosen the Mets as his team once both Chicago teams were out of the post-season, saying he had to be a Mets fan because we had lived for a short time in New York. I chose the Braves, not just to be contrary, but because I had been born in Atlanta, something I wasn't sure Jimmy had known before that afternoon.

Baseball proved a nice diversion—it was something we were both interested in, and I hoped by next spring I would have enough extra cash to buy us an occasional ticket to the ballpark. Chicago had two teams, the White Sox and the Cubs, and it was a shame we hadn't been to see either of them play in person.

We had a pleasant weekend, which was good, because I had a hunch I wouldn't have a pleasant week.

Drew McMillan called first thing Monday morning. I sat bleary-eyed in my office, staring at a cup of coffee that I'd had to set aside twice—once to get Jimmy ready for school, and now for the phone call—and pulled a yellow legal pad toward me.

McMillan had the name of a forensic criminalist. I had never heard the term before, and said so.

McMillan chuckled. "It's what you asked for, Bill. Someone who investigates crime scenes."

"I need someone who'll actually work this scene," I said.

"He has. He's worked half a dozen cases that the police wouldn't touch, mostly in New York State. But he's reputable, and expensive."

"Have you cleared the costs with Laura?" I asked.

"I quoted his rates when I first talked to her," McMillan said. "I figured if we got him, we'd be lucky."

"What about confidentiality?" I asked.

"He's being hired by us. Which puts him under lawyer-client privilege. I have a list of credentials and cases he's worked. You want them?"

"Yeah," I said, and used my teeth to pull the cap off my pen.

McMillan listed nearly two dozen cases going back five years before I finally told him I had enough. I would be spending most of the day at the library looking up this information, and McMillan knew it.

"Okay," I said when he finished. "Now tell me the downside of this guy."

"He's fair," McMillan said.

"So?"

"If the evidence points to something the client wants hidden, he doesn't flinch. He works it."

"I have to be there with him," I said.

"You can't," McMillan said. "It'll taint the investigation."

"I have no stakes in the outcome here," I lied.

"You're a Sturdy employee. That taints you automatically."

"I'm not," I said. "I contract with Laura. I'm an investigator, just like your criminalist is."

"Hmmm." McMillan paused, clearly thinking. "Let me check with him. That might make a difference."

"It better," I said. "Because I'm going to be at his side, examining everything right along with him, just like a police detective would do."

"At some point, they leave the evidence sifting to the professionals and go after the bad guys."

"I'm not sure there're going to be any bad guys to go after."

"You know what I mean," McMillan said.

I did. He meant that I would have to see where else the evidence led. I wasn't willing to concede any point on that, at least not yet.

"See if he'll work with me," I said. "You have a backup on this if he won't?"

"A few," McMillan said. "But Laura insisted time was of the essence. I've already got a flight booked to Chicago on Wednesday. She wants a meet with the whole team."

"We'll see," I said. Sometimes Laura got too formal. "She gave me the right to approve everyone. So let's not get ahead of ourselves, okay?"

"You got it," McMillan said. "But that might muddy the lawyer-client thing."

"You get to check that out," I said, looking at all the names and dates I'd scrawled across that legal pad. "It looks like I've got quite a bit of digging to do."

I finally got to my coffee—now cold—and made two slices of buttered toast as a late breakfast. Then I stared at the legal pad and contemplated my next move.

Going to the library would take me to the Loop. Even though I'd be blocks from Civic Center Plaza where most of the activity was, I would be close enough to make me nervous.

The hoopla around the trial continued. The violent branch of the SDS, which called itself the Weathermen, were planning later this week an action they were calling the Days of Rage.

They actually had posters up for it on telephone poles around the city. The one I'd seen most had a fist extended in a Power-to-the-People symbol, with the words *Bring the War Home—Chicago* along the sides. The dates ran along the bottom: *October 8–11*.

I'd already told Jimmy that he had to come directly home those days. I had no real idea what the Weathermen were planning, but I'd met a few of their kind last summer, and I knew they were dangerous.

They were already in the city. They'd had a few demonstrations, and made some speeches downtown. Another branch of the SDS, the supposedly peaceful side, were also giving speeches denouncing the Weathermen.

And all of this was supposedly in support of the Chicago Eight, as the media was calling the members of the Conspiracy Trial.

Still, I had to research the criminalist. I couldn't go to the University of Chicago libraries. Lately, they'd been asking for university identification to use anything unusual like the microfiche viewers. The University of Illinois Circle Campus was clamping down as well. In response to the violence and unrest that had become part of campus life all over the nation, universities were increasing security in the most unexpected places.

I hadn't tried Northwestern, but its location in Evanston meant that I would have to drive through the trouble areas. Besides, most of the student demonstrations so far had either happened in the Loop or in Lincoln Park, and I didn't want to go near either.

So I opted for the main library. I took the L rather than fight for parking downtown. The library filled the entire block between Washington and Randolph Streets. This was one of my favorite buildings in the entire city—a good thing, since I had spent a lot of time in it over the years.

The building had been built just before the turn of the century in a classic Chicago Beaux Arts style. The old stone façade had character, but it didn't reveal what was in the interior—two Tiffany domes, a sweeping staircase that led up to the second floor, and lots and lots of marble.

It smelled like a library too, dusty and rich, promising all kinds of delights.

Only I wasn't going for the delights. I was heading to the microfiche room to look up old newspaper articles. I started with the *New York Times* for the dates McMillan had given me, going through badly scratched photographic film of each newspaper, trying to find articles about the various trials, hoping for a mention of the criminalist.

After three hours of work, I had found a few, most of them having to do with his testimony. They all cited the same credentials, which had to be the ones he was using when asked about his background on the stand.

I finally gave up. There wasn't a lot I could learn this way, unless he had gotten into trouble. And since McMillan was promoting him, I doubted that I would have received any of the case citations that went badly.

I was about to return the last microfiche of the *New York Times* when I realized I had another option. I went back through the trial materials in the paper, getting the names of the attorneys on that trial. Then I made a note of which attorney had hired the criminalist.

When I had a substantial list, I went into the public records room and found the phone books for various metropolitan areas. Manhattan's was prominently displayed. I had more trouble finding the smaller cities, but after another hour had passed, I had the phone numbers of nearly a dozen attorneys, all of whom had contact with the criminalist.

I didn't feel as defeated. I left the library with plenty of time to take the L back home and to pick up Jimmy at the after-school program.

I stopped on Washington and peered west. If I walked just five blocks that way, I would be at Laura's offices. A knot of people had gathered in Civic Center Plaza near the spectacularly ugly fifty-foot-tall Picasso sculpture. I couldn't tell who the people were, but from their attention, it looked like someone was either giving a press conference or a speech.

That convinced me to stay away. I walked to the L, and headed home. I had phone calls to make anyway and questions to be answered before I hired someone to help me excavate what might become Laura's most important secret.

SEVEN

By the time I got to the apartment, I only had an hour before I had to pick up Jimmy. It was after five in New York: most of the law offices were closed, although I knew many lawyers worked later than that. I figured I'd have better odds of catching people in early in the morning.

Instead, I drove to the funeral home off East Sixty-third, where the mortician that Franklin had pointed me to worked.

Poehler's Funeral Home was in a transitional neighborhood. The Blackstone Rangers claimed the area as their territory, and legitimate businesses were starting to thin out. But some old-timers remained, partly because they had been in the area for decades, and partly because their services were still needed.

These days, Poehler's probably had more business than it could handle.

The building dominated one corner and made the street look more respectable than it was. I parked in the nearby lot, and as I got out, I realized that several buildings had broken windows or were boarded up. Even more were covered with graffiti.

But no spray paint had touched Poehler's brick walls—or if it had, the funeral home had paid a pretty penny to get it scrubbed off. Unlike the Loop, which was filled with people, the sidewalk here was nearly empty, and littered with broken beer bottles. I avoided as much glass as I could, but still checked the bottom of my shoes before going inside the funeral parlor.

The parlor's doors were made of solid oak. I actually had to brace myself to pull the door open. As I stepped inside, the scent of lilies and formaldehyde greeted me, a scent that always sent me back to my childhood, to that hideous afternoon when the Grand had smuggled me into a funeral home in Atlanta to whisper my good-byes to my parents before he sent me to my family upstate.

He'd taken me into the building hidden between four large, strong men, all vowing to protect me in case someone tried to take me away too. At the time, I didn't know—I wouldn't know for another twenty-nine years—that my parents had been accused of a major crime, and half of Atlanta's black community wondered if they had done it.

Even so, I had the community's support. My parents had been lynched by a white mob, never able to prove their innocence or even to answer the charges. And that alone made them sympathetic in the eyes of the community.

I squared my shoulders, and stepped along the dark burgundy carpet in the waiting area. A listing of this week's viewings was on a board near one of the doors, and farther down was a hand-scrawled list of the funerals, their times and their locations.

I was looking for a bell or some way to contact someone, when a man came out of the back room. He was wearing a black suit and a starched white shirt. He had a five-o'clock shadow and he looked tired.

"How may I help you?" he asked in a low tone. Not too sympathetic, not too friendly. Perfect to deal with someone who might be grieving or someone who was simply there to ask for information.

"My name is Bill Grimshaw," I said. "My cousin Franklin sent me here to speak to Tim Minton."

The man nodded as if nothing surprised him, then ushered me into a small room to the side. Heavy velvet curtains hung across the archway instead of a door. Inside were two upholstered armchairs and two matching couches, all set up in a square, so that seated people could see one another.

Behind the chairs were potted plants that climbed toward the ceiling, expensive vases on shining wooden tables, and a single vase with one perfect white rose.

The entire room smelled faintly of perfume, which did succeed in masking the hated odors of formaldehyde and lilies.

I was inspecting the rose—it was made from some kind of fabric, probably silk—when the curtains moved.

A slight man entered. He was wearing a blue chambray shirt with the sleeves rolled up. His blue jeans were stained with various fluid marks, and on his feet, he wore sneakers that had once been white.

He was younger than I was, probably in his late twenties, and moved with the grace of an athlete. He was too small to play most sports, but his lower arms were roped with muscle, perhaps from the job itself.

"You don't look nothing like Franklin." He was the first person to ever note that aloud, although I was certain a number of people had thought that in the past.

"I know," I said with a smile. "I don't look like any of my cousins."

Which was true, but irrelevant. I nicely dodged the fact that Franklin and I weren't really related.

"He says you got a project for me."

"So you're Tim Minton then," I said, extending my hand. "I'm Bill."

He took my hand reluctantly. His fingers were callused and covered with small scars. "I'm only talking to you because of Franklin."

"I know," I said.

"He says this could be something big." Minton was still standing near the curtain, as if he planned to bolt at any moment.

"He already spoke to you?" I asked.

Minton nodded.

I looked at the seating arrangements. "You mind if we sit?"

"I've still got a lot to do before I can go home," he said. "We got three viewings tomorrow."

But he walked to the nearest couch and sat in the middle of it, leaning forward, as if he couldn't contain his own energy.

I sat on the couch opposite him. "So you're the one who prepares the bodies."

"Most of them." He bit his lower lip. "The Poehlers help when they can, but they're better at the people stuff. The old man used to work with me. He can't no more. We're hoping to hire someone else, but hardly anyone wants to come down here."

I nodded. I wasn't sure how to approach him. I'd been thinking about this all day. Finally, I plunged in.

"Franklin told you that I'm an investigator, right?" I said.

Minton nodded.

"And he told you that I have a case involving a possible crime?"

"He said you can't go to the cops with it."

"Not yet," I said. "Although we might have to at some point—or some sort of authority—so any work that would be done on the victims would have to be something acceptable in court."

"Franklin wouldn't've called me otherwise." Minton tilted his head. "You interviewing me?"

"I'm making sure we're on the same page," I said. "Franklin said you were the best person in Chicago."

"Right now, I'm the only person in Chicago. At least for us." He didn't smile as he said that. "You worried I'd talk to someone I shouldn't?"

"Honestly, I've never done this before," I said, silently adding that I had never done this in Chicago. The Memphis people I had never had to quiz. "I'd be trusting you with something that could be big."

"I'd be trusting you too. Franklin says you're stand-up, but he also says some white woman calls the shots. So I'm a little leery. I don't work for white people."

"She's my client," I said. "But you'd be working for me. If I have to step beyond her on any of this, I will."

He looked at his folded hands. "She's not official or nothing, right?"

"You mean is she connected to law enforcement?"

"Yeah," he said. "Or a lawyer looking to make a buck on something that's got nothing to do with her."

I suddenly understood his hesitation. He didn't want to be an expert witness for a cause or a case that might compromise his ethics.

"She's not a lawyer," I said. "She owns the building where I found the bodies."

"Bodies," he said. "How many we talking?"

"I don't know," I said. "At least three."

He whistled. "Timetable?"

I shrugged. "Depends on who they are. I don't even know that. This discovery was a complete surprise to me."

"But you think something's up."

"Yes, I do," I said.

"You think a friend done this? Or your white woman?"

"No," I said, glad he didn't ask about Laura's family. "I think this is an old crime, and given the history of the house, which I'm not going to delve into, there could be some big ties, if you know what I mean."

He studied me for a moment. I wasn't sure he did understand me.

"Does something controversial bother you?" I asked.

"Hell, no," he said. "I'm getting John Soto tomorrow, if the city releases the body by then. Poehlers ain't handling him. I'm just doing the work for the family because they want another eye."

The name wasn't familiar to me. "John Soto?"

"Gunned down yesterday at the Henry Horner housing project. You haven't heard?"

I had heard something—a teenager had died near the project, shot by the police. But Henry Horner was on the West Side, and I had found myself listening to news reports lately and reacting by area. If someone died in a different part of the city, I had a smaller chance of knowing them—and so did Jimmy.

"Not enough, I guess."

"Traffic-light issue? Those kids being killed in that intersection near the projects? You ain't heard about that? Your cousin's in the middle of it."

I did know about Franklin's work. "He's been consulting with the people who want to get the city to put in a traffic light near the Henry Horner project. But he doesn't think the city'll do it. He's looking for alternate ways of accomplishing the same thing."

Minton pointed at me, as if I had answered a question right on a test. "The Soto brothers've been leading the protests about the light. Your cousin was none too happy with the actions. He prefers being behind the scenes."

Minton spoke as if Franklin had done something wrong by trying to find alternate ways to solve what sounded like a bad problem. Little children were killed at that intersection, the last two on separate days, one child on the way to school, the other on the way to a medical clinic.

"And now one of these brothers is dead?" I asked, because I hadn't tied the news of the shooting to the traffic-light issue. Franklin hadn't said anything either, but he often didn't on things he was working on for other people. Just like I rarely discussed my cases with him unless I needed his help.

"The sixteen-year-old. Cops say they stopped him for acting suspicious and he attacked them. Family and friends say he was shot and he wasn't doing a thing. I'm hearing that he was shot in the back, but none of us've seen the body yet. So I don't know for sure."

I nodded. "You're doing a back-up autopsy then, in case the family wants to do something against the city?"

"Yeah. Soto's older brother, Michael, wants to have everything covered in case. He's heading back to 'Nam in a few weeks and he wants to make sure as much of this's taken care of as possible before he goes."

I sighed, trying not to let the story go in too deeply, although I already knew it had. A young man fought to have a traffic light placed on a dangerous intersection. Because he held protests and drew attention to himself, he was dead. And now his brother was making certain that the city didn't cover things up.

"So," Minton said, "that's a long way of telling you the cops don't scare me. I'll do a report for the family, and if there's evidence that John Soto was in a skirmish or even caused something, I'll say it. If there's evidence that he was shot in the back from a good distance away, I'll say that. If the evidence is inconclusive, meaning I can't tell you if he was shot while attacking the police or while enjoying a Coke with his friends, I'll say that. You pay me to do the work, but the work is what it is. If the evidence says one thing, nothing you can do'll make me say something else."

"That's exactly what I want," I said. "In fact, that's exactly what I need. I'd like to hire you. Tell me your fees and how we can bring the bodies to you when we're ready."

"I'll come get them," he said. "It always helps to see how they were found. I'll take pictures too. Courts like that. Hell, people like that. They believe what they see."

I nodded, not saying that sometimes they could see the wrong things. He gave me his hourly quote, told me he'd bill me, and then gave me several ways to contact him. He wasn't afraid to come at odd hours.

That detail alone made me realize he had worked a lot of these sorts of on-the-side cases.

We shook hands, and as I left, I hoped we were doing the right thing. Because the more people I brought into this case, the harder it was going to be to back away if we had to.

And I was still worried that we might have to.

EIGHT

The next morning I started early, making calls before Jimmy was even awake. I took a break between calls, got him out of bed and into the shower, then made half a dozen inquiries while he got ready for school. It was my turn to drive Jimmy and the Grimshaw children to class, which I did, always on the lookout for the Blackstone Rangers street gang, who had given Jimmy and Keith Grimshaw trouble last year.

Nothing happened, which was the way it had been ever since school started. On days like this, I hoped that my devil's bargain with the gang had worked.

By the time I went through my phone-call list of lawyers, I had my second expert. Wayne LeDoux, the criminologist that McMillan recommended, had impeccable credentials. Attorneys who had hired him for their cases said he was thorough but expensive; attorneys who had gone head-to-head with LeDoux in court hated how well he stood up to cross examination and admitted (off the record, of course) that he was so unimpeachable they would consider hiring him themselves if they had a case that warranted it.

That was good enough for me. I called McMillan and told him I approved. I also told him we had someone to do the autopsies, and were ready to go whenever the experts could start.

I was making a lunch of Campbell's tomato soup and toast when the phone rang. It was Laura. McMillan had spoken to her. Apparently he had gotten LeDoux to come to Chicago on the next available flight.

She wanted all of us to get together at her apartment Wednesday night so that we could get this investigation under way.

I decided not to bring Minton—he didn't need to know much more than what he saw when he went into the basement—but agreed to come myself. I'd have to find someone to care for Jimmy, but that wasn't hard. The Grimshaws and I often exchanged babysitting duties and, for once, they owed me more than I owed them.

After Laura hung up, I went back to my lunch, feeling slightly unsettled. Experts rarely came to another city on such short notice. Of course, a man who dealt with crime scenes couldn't always control his own schedule—he would have to come when the scene still existed, not waiting until he had an opening in his calendar.

Still, I had the feeling that McMillan had hired LeDoux without waiting for my approval. I wasn't sure if I would confront him about that or not, but I did hold the suspicion in reserve. If the three of us—Laura, McMillan, and I—were going to work together on this case, we were going to do so on an equal basis.

Before that meeting, I had some logistics to figure out. We had to go in and out of the Queen Anne without drawing suspicion. If anyone at the rental agency or at Sturdy thought we were doing construction work in that building, they might get nervous. If they noticed us carrying items out of the building, they might get worried.

Somehow, we would have to do our work—photographing, removing the three bodies, taking evidence, and taking down the brick walls—without drawing attention to ourselves.

I figured there were two times we could work: in the middle of the night or during Jimmy's school hours. Both had advantages. Night provided its own cover. Most people slept and did not watch what was going on in a neighboring building.

But the moment a neighbor became suspicious, he would notice everything we did and maybe call the police. Since the neighborhood had white students as well as black families, there was a chance the police might actually show up. If they did, we would be in trouble.

Of course, at night no one could call the rental agency or try to track down the building's owners. And sometimes what seemed suspicious at 3:00 A.M. seemed normal or not worth the effort to contact authorities in the light of day.

Daylight brought its own problems. We would have to park in that alley. We would have to remove items from the building while people could see what we were doing. A call to the rental agency would show that no one was working on the building, which might lead to a call to the police.

But most neighbors in places like that didn't like to get involved. Most of them wouldn't be home in the middle of the day either. And most would accept the presence of a painters' van or carpet cleaners in the middle of the day if we could find a way to disguise our vehicles like that.

I preferred daylight, provided we could make it work, and not just because it was more convenient for me. People got nervous about nighttime activity, and I didn't want them to think we were robbing the place, selling drugs, or running some kind of illegal scam out of the Queen Anne.

By the time I had to pick up Jimmy from the after-school program, I had a short, typewritten plan that I hoped would work.

Wednesday morning, I woke to the news that a dynamite bomb had blown the police statue in Haymarket Square a hundred feet from the pedestal. Haymarket Square was on the West Side, past Greektown, a place we never went. I wasn't even sure I had seen the statue.

But the news unnerved me nonetheless.

I planned to keep the radio in the kitchen off while we had break-fast, but Jimmy had gotten there before me. He'd already put out the milk and cereal, taken raisins and the sugar bowl from the cupboard by the time I staggered out of the shower to make coffee.

He looked up at me, face taut. "Somebody's bombing stuff here now."

Our trip last June had ended when a bomb went off in a building I was in. I was injured, but not critically. I simply gained some scars on my legs and arms to match the one that ran down the left side of my face. For several weeks, though, I was black and blue and moved as if I had aged fifty years.

"I got news for you," I said, wishing I didn't have to. "They've been bombing things here for a long time."

"I don't remember nothing."

"Goldblatt's Department Store got bombed last Easter," I said, "and there've been other things."

Worse things, which I didn't want to explain.

"Then how come this one's all over the news?"

I sighed, rubbed my hand over my face, and wished I lived in calmer times. Poor Jim, all he got to see was the ugly side of human nature.

"It's all over the news for a couple of reasons," I said. "It's a police statue. Someone's issued a challenge to the Chicago Police Department."

"You know who?" Jimmy asked as he sat at the table. The hair on the back of his head was still matted. I would have to send him to the bathroom to clean up before he went to school.

"I have suspicions," I said. "I'm sure the police do too."

"Those Days-of-Rage people?" Jimmy asked.

"Probably," I said. "They promised four days of violence, starting today. Maybe someone got excited and started early."

Jimmy splashed too much milk on his cereal. It sloshed against the edge of the bowl. "If Haymarket's near Greektown, it's not by Lincoln Park."

"I know," I said.

"Can I stay home, Smoke?"

"You'll be fine at school," I said. "They're not coming down here."

At least not yet. The Black Panthers had spent the last few days trying to talk the Weathermen out of rioting in the park because the Panthers believed, with a great deal of justification, that the police would take out their anger in the ghettos, not against the rich white kids planning the so-called actions.

"What about you?" Jimmy asked that last quietly, not meeting my gaze.

"I'm working for Laura today. I'm staying as far away from those crazies as I can."

He raised his head. "Promise."

"Promise," I said.

He nodded, then finished his breakfast in silence. We listened to the disk jockeys on the radio discuss the radicals in town, the Conspiracy Trial, and the history of that statue, which had been erected by the police on the site of the Haymarket Rebellion.

The rebellion, the disk jockeys "reminded" us (knowing full well that most of us had no idea what it was), happened in 1886. At an outdoor rally to protest police violence against striking workers, someone threw a bomb that killed eight policemen and two bystanders. Several anarchists were arrested, although no evidence ever linked them to the bombing; four of the anarchists were hanged and a fifth committed suicide by placing a blasting cap between his teeth.

The statue honored the dead policemen. Blowing it up—with dynamite, nearly a century later—was an act of great symbolism. And the Weathermen faction of the SDS loved their symbolism.

I shuddered, bundled Jimmy off to school and hoped that he would think about other things all day, although I had a hunch that was unlikely.

It wasn't until I went into the back room that served as my office that I realized I wouldn't be able to keep my promise to Jimmy.

I was heading up the Gold Coast tonight, to Laura's apartment for that meeting. The Gold Coast was on the near North Side of Chicago, not too far from Lincoln Park, where the Weathermen planned to hold their first rally.

With great frustration, I picked up the phone and called Laura. I wanted her to change the meeting to my apartment, but she wouldn't. She felt that her place—a penthouse suite of one of the most expensive apartment buildings in Chicago—would be safe enough. She'd hired extra security after an attack last year, and they would be working tonight. So would her favorite doorman, who was more than capable of defending himself.

However, I did get her to compromise. I asked her to hold the meeting over an early dinner, at five-thirty instead of eight. Knowing this group of radicals, and having watched their self-serving speeches on the television newscasts for the last week, I had a hunch they'd want as much press coverage as possible.

They'd get that only after the Conspiracy Trial ended for the day, and the national press corps had time to make it from Civic Center Plaza to Lincoln Park. If we met at five-thirty, we would probably avoid the worst of whatever the Weathermen were planning—if, indeed, the police ever allowed them to leave the park.

Fortunately, I'd already asked Althea Grimshaw to pick up the kids from the after-school program. Jimmy would be happy when I got home earlier than planned.

If that happened, I would be happy too.

NINE

Laura's apartment building looked like it was set up for a war. In addition to the usual doorman, six security guards were stationed around the building's first floor.

Laura, who owned the building, wasn't taking any chances.

After more than a year of visiting her, I still wasn't used to the building's ornateness. My entire apartment building could have fit into the lobby, with its raised ceilings and black marble floors. Leather furniture that cost more than I spent in a year was arranged in casual groupings, although I'd never seen more than one or two residents sit in them.

Large glass windows on the east side overlooked Lake Shore Drive, and Lake Michigan beyond. This was one of the most spectacular—and expensive—views in Chicago, and the architect that built this place had taken advantage of that.

The newly hired security guards watched me as I crossed the lobby, but the head of security, who sat behind the desk near the elevators, pointedly greeted me by name. I said hello to him as well and pushed the elevator call button, shifting uncomfortably from foot to foot.

I was not a meeting sort of person. I preferred doing things to talking about them. But I recognized the necessity of planning ahead. We were about to do something tricky, and we had to proceed with caution.

The elevator doors opened, and the attendant, an elderly black man, grinned at me. He knew his presence made me uncomfortable. More than once I'd asked him why he stayed at the job. His answer was always the same: he liked Miss Laura.

I liked her too, but I wouldn't spend my days opening and closing elevator doors for rich people even if she asked me to.

"You think them kids is gonna bomb the Gold Coast?" he asked me as the elevator doors closed.

"I certainly hope not," I said.

"If they do, they's not coming here."

"Because of the extra security?" I asked.

"Because we's lucky. Judge Hoffman don't live here. He got an apartment in the Drake."

Judge Hoffman was the judge in charge of the Conspiracy Trial.

"That's expensive real estate for a judge, isn't it?" I asked. The Drake was on Michigan and Oak, with a view of Lincoln Park—and if your apartment was high enough, a view of Lake Michigan as well. The Drake was older than Laura's high-rise, and considered one of the premiere addresses in the city.

"His wife got money," the attendant said. Then he grinned at me. "Sometimes it be good to marry money."

The elevator stopped and he opened the door with a flourish. I was glad I didn't have to respond to his comment. He'd made it clear more than once that he thought I should marry Laura, for my sake, not necessarily for hers. I didn't want to have that conversation with him again.

I stepped into the space in front of Laura's apartment. The space, which I had no name for, wasn't exactly a hallway and it wasn't quite a foyer. Yet it was large and grand. It had marble floors, a mirror to make the space look even larger, and a huge vase of fall foliage on an expensive table that added a touch of elegance.

Laura's door was partially open, which made my stomach clench. She often did that when she was expecting someone, even though I had asked her not to. She claimed the building was safe enough. It wasn't. We both knew that any determined person could get past the security, but ever since her apartment had been broken into, she'd been struggling to regain her sense of safety.

Somehow, leaving that door open on certain occasions, seemed to do that for her.

I knocked and let myself in. The apartment did have a foyer, with an authentic oriental rug that I'd helped her pick out covering the black marble floor. Black-and-white photographs brushed up against each other on the walls. My favorite shot was a candid one of Jimmy that Laura had taken herself. She had caught him in a moment of laughter and he looked like the carefree boy I had always wanted him to be.

The place smelled of garlic and spices. Voices reached me from the main room. Then Laura's laugh, high and fluted, rose above them.

Apparently, I was the last to arrive.

I stepped into the living room and stopped, as I always did, mesmerized by the view. The room had floor-to-ceiling windows that showed Lake Michigan. At the moment, it looked gray and sulky. The sun would be down in about an hour, and the eastern sky was already taking on the shadows of twilight.

"Smokey." Laura stood up. She'd been sitting on the leather couch in the middle of the room. Her leather furniture was even more elegant than the furniture in the lobby. Plants dripped off every surface in the main room, which made it look like something out of *Architectural Digest*, while hiding the room's astonishing comfort.

Two men sat opposite each other on the large leather chairs. Drew McMillan faced me. He was wearing one of his stylish New York suits, with its wide jacket and slightly flared pants, and his black hair brushed the edges of his collar. He looked modern and expensive, as if he was the person this apartment had been designed for, not Laura.

Across from him sat Wayne LeDoux. He was older than the man in the grainy newspaper photographs I'd seen. His hair had gone gray and his cheeks were jowly. His suit had some wear on the sleeves. From the conservative black wool and the narrow lapels, it was clear he'd owned the suit for more than a decade.

I suddenly felt uncomfortable in my black slacks and white shirt. I hadn't even thought to wear a suit.

Laura came to my side. She was wearing long polyester slacks with bell bottoms. Her shirt flowed over the slacks like a short dress.

"Mr. LeDoux," she said. "I'd like you to meet our investigator, Bill Grimshaw."

It always sounded odd to hear her speak my fake name. Maybe it was the inflection in her voice, the way she emphasized the name Bill, just so that she would get it right.

"You're the man who found the bodies?" LeDoux's voice was deep and authoritative. No wonder so many attorneys had praised him. With that voice, he sounded like an expert right up front.

"Yes," I said. "I freelance, and one of the things I do on occasion is inspect buildings for Laura."

"I'm sure you're familiar with the corruption in the city of Chicago," McMillan said to LeDoux. "It extends to the building inspectors, who usually get bought off."

LeDoux nodded. He stared at the scar running along the left side of my face as if he'd never seen anything like it. I clearly wasn't what he had expected.

Laura touched my arm and guided me to the couch. I sat down, and she sat beside me, making it clear just with her actions that she supported whatever I did.

"We'll have dinner in a few minutes," she said. "I'm reheating. I ordered in."

I smiled at her. Laura could cook a few things, but she wasn't a gourmet by any standard. It was probably best that she had bought food from a nearby restaurant.

"Did you touch anything?" LeDoux asked me. It took me a moment to realize he wasn't referring to the food.

"I found the hidden room, touched the locks, the doors, and the light switches. The wall had caved in on one side, and when I used my flashlight to peer inside, I saw the bones. It took me a second to understand what I was seeing. For some reason, the skulls didn't register right away."

"Three of them," he said.

"Three skulls."

"On three skeletons?"

"I think so," I said. "I'm not sure. To my inexperienced eye, the bodies looked like they'd been tossed in this crawl space, or whatever you want to call it. I don't know if all the parts were there or if there were extra parts."

McMillan grimaced. His specialty was corporate law, although I knew he had consulted the criminal defense attorneys in the New York office to get LeDoux's name. McMillan just wasn't used to this kind of detail.

"But you touched nothing else," LeDoux said.

"As soon as I realized what I was looking at, I closed up the room, put the boiler room back the way I found it, and left."

"Excellent," LeDoux said.

"Smokey's had some experience working cases like this before," Laura said.

"Smokey?" LeDoux asked me.

I smiled at him. "It's a childhood nickname that seems to have stuck. My close friends and family use it."

LeDoux glanced from Laura to me and then over to McMillan. For the first time in the conversation, LeDoux seemed uncomfortable.

McMillan templed his fingers and leaned back in the chair. "Bill is one of the most able investigators I've seen. We're going to want him in that basement."

LeDoux frowned. He obviously wasn't happy with the idea of supervision.

"If nothing else," I said, "I can move materials for you when you're ready for that."

LeDoux frowned. "You believe there are other things to find down there?"

"I hope there isn't," I said. "But there's a lot of brick, and none of it has been done by a mason. It's slap-dash."

His lips thinned. McMillan watched us. Laura leaned against me, saying nothing.

"My examination of the foundation tells me the building has a full basement. But the brick walls off most of it."

"Unevenly," LeDoux said.

"And with no obvious plan, at least not one I could discern."

"In your short examination," LeDoux said.

"I wouldn't even call it an examination," I said. "I probably spent no more than five minutes in that hidden room."

"Good." He sighed. "We have an uncontaminated scene then. You did well, Mr. Grimshaw."

He was patronizing me, but I didn't mind. He was doing so not because of my color or my abilities, but because he thought I knew nothing about his field.

I would let him think that. It was easier than trying to explain myself to him.

A buzzer went off in the kitchen. Laura excused herself and walked there. McMillan stood as well, saying that he would help her.

LeDoux turned sideways in his chair so that he faced me more directly. "I do not mean to be rude, Mr. Grimshaw," he said. "But I prefer to work unsupervised."

"I understand. I'm not going to supervise you. I'll be helping where I can, but mostly I'm going to be observing. You're the criminalist. I'll trust you to handle the evidence correctly. But I'm going to be investigating. We need to know what happened here, when and why."

"You have no idea at all?"

"None," I said.

"No hints, no theories?"

"None," I said.

"Except that this is criminal."

I folded my hands together to keep them calm. "I think that's a fair assumption. Bricking three human beings into a wall is not a legal act."

"You think they were alive?"

I hadn't had that thought at all. The idea turned my stomach. "I have no idea. But I certainly hope not."

He nodded, once, as if confirming his own suspicion. I apparently had made assumptions that I hadn't realized.

"It's not so criminal an act to brick bodies into a wall," he said. "Perhaps they belong to unregistered aliens who died here or to someone who died unexpectedly. Perhaps this was a form of burial."

"That's against the law too," I said.

"Yes, but not so serious as murdering someone. You see?"

"I do," I said.

"Miss Hathaway tells me you found someone to perform autopsies. I'm assuming he's reliable."

"He is," I said. "He will come to the site when we're ready to release the bodies to him."

"I may want to supervise his work."

I couldn't imagine Minton allowing anyone to supervise him any more than I could imagine LeDoux letting me tell him what to do.

"He'll probably let you observe," I said.

LeDoux smiled for the first time. It softened his face and made him seem like a kindly old professor instead of a man who specialized in crime scenes.

"That's the answer I wanted," he said. "You were correct in your approach to this. We need a good team. Miss Hathaway has said she may bring in the authorities if the circumstances warrant it. I understand her position is precarious because of the shady nature of the business she is trying to repair. But I will argue for official investigations if her caution seems . . . unnecessary."

"I'll take that under advisement," I said.

His smile faded. "So there are things I don't know."

"Things you don't need to know," I said. "They might lead you in the wrong direction."

"Then you do have suspicions," he said.

"I have fears," I said. "I'm hoping your work will alleviate them."

He gave me a rueful look. "My work rarely makes things better, Mr. Grimshaw."

"In this case," I said, "it would be hard to make things worse."

TEN

Laura served dinner on her polished oak table in her formal dining room. She used her good china and her silver. She sat at the head of the table. I sat with my back to the windows, while the guests got the last views of the lake before night set in.

She had ordered authentic Italian food from one of the small neighborhood restaurants in Little Italy. Someone had come all the way up here to deliver it, which was one reason she had to reheat. We had an excellent lasagna, some meatballs in red sauce, and fresh bread, washed down with a Chianti that added a richness to the food.

Most of the conversation revolved around the case. I told LeDoux and McMillan about the problems we'd have working in that basement. Laura added some information of her own, making it clear that she suspected an employee or someone tied to Sturdy had placed the bodies there.

LeDoux, of course, reminded her that the building had owners before Sturdy bought it, and basements often showed ancient history. She nodded, having heard that argument from me, but clearly remained unconvinced.

McMillan was more concerned with the legal aspects. If a crime had been committed, he wanted to make sure that we weren't damaging a criminal case against someone.

Finally, LeDoux turned to him. "Any good defense attorney will take advantage of our unorthodox approach, Mr. McMillan. But if we can show that I have followed the same procedures the State of Illinois would follow in its investigation, we will alleviate much of what you're concerned with."

"How would we show that?" Laura asked.

"Other experts who would talk about cases in which techniques like this were necessary," LeDoux said.

"Like Emmett Till?" Laura asked.

"There wasn't this kind of investigation in the Till case," LeDoux said. "But you're on the right track. Cases involving the suspicious death of Negroes, particularly in the South, is one area in which experts like myself get called in all the time. Our evidence is often overlooked by the civil authorities, and our testimony is worthless if there is no trial. But at least someone is prepared to speak the truth, and that way, the truth is not entirely hidden."

Laura glanced sideways at me, as if his confirmation was something she had needed.

"Too bad no one takes those cases to trial with this evidence," McMillan said.

"The only good thing about murder," LeDoux said, "is that there is no statute of limitations. I have seen cases, mostly in New York, in which one prosecutor declines to pursue the court case, and the next prosecutor comes in, feels he owes something to that constituency, and re-ignites the investigation. If someone like me has preserved the evidence, then the crime scene continues to speak through the years, and often we have a successful prosecution."

"You think that'll ever happen in the southern murder cases?" Laura asked.

"Negro murder cases?" LeDoux asked.

His continued use of the word Negro bothered Laura, but it didn't bother me. It marked him as a man of a certain age, but it was clear that he had thought about these cases with justice in mind.

"Yes," Laura said, with a pointed glance at me. "The death of black people."

"There are several famous cases that haven't been prosecuted yet," he said. "I would love to see the men who bombed that church and killed those little girls a few years ago be convicted. There are others as well. Do I think that'll happen in my lifetime? I hope so, although

65

I doubt it. We were working toward enlightenment. Then someone extinguished the light."

"Dr. King?" McMillan asked.

LeDoux nodded.

"The movement continues," I said quietly. "It's just not as visible now."

"Or as unified," LeDoux said.

"Unfortunately," I said, "it never was unified."

"Still," LeDoux said, "every movement needs a leader—"

"And one will appear," I said. "Right now there's too much noise. We've been relegated to a back seat. We're not through. We're—"

The phone rang, startling all of us. Laura set her napkin beside her plate. "Excuse me," she said, and got up.

The nearest phone was on an end table near the kitchen. She picked up the receiver, stopping the bell in mid-ring.

"Yes?" she asked coolly, clearly letting the caller know that he was interrupting something.

We were silent. McMillan sipped his Chianti. I finished the meat-balls on my plate, glad that the conversation had ended. I normally didn't talk politics with people I had just met. Often, I didn't talk about it with people I knew well. Ignorance irritated me, and many white folks were ignorant of black politics. They understood it on a superficial level, gleaning what they knew from the broadcast news which, these days, was branding anyone who was not connected with Martin's Southern Christian Leadership Conference as a dangerous militant or an outspoken radical.

Laura's expression grew hard. "Is anyone hurt?"

We all turned toward her.

"All right," she said. "Please call when it's over."

Then she hung up.

"What was that?" McMillan asked.

"Apparently we're under siege," she said.

"What?" LeDoux asked as I said, "The Weathermen."

She nodded to me, then she turned to LeDoux. "We've been having protests over the Conspiracy Trial. Tonight there was a scheduled rally in Lincoln Park. It's turned violent. People running through the street below, attacking each other."

LeDoux looked at his plate as if he were alarmed. McMillan just shook his head. Laura's gaze met mine, her eyes bright.

"Honestly," she said, "I'd like to see how bad it is."

I had been in rallies that had turned violent before. And those were peaceful events. This one hadn't been planned as a non-violent protest. This one had been planned, as it said on some of the posters, to "stick it to the pigs."

"None of us is going down there," I said.

"How about standing on the balcony?" she asked.

She had a balcony off her bedroom.

"Let me check it out," I said. "If I hear bullets, we're not going out there either."

She nodded. I headed down the hall. It had been a long time since I had been back here, and nothing had changed. The artwork, with the little lights hanging above each piece, seemed as extensive as always. The nearby bathroom gave off the faint scent of Laura's perfume, and then I pushed open the door to her bedroom, trying not to think of all the wonderful times we'd had in here.

I passed the king-sized bed, brushing my fingers against the silk comforter that she used on cool fall nights, and pushed open the sliding glass door.

Immediately, the room filled with sound. Sirens, screams, and breaking glass. Flashing blue lights from police cars reflected off nearby buildings and, on a balcony across the way, clumps of people huddled, watching as we wanted to do.

But I heard no gunshots, smelled no tear gas.

"Well?" Laura asked behind me.

"There's not much to see." Still, I stepped onto the concrete. We'd spent a lot of time out here as well, sitting in the wrought-iron chairs and watching boats sail across the lake. Often we were talking about problems, but in hindsight it didn't seem that way. It seemed like idyllic moments, now gone.

I walked to the iron railing. I heard McMillan say something behind me, and LeDoux answer him, but I didn't pay attention to their words. Instead, I looked down.

A young man wearing a pith helmet and army fatigues hid between two parked cars. A teenage girl ran past, screaming, a brick in her left hand. Three police officers ran after her.

Another boy slammed a large club into the window of a building across the street, then jumped when he saw the police and headed toward an alley.

In the distance, voices rose in a ragged chant: "Ho, Ho, Ho Chi Min. Ho, Ho, Ho Chi Min."

"Didn't he just die?" McMillan asked as he stopped beside me.

"Around Labor Day." LeDoux remained near the door, clearly frightened.

Laura was on my left side, her hands on the railing. She peered downward, just like I was doing. "What the hell are they trying to accomplish?"

"Whatever it is," McMillan said, "they're not achieving it."

"Sure they are," I said. "They have our attention, don't they?"

"It's not that simple," he said.

"I think it is," I said.

Another scream, loud and long, echoed down the street. The boy who had been hiding near the car sprinted down a side staircase and disappeared into the alley.

Two more police appeared, dragging a young radical—male, female, I couldn't tell from this distance—by the arms, body limp in typical protest mode.

"What a mess," McMillan said.

"Look." LeDoux was pointing at a building to the west of us. Other people stood on balconies, and several of them were throwing cocktail ice on the young people below.

"That's constructive," Laura said. Then she sighed so loudly that I heard her over the sirens. "Anyone else in the mood for dessert? I have ice cream."

"Spumoni?" LeDoux asked.

"Spumoni," she said with a smile.

McMillan shook his head one more time at the street below, then said, "Why not?"

He followed the other two inside.

I remained on the balcony, watching the running figures disappear as they headed away from the streetlights. A slow-moving police car went by, clearly looking for more protestors.

If this protest had started in the park, they had already run several blocks to get here. The protestors were frightened and the police determined.

The meal sat heavily on my stomach. This was only the first night of the so-called Days of Rage. We had three more nights to go.

I had a hunch the violence would only get worse.

ELEVEN

By the time I left, a little after eight-thirty, the violence had moved to another part of the neighborhood. As I let myself out the back door of the apartment building, I heard sirens several blocks away. To the north, smoke rose against the dark sky, and I hoped the smoke was from bonfires in the park, not a burning building somewhere.

The air had an acrid tinge, and in the distance I could hear voices, but no more screams. I had parked half a block away, and as I looked up and down the street, I had no qualms about walking that distance in the open and unprotected.

Security had called Laura's apartment only a few minutes before, letting us know that the "action" had ended, and it was safe to leave the building. At my urging she asked them how long ago it had ended, and they claimed they hadn't seen anyone in the past fifteen minutes.

That was good enough for me.

The conversation had gotten stilted by that point, and I was paying less attention to it than I was to the time. I wanted to get to the Grimshaws', pick up Jimmy, and get him in bed before ten. I also wanted to get away from the fake collegial atmosphere that the dinner had engendered.

Working with LeDoux would be fine. He seemed more than competent. Socializing with him was another matter altogether. Although

69

I agreed with many of his opinions, I disliked how he presented them, and as the stress of the evening increased, I grew less tolerant of him.

I hoped that tolerance would return during the night, since we were heading to the Queen Anne first thing in the morning.

I crossed the back parking lot, past the dumpster, and walked to the sidewalk. In Memphis, after these things, I never went down the street because I was afraid I'd get arrested or worse. Here, though, it would be clear to anyone that I hadn't been involved. My hair was cropped too close to my head, my clothing was too nice, and I was too old.

I was also the wrong color. If anything, the police would assume I was a doorman getting off work.

Glass crunched under my feet. It littered everything—the sidewalk, the grass, the street. Most of the cars had broken windows, and so did many of the nearby buildings.

Laura's building was fine—she had been right to bring in the extra security; apparently they had stopped more than one kid from swinging a bat at the plate glass windows on the building's east side—but it seemed to be the only one.

As I reached the corner, I noticed a doorman, still in his uniform, sitting on the curb. He pressed a washcloth full of ice against the side of his face.

"You need help?" I asked.

He shook his head, then winced. "I just need someone to get those freaky bastards."

And then when he saw that his answer wasn't making me leave, he added, "I'm waiting for my ride."

I nodded to him and continued, turning onto the side street where I had left the van.

To my relief and surprise, its windows were intact. But it was the shabbiest vehicle on the block. The Mercedes and Cadillacs all sported broken passenger windows, and those vehicles with canvas tops had become the victims of someone's knife.

I wondered what the vandalism proved. Then I sighed. I didn't understand any of this—not on a deep level—and that concerned me. Maybe my lack of understanding was a product of my age and my upbringing. Or maybe I still clung to Martin's vision of non-violent resistance to a violent world.

I did understand how people like Black Panther leader Fred Hampton could talk about self-defense, how black people needed to protect themselves against the police brutality that hit our neighborhoods, often for no apparent reason.

But I did not understand wearing riot gear, gathering weapons, and planning to provoke the police, all with the intent of—what? Getting attention? Scaring the city? Protesting a trial where the defendants were accused of the very same thing: coming to Chicago with the intent to riot?

Although most sensible people knew the defendants were not guilty. Even the government-commissioned Walker Report, which came out last year, called the events at the Democratic National Convention a police riot.

Tonight was a planned action, a planned provocation, made worse by yesterday's destruction of the Haymarket statue. The Chicago police were already angry and confused, and most of them weren't sympathizing with anyone outside the blue brotherhood.

I had no idea what they did tonight in other neighborhoods, but here, near Laura's place, it seemed to me that the police were restrained. I hadn't heard gunshots and the air did not smell of tear gas.

Was that because the rioters were white? Or because the national press corps was nearby, ready to attack the Chicago PD one more time?

Maybe Daley had issued a different order than the one he'd issued during the riots that happened after Martin Luther King's assassination. Then Daley had told the police to kill all the arsonists and maim all the looters. Maybe this time he'd been reasonable.

He was a canny man. If he urged restraint this week, he would win this public fight.

So long as he didn't send his storm troopers into the ghettos. Like Franklin feared.

Like I feared.

So long as he didn't let the entire city take out their frustrations on us.

TWELVE

The next morning, the headlines screamed disaster: RADICAL INVA-SION and RADICALS RAMPAGE ON THE NEAR NORTH SIDE. I set our paper front-side down on the kitchen table and kept the radio off, but I didn't have to. Even though Jimmy saw the headline, he didn't asso-ciate the near North Side with Laura. He had no idea how close I had been to the riot.

He was more concerned with homework. Mrs. Armitage, his after-school teacher, had assigned him an essay on the Haymarket Riot, and he didn't understand the language of the book he had checked out of the library—socialists, anarchists, labor rally. I didn't help him because I'd been warned not to. Instead, I urged him to look up each and every detail until it all became clear.

He glared at me as if I had made the assignment and didn't talk to me all the way to school.

After I dropped Jimmy off, I picked up LeDoux at the Blackstone Hotel. The Blackstone was across the street from Grant Park. Most of the action during the Democratic National Convention had taken place here, and rumor had it that the radical protestors would stage one of their actions nearby.

I parked in the Conrad Hilton's lot across the street because I was familiar with it. I had briefly worked at the Hilton when I had first come to Chicago, thinking that a regular job would be better for both me and Jimmy. That assumption turned out to be a false one; I chafed at being an employee. I discovered that summer that I preferred getting into trouble on my own.

I met LeDoux in the lobby of the Blackstone. He had been waiting for me, cameras slung over his arms, and a thick black case near his feet. I carried the case as we headed back to the parking lot.

Then I opened the back of the van, had him stuff his case and cameras into a duffel, and gave him the painter's coveralls that we had agreed we'd wear. He slid the coveralls on in the back of the van, put on the painter's cap I'd bought him, and then climbed into the front seat.

The sky was dark, the clouds heavy, promising rain. That pleased me. Neighbors would be indoors and probably not paying a lot of attention to any activity outside.

When we got to the Queen Anne, I parked in the driveway with the back of the van facing the street. If anyone was watching us, I wanted them to see us remove the equipment so that they wouldn't call the rental agency and ask what we were doing.

Laura had told Sturdy's rental agency that she was hiring a few down-on-their-luck friends to paint and repair the interior of the Queen Anne. Because the company knew she had unusual friends (namely me), she had a hunch no one would question this news.

We all hoped this cover would work.

By the time LeDoux and I had reached the Queen Anne, rain dotted the windshield. The air was humid, and it felt like the storm would only get worse. I got out first, opened the back of the van, and pulled out the wooden ladder that I'd bought—it was the only piece of this new equipment that we'd probably use.

LeDoux joined me, took his duffel and a single paint can, and headed toward the back door like we'd planned. The billed cap, coveralls, and his poor posture made him look like a man who had spent his entire life painting other people's homes.

I leaned the ladder against the back stairs, went up them, and unlocked the back door. The stale odor of rot reached me first, and I winced. Then I stepped inside, relieved to find the place much cooler than it had been on my first visit.

My clipboard remained near the door at the top of the stairs. No one had been in the building since I had been here nearly two weeks before.

"Where're we going?" LeDoux asked.

"Basement," I said, opening the door farther. "Be sure to take the paint."

He grinned at me, then headed down the stairs. I went back out for some brushes, another paint can, and a tarp. Then I closed and locked the van, and came back into the house.

It still gave me the willies. That rot smell made the entire place feel unpleasant—or maybe it was my knowledge that three unknown people had been buried in that basement long ago.

When I went down the stairs, I found LeDoux photographing the stairs.

"We're not even close to the site yet," I said.

"I want everything documented," he said. "We don't yet know what we'll need."

So he photographed the door to the boiler room, the boiler room itself, the metal cabinet that led to the hidden room. He did a quick diagram of everything, marking the locations, telling me we would get exact measurements later.

When I opened the double cabinet doors, revealing the secret door, LeDoux whistled.

"I did not expect it to be so elaborate," he said.

Before we went through the secret door, he stopped me.

"The cabinet itself is evidence," he said. "Not only will it give us fingerprints, which we may or may not find useful, but somewhere on it we should find the name of the manufacturer. It should give us some kind of hint as to who felt the urge to hide that door."

"If this is the first cabinet," I said.

"We'll look for evidence of that as well."

He photographed everything about the cabinet, including the floor, before he let me step inside and open the secret door. As I unlocked the door, he asked, "Are you wearing the same shoes you wore the last time you were here?"

"Probably," I said. "I don't have many pairs."

"But you can't say for certain," he said.

"No."

"Before the day is out, I would like to measure them, take a print of the sole, and photograph them, just to keep them out of the evidence pile. I'd also like to see any other shoes you might have worn here."

I nodded, a little stunned. Previous forensic investigators had asked for my fingerprints (which I wasn't about to give LeDoux), but not my shoes.

I nodded, unlocked the door, and flicked on my flashlight. The room was smaller than I remembered, and dust motes floated across the beam of light. The damp, musty smell that I had noticed on my first visit returned just as strong as before, and I had to resist the urge to sneeze.

Then I stepped back, out of the cabinet, and let LeDoux go in first. He stood inside the door's frame, examining the entire area with his flashlight, one inch at a time.

"Think that light will work if we change the bulb?" he asked.

"We can try it," I said.

"Later," he said, and continued his meticulous examination.

I sighed, careful not to lean on anything, and waited for him to get done. Finally he turned the light toward the decaying wall, and froze in place.

"Oh, dear," he said faintly. "We do have a problem."

I resisted the urge to roll my eyes. "That's why we brought you here."

"No, no." He sounded fussy. "Your instincts of criminality were correct. That third skull—the one farthest away—has a gunshot wound through the cranium. Unless I miss my guess, someone shot that poor soul in the back of the head."

How had I missed that? A crushed or damaged skull was fairly obvious. One with a gunshot wound was even more obvious. Clearly I hadn't looked at the details as carefully as I thought I had.

LeDoux leaned forward, a gloved hand placed gently against the crumbling brick, his flashlight all the way inside the hole. The light reflected against his face, making his skin deathly white.

"Oh, dear," he said again. "And these poor things were tossed in here like yesterday's garbage. This probably isn't the primary crime scene, but it's a part of it. We'll have to investigate the house and see what else we find."

"The house has been apartments for decades," I said, "and judging by the look of these bones, they've been down here for a long time."

"That's a safe assumption, given the conditions. The walls would have protected them from the worst of Chicago's heat and cold." He stuck his head inside the hole. The light pouring out now illuminated the extra bricks and bags of mortar that sat in the only real empty space.

"Do you have a guess how long they've been here?" I asked.

"Not yet." He rocked back on his heels, and looked at me. His painter's cap, which he had forgotten to remove when we got inside, was slightly askew, and covered with mortar dust. "I'll have to get them out first to give you a real guess."

"How about a tentative one?" I asked.

He shrugged. "They could've been killed as recently as two years ago, or back when the house was built. I have no real idea. There are remnants of clothing that should give us an answer."

I clung to the idea that the bones could be as recent as two years old. That took Laura's father out of the picture, and while Sturdy would still have problems from this discovery, Laura herself would not be implicated.

"All right," I said. "Let's get them out, then."

"Not so quickly. I still have a great deal of work to do." He sighed. "We both do."

"I know," I said. "Measurements, photographs, footprints."

"Bits of trace evidence, seeing if we can find anything that will lead us to the killer, from something caught in the mortar itself to something dropped alongside the bodies."

"You're hoping for fingerprints?"

"I'm hoping for many things," he said. "Primarily, I'm hoping that those bits and pieces of clothing include wallets or some sort of identification. Quietly discovering who these corpses belong to without a driver's license or some other indicator is going to be hard. We'd be looking for dental records and at missing persons reports. Either the authorities will find out what we're doing, or we won't identify these corpses."

My stomach twisted. Three people had been tossed down here, missing for God knew how long. It would be nice to let their families known what happened to them.

Unless, of course, the families had put them down here.

"And then we have another issue." He stood, wiped his gloves on his coveralls, and pulled the cap down on his forehead.

"It seems to me we have another number of issues."

"You, Mr. McMillan, and Miss Hathaway, perhaps. But only one concerns me as well."

I waited.

"We're going to have to look behind each different bit of brick-work."

"You're afraid there's more bodies down here."

His gaze met mine, his pale blue eyes already tired and red-rimmed.

"Isn't that why you brought me here?" he asked me quietly.

"I didn't bring you. Drew did."

LeDoux shrugged a single shoulder. "But Mr. McMillan told me that a forensic examiner to remove the evidence was your idea. You brought me here because you were afraid."

"Afraid?" No one who had just met me had ever accused me of being afraid before. Usually it took someone years to realize that I felt fear, just like everyone else. "Of what?"

"Don't toy with me, Mr. Grimshaw," LeDoux said. "You think this is some uncaught killer's favorite burial ground."

"I'm hoping it's not," I said.

LeDoux nodded, then crouched, pulling his camera up to his face.

"I hope so too," he said as he got to work. "Three corpses are certainly easier to deal with than a dozen."

THIRTEEN

LeDoux's meticulousness drove me crazy. I thought I was a detail-oriented investigator, but compared to LeDoux, I was as sloppy and careless as Jimmy.

LeDoux photographed everything in that back room using only his flash and flashlight for illumination. He then went over the light socket itself before allowing me to try a new bulb. Once I put that in—and it worked (miraculously, I thought)—he photographed everything again, going through several rolls of film without focusing on the corpses at all.

Next he measured the entire area and drew his map, marking the measurements exactly. He showed me how precise he wanted me to be, then sent me into the boiler room as if I were a little kid assigned my first important task in life.

I felt that way; I had no idea how all these measurements and maps could be important, but LeDoux said they were, so I followed instructions.

He finished first, of course. He had a smaller area to cover. Then he oversaw what I was doing for a few short minutes before asking me if I wanted to break for lunch.

We went outside. The air was muggy, and it felt like thunderstorms loomed on the horizon. The low-hanging clouds confirmed that feeling.

We had agreed the night before to bring bag lunches, which we had left in the van. I opened the van's back doors, hoping the interior hadn't gotten too hot for our lunches, and was relieved to find that it hadn't.

I left the doors open, and we sat on the thin carpet, our legs dangling over the bumper, brushing on the gravel as we ate.

The hotel had prepared LeDoux's lunch. It was spectacular—a sandwich piled high with thinly sliced ham and cheese, celery and carrot sticks, an apple, and a thick piece of chocolate cake that looked almost perfect. My peanut butter and jelly looked like something Jimmy would hate, and out of pity (I think) LeDoux handed me the other half of his sandwich. I shook my head, but did take some carrot sticks when he offered them, and a bite of that wonderful cake.

"This is a nightmarish scene," he said as he wrapped up the plastic wrap the hotel had used for the vegetables. He stuck it into the bag, then grabbed the apple, obviously saving it for last. "You realize that, if my suspicions are correct, this might be too much for us."

"Too much how?" I asked.

"I'll need a place to store the evidence—somewhere cool enough and dark enough. Your friend the—"

I waved a hand so that he didn't say the word "coroner" or "mortician" or whichever version he was going to use. I wanted us to be careful outside, just in case a neighbor eavesdropped through an open window.

"—your friend," he said, understanding me, "will have to have a place to store his—um—things as well. And this might take a long time. Longer than I have. I have two testimonies scheduled this fall, with another pending."

"We're in no great hurry," I said. "At least, not at the moment. Unless something you and I find will make us hurry. So if you need to come back, I'm sure we can do that."

He nodded, as if he expected me to say that. "It's the organization I'm most worried about."

"I'll see what we can do."

"And the hotel," he said.

I looked at him.

"That riot we observed last night was most unnerving. I'm told by the hotel staff that these kids plan more such things all during this trial, so I should expect occasional lockdowns and warnings. I looked in the phone book this morning; it seems most of the good hotels are either near Lincoln Park or downtown, and neither seems safe. I was wondering if you or Miss Hathaway knew somewhere better, perhaps closer to this place."

I shook my head. "The hotels down here aren't places you want to stay."

He sighed. "I'm not sure I want to stay anywhere in this city."

"I'll talk to Laura," I said. "She might have a few ideas. After all, Sturdy does rent apartments. Would that work?"

"If I'm here for the duration, it might." He ate his apple slowly, lost in thought.

I put the rest of the food wrappings away, then glanced sideways at the neighborhood. So far, no one seemed to be watching us, and nothing seemed amiss.

Still, my stomach was a knot of tension, and the food hadn't helped.

"Do you mind if I ask you something?" he said.

"Go ahead." I adjusted my cap. It made my head itch.

"You and Miss Hathaway. You seem quite . . . familiar with each other."

I froze. I didn't know how this man would react to the truth—or even to a partial truth. He seemed open-minded for a man his age, and had shown no real objection to working with me. Yet some of the things he'd said the night before had grated on me.

"We've worked together for a long time," I said.

"So you've become friendly," he said.

"We're friends." My voice was tight, even to my own ears.

He put the apple core in his bag. "That's quite unusual, don't you think?"

"A white woman and a black man becoming friends?" I asked, with too much edge in my tone.

"I was actually thinking of the head of a company and one of her employees." He sounded bland, as if he hadn't realized he could have offended me.

"I'm not an employee," I said. "I work for myself. I knew Laura before she took over Sturdy."

"As a friend?" That bland tone again. I was beginning to become wary of it.

"As a customer. She hired me for some personal work, and was satisfied with the job."

"I see," he said, even though he didn't.

His brain was meticulous, and this didn't fit. So he would noodle it until he came up with an answer he liked.

"She met my son during that period," I said. "She adores him."

"Ah," LeDoux said, as if he'd discovered the secret of the universe. Maybe he had. That fit for him. Women couldn't help but like children.

My fist clenched, and I willed it open. I was going to have to work with him for some time. I couldn't let his attitudes infect me the very first day.

But they had. I couldn't hold back the next question. "Are you going to need an assistant for all of this 'duration'?"

"You, you mean?" He set his bag beside mine near the wheel well.

I shrugged. "That's who you got."

"I thought you were planning to go in whatever direction the evidence leads us."

"If I can," I said.

"Then you won't be here all the time," he said, as if I hadn't figured that out.

"But what about having someone else here with you?" I asked, hoping he would say no. I had no idea who I'd bring in if he did need someone. Malcolm Reyner, who used to be the person I brought in to help me on cases, had been drafted. If his timing was anything like mine had been when I went to Korea, he would be just finishing up Basic Training now, and would be shipped to Vietnam within the month.

"Most of this I can do alone," LeDoux was saying. "In the beginning here, I'll need you—we need to bring down enough of that wall so that I can get into the area where the—um—you know are. And we'll have to see the extent of what we're looking at. Once we know that, I suspect I'll only need help at certain designated times, and I can let you know when that will be."

"You're still hoping that this is limited," I said.

"Aren't you?" he asked.

I nodded, feeling overwhelmed. If that basement was a standard Queen Anne, it was huge. And we were only looking at a small portion of it.

"You note that the basement windows are blocked," LeDoux said, his voice lowered.

"I noticed that the first time I was here. They are all the way around the house, except for the windows in the boiler room."

He shook his head. "That's not a good sign."

"I know," I said.

He sighed. "I've come to scenes like this once or twice to double-check the police work. I've never done a multiple on my own."

"Is that what these are called?" I asked. "A multiple?"

He nodded. "The more gruesome the find, the more clinical the description."

I was silent for a moment. A multiple. Somehow that sounded worse to me.

"When should I bring in Minton?" I asked.

"He's our third?" LeDoux asked.

I nodded.

"Tomorrow," LeDoux said. "At the earliest. I'll be more concrete when we're done for the evening."

Tomorrow. We weren't going to move those bodies until tomorrow—at the earliest. Which meant that we had part of today and probably part of the next doing some meticulous thing that I was terrified of screwing up.

"So you won't need me right away," I said.

He studied me for a moment. "Not for the walls."

"Good," I said. "I'd like to have a look at the rest of the house."

"You haven't done that yet?"

I shook my head. "The boiler was running on a day like today. So I went to the basement first."

He raised his eyebrows slightly, as if imagining what that was like. "I'm not sure if that was a lucky break or not."

"Me either," I said.

"I wonder what you'll find upstairs," he said.

"Empty apartments, I hope."

He gave me a sideways glance, as if he thought I was being naive. "Rap on the walls. Make sure they're not hollow."

"I plan to," I said, even though I hoped I would find nothing. No more hidden places, no more bodies. No more potential for bodies.

"And measure things," he said. "Sometimes the best hiding places are quite creatively concealed, particularly in buildings this old."

I shuddered. What an unpleasant way to spend my afternoon.

And it looked like my future might hold a dozen afternoons just like it.

FOURTEEN

I knew I should start my search in Mortimer Hanley's apartment, but I also knew it would keep. I was off-balance enough from the morning's investigation and the lunch conversation. I wanted to reassure myself that the gruesome work was limited to the basement.

When I went back inside, I grabbed my building inspector's clipboard and Hanley's thick wad of keys. I made sure that LeDoux didn't need me for the next few hours. After he had reassured me—again—that he didn't, I went back outside, since the front door seemed to be the only way to get to the other apartments.

As I walked around the building, I looked at the windows, hoping that I had misunderstood what I had seen the first time. I wanted them to be merely dirty instead of boarded over from the inside, but it soon became clear that they were both dirty and covered.

This building had a full basement, and most of it was inaccessible. The queasiness in my stomach got worse.

I stopped looking at the foundation as I went around to the front of the building. I didn't want to look too odd. Too late, I realized I should probably have carried a can of paint or the ladder just for show.

I hoped the clipboard was enough.

The neighborhood remained quiet. The cars that were parked along the street were the same ones that had been there when we arrived. A quick glance reassured me that no one was peeking through their curtains.

Still, as I mounted the front stairs and unlocked the door, I felt conspicuous. It wasn't until I stepped inside that I realized I had braced myself for excessive heat. Amazing what the memory did. I could barely remember how the interior looked, but I could remember how stifling it had been.

It wasn't stifling now.

The entry seemed even darker than I remembered. I punched the ancient light switch and that filthy chandelier gave me its meager light. I had forgotten my flashlight, but I wasn't about to go around the house unless I actually needed it.

I decided to skip apartments one and two, and head up the oak staircase.

I would start at the top of this place and work my way down.

The staircase had been built to last. The stairs, though worn, were sturdy, and so was the banister. As I glanced at it, I didn't see any signs of repair: no spindles that had a different shape or were made out of a different wood; no cracks in the polished handhold. Even the steps seemed to be in good condition. No one had put another piece of wood across the top of one or shored up the bottom of another.

The staircase made a gentle curve to the second floor. The banister continued—obviously the second floor hallway had once opened to the entry below. The banister was against a wall now, although not touching it. There was a good foot of space between the banister and the wall itself, space that went all the way down to the first floor.

I would never have rented any upper-floor apartments to people with children, not with that hazard in place. But I'm sure no one thought of such things in the early years. I peered over the edge, missing the flashlight now, wondering what waited for me in that one foot space below.

Then I remembered the corpses in the basement and shuddered.

The chandelier's light did not reach the second floor, but apparently that light switch turned on all the hallway lights. The lights on the second floor were brighter, the fixtures dating from the 1940s. These "improvements" might have been the result of work done by Laura's father. I wondered if he had done the carpentry and electrical himself.

I pulled out the clipboard and made notes. A real electrician had to inspect this place, and someone had to repair that gap between the banister and the wall.

At the place where the staircase blended into the floor, becoming the hallway, stood the next door. It had a metal 3 on its front and four fairly recent deadbolts. I knocked for the hell of it. For all I knew, there could be squatters in here.

But the knock sounded hollow. If someone was squatting in there, they weren't home now. And if they were squatting, they hadn't brought a lot of furniture with them.

The thought of squatters made me shake my head. I had been thinking so hard about the bodies in the basement that I hadn't even recalled the possibility of living people upstairs. I'd been worried about that when I first arrived here, and completely lost track of it in the intervening days.

I knocked one last time, then pressed my ear against the door. Nothing so far. I would have to open each door before we got too far in our investigation, just to make myself feel more secure.

I continued down the hall. Another door to the left, marked 4, seemed to have been carved into the wall at a later date—obviously dividing up a bedroom suite or a larger area into something smaller.

Then at the end of the hall was the fifth apartment, with a grand door that seemed like part of the original construction. These last two doors only had regular locks, which looked flimsy compared to those deadbolts.

A narrow hallway continued past apartment five, leading (I suspected) toward the third floor. The hallway felt cramped and was dark—the light didn't extend from the main hall, and the fixtures above me either didn't work or needed new bulbs.

A window at the end of the hall provided what light there was.

When I reached it, I realized the window was original to the house, which meant that this hallway was. The stairs were to my right. Once, a door had covered them, but not any longer.

In the original design, these stairs had either led to the servants' quarters or to the attic. Sometimes those were one and the same.

Right beside the window was another light switch. I punched it on, but nothing happened. I peered up the stairs, seeing only darkness. I sighed heavily. Looked like I would have to go back for my flashlight after all.

86

Then something brushed against my cheek, making me jump. I reached up and found string. A pull-cord for a light switch. I pulled, and strong light filled the stairwell. This light bulb had been changed recently.

The stairs were narrow and sharp edged, made without the finesse of the lovely main staircase. If someone tumbled down these things, they'd end up more than scratched or bruised. They'd have broken bones, serious cuts, or both.

I made my way up carefully, using the wall as a support because no one had put in a railing. I made a note of that too before I started to climb. The stairs twisted and turned, narrowing the higher they got. I had to crouch halfway up, and when I reached the top I was nearly bent in half.

It was a relief to reach the end of the staircase, which opened into another hallway. This one was narrow, with high ceilings. The door at the end of the hall stood open, revealing a toilet and a bathtub, both old. The toilet had the shape of an old pull-flusher, and the tub had a clawfoot.

Obviously this had been the servants' quarters and hadn't been modified much. Four doors, two on each side of the hall, probably provided single rooms for apartment dwellers, allowing them to share a bath.

I looked for another doorway, one that would lead to the attic, but didn't find it out here. So I struggled with my keys, trying to find the one that opened apartment number 9.

It took some time. I nearly gave up and pushed the door open, breaking the lock, even though I knew better. I'd actually learned, in the course of doing this, that any action like that would make it easy for people to squat in the building.

Even though Laura had funded a charitable organization that helped squatters find real jobs and homes (something she put together after we discovered that the churches and Salvation Army were constantly full), it still took hours, sometimes days, of my time to help anyone who'd been living for free inside one of the buildings. I didn't always succeed either—for every person I helped, another ran away after seeing me, never to return.

I hated that part of the job.

The door finally opened, and a waft of stench blew toward me. It took a minute to figure out what it was: a combination of rust and mildew and loam. I struggled for a moment to find something that would turn on a light; I was surprised when my fingers found a modern switch, which I flicked upwards.

Fluorescents flickered on, taking a second to catch. When they did, they showed me a room filled with gardening equipment—rakes, shovels, and small pickaxes, all stacked against the back wall. I'd been right; this was a single room, and once upon a time it had probably been rented as such. But it hadn't served as anything but storage in a very long time.

I had no idea what anyone would need all this gardening equipment for either. There was no lawn here except for that small patch out front, which only needed mowing. And in no way was anyone going to carry a lawn mower way up here.

Canvas tarps, like painters' tarps, were stacked to my left, and beyond them, several rolled rugs. Some old chairs had been shoved against the wall. One of them had become a rat's nest—stuffing everywhere. I couldn't smell the rodents, though: I wondered if they were long gone or had simply not yet moved back inside for the winter because of this Fall heat wave.

I went inside, careful to prop the door open. For some reason, I didn't want it to close on me.

There were other tools in here, rusted and old, some of them so encrusted with dirt that I couldn't quite tell what they were. Others were obvious: hammers, nails, screwdrivers, several old saws. Cobwebs showed me that these hadn't been used in a long, long time.

Past the rakes, a utility sink had a board across the top and the faucets capped off. On top of the board were small screws, some kidney-shaped bits of leather, and small metal objects. I squinted, leaning forward, careful not to hit anything, and stared at the metal. Those were bullets.

I let out a small breath, then peered around again. Mixed with the rakes and shovels were a few rifles. Along the floor, some unattached barrels rested against a pile of dowels. And near the sink itself, some grips for handguns were stacked into a small pile.

LeDoux would want to see this room too. It was probably part of the crime scene—maybe even the murder site, although I didn't see any blood spatter on the walls or dried blood pools on what was left of the carpet. The room didn't quite smell bad enough either, but maybe that was because I had grown accustomed to foul odors after being in this building for so long.

Somewhere in this room, if the house continued to follow standard Queen Anne layout, which it had so far, would be the entrance to the attic. I didn't see it, but it could have been hidden behind one of the chairs or all the equipment.

Still, I could almost hear LeDoux, cautioning me not to do anything, touch anything, or step in anything.

I backed out of the room, trying to walk in the prints my shoes had left in the dust. When I got to the door, I removed the block and pulled it closed, letting the lock latch automatically.

Sweat ran down the side of my face, even though I hadn't been aware of being hot. Both my shirt and the coverall stuck to my back, and I felt grimy, just like I had on that very first day.

I stood in the middle of the hall and stared at the remaining doors, wondering what else I would find.

FIFTEEN

As it turned out, I found only empty rooms in the remaining third-floor apartments. The rooms were similar: they all had a utility sink and a tiny counter with a single cupboard hanging above it.

The floors were bare wood covered with dust, indicating that no one had been inside for a long time. A single window either overlooked the street out front or the alley in the back. The glass was clouded and dirt-streaked, and I dutifully marked on my clipboard that there might be dry rot and mildew around the frames.

I wasn't able to check the bathroom: the overhead light didn't work, and not enough light came in from the hall. I could tell that my initial assumption had been right: the bathroom hadn't been remodeled since it was installed in the 1920s. But as to cleanliness, dirt, and the interior of the medicine cabinet, not to mention a small closet off the side, I had no way of knowing, not until I came back up prepared.

The second floor provided more interest. The apartments there were empty as well, and, for two of them, just as dust-covered. These apartments were one-bedrooms with kitchens and their own bathrooms, some of them shoehorned into a very small space. Had there been no other problems in the building, I would have recommended these for cleaning and immediate rental.

The most interesting apartment—at least on this floor—was the one directly visible at the top of the stairs, the one with all the dead-bolts. It still smelled of Pine-Sol and Lemon Pledge.

This apartment sparkled. The floor had no carpet: someone had lov-ingly restored the hardwood floor. The windows looked new too, and the walls were freshly painted. A built-in bookshelf was the source of the Pledge smell. Its wood shelves looked as lovely as the floor.

I went in and explored, just like I had in the others. The main liv-ing area had an archway to the left which, as I went through it, sur-prised me. The windows curved outward, with a little built-in window seat below each one. This was part of the tower. I turned, saw a nar-row staircase leading up, and followed it.

The stairs opened onto a tower room, completely round, and com-pletely detached from the third floor. Windows surrounded me, giving me a 360-degree view of the neighborhood. The room itself was spec-tacular, and the only one in the entire building so far that made me feel even slightly comfortable.

If I hadn't discovered the horrors in the basement, I would have told Laura that she had a prime piece of property here. I would have wondered at the gardening tools on the third floor, and worried slightly over the gun parts and bullets, but they wouldn't have seemed sinister, not like they did now.

How many other crime scenes had I dismissed in other buildings I'd inspected, thinking them abandoned storage areas or forgotten equipment?

Probably quite a few.

I left the tower room, and went down the stairs into the main part of the apartment. To the right of the main door, two more rooms opened up—one holding a kitchen and, off it, a bathroom, the other a small dark bedroom with only one window.

These rooms told me nothing, except that the high level of cleanli-ness continued here as well. Had someone recently moved out and cleaned the place to perfection before Hanley died? Or did this clean-liness have a more sinister motivation, one that would hide the de-struction that murder often gives to a building?

I shuddered again, decided this was yet another problem for LeDoux, and left the apartment. I didn't lock the deadbolts. Instead, I made sure the door latch worked so that we could get inside easier.

The staircase down to the entry seemed darker than it had before. As I reached the first floor, I saw that the glass panels beside the main door had grown dark. Either a storm was coming or it was later in the afternoon than I thought.

I glanced at the watch Jimmy had bought me for my birthday and saw that it was nearly four o'clock. It was my turn to pick up Jimmy and the Grimshaw children from their after-school classes. Their teacher had made it clear at the beginning of the year she would stay in that old church no later than five o'clock.

I didn't have time to go through the downstairs apartments. Still, I took a few minutes to unlock them and peer inside, just to see if this building had squatters.

Both first-floor apartments were empty. The living rooms in each were covered in dust. No one had been inside in a long, long time.

I closed the apartment doors, then let myself out the front. A few of the cars that had littered the street were gone now, and one unfamiliar car had parked near the corner. I hurried around the building as drops of rain dotted my coveralls.

I would save Hanley's apartment for the following day.

As I hurried down the basement stairs, I checked my watch again. Barely enough time to drop off LeDoux and pick up Jim. But I would make it, if we hurried.

I found LeDoux dusting the cabinet for prints. He insisted on finishing, claiming he only had one more to go, even though I stressed the time urgency. It took him five minutes to dust the print, photograph it, and then use a piece of tape to remove it. He taped the print to a slide, then put the whole thing in his evidence bag, marked Cabinet Boiler Room 1.

"Now?" I asked.

He stood, wiped his hands on his coveralls, which were finally looking as dirty as they needed to, and handed me a torn sheet of paper.

"Here's the make and model of this cabinet," he said. "It's fairly recent, judging by the label itself. I think you should start there."

I bristled at his suggestion, but said nothing. We wouldn't be working together long. If this continued, I'd have to speak up, but for now I had to keep LeDoux happy.

I nodded, folded the note, and clipped it to my board. The cabinet wasn't a priority, yet. Those apartments were. I'd make certain I had my flashlight in the morning, when I'd start in that third-floor bathroom.

We left. I made certain both doors into the house were locked tight.

I also locked the basement door for good measure. As we drove back downtown, LeDoux pulled off his coveralls and tossed his painters cap on top of them. At my instruction, he bundled them into a ball and tossed them at his feet.

Maybe by the end of the week they'd look as used as most painters' clothing.

I took back roads as long as I could, but eventually we ended up on Michigan Avenue, waiting in traffic. I had factored that into my timing; still, I found myself tapping the steering wheel impatiently.

LeDoux shook his head slightly, as if he couldn't understand me. I wasn't sure I understood him either.

"You find anything in the house?" he asked, much later than I expected him to.

"No one's living there. It looks like someone recently moved out of number three."

"How recent?"

"Within the last few months," I said. "I'll know more tomorrow."

He nodded and kept staring out the window at the other cars, trapped like we were between the tall buildings and Grant Park. Police lights reflected off passing cars. I glanced in their direction, saw a squad car parked on one of the paths as if it were blocking someone's way.

My fingers tightened on the steering wheel. The park looked different than it had in the morning—more litter, a lot of paper, a few ripped signs.

I glanced ahead, made sure the way to the hotel was clear, and concentrated on getting us there.

"What's that?" LeDoux asked, tilting his head toward the park.

We were past the police car now, nearer to the Logan statue and the site of the main police riot during the Democratic National Convention, the horrendous one, the one the entire nation saw on television.

A reporter stood near the fountain, a camera crew trained on him, an equipment truck blocking part of Michigan Avenue. The camera lights made it seem almost like nighttime, even though the sun wasn't due to set for another two hours.

"That protest must not have gone well this morning," I said.

"Another one?" he asked.

"We're going to be treated to four days of them," I said. "And that's if these Weatherpeople do what they promise."

"You don't think they will."

"I think they'll do whatever they believe they need to do."

He shifted in his seat. "I want to stay somewhere else."

"I'll talk to Laura," I said.

"How about I call Miss Hathaway?" He sounded as if he didn't believe I could handle something that simple.

Or maybe I was overreacting. I turned left on Balboa, made myself concentrate on driving. This time, instead of going to the Hilton's lot, I pulled up behind the Blackstone Hotel.

"I'll pick you up in the morning," I said. "Same time, same place."

"See you then." He got out of the van as if he couldn't wait to be shed of me. He hurried along the sidewalk, looking both ways like he expected an attack.

I sighed and kept driving down Balboa to State. The traffic wasn't quite as bad here, and as I got away from downtown, the traffic got lighter.

I turned on the radio and turned the dial until I found news. The newscaster played tape from the morning rally.

Apparently the group that held the rally in the park was all female, all a part of the Weathermen. I heard snippets of a woman's speech—something about the martyrdom of Che Guevara in Bolivia two years ago, and comparing that with the sacrifices of the Chicago Eight now on trial. The woman called for violence, to remind the "pigs" of the pain they'd caused, and then her voice faded out to be replaced with chanting and the sound of nightsticks against gloves.

The entire thing sounded awful, but the reporter who covered it claimed the marchers were just scared little girls who didn't know what to do when faced with a police line.

That speech didn't sound like something a scared little girl would say, but what did I know? I didn't understand any of this.

By the time I reached the church, I had turned the radio back to WVON, letting Ruth Brown's sultry voice and racy lyrics ease my frayed soul.

The kids poured out of the church, Jimmy first with his best friend, Keith Grimshaw, beside him. Jonathan Grimshaw, the oldest at fifteen, held the hands of his sisters Mikie and Norene. Lacey brought up the rear, wiping the makeup off her face with a Kleenex as if she thought I didn't see her.

"You're late," Jimmy said as he pulled open the back door.

94

"I've got five minutes according to my very nice watch," I said.

"Mrs. Armitage was fretting," Keith said, sounding more like his mother than the eleven-year-old imp he usually was.

The boys crawled in, followed by Jonathan and the girls.

"Tell Lacey she's sitting up front," I said.

"Forget it!" Lacey was thirteen going on trouble.

"Up front or you're walking, Lace," I said, making a threat I knew I couldn't live up to.

She sighed so theatrically I could hear her over the engine and Ike Turner. Then she stomped around the van, pulled open the passenger door, and glared at the coveralls on the floorboards.

"What's that?" she asked, as if it were a live thing.

"Just some clothes," I said. "Throw them in the back if they bother you."

She wrinkled her nose, shoved at the clothes with her high-heeled foot, then got in. As she pulled the door closed she said to me, "You look weird."

"I've been working."

"You don't usually dress like that."

"I will be for the next week or two," I said. "You missed a beauty mark on your left cheek."

Her hand came up before she realized what she'd done. Then she looked at me as I started the drive home.

"You're not going to tell my dad, are you, Uncle Bill?"

"That you've decided to ignore his wishes? Why would I do that, Lace?"

She rolled her eyes at my sarcasm. "You don't understand."

"Surprisingly, I do," I said. "You just don't know the kind of men who go after little girls like you."

"I'm not little." She was right; she wasn't little any more. Her body had filled out.

I sighed, wondering how deep to get into this. "Has your mom talked to you?"

Her cheeks flushed redder than any rouge could ever make them. "Uncle Bill," she breathed.

"About boys and girls," I added, realizing she was thinking of the other mother-daughter talk.

"I know all I need to know."

I bit my lower lip, then leaned back just a little. Behind me, Norene was holding court, telling everyone about the importance of second grade. Mikie was trying to stop her by reminding her that everyone else had gone through second grade.

Keith and Jimmy were egging the girls on, and Jonathan wasn't saying a word. I wondered if he was listening to Lacey and me.

"Lace," I said, "if you continue to ignore your dad, you could get into real trouble."

"I don't get into trouble, Uncle Bill," she said. "I know what I'm doing."

At thirteen. Sure she did. But what could I say? I hoped that Althea had told her about condoms, but I doubted that she had. And I couldn't figure out a way to do so.

The voices behind me continued. I turned on to the Grimshaws' street.

"Lace, listen. I know you think you'll be all right—"

"Uncle Bill, I will. Honest."

"But," I said, "if something should happen, if some guy hurts you or wants you to do something you don't want to do, you come see me, okay?"

She looked at me, surprised. Apparently no one had ever said anything like that to her before.

"Okay," she said, sounding confused.

I pulled up in front of the house. She had the door open before the van had fully stopped. She was slipping off her high heels and hurrying, barefoot, across the sidewalk toward the porch.

The back doors opened and the remaining Grimshaw children spilled out, chorusing their good-byes. Only Norene took the time to wave at me—her braids askew, like they always were this late in the day—before she ran toward the house.

"Come up front, Jim," I said. "I'm not chauffeuring you home."

He liked riding in the back of the van, able to lie flat and read or sit with his back against the wall. We'd had arguments about that before.

This afternoon, however, he didn't argue. He slammed the back doors closed and slid into the seat Lacey had just vacated.

"How come you're so worried about Lace?" Jimmy asked. "She just wants to dress the way she likes, not the way Aunt Althea thinks is right."

"There's more to it than that," I said. "Things Lacey doesn't understand yet."

"You mean like my mom?" Jimmy asked.

I looked at him, glad I hadn't started the van. He was looking at his hands.

His mother had been a prostitute. She hadn't known who Jimmy's father was. For a while she had tried to raise her sons alone, but she was never reliable. I remembered seeing Jimmy on the street when he was as young as three, begging for food. I used to take him to nearby restaurants for warm meals. That was when I learned that his mother would take off for weeks at a time, leaving him in the care of his older brother, Joe.

Joe eventually joined a gang and started dealing drugs, abandoning Jimmy too. And when he got evicted from his apartment for lack of payment, I helped him find a foster home.

That might have worked, if it weren't for Martin's assassination. Jimmy had been across the street, and he'd seen the shooter, a man who wasn't James Earl Ray.

That's when I took Jimmy, left Memphis, and came here. From that moment on Jimmy was my son, and he'd remain mine until the end of my life.

But we'd never talked much about his mother. He hadn't said much and I hadn't asked, thinking he'd talk to me when he wanted to.

"What do you mean, like your mother?" I asked gently, glad I hadn't started to drive away yet, so that I could pay attention to Jim.

"My mom, she used to dress like Lace when she went to work." He said that so matter-of-factly. "I been wanting to tell Lace, but I can't, since you said we can't say nothing about Memphis."

I nodded. So that was Jimmy's dilemma. Of all the children I'd just had in the car, he was the only one who understood why Lacey's path was dangerous, and he had no way to talk to her about it.

"She wouldn't understand," I said. "She thinks you're my biological son. We've always said your mother is gone, which is true, but most people think that means she died. Lacey can't imagine a woman like your mother."

"I know." Jimmy was still looking at his hands. "You don't think Lace'll end up like my mom, do you?"

I put a hand on his shoulder, suddenly understanding his fear. My fears for Lacey were bad, but his were worse.

"She won't end up like your mom," I said. "She has too many friends and family for that. But she could get hurt."

Jimmy raised his head and looked at me, his eyes wide. "Some trick'll hurt her?"

The word stopped me, but only for a moment. "Some boy'll hurt her. He'll think that she wants to do what your mom used to do. Lacey won't understand and—"

"He'll just do her. I know." Jimmy sighed.

I felt out of my depth. Sometimes I couldn't even imagine what this boy had seen.

"We can't talk her out of dressing like this," I said. "We've been trying for nearly a year."

"Uncle Franklin took her makeup away, but she just borrows it from the girls at school," Jimmy said. "Even Jonathan says she looks awful."

"She'll do what she wants," I said, hoping my tone at least would reassure him. I was trying to keep my voice as steady as possible. "But if she does get into trouble—if she starts crying a lot, or acting really angry for no reason, tell me, okay?"

"What if she don't want me to?" he asked.

"Tell me that too."

"Feels like tattling," he said.

"If someone just—does her—" I hated that phrase, but he obviously understood it from his past "—then she's not going to want to tell her parents. Maybe she'll tell me. We can make sure it won't happen again. We'd be protecting her, Jim, not tattling on her."

He nodded. Then he leaned back and closed his eyes. "Even my mom said it was nasty when some guy didn't listen. And she said she usually liked nasty."

I clenched a fist against my thigh. She had no right to say things like that to her son. To her nine-year-old son. She hadn't even been around for Jim's tenth birthday.

But she had a point. And for the first time, her words were helping me with Jim. I wasn't going to take that understanding away.

"I'm sure Lacey's parents will keep trying to talk to her," I said. "But keep an eye out, Jim. If the talking doesn't work, she's going to need all the help she can get."

SIXTEEN

The conversation with Jimmy left me shaken up. I remained awake long after he went to sleep, wishing I could wipe that hideous childhood from his mind.

I had no idea how it would affect him in his teen years. I hadn't wanted to think about how his mother's behavior would influence his own when his hormones took over his body.

I often mentally criticized Althea for not having the right talk with Lacey, but I hadn't talked to Jimmy either, and I wondered if I was running out of time.

At ten o'clock I turned on the local news, hoping to distract myself with the weather. I settled onto the couch, noting that the springs were nearly gone, and put my feet on our scarred coffee table.

The lead story was about the rally in Grant Park. I was startled to learn that less than one hundred women had gathered there. On film, the entire thing looked ridiculous: a group of young women wearing crash helmets and biker suits carried clubs over their shoulders like they were cave women. Apparently their mission had been to go to the Army Induction Center and "free" the poor draftees, but no one made it out of the park.

The phalanx of police officers along the edges of the park reminded me of the groups I had seen a year ago during the convention—police in their riot gear, lined up like they expected trouble—and if it didn't start, they might help it along.

It was only a matter of time before more people got hurt. After the melee the night before, Governor Ogilvie had called out the National Guard. Shades of Memphis during my last few weeks there. I never did get used to the Guard patrolling the streets in tanks, guns slung over their arms like they intended to use them.

I'd learned there—and it had been repeated all over after Martin was assassinated—that young men with guns always looked for an excuse to use them.

A shiver ran down my back just as the report switched. The anchor segued away from the Weathermen, talking about the groups of young people who did not support them, including a whole other branch of the SDS called the Revolutionary Youth Movement Two. I was beginning to think I would need a scorecard when Black Panther leader Fred Hampton appeared on my television screen.

Hampton was standing in front of the Panther headquarters on the West Side, wearing some dark glasses that made him seem older than a young man barely out of his teens. He also looked burlier than I remembered, or maybe that was just what the cameras did to him.

The anchor sounded surprised in his voice-over as he informed Chicagoland that the Black Panthers did not support the Weathermen. In fact, the anchor said, the Weathermen's actions were too violent for the Panthers.

"We believe that the Weathermen's action is anarchistic, opportunistic, individualistic," Hampton said, in the church rhythms that made Martin so easy to listen to. "It's chauvinistic, it's custeristic, and that's the bad part about it. It's custeristic in that its leaders take people into situations where the people can be massacred. And they call it revolution. It's nothing but child's play. It's folly. We think these people may be sincere, but they're misguided, they're muddle-headed, and scatterbrained."

He sounded scared to me, and I remembered what someone had said, that Hampton believed the police (and now the National Guard) would take out their frustrations on the black community, not on the suburban white kids who were starting it all.

I wondered if he'd considered the effect of having the Black Panther leader say that the Weathermen were custeristic gave the Weathermen even more power. They suddenly had a validation that they hadn't had before.

They even scared the Black Panthers.

I was certain Hampton had continued with his speech, maybe even discussing the effects of the Weathermen "actions" on the black community, but of course the local newscasts didn't air the rest of his comments.

The news segued into a story about four society women getting Judge Hoffman to let them into the gallery of the Conspiracy Trial.

I sighed, got up, and turned the damn thing off before the weather, just as the announcer told me that Joe DiMaggio was going to Vietnam.

As if a baseball player could stop a war.

Or society women could view the trial of the century as if it were a show put on just for them.

Or a black man could say something sensible and expect fair press coverage.

I wandered off to bed, knowing I would lie there for a long time, wide awake, worrying about all the things I couldn't change.

SEVENTEEN

That morning, LeDoux was the one who added to our wardrobes. He came out of the hotel carrying a box under his arm. When he got to the van, he motioned me toward the back.

The box was full of cheap cotton gloves.

"I special-order them," he said. "They become essential in my line of work."

He preferred the latex gloves that some hospitals used, but those were expensive, so he hadn't brought any to Chicago. But his office in New York had shipped these and they had arrived yesterday.

He handed me several, urging me to stuff extras into my coveralls so that I could touch things without worrying too much about destroying the evidence.

He gave me specific instructions on how to use the gloves, and then gave me some plastic sandwich bags to store each pair in when I was done.

"Don't wear the same pair in different apartments," he said. "Mark each bag with the apartment number, so that I know where the gloves came from. You might acquire trace evidence that we don't get any other way, and I'll need that. I might also have to eliminate some cloth from the gloves in the fiber evidence, should I collect any, and I'll want to see if your gloves are ripped or torn."

As we changed into our coveralls and then got into the van, he continued to explain the importance of gloves to crime-scene work. I tuned him out at some point. While I realized his efforts were extremely important and his attention to the most minute detail critical to any case that we might build down the road, I really didn't care about dust layers and grease smudges, and the importance of matching dirt to dirt marks.

The day was cooler than the day before, and the promise of rain held. Only it didn't feel like the sky was dripping humidity. The air had an autumn chill which I welcomed.

We drove through the Loop, avoiding the worst of the traffic. When we hit Bronzeville, LeDoux switched topics. He wanted to know if I had spoken to Laura.

In all the turmoil of the night before, I had forgotten to call her. LeDoux nodded, as if he had expected that of me, and proceeded to tell me about his conversation with her.

Apparently, Sturdy kept a few furnished apartments in their high-end complexes for visiting businessmen. It was less expensive for the company to do this than rent hotel rooms for a month or more.

According to LeDoux, McMillan had often made use of these apartments when he was in Chicago, before he actually bought one of his own.

LeDoux would be staying on the Gold Coast. Laura would meet him after we finished work this evening and take him to his new place.

"It's not great," he said, "but at least I'm away from the Loop and whatever those crazy kids were doing."

"Those crazy kids were in the Gold Coast two nights ago," I said, in case he didn't know what part of town Laura's apartment was in.

"Yes, but those buildings had security. The hotel actually went into something they called lockdown during the riot yesterday morning; they locked the building tight and wouldn't let anyone in or out."

That was a new policy since the convention, and one hotel patrons probably hated.

"If you'd brought me back at lunch," he was saying, "I wouldn't have been able to get into the hotel, let alone my room."

I nodded. I wouldn't like that either. "Most of those buildings don't have hidden parking areas, so I'll be conspicuous picking you up. We should probably meet somewhere else. Have Laura show you a nearby restaurant where you can have a good breakfast, and I'll pull up outside at a designated time. All right?"

He nodded, looking out the window at the changing neighborhoods. "This city is such a damn mess. It'd be a lot easier if I could just travel on my own."

"Not down here," I said, as we took the last turn before we reached the Queen Anne. "Any car you drive would be conspicuous, and so would you."

"I know." This time his words were soft. I empathized. I wouldn't be in Chicago either if I could have found a better place to live. But LeDoux probably had a better place to live. He wasn't protecting a fugitive child, and he was white. A lot of smaller cities in this country—a lot of smaller towns—weren't really touched by the violence that seemed endemic in the larger ones.

I parked the van in the same spot that I had the day before. We carried a few more paint cans to the door, which I unlocked with ease. The place looked undisturbed yet again.

I wondered how long that would last.

It only took a few minutes to get LeDoux back to work. For all his complaining about Chicago, this Queen Anne intrigued him. He wanted to collect all its secrets.

As I gathered my flashlight and my clipboard, I turned to him. "Did you talk to Laura about evidence storage?"

He had returned to the side of the cabinet, crouching just where I had found him the night before. His lips thinned in disgust. "I forgot. Did you?"

"No," I said. "I'll take care of it later."

"We're all right at the moment." He glanced at the open cabinet doors. "But I have no idea how long that will last."

"I'll see what I can do," I said.

Then I left the basement. I stopped in the back entry, near Hanley's apartment, and ran the flashlight along the walls. Victorian houses usually had a servants' stair off the kitchen. Since Hanley's apartment had been built over the site of the original kitchen, the stairs had to be somewhere nearby.

But they weren't in the entry, and I still wasn't ready to look in the place where he had died.

So I went back outside, grabbed my toolbox from the van, and walked to the front of the building. I let myself in, feeling less conspicuous than I had the day before.

I wasn't sure if that was a good thing, if I was getting used to this neighborhood. It certainly didn't seem much different than it had been the day before, but I couldn't look around. I had done that the day before, and if I did it every day, I would look suspicious.

Once inside, I closed and locked the door, then left the toolbox in the entry. This time I didn't turn on the lights, preferring to use my flashlight. I hurried up the oak stairs, then took the narrower stairs to the third floor.

My heart was pounding, and it wasn't from the exertion. I didn't like it up here, and I wasn't sure why. I went all the way to the end of the hall and stopped at that bathroom, using the flashlight the way I'd seen LeDoux use his, as a way of examining each bit of flooring and every inch of wall.

The bathroom was as filthy as I had thought. The claw-footed tub had some kind of brownish-black goo lining its porcelain surface on the inside, and all sorts of scratches and scuff marks on the outside.

The water in the toilet was brackish and brown. I debated lifting the lid on the storage tank to see if that water had rust in it, then decided against it. Just the condition of the tub alone convinced me that LeDoux would have to examine this room. He could take care of the lid.

An ancient medicine cabinet stood partially open near the toilet. I was glad for the gloves as I used my index finger to pry the cabinet open the rest of the way.

A surprising number of things greeted me, some that I expected, and some that I didn't. I expected the aspirin and the Mercurochrome, but not the two dozen other pill bottles that seemed to be arranged by type, although they weren't marked. The tweezers seemed normal to me, but not the small pair of pliers. And what was a medicine cabinet without Band-Aids—only this one had treated bits of gauze as well, all of them separated by some kind of paper.

I eased the cabinet closed and turned to the built-in linen closet. That door I had to pry open. There were no towels or sheets inside. Instead, the top rows held empty jars with rusted metal screw-tops, as if someone had planned to use them for storage (for the nails in apartment nine or for the bullets?).

The jars made some kind of quirky sense—tenants left the darndest things—but the rest of the closet held items I'd never seen in an apartment building before, at least not in this quantity.

One entire shelf held adhesive bandages, sterile roller gauze, and adhesive tape. Next to those were light, stiff boards that took me a moment to recognize. When I was in the service, we'd had them in our field medical kit so that we could make impromptu splints.

Then there were the bottles: rubbing alcohol (nearly a dozen), hydrogen peroxide (five large bottles), iodine (more small bottles than I could quickly count), and Phisohex (which seemed to fill up one entire shelf all on its own).

Forceps, tongue depressors, and thermometers lined the front of a lower shelf, with more items behind.

I let go of the door, watching it close on its own, and finally remembered to breathe.

I was looking at medical supplies—for what, I didn't know. But a normal home only had a few of these things, and an apartment complex, even with a shared bathroom, generally had none.

At least that I had ever seen, and I'd been inspecting these places for almost a year now.

The entire thing disturbed me more than I could say, and so did the pile of dirty rags that filled the corner behind the door. To my eye, the brownish-red substance on those rags was blood, but I knew from experience that substance could be a lot of things.

I'd been put in mind of blood by the bodies downstairs and the medical supplies up here.

I made myself examine the rest of the room, finding more cobwebs and dust than I cared to think about. I had no idea how old any of this stuff was, but I was certain LeDoux would figure it out. He'd probably read every label and would make a report that noted how long each bottle had been inside that closet.

As I left the bathroom, I remembered to remove that pair of gloves. I grabbed one of the plastic bags that I'd shoved in the back pocket of my coveralls, wrote on the white label that LeDoux (or someone) had pasted onto the outside "third-floor public bathroom," and dropped the gloves inside. Then I closed the bag, pressing down on the piece of tape, and dropped the entire thing in the hallway outside apartment nine.

I'd forgotten to bring one of the grocery bags that LeDoux also insisted we carry.

Then I put on another pair of gloves, unlocked apartment nine, and stepped inside.

It smelled just as bad as it had the day before. I sneezed, covering my mouth with my arm. I turned on the fluorescents and waited for them to catch. This time, I vowed to ignore the tarps and the bullets and the gardening equipment and examine the walls of the room.

I used my flashlight to look for any suspicious cracks or lines on the walls. Mostly they were covered with old newsprint or good-girl art taken from old calendars. I couldn't see much. So I started beside the door and rapped on any available wallboard that I could see.

Dirt occasionally fell to the floor, and I dislodged one clipping. The clipping slipped behind a box of bolts, and I decided to leave it all for LeDoux.

I was only going to be able to touch three of the four walls. The one farthest from me was buried behind all that equipment. To reach the third, I had to reach over those upholstered chairs that, up close, smelled of rodent droppings and terrible mildew.

The paint was a different color here, grayer—older, perhaps. I braced my right hand on the back of the nearest chair, and then knocked. The sound wasn't hollow. It was barely a knock.

My fingers hadn't hit plaster and lath; they'd found particle board.

I stepped back. This was the interior wall, but it shared a corner with the outside wall. I silently apologized to LeDoux, then slid the two chairs out of my way. I rapped on the interior wall again—yes, particle board—and then on the exterior wall, which was clearly plaster and lath.

The walls didn't line up well either. The particle-board wall had warped and moved about an eighth of an inch away from the exterior wall.

I trained my flashlight on that tiny crack, then peered inside. I couldn't see much, but something reflected white at me.

My stomach churned. This place seemed to always make me queasy. I didn't want to pull that wall aside, but I was going to. And I wasn't sure I would like what I found inside.

It didn't take a lot of strength to knock a good-sized hole in the particle board. I didn't even have to set down my light. I looked inside, afraid I'd find more bodies, but all I saw were yellowish-white walls, a dust-covered wooden floor, and a door.

Another hidden door.

There had to be a better way to get inside, but I couldn't see it. I widened the hole until I could step through it, letting the pieces of particle board fall inside the hole instead of out (that way LeDoux would know what part came from my destruction and what came from things that had happened before we arrived).

First I leaned in and let the flashlight explore all the angles of the cubbyhole. There wasn't much to see—just someone's desire to hide yet another door from prying eyes.

Then I stepped inside and looked again. Cobwebs on the ceiling indicated that no one had been in here for quite a while. There was a small space behind the particle-board wall.

It had been engineered to slide back. If I had tried hard enough, I could have slid it toward the apartment's door, and then stepped through without doing any damage.

Someone had designed this to give easy access to the door hidden by this wall. But that same someone hadn't wanted anyone to know the door was there.

I tried the knob. The door was locked, just like I expected.

I fumbled through the ring of keys, trying almost two dozen before I finally found the one that worked.

The lock clicked, and the door actually creaked open, sending a shiver along my spine.

I shone the light inside, surprised to see a landing. Narrow stairs ran down to the right, and up to the left.

The servants' staircase. I had a hunch it ended in Hanley's apartment on the first floor.

I opted to go up first.

But again, before I did, I propped this door open, then left it, went into the main part of the apartment, and propped the apartment door open as well. If LeDoux came looking for me, he would at least have an idea where I had gone.

I walked back in the hole. Butterflies had replaced the queasiness. I was breathing too shallowly—the smell and the dust caused that—and I was feeling lightheaded.

I made myself take a deeper breath, even though I really didn't want to taste the fetid air.

The stairs leading up were so tiny that I had trouble fitting my shoes on them. I had to climb up on the balls of my feet, once again using the wall as a banister.

The air smelled stale up here, dust-filled, and old in a way that I couldn't describe. That pervasive odor of rot was here too, but not as offensive as it had been in some other places. Just a lingering afterthought, as if this part of the building had once housed something awful, but did no longer.

The stairway turned and opened under the eaves. I had to crouch to keep from bumping my head. The edges of the walls were unfinished—newspapers and some kind of material peeked out from behind the wallboard, obviously an old-fashioned source of insulation.

Gravel and dirt lined the edges, and along the very side I saw mouse prints, hundreds of them, along with black flecks of mouse droppings.

I had to remain bent at the waist to get all the way into the room. I braced a hand against the ceiling, and when it became clear that I could stand, I did.

Tables surrounded me. Tables covered with things—jars filled with buttons and campaign pins and marbles. Folded bits of clothing, blankets, and coats. Socks rolled up the way my mother used to do when she'd put them in my bureau drawer, and underwear that looked used.

Beneath the tables, open boxes. The one nearest to me was filled with newspapers—not clippings this time, but entire editions of the *Chicago Tribune.* Another box held the *Chicago Record,* and a third held the *Chicago Times.*

The boxes trailed back into the darkness, filled not just with newspapers, but magazines and snapshots as well. I felt vaguely overwhelmed and hoped that most of this was just items abandoned by previous tenants.

But of course, I wasn't that lucky.

I turned and banged into the table behind me. A jar tumbled toward me, jingling as it fell, and I caught it.

At first I thought it held stones in the bottom, maybe a child's collection of something, and then those stones reflected my flashlight beam.

I turned the beam on the jar completely, brought the jar closer so that I could see it clearly, and then nearly dropped it.

What I had thought were stones were teeth.

Gold caps, gold fillings, and bits of loose gold.

Some of the fillings hadn't been removed from their tooth. The tooth remained at the bottom of the jar, bits of tissue hanging off the jagged ends.

The queasiness was back full-force. I set the jar down, careful not to dislodge it again, and made myself breathe evenly.

The table I had bumped into was a worktable. In the very center someone had carefully laid out a blotter, placed a lamp beside it, and set tools along the right edge.

Behind the table, a straight-backed chair with no cushion had been pushed up close, its wooden seat worn smooth from use. A few empty jars sat to the left side, a few full jars to the right.

This was the only table with nothing stored beneath it.

I made myself look at the tools. A dental pick, tweezers, and another pair of pliers. Some jeweler's cloths lay to one side, and beside them, one of the bottles of hydrogen peroxide. A small bowl was placed on top of the peroxide, upside down, obviously intended for use whenever the owner of all this stuff returned.

I scanned the flashlight over the end tables behind this main table. More jars, these holding jewelry, separated by rings and watches and pins.

The window behind all of it had been boarded up except along the bottom—perhaps so that it could be opened a crack in the heat of the summer—and along the back wall, hats. Dozens of them, all hanging on pegs. Bowlers and stocking caps and fedoras. There were a few straw hats and a haymaker, as well as billed tweed caps. Along the bottom were several garrison caps and a few other military caps, the foldable kind used in both World Wars.

I let out a small breath, feeling shaky. Maybe the air was bad up here or maybe the sheer numbers were starting to overwhelm me.

A bulletin board had been pasted on the eave wall beside some of the caps, and on it someone had pressed papers—pictures, cards, postcards, letters. I couldn't get back there, not without disturbing everything else, but knew I would have to as soon as I could get LeDoux up here to photograph everything.

Then my light caught another table, the one directly behind the worktable, and I realized that one was a worktable too. Only on it were gun parts, oil, a cleaning rod, and a repair kit like the one I had had in Memphis. A grip lay on its side, unattached, and a barrel with a dent along the edge sat in the middle of yet another blotter.

This was clearly a workroom of some kind, but all the clues kept miscuing me. What kind, exactly? The teeth implied one thing, the gun another, the hats yet one more. And then there was the newspaper storage, not to mention the medical supplies downstairs.

What kind of business had been run out of this place? What had been going on?

I turned all the way around—carefully this time—and headed back down the stairs. Much as I didn't want to, I would have to consult with LeDoux. We would have to make decisions together on all these finds, how we were going to investigate them, and then what we would do with the remaining pieces.

I would also have to call Laura and update her.

She wouldn't welcome this news, any more than I did.

I shuddered and went down through the cobwebs, all the way to Hanley's apartment.

EIGHTEEN

The stench of decaying flesh grew worse the farther down the stairs I went. I knew it would; no one had cleaned Hanley's apartment after finding him there during a heatwave, dead for more than a week.

I went down the stairs carefully, the flashlight in my right hand. I didn't touch the walls for balance here; I didn't want to think about what could be on them.

Halfway down the first flight, a cobweb brushed my face. I jumped, brushed the web away, and kept going, my heart pounding. I had put this off for a long time—going to Hanley's apartment, seeing what kind of damage his decaying corpse had done. Now I would have to face it.

There was no landing on the second floor like there had been on the third. Apparently servants weren't supposed to enter the second floor unless they absolutely had to. There was a door, but it had been boarded over and painted shut a long time ago. The nails in the boards had rusted. No one had used this door since the building was converted to apartments decades before.

I continued down. The stairwell seemed even darker than it had above, even though I knew that was a figment of my imagination. The stink grew worse. The air was actually coated with it, and it felt like it had gotten on my skin.

At the bottom of the stairs there was a narrow landing and a brand-new light switch—at least, brand-new in the context of this house. The switch had been installed in the last five years. I flicked it on just to see if the light bulbs worked.

They did. The entire stairwell lit up, revealing unfinished walls and rough wood stairs. The cobwebs were thin, not the kind that had been woven and rewoven year after long year. These webs came from spiders that felt free to build, but only recently. Some were so thin I hadn't felt them as I broke through them.

Now I felt crawly, and I willed the sensation away.

The door in front of me had a shiny new deadbolt, as well as a brand new knob. It was a hollow-core door, obviously a replacement for an older door, and it locked from this side.

I turned the deadbolt, then turned the knob and opened the door. A waft of heat hit me, and that stink, even worse than before, oily and grotesque.

My eyes watered. I blinked, forcing myself to breathe, knowing that the only way to deal with the smell was to get used to it.

The door opened into a good-sized kitchen, clearly remodeled from the house's original kitchen. A stove stood next to the wall and a deep sink stood under a window. The table in the middle had the remains of a meal on it. The food was green and covered with flies.

More food rotted on the counters, all of it unidentifiable, except for a bunch of bananas, thin and black and melting into a puddle on the linoleum. There were no dirty dishes in the sink; Hanley had been neater than I expected.

The *Sun-Times* and the *Tribune* sat on the table as well, yellowing in the sun that had poured in from that window. The newspapers were unopened, probably dating back to the day Hanley had died.

I closed the door to the stairwell, then turned to look at it. The door looked like any other; its placement in the remodeled kitchen suggested a closet door or a door that led into a small storage area, not one that opened onto a narrow stairway

I checked the knob. It locked automatically. If I remembered, I'd come back and thumb through my keyring until I found the key to the deadbolt.

For the moment, though, I had to get out of that kitchen. I went through an archway into a room I guessed had once housed the ice-box. A refrigerator was plugged into the wall nearest the stove, but the rest of the room had filing cabinets and keys hanging off the wall.

A desk stood near another small window. Piled on top of the desk were bills, their envelopes also yellowing in the sun.

I couldn't tell where the heat was coming from. I'd checked the stove as I passed, and it was off. This room was just as warm as the kitchen had been. Sweat trickled down my back.

A narrow archway opened into yet another room. This archway had been cut into the wall later—in the original flow of the house, no one had been meant to go from the icebox room to what had to have been a back parlor.

It had been Hanley's living room, and I finally found the source of the heat. This room had electric heaters built into the wall; it wasn't on the boiler system at all. The heaters had been cranked up to high, and no one had shut them off. Apparently no one had noticed when they came to pick up the body.

I shut them off now, thankful that the building hadn't burned down. I opened a window, as much for the heat as the smell, and felt relief as a cool breeze floated in.

The living room had a narrow couch with sagging cushions, two cheap blankets wadded on one side and a pillow on the other. The coffee table housed a collection of coffee cups, all half full, two empty Kleenex boxes, and a lot of wadded-up tissues, as well as four plates, two bowls, and a spoon that all bore stains from the food that had once been on them.

A console television—the most expensive item in the room—was pushed up against the far wall, but its top was curiously bare. Most people placed photographs on top or mementos, but Hanley hadn't even put a *TV Guide* up there.

The television sections from the *Tribune* did sit in a basket beside the couch. Hanley had apparently spent a long time there while his health got worse.

This was a one-man apartment. There were no other chairs, no place for a visitor to put up his feet. The remaining door led to the bedroom. The bathroom was off the bedroom, a tiny afterthought without a window, and barely enough room for a shower.

I couldn't stay long in the bedroom—the smell was eye-poppingly bad in there. The blankets had been pulled away from the bed and a large stain covered the bottom sheet. I did make myself check the walls for another electric heater, but I didn't find one.

Then I frowned, wondering how the mailman would have seen

Hanley if he had died in here—which the stench and the stain told me he had. The window was covered by a shade and curtains: when I raised them, I saw only the building next door.

There was something odd about this entire setup, but I wasn't confident enough in my memory to be sure about the story of Hanley's death. Laura had told me how they'd found Hanley. She had heard it from someone else who had heard it from someone else.

Perhaps she had gotten the story wrong, the way children did in a game of telephone.

Or maybe there was a different version of the truth.

Aside from that bed, the apartment had nothing unexpected—no tools, no guns, no jars filled with teeth. It looked like what it was: an apartment of a man who had lived most of his life alone, managing other apartments.

I'd search drawers and closets when I got the chance, but I didn't expect to find much else. I had a hunch all the scary stuff was on the third floor—and in the basement.

That thought reminded me that I had to go back down there to talk with LeDoux. Instead of going out the apartment's front door and down the nearby stairs, I backtracked, locking off the hidden staircase as I went. I didn't remember to remove my gloves until I was all the way outside apartment nine.

Then I removed the gloves, bagged them, and labeled that plastic bag as "Nine, Hidden, Manager." If LeDoux wanted to know exactly what that meant, he'd have to ask me.

I put on the third pair of gloves for the past hour, then went down the main flight of stairs, and out the front door. A police car drove by, going slowly. My stomach clenched.

The officer in the passenger seat raised the bill of his cap so that he could see me better. I resisted the urge to lower my cap. Instead, I pretended I hadn't seen him and headed down the side of the building, hoping that that tiny interaction hadn't called too much attention to our activity at the house.

It seemed odd for the police to cruise this neighborhood in the middle of the day—particularly a day like this, when the entire city was dealing with the Weathermen and the protests.

But I didn't live here, and I hadn't worked here long enough to notice the neighborhood patterns. I hoped that no one had called the police to check us out this soon.

When I reached the basement, I was covered in a fine layer of sweat despite the day's cooler temperatures. LeDoux was standing just inside the hidden door. When he saw me, he wrinkled his nose.

"Where'd you find that smell?" he asked.

"Manager's apartment," I said, "just like I expected."

"Whew," he said. "We're going to have to take care of that."

I nodded.

Then he frowned. "Thought you were going upstairs."

"I did. I found the servant's stairs." And I proceeded to tell him about the second hidden door, the stash in the attic, and the staircase that led to the manager's apartment.

"I don't like where this is leading," LeDoux said.

"Have you seen anything like this before?" I asked.

"Not exactly like this, no," he said. "And we still don't know what we're up against, although it seems to me you're going to have to do some preliminary research."

"On Hanley."

He nodded, then peered at the crumbling brick wall. He hadn't moved any of the bricks, and so far had not gone inside the area where the skeletons were.

"You want me to help you with the wall?" I asked.

He bit his lower lip. "I've been debating how to proceed. I couldn't decide between handling this area or figuring out what else this basement held."

He turned, then grabbed my flashlight and flicked it on. The beam centered on the other brick walls, their uneven construction even clearer in the light from the overhead bulb and the scrutiny LeDoux was giving them.

"I think we need to know," I said.

"I think we *do* know," he said. "I think we're just afraid to find out that we're right."

NINETEEN

We skipped lunch. I doubted either of us could have eaten anyway. Even though I wasn't hungry, my queasiness had vanished. Instead, I felt an odd bleakness.

We had found evidence of a huge crime, perhaps several crimes, and we only found it because the perpetrator was dead. The only justice those three skeletons would get was a real burial after we identified them.

If we could identify them.

LeDoux and I didn't talk much. He outlined our plan of attack on these brick walls as if he were a general and this was D-day. I didn't mind. I needed to do something physical.

My task was simple: I had to remove a single brick from each of the differently made areas so that we could look inside and see if any other surprises awaited us.

I started all the way to the left on the long wall facing us. I squeezed in beside the bricks and mortar that were down here to build more walls and crouched. LeDoux wanted that single brick to be removed about a yard from the floor. That way, we could see what was on the floor and have a sense of what was above the floor as well.

Removing the brick took more work than I expected. I had to carefully chip out the mortar, then get my fingers on the side and pull the brick toward me. Mortar fell into the hole—there was no way to avoid that—and part of the brick itself crumbled into my hand.

LeDoux didn't watch me work. Instead, he was moving the supplies and stacking them against the wall behind me, making room to store any bricks we removed. We would have to label them, of course, and we were both wearing gloves, just in case.

At first I had protested, but when the edges of the brick caught my fingertips through the material, I was grateful to have something protecting my hand, thin as the cotton was.

I finally got the brick out. LeDoux took it from me, put it in a bag along with all the crumbly pieces that had caught in my palm, and set the bag—well marked—along that far wall.

By the time he came back, I had already picked up my flashlight, and shone it inside the hole.

Another brick wall greeted me. It looked like it was about a foot away, and from what I could tell in the circle formed by the flashlight's beam, this new brick wall was different from all the others we'd seen.

"Allow me," LeDoux said as he crouched beside me.

I moved aside. There was no way both of us would be able to see inside that tiny hole.

He used his own flashlight as I went to the next brick. He'd marked the ones he wanted removed. I ran a screwdriver around the edge of the brick, noting that the mortar here wasn't as crumbly. It also didn't seem to have the same consistency—or lack thereof—as the previous section.

The brick itself was wider horizontally than the previous one, but narrower vertically. I turned to LeDoux to ask him if he wanted me to remove a second brick, only to find him in a half-standing position, pointing his flashlight downward.

"You okay?" I asked.

He glanced at me, his skin paler than it had been before. "I think we need to remove a few more bricks."

I got up, took my own flashlight, and peered in. The floor was covered with what looked like discarded clothing.

"How many bricks would you like me to remove?" I asked.

"These." He touched two more beneath the one we'd already removed.

I edged the mortar and gave LeDoux my screwdriver. He worked on the other brick. In a few minutes, we managed to loosen them both. I cleared the rest of the mortar away, and then gave him the bricks, one by one.

He clutched them to his chest as I trained my flashlight inside. The pile on the floor still looked like old clothes to me. Until I saw the easily recognizable bones of a hand peeking out from underneath a flannel shirt.

I kept the light on that hand, the tiny bones perfectly intact and arched downward, as if the skeleton's owner had been trying to claw his way out of that tiny space.

Oddly, there was no smell here. Just a dry-as-dust odor that might have come from the bricks.

"Is that what you saw?" I asked.

"No." LeDoux nodded toward the right. "Against the wall."

He meant the built-in wall. I moved my light over, and caught what looked like flattened white stones.

I shook my head.

"In the corner," he said with some impatience. "Against the wall. Toward the back."

Then I saw it. Teeth and part of a jawbone. The remains of someone's mouth. Only the bottom part of the jaw had jagged edges. It had been broken off.

"This person was dismembered?" I asked. I could hear the disbelief in my voice. I hadn't realized that was how I was feeling, but it made sense. I didn't want to know this, so I hadn't seen the pieces of the body until LeDoux pointed them out to me.

"No," he said. "The parts are where they should be. But I think we're going to find that this poor unfortunate's skull was completely shattered. Once the skin holding it together was gone . . ."

I nodded. I did understand, even though I didn't want to. "He's in there alone?"

LeDoux shrugged. "We can't tell, not from this."

I raised my head, my eyes sore from staring into that blackness. No one had looked into that space in years.

"You think each one of these places is a tomb."

LeDoux sighed. "Let's see."

"There's more brick behind this one," I said.

"I know," LeDoux said. "Let's just do the ones we can see at the moment."

I stood, feeling a little lightheaded. I hadn't been breathing while I crouched down there, looking in. A crushed skull, a bullet wound to the head. These were not accidental deaths.

These were something else.

I moved to the next part of the wall, and finished removing the long, narrow brick. I had to tell LeDoux I was done; he was still looking inside the first hole we'd made.

He glanced at my work. "A bit more, I think. Like this one."

So I removed three more bricks. A swampy smell of decay floated around me, not as bad as it had been in the apartment, but there, almost like a memory. I trained my light inside. An eye greeted me, bloated and almost unrecognizable. I yelped and skittered backwards.

LeDoux looked at me, frowning, as if he hadn't expected a reaction like that from me. I wasn't sure I had either.

He moved to the open space, peered in, and made an involuntary sound of disgust.

"This one's newer," he said.

"How much newer?" I asked.

He shrugged. "There are a few in here. They're not full skeletons yet. But that could be the effect of being crammed into such a tiny area."

Then, almost to himself, he added, "This one's going to be a mess."

As if the rest of them weren't. I glanced at the wall, counted the changes and the marks, and figured we had six more areas to open.

I began removing bricks.

TWENTY

By the fifth opening, I had found that place inside myself that had helped me survive Korea. It was protected, analytical, cold. I had a job to do, and I was going to do it, no matter what I came across.

The third opening had had a single body in it again, this one in women's clothing, both femurs broken, but nothing else obvious—at least until we got the entire tomb open.

The fourth opening held another single body with most of its flesh intact, but seeping and swollen as if it were filled with water. The fetid smell barely registered for me. That was when I realized that I had become detached.

"I have no idea how one man could have done this," I said. "Or why."

"It's not my job to ask why," LeDoux said. His tone had gone flat, just like mine. He was just working now, not reacting.

"How is part of your job, right?"

"I don't speculate."

I wanted to snap at him. I needed speculation. I needed conversation, anything to keep my mind from weaving scenarios that made this basement even worse than it was.

"But," he said, "I do know that these types of things are more common than we like to admit."

So he did understand. Or maybe LeDoux needed to talk too, just to keep himself from speculating, which was, as he mentioned, one of the worst things he could do.

"These types of things?" I asked, wondering exactly what he meant.

"Mass murderers. They're much more common than generally understood."

"Sure," I said, not really believing him. "Hitler, Stalin. You look through history and you find—"

"No." LeDoux cut me off as if I were a particularly poor student. "Killers with more than one victim. With a dozen, maybe more. Killers we've never heard of. We're discovering just how common they are."

"With no one noticing?" I asked. "I can believe a few victims, but dozens—"

"It's not a stretch if you think about it." LeDoux was photographing the third hole, documenting our laborious work. "Jack the Ripper killed—what? Five prostitutes in the space of a few months? Then what happened to him, hmm? Was he killed? Did he go to prison for another crime? Or did he move to a new killing field?"

"No one knows." I knocked some mortar from the side of two bricks. I was getting more efficient, even though the work was getting harder. This mortar had a solid texture, and I was finding it difficult to scrape it aside.

"That is the point," LeDoux said. "No one knows."

He set his camera down, then looked in the hole again and sighed. I didn't know if he felt sadness for the woman inside or if he was just thinking about the work that faced us.

"Jack the Ripper's famous," I said.

"Jack the Ripper was a taunter. They're rare. Most of these mass killers work in silence, I think, not seeking any publicity at all."

Some of the mortar toppled inward. I winced, wondering whose grave I had disturbed this time.

"There are others from all over the country, people you've never heard of."

"You keep saying that," I said, letting some of the irritation I'd been feeling at LeDoux grow.

"You need something sensational to make the news," LeDoux said.

"Like a basement full of bodies," I muttered.

"Like *discovering* a basement full of bodies," LeDoux said. "And yes, I remember the agreement. I'm not going to disclose this to anyone. If I did, we'd never find out what was down here."

That wasn't my priority. My priority was Laura. But he already knew that.

"A basement full of bodies," he said musingly, "or a taunting letter to the editor like that creature in California is doing—"

There was a man who was sending letters to the California papers, claiming to have murdered people in the San Francisco area.

"They've lost that battle, by the way," LeDoux said. "They've given him a name. The Zodiac. These creatures love names."

"You said a lot of these people work in silence," I said.

"I believe most of them do." LeDoux rose up again on his haunches, just enough so that he could see the floor of opening number three.

I managed to loosen more mortar. If I got one more side, I'd be able to remove my first brick of this section.

"And then there are the accidental sensationalists. Chicago had one a few years ago—what was his name? The young man who killed all the nurses?"

"Speck." That had been before I moved here, but I'd heard of it. People still talked about it, with fear in their voices. "He killed eight nurses in a single night."

"Like Starkweather in—what was it? Kansas?"

That had been in the 1950s. The case had dragged on for what seemed like forever.

"It was like these men just snapped and took people with them." LeDoux made some notes on his clipboard. "But the mass killers who work in silence, they're the dangerous ones."

"Why?" I asked.

"Because they're smart." He leaned back and looked at me. Then he swept a hand toward the wall. "If we're right, this man has been killing for decades. *Decades*, Mr. Grimshaw. And we're only figuring it out because he's dead. The Grim Reaper stopped him. We didn't."

"If Hanley is the one who killed them all."

"That stairway and your discoveries today suggest he was."

"But that's an assumption." I got the last brick free. More bodies, crammed into the space, flesh still on the bones. A waft of rot came toward me and my eyes watered. "I thought you weren't going to speculate."

"I wasn't. I'm sorry." He sighed. "More?"

I nodded. "Right up close."

I moved away, then stopped at the sixth section of wall. It looked different too—the bricks were small and evenly made. Machine-made bricks instead of handmade bricks. None of the previous sections had used them.

"Do we need to open these last three?" I asked. "We know what we're going to find."

"Now *you're* speculating," LeDoux said.

I brushed the back of my glove over my face. The fabric, which wasn't white any more, came away a dull gray.

"How could anyone live with this stink? There were apartments in here." I couldn't imagine it. I couldn't imagine any of it.

"The brick blocked a lot of the smell. If you'll note, he even thought to brick the ceiling of each crypt. But this building does have an odor. I noticed it when we first arrived."

"I blamed it on Hanley dying in here and rotting for a couple of weeks."

"Me too." LeDoux finished marking the clipboard. Then he picked up the camera and took shots of section four. "Although it stands to reason that the place always smelled slightly foul and the tenants blamed it on each other. I'm sure you've been in a building that had awful cooking odors or tenants who didn't bathe much."

I had, and recently too. The stench of urine in some of the buildings I'd inspected had been overpowering. And those places had been uninhabited for months, sometimes years.

He was saying, "People don't question much, especially if they have no other choice."

"I suppose." I stood. My knees cracked. I'd been crouching too long. "You haven't answered my question, so I'm going to make the decision. Those remaining sections'll have to wait."

He let the camera fall against his chest. "Probably wise. Each one of these sections has brick behind it. Different brick."

I had noticed that and then put it out of my mind. I still didn't want to think about it.

"If we don't report this," LeDoux said, "this work could take months."

I nodded. It was up to me now. I had some outside investigating to do. If I could find out Hanley's history, figure out—with Minton's help—who these bodies belonged to and what had happened here, at least with the ones we'd found, I would have enough answers. I would know if Laura could bring the police in.

"I think if we excavate all of this at once, we'll be overwhelmed," I said.

LeDoux crossed his arms over his camera strap, clinging to the clipboard with one hand. He did not look happy, and I didn't blame him. I wouldn't want to be responsible for all of this on my own either.

"Besides," I continued, "we might lose a lot of evidence in all the brick and mortar debris if we go too fast. Let's see what we can find out about what we've already found and go from there."

"I have days just on this area alone," LeDoux said, "not counting what your pathologist will do with these corpses."

"I realize that," I said.

He sighed. "What are you thinking?"

"If it was Hanley all alone, like you mentioned, then Sturdy's off the hook," I said.

LeDoux shook his head. "He was their employee."

"But when would they have gotten the chance to inspect this? Besides, I suspect most killers are someone's employee. The employer doesn't get blamed when a man murders his wife. Sturdy won't get blamed for this."

"In their building? Right under their noses?"

"Their PR people should be able to handle it," I said. "People will be more caught up in the whos and hows than the employer."

"He's dead," LeDoux said. "Someone will have to take the fall."

"And you think one of Chicagoland's greatest companies, with ties to the mayor and the city, will take that fall? Especially considering how many employees it has and how many pies it has its fingers in?"

"Put that way, I see no reason to avoid the press now," LeDoux said.

"Stock prices," I said. "And uncertainty. At the moment, you and I suspect Hanley acted alone. If something proves otherwise, if this does go back into Sturdy's past, then the situation could become more dire."

"And what if Hanley knew nothing?" LeDoux asked.

"Tell me how he knew nothing with that staircase," I said. "And the keys to this back door."

LeDoux nodded. "It does point to him."

"It does," I said. "Now let me prove it."

TWENTY-ONE

We quit for the day soon after that. I think neither of us could continue, although we both made noises about being tired, needing showers, wanting time to complete some outside tasks. Even though it was only three in the afternoon, I needed to be shed of that place.

So did LeDoux. Instead of driving back with me, he offered to take the L. I didn't want to be in the van with myself either—not with that rotting stench still on my coveralls, on my skin—but I had no choice.

I drove LeDoux to the nearest L stop. He had taken off his coveralls. In his blue jeans and T-shirt, he looked younger than he was. I convinced him not to carry his cameras or his cases—he was going through a few bad neighborhoods as the L took him back downtown—and then I waited until he boarded the train before driving to my apartment.

I had peeled off my coveralls as well and stuffed them in an evidence bag. I wasn't keeping that bag, though. It would stink up the van. I would have to clean the seats as it was.

Before going into the building, I tossed the bag in one of the garbage cans around back. Then I hurried up the stairs to my apartment, peeled off my clothes and put them in another bag for the garbage, and climbed into the shower.

The hot water felt good and I stayed under it much too long. As it grew tepid, I realized that I might get the smell off my hair and my skin, but I wouldn't get it out of my nose. That would take time.

I had a hunch I wouldn't be eating well for a while.

I got out, toweled off, and dressed, taking a minute to go outside with my clothes, tossing them on top of the coverall bag. Then I went back inside, picked up the phone, and called Laura.

"You're done early," she said.

"We found some things," I said.

She sighed. "Is it bad?"

"What we found—" meaning the bodies "—yeah. The implications—" meaning her father's involvement "—maybe not so bad."

"I wish you could explain that to me," she said.

"I will, just not now. I'm going to need records."

"Just tell me what kind and I'll get them."

"Thanks," I said. "We'll also need a place to store things."

"Things?" she asked.

"The stuff your friend is working on," I said. "He'll need a dark-room at the very least."

"I have to pick him up in an hour. We'll see what we can work out."

"Let me know where you drop him off," I said, "and where I can pick him up in the morning."

"How about I come see you tonight, after I'm done?" she said.

"Jimmy would love that," I said, then silently cursed myself. *I* would love that. I should have said that first. Now it sounded awkward.

"He might be in bed when I get there," she said.

"Having dinner with someone else?"

"I think it's rude to pick a man up at his hotel and not have dinner with him, don't you?" she said.

"I think rude is allowed at times," I said.

She laughed. "I don't. I'll be there late."

"I'll be waiting."

I hung up, envying LeDoux his dinner with Laura and worrying that he would tell her the wrong things. But I couldn't do anything about that. If she had questions, I would hope she'd ask when she saw me.

In the meantime, I had a van to clean, a son to pick up, and dinner to cook. For a little while I'd pretend my life was normal, even though it was anything but.

TWENTY-TWO

Laura arrived after nine, looking tired. She still wore her corporate uniform, a conservative blue dress, too much makeup, and low-slung blue heels. Jimmy was up, waiting for her. He was watching *Bracken's World,* a show he'd become addicted to, although I wasn't exactly sure why. I didn't like it: who cared what happened at a Hollywood studio? But it was on late on Fridays, in the same time slot that *Star Trek,* which Jimmy loved, had had. We had gotten into the habit of letting him stay up late on Fridays, and he argued that we shouldn't change it.

That, more than anything, I thought, explained his love for *Bracken's World.*

He gave it up the moment Laura walked through the door. He ran to her and hugged her, and she wrapped her arm around him, relaxing into the hug as if she'd needed it.

I took her purse and set it on the table. "LeDoux told you?"

She nodded over Jimmy's head and gave me a sign that we both knew meant we'd discuss that later.

Jim broke free of the hug. "You want some pop?"

"I'd like a Scotch," she said.

He raised his eyebrows in surprise. Laura drank, but generally not around Jimmy. It wasn't a political thing, more like habit. She wanted to be on her best behavior with him.

"Smoke's got to get that," he said.

I did. We talked, mostly about Jimmy's day and the stuff he'd learned all week about the Haymarket riots.

"Did you know," he said to her, "that without them—right here in Chicago—we wouldn't have an eight-hour workday?"

Most of us didn't have one right now, but neither Laura nor I mentioned that. We let Jim tell us about ancient history, all sparked by the Weathermen bombing, and then we coaxed him to bed. Laura had to promise to read to him—something he hadn't asked me to do in months—and she did, disappearing into his room to read something out of the middle of *The Hobbit*.

I cleaned up the living room and was about to shut off the now-forgotten *Bracken's World* when the local news began. The Weathermen had apparently retreated today; a planned boycott of schools by the students had failed (something I hadn't even heard of) and some rally got called off. RYM-II, the other branch of the SDS, held a demonstration at Cook County Hospital to protest the "exploitation of women" and the hospital's "butcher-shop" techniques.

That brought up too many bad memories from the previous spring, and I shut the television off. By the time Laura came out of Jimmy's room, I had another Scotch for her and a glass for myself.

"It sounds horrible," she said, without preamble.

"It is," I said, sinking onto the couch. I couldn't tell her how grateful I was that she had come, not because we had to do some planning, but because I had to talk with someone other than LeDoux.

"What're we going to do?" she asked, swishing the liquid around in her glass.

"Take it bit by bit," I said. "See what else we can find."

She sat down beside me. "I think you've found more than enough."

"Your father might not have been involved," I said. "In fact, there are good odds now that he wasn't."

"Small comfort," she said. "We've been renting apartments over an active graveyard."

It was worse than that. Renting apartments that placed people in close proximity to an active murderer. But I didn't say that.

Instead, I took the drink from her and set it on the coffee table. Then I took her hand.

I knew platitudes wouldn't comfort her. She understood how awful this was, even without her company's involvement.

"Now this becomes a battle for information," I said quietly. "If we can find enough that implicates Hanley and keeps your father out of it, we can call in the authorities. This'll become a police matter—"

"And headlines," she said. "Oh, so many headlines."

"And headlines. But you have PR people who can handle that."

"Handle it." She shook her head. "Now you sound like the bastards who used to run the company. This isn't handleable, Smokey."

"It is," I said. "It's awful, it's gruesome, and it's horrible. You say that. You let your shock show. And you vow you'll do whatever you can to help the families of the victims."

"Victims," she repeated softly.

"You live up to that promise, and you have your publicity folks make it clear whenever you help someone connected to that house."

She looked at me, her expression fierce, but she didn't pull her hand away. "I don't advertise charity. You know that."

"You have to break that habit for this place. To save—how many people work at Sturdy now? A thousand jobs?"

"More," she whispered.

"You save them, and the shareholders' investments, and by this time next year you'll be able to go back to your anonymous works." I knew how important they were to her. I also knew that she would be in the fight of her life, even if her father hadn't been involved.

"And the house?" she asked.

"You tear it down."

"I was thinking it might be easier to raze the whole thing and be surprised by what we find." She stared at the ceiling. "Pretend we had no idea."

"You thought of that on the drive over, or did LeDoux suggest it?"

"He warned me that this would cost a lot of money, and his actions, no matter how careful, could interfere with prosecution."

"I don't think there will be prosecution," I said. "Hanley's dead."

"If he's the one who did it."

"You wouldn't have a lot of doubt, Laura, if you'd seen that attic and that staircase."

She turned her head toward me. "So raze the house. Then we can blame him and—"

"If we tear down the house, we open all the questions again. The proof, what little of it we have, would disappear and people would wonder how Sturdy was involved."

"They'd know we weren't," she said. "Otherwise we wouldn't have torn it down."

"You're expecting logic," I said.

She smiled. I'd said that to her before, in other contexts. She knew it was a failing, and yet she persisted. One of the things I loved about her was the way that she mixed naïveté with savvy, all of it caused by a willingness to believe the best of people.

I didn't know if I ever believed the best of people. I couldn't quite imagine how to go through life that way. I suspected I would have been perpetually disappointed.

"So we excavate," she said. "That's Mr. LeDoux's word. He says it'll be costly."

"He'll need a place to store his evidence."

"I know," she said. "He also mentioned that we'll need a place to store the bodies. He doubts any funeral home will be able to keep them for an indefinite period of time."

No wonder she wanted the police involved. I hadn't even thought of the body storage.

"Did he have any ideas on how to do that?" I asked.

She shook her head. "But I've been thinking about it. I've been worrying about laws—I don't know if it's illegal to store body parts in a warehouse."

I winced.

"I think we might be better off in an old medical building or a funeral home, some place already zoned for this sort of thing."

She had been thinking about it.

"Does Sturdy have something like that?" I asked.

"No," she said. "But I do."

I sat up in surprise. "*You* do?"

She frowned at me. "I own properties in my own name. My mother insisted. You know that, Smokey. I own my apartment building."

"I just thought it was the only one."

She shook her head. "When I got married, Daddy gave me a bundle of properties, all for me. Not for me and Addison. Just me. Mother wanted to make sure I was protected. She never really liked Addison much."

"Addison," I repeated. Laura never talked about her ex-husband. This was the first time I'd heard his name, although I'd read it. I just didn't realize how snobby the name sounded when spoken out loud.

She smiled, hearing my tone, and perhaps sensing my disapproval. "I was young."

"Clearly," I said.

She closed her eyes and leaned her head back again. "He was a nice man."

"Just not nice enough for you?"

"A little too . . . bland . . . for me. I don't know. He sent me a rather perplexed note when I took over Sturdy."

My heart skipped a beat. She hadn't mentioned that before. "Perplexed?"

"It was nice. He wished me well. I could just tell he'd had no idea I ever wanted to be anything but a wife."

I couldn't imagine Laura as a wife at all. She wasn't arm decoration or a homemaker. She clearly loved Jimmy and was willing to give him her all, but she didn't cater to him.

I reached for my Scotch, amazed at my reaction. I hadn't realized that I never thought of Laura as a traditional woman. I thought of her as unique, one-of-a-kind, someone who had never fit into society's roles.

"Surprised you, didn't I?" she said, looking at me, her head turned sideways.

"I keep forgetting you were once someone's wife," I said.

"Not someone. Addison Lake's. I was a society matron who held the right parties and gave to the right charities. I managed a large household and I was expected, at the right moment, to have at least two children, the first of whom had to be a son."

"As if you could plan that."

She chuckled. "It would have been Addison's responsibility if the first one had been a girl. That's one of the comforting things about biology. Gender is the male's job, not the female's."

Comforting. She was making light of something that had clearly been part of a large argument.

"I didn't realize you wanted children," I said, feeling awkward. Was our on-again, off-again relationship keeping her from a life she wanted?

"I'm not sure I do," she said. "I was never sure. And I'm really uncertain now. I think I'm doing more for children in this city right where I am. If we can clean up the slum housing that Sturdy owns and keep up Helping Hands, I might be making more of a difference right there."

I didn't know what to say. I wanted to ask her more, and yet I didn't want to hear her answers. I didn't want her to say that I was the roadblock I feared I was—or worse, say that I wasn't. I didn't want to put the idea in her head if she hadn't thought of it, and conversely, I didn't want her to think I wanted something more than what we'd had—when things were good, that is.

So I settled for, "You can have children and keep your job, you know. Black women do it all the time."

She smiled at me. "And white women, although no one talks about it."

Then her smile faded. She swirled that drink again. She'd been nursing it since she arrived. I'd been nursing mine too, which showed just how unsettled both of our moods were.

"How did we get from that horrible house to this?" she asked.

I took her cue and let her change the subject. I guess I wanted to get off that topic as well.

"I know you've been checking the records," I said, "but I'm going to need to see what you have on Hanley. Everything, from his employment applications to his pay stubs to notes in his file."

Disappointment flitted across her face, so brief I almost missed it, and then she squared her shoulders, coming back into the conversation we'd run from, finding refuge from a conversation we'd avoided for more than eighteen months.

Should I have gone on? I didn't know, and now it was too late.

"My father hired him," she said. "Isn't that what we needed to know?"

"No," I said. "We need much more than that. How independent he was, and what he did. We don't even know the occupancy rate of the house. Maybe it was always poor. Can you find that?"

"That'll take work," she said. "I'll try."

"It has to be somewhere."

"At some point, people are going to notice my interest."

"I know," I said. "We just have to stay ahead of them."

"I'll be ready," she said.

But neither of us knew what she had to be ready for. This was all unknown, and worrisome. Disturbing, she had called it when she came in, and it was that. It was disturbing, and had grown more so each day we spent in that house.

She put her hand on mine. "Why does this scare me so, Smokey?"

I threaded my fingers through hers. I didn't have an answer for her, and I didn't want to tell her that it scared me too.

TWENTY-THREE

The next morning I picked up LeDoux at a restaurant in Old Town. He waited under an awning, arms clutched around his thin shirt. It was pouring rain and fifty-some degrees, and it finally felt like fall.

I hadn't planned on working Saturdays in this job, but LeDoux and I had agreed we'd spend the morning at least preparing for the mortician. Jimmy was at the Grimshaws—he and Keith had a joint homework project which intrigued them: they had to bring a million of something to their after-school class later in the week.

I was glad the entire thing fell to Franklin and Althea. I didn't mind helping Jimmy with his practical math homework—showing him how to use a budget, how to calculate a grocery bill—but I really didn't want to spend my entire weekend counting something.

Neither did Jim. He made me promise I'd be back right after lunch. We had a date I didn't dare forget.

The World Series started this weekend and his new team, the Mets, were in it. They'd creamed the Atlanta Braves, and now planned to do the same to Baltimore.

I hoped they did. I needed something else to think about besides corpses and built-in tombs and hidden secrets. I wanted something to celebrate, even for a few hours.

I dropped LeDoux, already in his coveralls and cap, at the house, along with that big ring of keys. He would work the first area we found, take whatever evidence there was from the cubby near the skeletons, and then we'd let Minton take them away.

I drove on to Poehler's Funeral Home. Saturdays, apparently, were big days at funeral homes. When I had spoken to Minton before I had left the apartment, he told me to go around back where the hearses parked. He said he would leave the door open for me.

I parked in a bottle-strewn alley, next to a shiny hearse. Another was parked in front of the funeral home, the back doors of the vehicle wide open. Apparently it was taking a body to a church for a funeral later in the day. Minton had said most of Saturday was about transportation or viewing; he figured he'd have some time to spend with me, barring any emergencies.

The back door was propped open, by a brick, of all things, and I slipped inside, wincing at the smell of formaldehyde and flowers. I sighed and went down the back stairs. My parents would be with me in every funeral home I walked into for the rest of my life.

Three bodies covered in sheets rested on stainless-steel tables. The stench of formaldehyde was stronger in here. Minton stood near the back. He was sliding on a white doctor's coat, his hands already covered by gloves.

When he saw me, he grimaced. "I forgot."

"I take that to mean you can't come with me," I said.

He glanced through another door, as if he thought someone overheard us.

"I have an emergency peek," he said. "I didn't know about it when I talked to you."

"An emergency what?"

He beckoned me to come with him. In a narrow room just off the main room, a man had been laid out on yet another stainless-steel table. This room was claustrophobically small and had none of the equipment that the main morgue had.

"Why's he here?" I asked.

"He's not here," Minton said. "He's with me."

I looked at him, not entirely understanding.

"Like your job."

Then I nodded. This one was off the books too. I walked over to the body. The man was maybe in his twenties, but young enough to still have some acne around his chin. He had a buzz cut, which was unusual for this part of Chicago. His face was the only part of him that looked halfway normal. His torso had been opened and then sewn back shut in the traditional autopsy Y.

"You're done, then," I said.

"Haven't started," Minton said. "He's just come from the police."

I looked up at him. "The police are here?"

"Hell, no. He came in that hearse out there. The family's got him set up at a different funeral home, not far from here. Some folks just thought he should see me first."

"What folks?" I asked.

Minton gave me a faint smile. He clearly wasn't going to answer that question.

"What happened to him?"

"That's the question," Minton said. "You didn't hear the news yesterday?"

I shivered, remembering that snippet I'd heard the night before. "Just a piece of it."

He nodded. "This here's Michael Soto."

"I thought you had him earlier in the week," I said.

"That was his brother, John. Michael here brought him to me last Sunday."

"The Henry Horner traffic-light issue," I said.

Minton nodded.

"And now this boy's dead?" I felt cold.

Minton shrugged one shoulder. "The police say he charged them, him and two others, after committing a robbery."

"You don't believe it."

"No one believes it," Minton said. "Michael here is an Army sergeant."

"He's the one you said was in 'Nam." I remembered now.

"Yeah," Minton said. "He knew better than to rob a convenience store or go after the police."

I sighed. "They shot him because he questioned his brother's death?"

"Most like," Minton said. "I get to look at him quick enough to see if his wounds correspond to their stories. I only got about three hours. Can you get me after noon?"

I almost said yes, and then I remembered my promise to Jim. "Not this afternoon," I said. "How's Monday morning?"

"Probably hectic if this weekend's anything like last weekend. But I'll make time for you."

"I'll be here," I said.

He nodded, but he wasn't looking at me any longer. He was looking at Michael Soto, an Army sergeant who found the streets of his hometown deadlier than the jungles of South Vietnam.

I turned around and left, wondering how a family dealt with the loss of two boys in the space of a week. Two nearly adult boys with good hearts, who had been murdered by the police.

TWENTY-FOUR

The Mets lost.

It was a heartbreaker, almost as if the team that Jimmy and I had watched during the last week had vanished, replaced by a bunch of minor leaguers.

Jimmy took the loss philosophically. He had hope—the best three out of five, he reminded me—but I was oddly devastated. I'd been hoping for something joyful, something upbeat.

Instead, I'd gotten a 4-1 loss that boded poorly for the games to come.

But I didn't say anything to Jim. I was afraid I'd sound even more bitter than I felt.

My meeting with Minton had shaken me. The body of poor Michael Soto reminded me just how much I hated this city—how much I hated most cities, after this summer had shown me that Chicago was not unique.

Then I'd gone back to the house, where I took out the bricks on the remaining sections while I waited for LeDoux to finish fingerprinting and measuring and searching the tomb where we'd found the first three.

And sure enough, those remaining areas had bodies as well. One in such a state of preservation that he looked almost alive—not like Michael Soto, who seemed (if you didn't look at that Y incision) like he could wake up and get off the table at any moment—but like someone who'd only been dead a few days although, fortunately, he didn't smell that way.

I was startled enough to call LeDoux over. He groused, but came, holding his flashlight like a club.

"What do you make of this?" I asked, shining my light on the corpse's graying face. In life, he'd been a rather heavyset black man. In death, he seemed a little sunken, and quite sad.

LeDoux stared at the corpse for a moment, frowning. Then he said, "This one's fairly recent."

"That's what I thought. You think just before Hanley died, he killed this guy?"

"No." LeDoux's answer was curt. "By fairly recent, I mean he's been down here for less time than our skeletons there."

"How much shorter?" I asked.

"That's for your invisible friend to figure out." LeDoux was unhappy that Minton hadn't come. I didn't explain why, figuring Minton's side work for the Soto family was none of LeDoux's business.

"Do you have a guess?" I asked.

"Five years, six. Maybe a dozen. Maybe last year. I really don't know."

"He could have been here that long?" I asked. "I thought bodies lost their flesh when that much time passed."

"As I told you the other day," LeDoux said, using the tone professors used with particularly dumb students, "it all depends on the conditions under which the body was stored."

"The condition is the same as all the other bodies," I said.

"Nonsense." He frowned at me as if he had expected better. "This little nook is as different from the one next to it as an expensive casket is from no casket at all. The brick is different, the mortar used is different, the airflow, if any, is different. And I would wager that this poor soul had a concrete floor, while our friends over there—"he nodded at the skeletons. "—were resting on the actual ground itself. More bug activity, more variation in temperature."

"It's not just a time difference?" I asked.

He sighed, and pushed past me, shining his light down the hole. "I was right. Concrete."

I had to look as well. Only the heavyset black man filled this space.

He still had his shoes, pointed-toed oxfords, which seemed awfully expensive. Past the shoes there was a floor. A real floor, concrete, like the visible part of the basement had.

"You think this was put in when the boiler got put in?" I asked, my stomach knotting. If that was the case, that tied this body back to Laura's father. The boiler dated from the 1940s when he worked on the premises.

"No way to know until I get down there," LeDoux said. "And at this rate, it'll be a while."

That phrase, more than anything, made me bite back anger. LeDoux wanted to work evenings and weekends until we had this place cleared out. I couldn't, even if I wanted to.

It had been a mistake to tell him that Jim and I planned to watch the World Series. LeDoux saw that as frivolous, a waste of his precious time.

When I refused to work Sunday as well, he pointedly asked me if it was because there was another baseball game.

There was, and Jimmy and I planned to watch it, but that wasn't why I had said no.

"Church in my community," I'd said to him, "sometimes lasts all day."

That sentence was true, but the implication—that I would be in a pew, participating in the service—wasn't. Jimmy would be there. I believed that his church attendance with the Grimshaw family was almost more important than his schooling. The black community's heart was its churches, and even if Jimmy became an agnostic like me, he needed to know where he could go for help—real, physical help—any time he needed it.

LeDoux had raised his eyebrows, muttered something about having trouble believing that I was a church-going man, and then went back to work. He stayed until I threatened to drag him out of the building, and then, rather sullenly, asked me how he should spend the rest of the day.

I recommended the Series, which I now regretted. LeDoux was from New York, unlike me or Jim, and might have had an even greater stake in the Mets than we had.

"You know," Jim said when the game was finally over. "It's not fair."

"What's not fair?" I asked. There'd been some bad calls, but all in all, it had been a good ballgame.

"How you get your hopes up and then something comes in to smash 'em down. I hate that, Smoke."

I nodded. "At least you still have hopes," I said.

TWENTY-FIVE

E arly Sunday morning, someone knocked on my door.
I debated answering, feeling irritated. I had just gotten back from dropping Jimmy at the Grimshaws' so that they could take him to church. How could someone else know that I had planned to use the next few hours to catch up on my sleep? My little adventure in the basement had brought back the nightmares I'd had since I'd come home from Korea, and I often spent the wee hours pacing.

I went to the door and peeped through the spyhole. Two men stood outside. They wore black leather jackets and one of them had on sunglasses indoors.

The men looked familiar, but it was hard to tell in the peephole's fisheye.

I knew they'd heard me. They'd both moved slightly when I leaned against the door.

"What do you want?" I asked.

"We'd like to hire you," said the man toward the back. His voice was unfamiliar.

I sighed, debating whether or not to open the door. I didn't need the work—this job from Laura would take most of my time for the foreseeable future—but I really did want something else to think about: kind of a rest job that would allow me to concentrate on a different problem for a while.

I unlocked all three deadbolts and pulled back the chain. Then I opened the door—and immediately tried to push it shut.

The man in back, the one who'd spoken, put his foot in the door. "Do us the courtesy of listening to us," he said.

But I wasn't looking at him. I was looking at the tall, broadshouldered man with the familiar face. He pulled off the sunglasses and smiled at me, and that smile had as much charm as I remembered.

Fred Hampton, chairman of the Illinois Black Panther Party.

He was the last person I wanted in my home.

"We really do want to hire you." He had a deep voice that resonated even when he wasn't doing public speaking. He was only about twenty or so, but he had more physical presence than anyone I'd met since Martin.

I blocked the door with my body. "I don't need the work."

"Then why didn't you jus' tell us to fuck off?" the other man asked. "Seems to me you needed the work until you figured out who we was."

Hampton glanced at him, a calculated look instructing him to shut up. "This is William O'Neal. He's my bodyguard. My name is Fred Hampton. I'm with the—"

"I know who you are," I said. "I'm not going to do any work for you."

"You don't like the Panthers?" he asked.

"I don't like anyone who draws the wrong kind of attention to our neighborhood."

"Our offices are on the West Side," he said, "not down here."

"I know," I said. "And whenever you make one of your pronouncements, the cops show up here too. You have an 'action' like you did at Cook County Hospital the other day, and the cops knock some heads on Sixty-third and Woodlawn. We're tied together, your neighborhood and mine, and you know it."

He gave me a half smile. "You been following what I do."

"It's hard to miss." I kicked O'Neal in the shin, and he yelped, pulling his foot away. I shoved at the door, but Hampton caught it with the flat of his right hand.

"Do me a favor. Hear me out."

"No," I said. "You bring cops and FBI wherever you go. I don't want any informant telling them you've been inside my place, especially if you stay longer than ten minutes."

Hampton leaned back slightly. He was slimmer than I was, but just as tall. He had no obvious weapons on him, but he didn't look very muscular either. I could probably shove his arm out of the way, push him backwards into that so-called bodyguard, and get the door closed in record time.

"If someone's watching," Hampton said, "and they probably are, they've already seen us coming into the building."

"But they don't know where you went," I said, realizing the argument was weak.

"It wouldn't be hard to find out, would it?"

He had a point. They were already here. If the police investigated the tenants, they'd figure Hampton either came to see me or the grandson of the lady upstairs. The grandson was a member of the Blackstone Rangers, the street gang I'd made a deal with and that Hampton had negotiated a truce with last spring.

"All right," I said. "You have five minutes. Your 'bodyguard' has to wait outside, though."

"Don't lock the bolts," O'Neal said. "I wanna be able to come in if there's trouble."

"I didn't mean outside the apartment," I said. "I meant outside the building."

O'Neal looked at Hampton. Hampton nodded to him.

"I don't like this," O'Neal said, but he clomped his way down the stairs just the same.

I waited until he stepped outside before I opened my door all the way to Hampton. He gave me a boyish grin and stepped in. He had a loose, angular way of walking that suggested comfort. But it was as deceptive as the walk of a large cat. That comfort hid a preparedness. If I had gone for Hampton, he would have blocked me. Hampton seemed to see his surroundings as clearly as I did.

I shut the door behind him and locked the top deadbolt for good measure. I didn't want O'Neal to come back here and barge his way in.

Hampton took in the dirty dishes at the sink, the opened Sunday paper, the boy's jacket hanging on the coat tree.

"Family man," he said.

I didn't respond. I wasn't going to give him any information about myself. I also didn't take him down the hall to my office, like I would have any other potential client. We remained right in front of the door so I could usher him out quickly if I had to.

"I approve," he said. "I'm gonna be a father myself in December."

That surprised me. I hadn't thought of him as much more than a creative and eloquent street thug, a young man who had one foot in the gangs and another in a rising political movement. In the past few months, I felt like he'd moved closer to politics, but he still liked guns and violence too much for my taste.

"You're wasting your five minutes," I said.

He nodded, grabbed the front of the paper, and turned it over to reveal the headlines. More frightened reporting about the radicals and their Days of Rage. Only this time the reporters had something to discuss—in yesterday's riots downtown, a district attorney working on the Conspiracy Trial had been critically injured. More than a hundred demonstrators had been arrested, and the police were taking credit for the riot's fifteen-minute duration.

"We're not dangerous like them," he said. "We don't agree with them."

"I know," I said. "I heard you call them custeristic."

He smiled. "You do keep track."

"I need to know what's happening in my community," I said.

His smile faded. "Then you know about the Soto brothers."

I thought of the young man on that steel table, his hair cut off by the U.S. Army, his friends and family so frightened of the police they were paying for a second autopsy in the hopes of gathering some wrongful death evidence, evidence that might help them down the road.

"Yeah." I kept my answers terse. I didn't want to let him know how I felt about anything.

"You know the cops killed them."

"Both sides agree on that," I said.

He stuck his hands in the pocket of his black jacket. "You and I both know that those brothers didn't provoke the cops. They were targeted."

"I suspect it," I said. "I don't know it."

He grinned at me. That grin was winning; no wonder people liked him. "That's what I heard about you. You're thorough."

Not as thorough as LeDoux. "You've heard about me?"

"I asked around. I wanted the best, someone discreet, someone who could handle a crisis, someone a little unorthodox who'd be willing to work with the Panthers. Everyone said that was you."

"Everyone was wrong," I said.

146

"Look." He took his hands out of his pocket and spread them open in a movement of supplication. "We're not as bad as folks make us out to be."

"I know," I said. "But you're visible."

"And you're what? Invisible?"

"I don't like trouble," I said. "You court it."

"No one's gotta know that we're tied. We hire you, one job, and we'll pay you. We got a backer who'll pay for the answers."

"Why don't you investigate this yourself?" I asked. "You've got the manpower."

"But not the expertise," he said. "We want hard-hitting, real evidence, more than eyewitness accounts, something I can take to the mainstream media. I got their eye right now. They talk to me and listen to me—"

"And put you on the ten o'clock news where your celebrity goes to your head."

He laughed. "You are hostile, man. You are more hostile than the tough guys who come to me, wanting to off the pigs."

"I'm not taking your job," I said.

"It's the only way the Sotos is gonna get justice and you know it. White folks don't care that black kids die when they come home from school, just trying to cross the street. John was trying to change that, so he got murdered. Michael, he says John's cause is a just one, and he gets murdered. Why's that? Because the police are hiding something about that streetlight? Or because the police don't like uppity niggers?"

"The police have never liked us," I said.

"Right back to the moment Lincoln freed our black asses."

"Oh, probably long before that," I said.

He tilted his head. "Your politics are in the right place. It wouldn't hurt to work on this case."

"It'd hurt my family," I said. "I'm staying of it."

He studied me for a moment, as if he was trying to figure me out. "We've met before."

"I've heard a few of your speeches," I said.

"So you know about the Free Breakfast for Children program, the Free Clinic, everything we're trying to do to build up our community."

"I know," I said.

"And you still won't help?"

"Taking on the police is . . ." I paused for dramatic effect. ". . . custeristic."

His smile was long gone. "The cops're targeting us."

"They'll target any black man who parades around in a pseudo-military organization and shows off his guns. We frighten them. No sense in provoking them."

"We're not provoking," Hampton said. "We're just standing up for our own."

"You don't need the news media to help you stand up," I said.

"Is that what's bothering you?" he asked. "I can guarantee no one'll know where we got the information. I'll be the only one who'll deal with you."

"You and that bodyguard," I said.

He nodded.

I might've actually trusted Hampton if I hadn't seen him with the bodyguard. I didn't like the other man. He seemed shifty, although I couldn't say why.

I said, "Your five minutes are up."

"Look, Grimshaw—"

I started at his use of the name I was using. It brought home that he had found out about me, and that startled me.

"—what we're proposing isn't that new. We're not the first black men—hell, we're not the first Chicagoans—to take up arms against the pigs to defend our homes. It's a proud tradition here, going back to World War One. I got brothers whose grandfathers stood on the roofs of houses not far from here and shot at any pig that ventured into the South Side."

I hadn't heard of any of this, but that didn't surprise me.

"So how come you're advocating the same thing fifty years later?" I asked. "You'd think, if that strategy worked, things would've changed."

His eyes sparkled. He clearly liked debate. "If I had more than five minutes, I could convince you, I could win you over. The political theorists—"

"Mostly sat around in European coffee shops and played chess while other people fought their battles. I don't need to reread Mao's *Little Red Book* or get yet another lecture in Marx. I do need you to get out of my apartment."

"What about Machiavelli?" he asked. "You got to outsmart the other guy, outmaneuver him."

"And that worked so well for Machiavelli," I said. "He died in prison. I'm not sure you and your friends'll make it to prison before someone kills you."

The sparkle left his eyes. I wasn't sure he'd ever spoken to anyone who'd read the same books he had, and had longer to think about them.

I'd tried the idealistic route. It took me down a similar road. Only mine ended in Korea, with friends getting shot around me.

"That's why I came to you, man. We're gonna defend ourselves if we get attacked. But we're getting attacked all the time now. Our offices got invaded ten days ago. The pigs arrested six brothers on trumped-up murder charges, even though they barged into *our* place and set fire to *our* files and destroyed food and medical supplies. *Medical* supplies, man, for poor people. What kind of justice is that? We're peace loving, but we're American. We believe in the right of self-defense."

"I'm not arguing with that right," I said. "I'm exercising it myself by asking you to leave. Your very presence here endangers my family."

He leaned closer to me, an intimidating move, designed to get me to physically back away. I stood my ground.

"Listen, man. In June the police raided our offices and set fires. In the middle of July, they murdered Larry Robertson. At the end of July, they come back and claim we started a gun battle—hell, we just returned fire—and then, last week, they come again. And that doesn't count Cox, who got beaten to death in the Eleventh District Police Station, or Green, who got shot when the police busted into his house for no reason at all, or Medina, who was just driving his car when the cops pull him over for a burglary he wasn't nowhere near, and they shot him in the goddamn stomach, killing him. That's just the month of May, Mr. Grimshaw. I can tell you about June and July and August and September, but hell, that'll take all day, and that'll really use up my five minutes."

"You've already used it up and then some," I said.

"You don't care? You don't care about the so-called gang-related shootings the cops do that usually happen to non-gang members? You don't care?"

"I care enough to keep my family away from organizations that require their members to wear some kind of uniform, talk about their leaders as 'chairmen,' and egg on the cops."

He paused, as if he were going to say something else, then shook his head. "You should look beyond the clothes."

"I do. I don't believe in provoking people who already hate us."

"We don't provoke," he said. "We organize."

I shrugged, but said nothing.

He walked to the door, put his hand on the knob, and then looked down at it, as if he were considering his next few words. It was an excellent theatrical maneuver, and if I hadn't already seen him at rallies and on TV, I would have thought it spontaneous.

"At some point," he said, raising his head, "people've got to do something. Keeping silent is just what the pigs want."

I didn't respond.

His gaze met mine. "We can't get the mainstream press to cover what happens here and on the West Side. They're run by rich white people who think every nigger's a crook, and every black man rapes white women, and every black woman's a whore. So who cares if the pigs are shooting us, hmm? We deserve it."

I'd made this argument myself. It had a lot of truth. Too much truth.

"I was asking you," he said, his voice lower than it had been since he'd come into the apartment—his real voice, probably, the one he used with his friends and family—"to help us on a pretty straightforward case. Michael Soto's a war hero, for crissake, and John was a good kid who just wanted to save the lives of littler kids. These guys didn't deal dope or steal or whistle at white women. They were good citizens who were murdered for poking their heads out of the hole the Man forced them into."

I didn't move. I didn't dare. I didn't want Hampton to see he was actually reaching me.

"These two guys—men, really good men—were murdered. And I was asking you to help me find evidence of it. Good, hard evidence that I can bring to the media, to let the white folks know that good black folks're dying down here. We're being massacred, and no one seems to care. Not even fucking house niggers like you."

He yanked the door open and walked through it, slow enough that I could have stopped him if I'd wanted to.

Then he turned before closing the door. "You know where I am if you change your mind."

"I'm not going to," I said. "And calling me names won't convince me to."

"I'm not calling you names," he said. "I'm just pointing out where complacency leads."

Then he pulled the door closed.

I listened to him stomp down the stairs, and then I walked to the door and locked the deadbolts.

I leaned on it, my heart pounding. I'd given similar speeches, and meant them. Hell, I had given similar speeches this past year.

I believed in taking action, I truly did. And it had taken all my restraint not to agree to take Hampton's case. I'd seen Michael Soto's body. I knew the man had been murdered, and I knew why.

Hampton was right. The Soto brothers had aggravated the authorities by making "uppity" demands and not staying in their place. These two men were object lessons—clear object lessons—to the entire Henry Horner housing project, and if someone didn't stand up to that lesson and call it wrong, then people would absorb it, and stop standing up at all.

Had anyone else brought this to me, anyone—even Minton—I might have considered it. I would have tried to ignore the public nature of the case. I would have taken the evidence—if there was any—to a reporter friend of mine, Saul Epstein, who'd won some national journalistic prizes with the last story I took to him.

But I couldn't link up with Fred Hampton. He was too visible. And his people were targets, just like he'd said.

If I were alone, I could be a target. But I had Jimmy.

And Jimmy always had to come first.

TWENTY-SIX

Another knock on my door made me start. The police? The FBI? What the hell would I tell them? And how would I get them off my back?

"Bill?" It was Marvella Walker, my neighbor from across the hall.

I let out the breath I'd been holding. I turned around, peered through the spyhole again, and saw that she was alone. I unlocked the deadbolts and pulled the door open for the second time that morning.

"You should be in church," I said, trying to keep my tone light.

"I could say the same about you." She gave me a worried look. We had a checkered relationship, she and I. When we first met, she hadn't approved of Laura, saying some things that I thought would end our friendship.

But her cousin had nearly died one night, and Laura had saved her life. From that moment on, Marvella and Laura became friends; not good friends, but friends who understood each other. During that period, I realized that I had underestimated Marvella as well.

This morning she managed to look stunning, even though she had clearly just woken up. She was wearing a batique caftan that looked authentically African, and her eyes were late-night puffy. She'd run a pick through her ever-expanding afro, but it hadn't done a lot of good. Tufts still stood up in the back, a sign that she hadn't looked in the mirror yet.

"I saw your visitor," she said.

I bit back a curse. I had hoped that somehow no one had seen him. "Everything okay?"

I shook my head. "I didn't ask him to come here. He wanted to hire me."

"Really?" she asked.

I nodded.

"You didn't take the job?"

"He's too high-profile for me. I don't want anyone thinking me or Jim has anything to do with the Black Panthers."

Marvella let out a small breath, almost as if she'd had a realization— and maybe she had. She knew me a lot better now than she had last year. She'd seen me at my worst, and she knew what I was capable of.

"You think everyone's gonna know he came here to see you?"

"I don't think he talks to Blackstone Rangers who aren't in the Main 21." The Main 21 was the Stones' ruling council.

"That kid hasn't lived upstairs in months," she said.

"See?" I said. "Who else would he visit but me?"

She put a hand on her hip, and gave me a sultry smile. "Why, Officer," she said, in a good imitation of a Georgia accent, "that sweet boy just come to see me. Even revolutionaries need a little . . . comfort now and then."

I grinned in spite of myself. Marvella wasn't a hooker, and to my knowledge she'd never taken a young lover. She had, however, been married several times, and she had mastered a look that went all the way down your spine.

"Nice try," I said, "but that young revolutionary is going to be a father in a few months."

She let her hand slide off her hip, and the entire pose went away with it. "Who would have thought? I thought he was making war, not love."

"Apparently he's doing both," I said.

"And he's not afraid to bring a child into his gun-soaked world?" she asked.

"I have one in mine." That came out bitter. I hadn't meant it that way. I'd meant it as banter.

Marvella's gaze softened. "I've never seen you with a gun, Bill."

I had one. I kept it in the glove box of my van because I didn't want it in the apartment.

"That doesn't mean I haven't used one," I said.

"But you're not carrying it around like it's the Second Coming of Christ."

"Neither is he," I said, not sure where this urge to defend Hampton had come from. Maybe that last speech he'd given me. Maybe the guilt I was feeling for not taking the case.

"Sounds like he got to you," she said.

"He had a good argument," I said.

"And you're still resisting."

I nodded.

"Good for you." She ran a hand through her tufted hair. "Now, I'm going back to bed. I had a late night, and I planned to sleep until noon. Your friend got in my way."

"Mine too," I said.

Her sultry smile returned. "If we're both going to bed, we may as well share."

A little shiver of shock ran through me. Marvella hadn't flirted with me in months—not because we'd worked together, but because she'd gone through a lot of family tragedy. I hadn't seen her smile like this since December.

"You seem to be better," I said.

"I heard from Val," she said, referring to her cousin, Valentina. "She's settling into California, wants me to join her."

"Are you going to?"

"And miss all the excitement around here? You've got to be kidding." She flicked her caftan at me, that light mood helping mine. "Sure you don't want to change your mind?"

"I'm sure," I said.

"You'll regret it," she said.

"I'll just add it to my list," I said. That list seemed to be growing longer by the minute.

I only wished it was full of offers like Marvella's instead of missed opportunities like the one I'd had to turn down with Hampton.

I should have recommended someone else to him, but I hadn't thought of it at the time. All I'd wanted was to get him out of the apartment.

Maybe I'd talk to Minton. He was in contact with the family. He could point them to one of the other fine detectives who worked the Black Belt.

Maybe then the Soto brothers would find some justice.

TWENTY-SEVEN

The next morning, a black sedan followed me as I drove to the Grimshaw house to pick up the children. The tail was so clumsy that even Jimmy noticed, nodding his head toward the side mirrors I'd installed for safety and asking, "You see that car?"

"I do," I said.

"You gonna lose him?"

He'd definitely been watching too much television. The new after-school teacher didn't assign as much homework as Grace Kirkland had, and I hadn't taken the time to fill in the gap.

Looked like I was going to have to.

"What's the point?" I asked. "He'll see my exciting taking-the-children-to-school routine."

"How come you got a tail?" Jimmy asked. "Is it that job for Laura?"

I didn't want him to worry about that. "No, I think it's connected to a job I turned down."

I hadn't told him about Fred Hampton, and I didn't plan to. Jimmy'd seen Hampton speak once too, and was a bit too awestruck for my taste. I wanted to keep them as far apart as possible.

"How come you turned it down?" Jimmy asked.

"Because I had a hunch the guy who wanted to hire me was being watched. Now I know my hunch was right."

"What're you going to do?" Jim's voice wavered just a bit. He tried, gamely, to put up with my work, but I'd been injured too many times, and his life had been too unstable. He was terrified that I would die, and nothing I could do would make that fear go away.

"I'm going to let him follow me for a few days," I said.

"Why?" Jim asked. "Shouldn't you shake him?"

I shook my head. "Shaking him would be more suspicious. Instead, I'll let him see that I'm a hard-working American, and he can go bother someone else."

Jim grunted, and the conversation was mostly forgotten by the time all five Grimshaw children had settled in the van. Jimmy did double-check the mirrors once or twice, and I heard him whisper to Keith that we were being tailed, but he didn't sound alarmed by it.

I was, a lot more than I'd let on when I spoke to Jim. I didn't want the tail to run a background check on me and discover that there wasn't much to know about Bill Grimshaw before 1968. I also didn't want him to follow me to the Queen Anne.

I would have to lose him, but I'd do it in the natural flow of traffic and make it seem accidental.

I also did a few uncharacteristic things. I sat in the school parking lot longer than usual, as if it were part of my routine, just so that sedan would get a bit complacent. Then I took off quickly to make him worry that I'd spotted him and decided to lose him.

Finally, I waited at a nearby stoplight until I saw him round the corner, easing his mind (I hoped) so that he simply thought I was an inconsistent driver instead of an alert one.

I stopped at the apartment for a few minutes, packed my lunch and ostentatiously carried it to the van, along with a briefcase filled with another new coverall. Then I sat inside for a few minutes, got myself settled, and listened to the traffic reports on WVON.

The best place to lose the tail was downtown. By the time I pulled out, I had planned my route and my backup, in case my first attempt didn't work.

It did work. I didn't have a black sedan—or any other kind of car—follow me to the restaurant where I picked up LeDoux. That relieved me. The tail wasn't the sophisticated kind the FBI sometimes used, the kind where one car traded off with another because they were in radio contact.

LeDoux got into the van, looking tired. His normally neat gray hair was mussed in the back, as if he'd forgotten to comb it. He had purchased some casual clothes—tennies, jeans that were so new they crinkled as he moved, and a denim workshirt.

He looked like a man who was trying to dress down, instead of someone who was comfortable in his grubbies.

As we drove off, I checked my mirrors. Nothing suspicious. No one had seen me pick him up.

He leaned his head against the back of the seat. "You got me watching baseball."

I grinned. The Mets had won the day before. Jimmy had danced around the living room as if he were a diehard New Yorker instead of a transplanted child of the South, and I had to admit, the win gave me that momentary feeling sports sometimes meted out—that you could do anything if you only believed.

"It was something, huh?" I said.

"Christ," he said, running his hand through his hair, explaining the mussing. He'd obviously been having this conversation all morning, probably to anyone who would listen. "Made me wish I wasn't alone. I was screaming like an idiot in my apartment."

"I think half the world was screaming like that," I said.

"And the other half were Baltimore fans? How could that be?" LeDoux asked and gave me a real smile—a warm, friendly smile—for the first time since I'd met him.

"Forgive me," I said. "I wasn't thinking clearly."

He laughed, and we talked about the game for the rest of the drive. Almost as if we were two painters heading to their job for the day. It felt odd, having this camaraderie with LeDoux, but it felt good at the same time.

I kept my eyes on the mirrors as I drove, but no one else followed us. I had lost the sedan for the time being, but I knew if I went home, the watchers—whoever they were, whatever government organization they belonged to—would find me again.

The Queen Anne looked as foreboding as it always did. The early morning cloud cover didn't help. The air was pregnant with moisture, and the slight wind had a chill that suggested an impending storm.

LeDoux and I went through what had now become a routine, taking in ladders and toolboxes and extra gallons of paint. He'd slipped on his coveralls in the van and tugged his painter's cap over his head like an old pro.

We got inside, the faint smell of death assaulting us, and the laughter faded as if it never was. I had managed not to think about this place through most of the weekend, and it had felt good.

Once LeDoux was set up, I got back into the van and headed to Poehler's. Minton was standing in the back, smoking a cigarette. When he saw me, he dropped it and stomped it out.

"What do I need?" he asked, leaning into the driver's window.

"Body bags. Transport."

"Gurneys?"

"At least one," I said.

He frowned. "What're we talking here? How many dead are there?"

"I don't know," I said quietly.

He stared at me for a minute. "Jesus, man, what is this?"

"You'll have to see. And we're taking the van."

He chewed on his lower lip, just like Jimmy did when he was nervous, then he nodded. "You gotta help me carry a few things."

I parked right where I was, pocketed the keys, and followed Minton into the funeral home. No one was working this early in the morning, which surprised me. I would have expected a mortician dealing with one of the bodies resting on the tables.

When I mentioned that, Minton said, "Monday's our slow day. Most folks take it off. The weekends're always busy, and even though Death never rests, we do."

"Or at least some of you do," I said rather pointedly. He wasn't resting.

"Yeah, well," he said. "Some of us are on a mission to save the world. Being a superhero and a mortician doesn't leave you a lot of time for sleep."

He'd meant that as a joke, but I knew what he was referring to. He was still shaken by the Soto case.

He handed me several body bags, and I slung them over my arm. They felt like garment bags, only heavier and longer, and I knew I wouldn't carry clothes in quite the same way again.

"You find anything on Michael Soto?" I asked.

"Any unrefutable proof that he was murdered?" Minton's voice was bitter. He was facing away from me, rummaging in a closet of stuff. "Besides the bullets in his body, you mean?"

"You know what I mean," I said.

"Yeah." He stood up. He had a box of gloves, and some evidence bags just like the ones LeDoux used. "Short of finding a note inside the poor guy saying that he'd been shot in cold blood, there's no way to prove that the shooting was one kind or another. It's all circumstance. We said versus they said. And I can't show whether or not Michael Soto was carrying a gun. All I can show was what direction he was shot from, how close the cops were, whether the evidence jibes with what they say."

"Does it?"

He shrugged. "They're not talking much about the actual shooting itself. Only that he had a gun and was planning to use it. Until I learn whether they say they were ten feet away or two feet away—if they ever say it—I can't figure out whether the evidence jibes or not. And if they're smart, they're gonna stay quiet about the whole how-when-what part of the case."

We stared at each other for a moment. Then he clasped the box of gloves to his chest.

"Hear you had a visitor Sunday," he said.

"Yeah."

"Hear you said no to taking on the Soto case."

"Yeah."

"How come I should help you then? Hmmm? Those brothers were good men."

"You're friends with Chairman Hampton?" I asked.

"Fred's a good guy. He gets written up as this big revolutionary, but he just cares about people. He's trying to save the world, just in his own way."

"He's fond of guns," I said.

"He's fond of self-defense, and who can blame him? He was an honor student once, you know that? Star athlete, one of the most popular kids in his community. He was going to college, prelaw, before all this."

"He should've stayed there," I said.

Minton shook his head. "A couple things happened—nothing major, stuff we've all gone through—and he lost his faith in the law. He come to realize that the only ones who'll ever take care of us is us, just like you and I are now."

I was beginning to like Hampton more than I already did, which was more than I wanted to. Staying out of cases like this was not my strong suit, but it had to be this time. Too many police, too many journalists, too much explaining to do.

"I know Hampton's trying, and I know you want some justice for the Sotos." I ran my hand over the body bags, trying to smooth them out. "It's just too high-profile for me."

"High-profile?" Minton said. "Since when is that a consideration?"

"Since I became a father." It was the first time I'd ever used that word in that context, but it applied. Jimmy was my son, just not legally, because we didn't dare make it legal. But I was as committed to him—more committed to him—than any real family he had.

"Your kids'll thank you for taking this on," Minton said. "Someday—someday soon, I hope—we'll get these dirty cops. We'll stop them, we'll show the world what they're doing, and things'll change."

I stared at him for a moment. He believed that. He'd just autopsied two boys shot by the police, probably for no reason except that they were "troublemakers," people who didn't know their "place," and he thought that someday, someone would stop that.

"I hope you're right," I said. "But until things do change, I've got to keep a low profile."

"For heaven's sake, why, man? What'll it gain you? More dead kids, that's what. And if you're not careful, one of those kids'll be your own."

I stared at him. Minton flushed, but didn't look away.

"What're you doing this for?" I asked him. "This work. How come you're not a detective or a Panther? How come you're in this basement on your day off, coming to help me with a case that could be as important—just not as high profile—as the Soto brothers?"

"How come I dig through the evidence?" he asked.

"Not just the evidence," I said. "The evidence as it manifests on dead bodies."

He sighed and grabbed a small bag of equipment, slinging it over his shoulder. For a moment, I thought he wasn't going to answer me.

Then he said: "Emmett Till."

I looked at him. Was poor Emmett Till Chicago's only frame of reference in the recent race wars?

"What about him?" I asked.

"You know what happened, right?"

"Yeah," I said. "I know."

Probably better than he did. Definitely better than he did. My parents died a death very similar to Till's. And so many other people I'd met over the years had died the same way and for the same kind of non-reason.

"Then you understand," he said.

"No," I said, "I don't. I understand joining the Southern Christian Leadership Conference or the National Association for the Advancement of Colored People. I understand marching. I understand protesting. I don't understand how Till brought you here."

Minton sighed, then nodded toward the door. "Let's get to your van before someone shows up for work."

With his free hand, he grabbed a gurney and wheeled it toward the small freight elevator. When we reached it, Minton pressed a button, and the doors opened. We stepped inside. I helped him bump the gurney over the gap between the doors and the wall.

The elevator smelled of damp and rot, just like the Queen Anne did. No formaldehyde here, no pretext, no made-up corpses. Just the smell of death, old death, decaying, half-forgotten, and never completely gone.

He pressed the top of two buttons and the door slid shut. "I went to school with Emmett. He was a good kid. Quiet, but fun. His eyes always twinkled, you know?"

I wanted to ask if Minton thought Till had actually whistled at that white woman. But he continued before I could say anything.

"He, ah—." Emotion I hadn't heard from him before, the kind a little boy felt for the loss of a friend, strangled him. Minton shook his head as if shaking off the feelings, then started again. "Did you see him?"

"After he was dead?" I asked.

"Yeah."

I shook my head. "I hadn't moved here yet."

The elevator bumped to a stop, then bounced for a moment before releasing us. I glanced at Minton, who seemed unconcerned by the malfunction.

He grabbed one end of the gurney, pushing it out of the elevator and onto the ground floor near the freight doors. I wondered, for just a moment, if funeral homes called those wide double doors freight doors, then decided they probably didn't. They probably had some euphemism, something that sanitized even the transportation details of death.

"What made Emmett's death so powerful," Minton said as he

headed toward those doors, "wasn't his youth or what he did. It was how he looked. And what they did to him."

Minton paused, his hand on the red switch that would automatically swing the freight doors open.

"You couldn't look at Emmett's body and believe that his death was easy. Everything those bastards did, everything, was imprinted on him. His eye was coming off, for god's sake. His face was smashed. He barely looked like Emmett at all."

Minton slammed his fist against the switch, activating it. The doors creaked as we started to move.

"My momma, she made me get in that line of people coming to view his body. I didn't want to, and my dad said I was too young. 'The boy needs a childhood,' he said, but my momma said, 'Emmett Till had a childhood and they stole it from him. Our boy needs to know what could happen to him.'"

"That's harsh," I said, even though I understood both impulses. If I could hide the filth of this world from Jimmy, I would have. But I would have had to have gotten him when he was an infant. By the time he was two, he'd seen a lot. By the time I met him, he'd probably seen more depravity than I could even imagine—and not much of it came from whites. Whites were the great unknown in his life, until he met me.

"It may be harsh, but my mom was right."

The doors had opened. Rain pounded the parking lot, huge fat drops that sounded like they were landing with the power of hail.

Minton grabbed the gurney and shoved it out the door. I hurried ahead of him and opened the back doors of the van. Together we lifted the gurney inside.

"I expect you want me to wear one of those coveralls," he said, nodding toward mine.

"Yeah." I set down the body bags and grabbed one of the last of the coveralls, handing it to Minton. He nodded.

He set his equipment inside, then we closed all the doors and ran to the front of the van.

I started it up, shut off the radio, and turned on the wipers. Then I drove out of the alley and onto the street.

"I still don't get why you didn't become an investigator," I said. "Or even a reporter. It was the journalists covering that funeral who really got the nation's attention."

"No," Minton said. "That was Mrs. Till. I'd never seen anyone so angry. She wanted the world to see what happened to her son, and by God, the world saw it."

In still black-and-white photographs. A lot of the southern papers didn't carry the story, but I saw the photographs in the *Defender*, which a lot of people subscribed to in Memphis.

He shook his head, lost in his memories. "My momma took me to that line, and we threaded past that casket to pay our respects. That was the first time I saw anyone dead, and it was a boy I knew, and he hardly looked human any more."

I wanted to close my eyes against the images that rose. I'd seen victims of southern "justice." That was how I'd learned some of these behind-the-books techniques in the first place.

"I didn't just learn about death or excessive cruelty that day, Mr. Grimshaw. I learned that bodies talk."

I glanced at him. He was staring at the buildings going by, places with their own secrets, filled with people who lived mostly quiet lives.

"Emmett Till's body didn't just talk. It screamed. And because it screamed, the white world finally listened."

A little. They listened a little. Not enough to stop all the racism and prejudice and cruelty. But enough for some folks to say that the violence was unacceptable. Loyce Kirby, my old partner, had been teaching me the detecting business during the Till uproar.

He said it was kinda like white folks had just discovered their neighbors were beating their dogs. You had to stop the cruelty because you saw it. But they never did see blacks as human. Just dumb animals who couldn't defend themselves.

"So you went into the body business," I said.

"At first I thought I wanted to heal them," Minton said. "But then I figured out that you couldn't step in. A woman could come in, beaten by her husband, and you could patch her up. But then she'd go home to the same bastard who hurt her in the first place and you couldn't do a damn thing."

I shook my head. "Waiting until he killed her so that he could be brought to justice isn't good either."

"I can't stop people from killing other people," Minton said. "I can help prove that they've done it, and maybe stop a future crime. And that's all I can do."

"That's enough for you?" I asked.

He glanced at me, his eyebrows raised slightly. "Solving old crimes for a white woman? That's enough for you?"

"Touché," I said.

We pulled onto the Queen Anne's block.

"She's doing good works," I said of Laura, not wanting Minton to back out of this. "Like I told you—"

"I know what you told me. I investigated it as best I could, and I agree. But I also hear she's someone special to you. And she's high-profile. So I don't get your argument on the Soto case."

"You should if you think about it." I pulled the van into the back and shut off the ignition. "Laura's been high-profile for a long time. Because she's white, she gets invited to luncheons for her fame. The Soto brothers were high-profile for—what? Three months? And for their efforts they got gunned down."

"Fred's been high-profile longer than that," Minton said sullenly.

"And he's been arrested—"

"For stealing ice cream. They called it a felony, and he didn't do nothing. He wasn't even there."

"—and his offices have repeatedly been broken into, and his friends have been killed. Do you have a family, Tim?"

"My folks," he said.

"A wife? Kids?"

He shook his head.

"Then you're free to act on this stuff. Me, I gotta pick and choose. Because if the cops gun me down, my little boy's got no one. And if the cops want to get to me without killing me, guess who'll they'll go after? I don't want to see my son on your table."

Minton sighed. "It's just that everyone says you're the best, man. Everyone."

"Maybe I am. But I can't help on this one. I can recommend a few folks. But that's all I can do."

"Fred won't trust just anyone."

"That's smart," I said.

"Maybe we'll just look into it ourselves," Minton said. The "we" and the "our" unnerved me a little.

"You're a Panther?" I asked.

"I don't wear the leather or carry the guns," Minton said. "But I believe in Fred. I'm gonna help at the Free Clinic when I can. I have enough pre-med to do some basic first aid. He's right about community first."

"Family first," I said. "Community second."

He grabbed the door handle. "You know, Mr. Grimshaw, for all your talk of family and non-violence, your body says something different."

I glanced at him, surprised.

He touched his left cheek with one finger. "That scar you have right here? It's fresh, less than a year old. It came from a knife, and it was sewn up by a professional. Family men, they'd find a way to cover it up. You wear it like a badge. It says, 'Don't fuck with me because I'm mean enough to survive anything.'"

He saw me a little too clearly. I needed to push him away.

"So don't fuck with me then," I said, and opened the van door.

TWENTY-EIGHT

The tension between me and Minton increased as we walked into that awful house. He took a sniff of the foul air as we stepped into the back entry and said, "Someone died here not too long ago. I thought these were old bodies."

"The manager died here in September and didn't get found for a while," I said. "That's why we're here in the first place."

He nodded, waited for me to open the door at the top of the steps, then followed me down. Halfway to the basement he muttered, "This's creepy as shit."

I'd felt that way from the beginning, but I didn't say anything. He'd have to work in here same as I did, same as LeDoux was doing.

We went through the open cabinet doors into the hidden room. Minton was looking around like a kid at his first visit to a carnival's haunted house, almost as if he expected someone to jump out of the shadows at any moment.

LeDoux was inside the first section we'd found. He was crouched over one small corner, a pair of tweezers in his gloved hands. "It's about time," he said.

"Christ on a stick." Minton was staring at everything, eyes wide. "What'd you think happened here?"

"I don't know, but I certainly don't appreciate the language," LeDoux said primly.

Minton shot me a can-you-believe-this-guy? look. I ignored it, and swept a hand toward LeDoux.

"The first body we found was in here. The rest are in those opened areas."

"And there's probably more behind them," LeDoux said. "This is a big room, and we've only scratched the surface."

Minton winced.

"You done?" I asked LeDoux.

"Yeah," he said, coming out, a flashlight in one hand, an evidence bag in the other. He must have put the tweezers in the pocket of his coveralls. "It's all yours, Mr.—?"

"Minton." Minton extended a hand. "Sorry about the language. Grimshaw told me there were some long-dead folks here, but he didn't explain much more. I wasn't prepared."

LeDoux looked at his hand, and I prayed that he'd take it. The last thing I needed was a fight between my acting coroner and my acting criminalist.

"I don't think anyone could be prepared," LeDoux said after a moment, and then shook Minton's hand. "Something awful happened here, and the worst of it is, I don't think it happened all at once."

Minton nodded in just the same way LeDoux did when I made a statement before he'd had a chance to examine the evidence.

"Body's in there?" Minton asked, then didn't wait for an answer.

He slipped inside the hole that we made, careful not to touch anything. He had to duck to avoid hitting his head on the lower bricked-up ceiling. He crouched near the skeletons, poking one of the skulls with his fingers.

"You guys move anything?" he asked.

"Not around the bodies," LeDoux said. "I've taken some bits of fabric, paper, and small hairs from the area near your feet. I also took many items from around the opening, and some scrapings off the walls."

"Fingerprints?" Minton asked, but he sounded distracted.

"In the mortar, etched forever in time," LeDoux said. "That's the fortunate part. The unfortunate part is taking fingerprints off such rough brick. I only got partials."

"Hmmm." Minton clearly wasn't listening any longer. He was crouched over the bodies, touching them gently. "I'm going to need my camera, Grimshaw."

168

"I took photographs," LeDoux said.

"Department of Redundancy Department," Minton said. "Grimshaw here hired me to be thorough. That includes pictures. No offense."

"None taken." In fact, LeDoux looked happy that Minton wanted to take his own photographs. These two shared an attention to detail that made me feel as if I was careless.

I went back to the van, grabbed a bag of Minton's equipment, and slung it over my shoulder. The rain had lessened a little, but it was cold, and I was getting tired of moving around in it. The shoulders and back of my coveralls were already soaked, and some of the water had worked its way through to my shirt.

If this kept up, by the end of the day I'd be drenched.

I went back inside, handed Minton his camera, and moved out of the way. LeDoux watched for a few minutes, then turned his attention to the next section that we'd opened.

"What can I do?" I asked, hating to be idle.

"Nothing for a while," Minton said. "There are at least three bodies here. I'm going to have to do some preliminary work before I can move them."

"I'm sure this isn't the only thing taking your attention," LeDoux said to me. "I can help Mr.—Minton, is it?—until it's time to load the van. Then we'll need you."

I probably could have examined the files in Hanley's apartment, but I didn't want to, not until LeDoux had gone over the entire area. Or at least, that was my rationalization. I knew, deep down, I didn't want to spend my day in that stink.

"Everything I have is off-premise," I said. "When should I be back?"

"How many others are there?" Minton asked.

"We're not sure. But you have eight different areas to examine at the moment," LeDoux said.

"Jesus," Minton said, and then he looked over his shoulder. "You're just going to have to put up with the language. I've never had a scene like this before."

"None of us have, son," LeDoux said softly.

I glanced at him. Minton gave me a shaky smile, and then shrugged his shoulders.

"How about four, five, maybe six hours," Minton said. "I'd like to finish today. I have a lot to do at the Poehler's tomorrow, not counting the extra work this's going to be."

"I'll be back in five," I said, figuring that would give me enough time to load the van, transport these two, and pick up Jimmy.

Then I fled the basement.

By now, Laura should've gotten some of that information on Hanley. I also wanted to investigate his death a bit closer.

And to do all those things, I needed my phone.

I headed home, even though I knew I'd pick up the tail once again.

TWENTY-NINE

I pulled over and took off my coveralls halfway home, throwing them and the painter's cap into the back of the van. Then I drove to the apartment, noting with no surprise the black sedan parked halfway down the street.

I almost saluted the driver, but thought the better of it. I'd spent the morning convincing him I was an average Joe going about my day. I didn't want to blow that image by letting him know I'd spotted the tail.

The apartment was excessively warm. The landlord had turned on the heat, probably inspired by the rain. I sighed in irritation. The radiators had never worked properly in this apartment, and throughout the winter I usually had to have a window open. I didn't want to do that on such a stormy day, but I knew I had no choice.

I opened the window in the living room, made myself a corned beef sandwich, and ate the first bite in full view of the street, just so that the tail could guess why I'd come home.

Then I went into my office and started to make calls.

First, I called Laura. Her secretary put me through immediately, which had become unusual.

Laura sounded harried. But she had managed some of the investigating I'd asked for. Apparently she'd done it on Sunday, while Jim and I watched the game.

"I've a packet of materials for you," she said. "I've double-sealed it, marked it confidential, and left it with Judith."

Judith was her secretary.

I opened my mouth to protest leaving documents for this investigation with someone else, then realized it was already too late.

"I would give them to you myself," Laura said, "but I'm still working with the Model Cities people. It's a mess, Smokey."

It seemed like everything was.

"Can you remember off the top of your head the date that the manager was found?" I was being deliberately vague.

"You started, what? September twenty-second or so?"

"Something like that," I said.

"Then it would be a week before that. Whatever that was." Her tone had shifted, become more guarded. Someone had come into her office.

I ended the call as quickly as I could. Then I dialed another number I knew by heart, a number for a police officer at a nearby precinct. Jack Sinkovich wasn't a friend, although he might call himself one. I'd met him during an investigation more than a year ago. He had proven himself to be reliable on more than one occasion, and his willingness to buck the dominant culture of the police department had gotten him two warnings and a reassignment to the desk.

Only when my call went through, someone else picked up Sinkovich's phone. I asked for Sinkovich, wondering if I'd gotten the wrong number, and the voice on the other end—a disgruntled detective whose rank I'd caught but not his name—told me that Sinkovich had been reassigned again.

"Can you tell me how to reach him?" I asked.

"He's not gonna be near a phone for the foreseeable future," the detective said.

"Where can I find him, then?"

"Can't," the detective said. "I'll let him know you called, Mr.—"

"Just tell him Bill called," I said. "He'll know who that is."

Then I hung up and frowned. Sinkovich was undercover again, which was a surprise. He'd upset the brass enough that I would have believed the other detective more if he'd told me that Sinkovich had been fired rather than hinting that he was undercover.

Which made things difficult for me. As of last spring, I had two contacts in the police department. Now I had none.

And I needed one. I had hoped to get Sinkovich to pull the sheet on

Hanley's death. There had to be a report—that infamous mailman had to have called in the death itself—but now I had no access to it.

I grabbed my phone book and looked up the number for the central post office. When I got through, I asked for the name of the mailman who had the route that included the Queen Anne.

"Why?" asked the suspicious voice on the other end.

I hadn't really thought this through. I wanted to talk with the mailman about Hanley's death and had planned to get his name through the police report, but I couldn't very well tell the postal employee that.

"Because he did something nice for my son," I said, "and I just wanted to make sure you folks know how pleased my wife and I are with the service we've been getting. Too many people call and complain."

"That's for sure," the voice said, sounding less suspicious now. "I can take the information if you'd like."

"I'd actually like to write a letter," I said. "It's always better when you have things in writing, right?"

"Yeah." The voice seemed almost pleased now.

"I figured I could put down his route, but it's better if I have his name. The incident happened in the middle-end of September, if that makes a difference. You don't switch routes or anything, right?"

I could hear paper shuffling. "Only when someone retires," the voice said. "We even discourage substitution. Neither rain nor snow, you know."

The way he said it, it rhymed—that good old Chicago accent.

"I know," I said.

"Here it is. You're wanting Carter Doyle. You need me to spell that?"

I didn't, but I asked, just for good form, and dutifully took down the name. Then I thanked the anonymous voice and hung up.

It never ceased to amaze me how much information I could get just by being polite and having the right cover story. The phone was my best weapon—sometimes I learned things I never suspected, from people who wouldn't have given me any time at all face to face.

I found Carter Doyle's address in the phone book—my second best tool—and jotted it down for later.

First, I had to get to Laura's office and pick up the packet on Hanley, and find out what surprises might lurk in there.

I finished my lunch, rinsed the dishes, and left the apartment. I let the tail follow me downtown. I parked near the library, ostentatiously plugging pennies into a meter until I saw the tail circle past me, unable to find a nearby spot of his own.

I made sure he saw me go into the library. Then I wandered through the stacks, peered through the dirt-encrusted window on the second-floor landing, and watched the tail finally snag a space. As he plugged the meter, I headed out a different door on the far side of the building, and walked to Laura's office.

It was still raining, but not as heavily. And now I blended in. I wore a felt hat and a black raincoat. I also carried a briefcase, so that I could put Laura's information inside without anyone seeing what I was carrying.

The building was across from City Hall. Outside the building, a handful of protesters walked in the rain, holding signs that read *Free the Chicago Eight* and *Stop Nixon's Dirty War*.

No one seemed to pay them any attention. Most people ran from building to building, carrying umbrellas or newspapers over their head even though the rain wasn't that heavy.

I had become used to it in my short walk, and merely shook it off my shoulders as I went inside Sturdy's building.

Judith smiled when she saw me. Laura had hired her over the summer. She was a heavyset young woman who had an air of competence to her that the secretary Laura had inherited hadn't had. Judith wore her hair in a modified beehive—it didn't stand as tall as the style seemed to on older women—and she wore dark, horn-rimmed glasses that hid half her face. I often felt that if she pulled her hair down and changed her glasses, she would have been a lot more attractive.

"Miss Hathaway left this for you," Judith said, handing me a thick envelope that had been crisscrossed with masking tape. If anyone had wanted to get into it, they would have had to repackage the entire thing. Maybe Laura wasn't as careless as I had thought.

I put the entire thing in my briefcase, thanked Judith, and left. I walked back to the library and went inside the way that I came.

Then I found a hidden table deep in the stacks and started to read.

THIRTY

Mortimer Hanley had not filled out an employment application. Laura had left me notes, annotating her assumptions as she had gone through the various files. She believed that Hanley's application had been lost to time, but I believed he had never filled one out.

Earl Hathaway had hired Hanley for other reasons, probably because they had known each other and worked together long before Hanley started managing the Queen Anne.

Most of Hanley's early records were buried in a set of accounting books that Laura had included. She had paperclipped a note to the top one which read *I'll need this back as soon as you're done with it.*

I sighed deeply—I had known that I wouldn't have these records long, but I didn't like the confirmation—and dug my legal pad and pen out of my briefcase. Then I started to thumb through the books.

The first accounting book dated from just after the war to 1947. The information on each ledger line was filled out in a cramped hand, as if the person who wrote down the figures wasn't used to writing anything.

I guessed, since Sturdy hadn't incorporated yet, that Laura's father kept these books himself, although I would have to check that with her.

The ledger didn't have a lot of information. Mortgages paid on various buildings, all identified by address; incoming rents, again identified by address; outgoing fees, most of which had an address but not an identification, so it was impossible to know what the fees were for.

The ledgers balanced, sometimes painfully—where I could see, even though I wasn't an accountant—with an added expense that made sure the business had no profit or at least, a profit that could be taxed. It was many years too late to investigate now, but I would have wagered, had I investigated, that I wouldn't have found a receipt for that added expense. Someone had just made up a number and written it in, hoping that no one would notice that the number just happened to be the one needed to zero-out the business.

Obviously, Earl Hathaway hadn't been an accountant, and this practice changed in the next accounting book, which only covered 1948. The cramped hand had disappeared, replaced by a sure and slanting penmanship that suggested more education.

The income and expenses were better identified. And in January of 1948, I noted something odd: in addition to the rent paid for apartments one through nine at the Queen Anne, I also found rent paid for apartments eleven through twenty. That money arrived in one lump sum, and was labeled cash rents received.

I leaned back in my chair, lost in the smell of the library's musty books, and ran through that building in my memory. Even with the manager's apartment being rented, the attic room, and the storage areas on the third floor, in no way could that building house ten more livable apartments.

Apartment rental standards had changed since 1947, but even if some of the rented spaces were closets, there still wasn't enough room for people to live. Unless the basement had once been subdivided into apartments. Maybe the entire building's apartments had been reconfigured.

I wouldn't know that unless Laura had given me all the books pertaining to the Queen Anne. All I'd asked for were the materials involving Hanley.

At some point I might have to get her to go for those files. Or I would have to risk exposure and go to the records office for building permits and official changes made in that Queen Anne.

Still, this finding bothered me. It was subtle, unlike the material in that first ledger, and it suggested something else was happening at the Queen Anne, some kind of payment, some kind of bribe, being paid as "rent" and hidden in the doctored books.

I leaned forward and went back to that earlier ledger. None of the rents paid were marked as to which apartment had paid them, only which address they came from. I took the last month, December 1947, and counted the rents that came in from the Queen Anne, and found ten, one of which was a cash lump sum that matched the amount I found in the 1948 book.

That "rental" payment existed all the way back to the beginning of the ledger, although in 1946 it hadn't been called rent. Then the deposit was simply marked C.P. It came in on the same day of every month.

I skipped ahead. Each ledger she had given me—and she had given me through 1951, the year before Sturdy incorporated—had that payment. It was the only payment that didn't fluctuate, and it never missed a date. Not even, I realized, on weekends.

The fact that the payment hadn't missed, even on weekends, bothered me more than the missing apartments did. So did the initials C.P. Because that led me to believe that apartments 11-20 were invented for people who had never visited the Queen Anne, and who would never know that those apartments didn't exist.

The payment also predated Hanley's appearance on the books. He started showing up in May of 1947, a regular salary paid in monthly increments. I didn't find that unusual either, until I saw a correction to the bookkeeper's neat scrawl in January of 1948. The word "salary" got crossed off, and above the cross-off, someone—the person with the cramped hand—had inscribed "commission." From then on Hanley's payment, which also ran to the end of 1951, was labeled as commission.

I glanced at my watch. I had to leave if I was going to help Minton and LeDoux finish up before I had to pick up Jim. Which was probably good. I needed time to digest those numbers. My brain was crammed full of them, all of them contradictory and confusing. I almost wished Earl Hathaway was alive so that I could question him about his early business practices.

I packed everything in the briefcase, closed it, and headed out of the stacks. High school students had arrived, doing homework on the oak tables in the main room, and occasionally being shushed by the librarians. Most of the older patrons who had been in the library that afternoon were already gone.

I scanned for familiar faces—an old habit—and wondered if the tail had come inside to keep an eye on me, or if he had waited in his car as per law-enforcement regulations.

I guessed I would find out soon enough.

The rain had stopped, but the sidewalk remained wet. Water dripped off building cornices, and passing cars drove through puddles, splashing bypassers.

By the time I reached my van, my feet were wet and I was more tired than I would have been if I had spent the day in that basement, lifting bricks and bodies for Minton.

My parking meter had expired, and a soggy ticket adhered to the van's windshield. I pulled the paper off and looked at the numbers bleeding into each other from the rain. They looked as fuzzy as the numbers had on the ledgers inside my briefcase.

If Hanley had a free apartment, how come he had received a salary? And if Hathaway had changed the payment notation from salary to commission so that he wouldn't get in trouble for failing to pay taxes—and did someone have to pay employment or social security on a commission? I didn't know for certain—why hadn't he changed his practices in 1948 or 1949? Why not change the notation back to salary, remove the taxes, and ensure that everything balanced?

I hoped the rest of the file that Laura had given me had the information I needed. Because, at the moment, the more I learned about Hanley and the Queen Anne, the more confused I got.

THIRTY-ONE

The tail followed me down Michigan Avenue into Bronzeville. It was the same car, and it looked like the same driver. I still had no idea if he had followed me into the library, but if I had to guess, I would have thought that he hadn't.

Still, I had to lose him on the drive back, which wouldn't be as easy to mask. Most people didn't drive south in rush hour. Many of the people who lived in Bronzeville, Bridgeport, and the near South Side took public transportation. People from the suburbs and the Gold Coast drove, making most of the afternoon rush hour traffic head north.

So I had to do some creative driving, heading west farther than I wanted to find a small tangle of roads near the stockyards. I arrived just as the shifts were changing, which added a confusion of traffic, and I slipped through it, gunning the van when it wasn't appropriate and making a few illegal U-turns.

I suspected I had lost him there, but I knew I had lost him when he didn't show up behind me in the relatively minor traffic near Fiftieth Street.

Still, I drove through some of the back roads of Hyde Park, pausing too long at stop signs and pulling over now and then to see if anyone in a black sedan appeared behind me.

No one did, but a police car passed me. As I glanced inside, I thought I saw the same two cops I'd seen the previous week.

They didn't notice me. They drove by, and although I checked my rearview, they didn't follow.

I made my way safely to the Queen Anne.

LeDoux and Minton were still in the basement, still working the first crime scene. I had joined them, after I donned my coveralls and cap in the van, and was startled to see that they hadn't made much progress at all.

I mentioned that as politely as I could.

"Actually, we've made quite a bit of progress," LeDoux said.

He handed me a rolled-up grocery bag. I opened it and looked inside, discovering several small, full evidence bags. I pulled one out. It held a faded box of matches, the logo almost unreadable. The label attached to the plastic bag written in LeDoux's characteristic scrawl read:

Right Pocket
Tan? pants
Skeleton one [see drawing]
item 105A

"I assume you know what this tag means," I said.

He nodded. "This," he said, sweeping his hand toward the first crime scene, "is area A. We'll go as far down the alphabet as we need to."

I set the matchbox in the bag beside the other evidence. "I thought you'd have to process all of this for fingerprints and stuff. You haven't finished that, have you?"

"Heavens, no," LeDoux said. "I really don't want you to touch anything but the evidence bags. But write down the information. Both Tim and I thought, however, that you could find out things about these victims from these items."

"No ID, then," I said.

"Nothing we can use." Minton's voice floated out of the crime scene area. "Some letters, some torn pieces of paper, a few wallets with money but no real ID."

A group of flashlights surrounded him, washing out his skin and making him seem larger than he was. He was still crouched near the skeletons, only he had a long box near him and he was lining it with paper.

"What're you doing?" I asked.

"Packing these men up," Minton said.

I wasn't sure what to respond to first—the fact that he had figured out gender or the fact that he wasn't using a body bag for each skeleton.

"We have tarps," I said, before I actually made a conscious decision.

"Hmmm?" Minton asked.

LeDoux was looking at me strangely as well.

"Tarps. To cover the body bags. It'll look like we're carrying out painting equipment if we're careful," I said.

Minton let out a small laugh. It had surprise but no real humor in it. "That's not why I'm using the box. This is the preferred way to carry old bones. If I put them in a bag, they'll knock together and chip."

He held up a femur. It looked yellow in the odd light.

"See?" he said. "It has no connecting tissue, nothing to hold it to the other bones."

"So you can't tell which body it belongs to?"

"I can guess," Minton said. "I'm going to try to put the right bones with the right person. But I'm not going to be entirely sure until I get back to Poehler's. There's been some animal activity—mouse or rat, I can't tell—"

"Don't worry," LeDoux said, apparently seeing my expression. "It was a long time ago."

"—and some of these parts have been moved around."

"But we've already made one discovery." LeDoux actually sounded pleased.

I glanced at him.

"The bones are old," he said.

"How old?" I asked, feeling the muscles in my shoulders tighten, hoping they wouldn't implicate Hathaway—not for his sake, but for Laura's.

"These bones are yellow and brittle," Minton said. He had set a femur at the bottom of the box and was packing soft white cloth around it as if it were the most precious thing he'd ever seen. "They flake easily and are very fragile."

"Which means what?" I asked.

"These bodies have been here thirty or forty years minimum," Minton said. "Probably closer to forty. The area's pretty dry, and except for some early bug activity and those long-ago mice, they've been relatively unmolested. The exposure to air's pretty minimal, so decay would have taken longer, and the walls—especially basement walls—would have protected them from the extremes of Chicago's weather. So it would take longer for them to reach this condition."

"Forty years," I said numbly. Forty years ago was 1929. Earl Hathaway hadn't even stolen his name yet, let alone moved to Chicago. I had no idea where the man was in 1929, but I would have wagered everything I owned that he hadn't been anywhere near the Windy City.

"They're probably older than that," LeDoux said, "given some of the items we found."

"Items?" I asked, feeling like I'd missed a great deal.

"One of the letters," LeDoux said, "has a date of 1917."

I frowned. "Letters."

"In your bag. And no, you can't remove it, but I packed it so that you can read it. If you'd like, I'll supervise you while you take down the information."

LeDoux always managed to sound condescending, even when he wasn't trying to.

Minton looked up from his packing and grinned at me. Since LeDoux was calling him Tim now instead of reprimanding him on his language, I assumed they had come to some kind of truce.

"These bodies could have been down here longer than forty years?" I asked.

"Sure," Minton said. "They might even date to the turn of the century. I don't think the smaller bones would still be here if they were older than that. Eventually we do turn to dust, just like the Bible says, but I'm only guessing. I've worked with some old bodies, mostly identifiers from unmarked graves, but never anything quite like this."

He'd clearly gotten over his revulsion at the site and had moved to intellectual intrigue. I couldn't quite get past the way he was laying the bones in that box, as if he were disassembling a puzzle.

"The lack of connective tissue," he said, "the condition the clothes are in, the things we found near the bodies, like that book—"

"Book?" I asked.

"It's more of a notebook, really," LeDoux said. "The kind you'd put in your breast pocket and use to keep track of spending or something."

"And it's in here?" I peered into the grocery bag.

"No," LeDoux said. "I'm keeping it. It's too fragile for any kind of handling. I'll go through it and see what I can read out of it, and then I'll give you that,"

"Sooner rather than later," I said.

He looked pointedly at the rest of the hidden room. "It's hard to prioritize."

"Plus you have a lot of gems in that grocery bag." Minton folded up more cloth, making barriers that seemed unnecessarily deep to me. In each tiny area, he put one small bone. It took me a moment to recognize them. They were the small bones of the fingers.

"It'll keep you busy for a while," LeDoux said.

As if they wanted me out of here. They probably did. I was the one who was unnecessary.

"You think the other bodies are forty years old?" I asked.

"No," LeDoux said.

Minton looked up from his work and glared at LeDoux. "You'd be surprised. I've seen bodies I've known were in the ground since the 1890s that are in the kind of shape some of those bodies are in."

"You've looked at them then?" I asked.

"I peered through those openings you made," Minton said.

"The bodies you saw in those graves," LeDoux said, "had been embalmed."

"Not all of them," Minton said. "Embalming was not an exact science eighty years ago, nor was it used in all cases. Some of these bodies were in wooden caskets. It just depends on the ground conditions."

"Which are pretty benign in this basement," I said.

"You got it." Minton put a lid on that box, scrawled on the top of it, then handed the box to me. "Be careful."

"Where do you want it?"

"Near the stairs'll do for the moment," he said.

I carried the box, labeled *300A Human Male Skeleton [bones missing—skull in box 300AA]* and signed by Minton. The box seemed to weigh nothing, even though I had watched him put several dozen bones in there. Amazing what a human being was reduced to after so much time.

I found it hard to believe that this body had been dead as long as I had been alive. Forty years. Maybe more.

That meant Hanley hadn't killed these people. Had he known about them? He had certainly known about the attic room. Many of the clippings up there were more recent, and I would have wagered that some of those teeth were recent too—the fillings looked like fillings done in this century, not at the turn of the last one.

I had no idea what the condition of dentistry in Chicago had been in 1929, but I would have wagered that it wasn't very good. Dentists had made a lot of advances in the last ten years, advances that I'd personally experienced.

I set the box down near the stairs, making sure that no one would accidentally step on it, and then went back to the hidden room. LeDoux handed me a smaller box labeled *300AA Skull of Unknown Male* and signed by Minton.

I carried that box, which was even lighter, to the stairs as well, and glanced at my watch. I'd have to get these men to work quicker, or I was going to have to pick up Jim, drop him unplanned at the Grimshaws, and come back.

But Minton was nearly done with the third box by the time I'd returned. LeDoux handed me a fourth—*200AA Skull of Unknown Male*—and I realized that Minton had boxed up the skulls first and was working on the other bones second.

"You're sure these are men?" I asked when I came back the third time.

"Yeah," Minton said. "All three pelvises are here. They confirm what at least one of the craniums didn't—that these are men."

"You think maybe there are four bodies here, if one of the craniums isn't male?"

"I didn't say it wasn't," Minton said. "I just said it wasn't immediately obvious on one of them. He was probably young. Tests'll confirm that. He had all his teeth. But the things I look for—the front nose angle, the curve of the eyebrow, the thin cranium wall—weren't immediately obvious in this one skull. All three pelvises were definitely male, though, just at a glance."

LeDoux handed me the fourth box—*100AA Skull of Unknown Male*—and prevented me from asking a question I wasn't sure I wanted to know the answer to—how did one tell the difference between a male and female pelvis?

"How much longer?" I asked when I came back. "I have to pick up my son in less than an hour, and if I have to drive you both back—"

"Almost done." Minton scrawled on top of the second large box. "This's going to take me days, Bill."

184

"I realized that when I got back here," I said.

"We're going to have to juggle it with my own work schedule. I'll probably have to work nights."

"I really don't want the neighbors to see lights here," I said. "I'd prefer it if you can come in the afternoons. Can you switch hours at Poehler's?"

"I'll see," he said. "There're just fewer questions if I bring the bodies in to the funeral home at night."

"If we get you a different workspace for these bodies, would that help?" LeDoux asked. I knew he had already discussed this with Laura, but I didn't think they had the space set up.

"Yeah, it would. Poehler's doesn't mind if I do side work, but this much—and all of it obviously old—would raise some questions."

He handed the fifth box to me. I carried it out and set it near the others. How many days would I be doing this? This work was surprisingly similar to carrying real bodies out of the trenches in Korea. Even though those bodies still had flesh—some of them were still warm—they weren't human any longer. They were parts and materials, things that could be—and eventually would be—stored in a box.

Then I went back and waited while Minton packed the sixth and last box. I opened the grocery bag one last time and peeked into it. I wasn't quite sure what to do with it: if I brought it home, Jimmy might get into it and the evidence would be compromised.

"I'm going to leave this here," I said to LeDoux. "Laura hasn't told us where we're storing the evidence yet, and my home office is too open."

LeDoux nodded. I'd spoken about Jimmy enough that LeDoux understood what I meant.

"I'll go through it all tomorrow and make notes. That way the evidence never leaves your custody."

"That's probably better," LeDoux said.

Minton finished placing the small bones in the last box. He always ended with the bones of the fingers. Apparently he had quite a system.

He handed the box to me. It seemed even lighter than the others.

I mentioned that.

He nodded. "This one seemed smaller. Remember? I told you we had a younger one? This is it."

Not him. It. Maybe that was how Minton handled such old death.

I knew I couldn't do his work, but I also knew I couldn't call that boy it and not him.

The label on the box was as neat as the others: *100A Unidentified Male.*

It would be my job to identify these men. My job to find out who they had been. Some of that would come through the items in the bag. The rest through legwork.

I couldn't imagine that Minton would find much that would help me. And if the bodies were as old as he said, I doubted these poor souls would have dental records in some kind of file.

"Are we done for the day?" I asked.

Minton nodded and started turning off flashlights.

I carried the box up the stairs and to the van. The walk felt oddly ceremonial—like a funeral procession with only me left to mourn.

THIRTY-TWO

Even though I'd left the grocery bag of evidence at the Queen Anne, I still had a lot of material to go through. I had spent the entire drive from the Queen Anne to the funeral home to LeDoux's new apartment convincing myself that nothing had yet disqualified Hanley as our chief suspect.

Maybe he had known about earlier killings. Maybe he had committed them himself. I still didn't know his age or what he had done before he had come to work for Earl Hathaway.

Maybe Hanley had some kind of connection to the house's previous owner.

Anything was still possible. I had to keep my mind open.

I also had to keep my eyes open. I made sure I drove slowly through my neighborhood on the way to pick up Jimmy so that the tail would see me and follow again. Sure enough, I picked him up and he spent the rest of the afternoon tracking me.

We went to the church where the after-school class was held, to the Grimshaws' to drop off their children, to a nearby market for that night's dinner, and then home, where we stayed.

All the while, Jimmy watched through the back window, reporting on the driver of the sedan.

He started with, "It's some white guy." A few minutes later he added, "He's wearing a suit!" as if that were strange behavior late on a Monday afternoon. By the time we stopped at the market, Jimmy told me, "He's got a buzz cut too. Is he military?"

"Police, probably," I said.

That satisfied Jimmy for the rest of the drive home.

Satisfied me too. There was nothing unexpected about the driver's appearance or his behavior. I only hoped that by the end of the week he'd be gone, convinced that I had nothing to do with the Black Panthers.

That night, while Jimmy struggled over some math equations that would lead him (and Keith, his partner) to a container filled with one million poppy seeds, I struggled with equations of my own.

The math on the Queen Anne changed in 1952, the year Sturdy incorporated. That year, the business had gone legit or, at least, had to respond to shareholders and a board of directors.

Laura and I both knew her father had kept two sets of books—the one that got scrutinized by outsiders, and the one he kept for himself. Unfortunately, we hadn't found all of them, and she hadn't included any in this packet, which made sense, considering I had only asked for things that pertained to Mortimer Hanley.

The changes on the Queen Anne's accounts were vast. The apartment numbers went from one to twenty to one to ten. The tenth was marked as comped, and the comp went to Hanley. A notation along the side mentioned a missing Social Security number, which led me to believe that the new bookkeeper, whoever he was, had decided that Hanley's free apartment ranked as a salary.

The lump-sum payment for apartments eleven to twenty had disappeared as well. There was no remodeling expense attached to the building, and nothing that showed where that payment went.

There was also no cash compensation to Hanley.

I cross-checked the books. Hanley's initial salary, the one that Hathaway had marked as "commission," had been about fifty dollars less than the lump-sum payment which came in every month. If Hathaway had been smart—and I knew he had been—he would have had funneled that money to Hanley himself.

If that money had gone to Hanley, then it stood to reason that the cash payment was somehow affiliated with the Queen Anne.

If the cash payment vanished and Hanley lost his compensation, then I had to assume that the money had nothing to do with the house.

I would have to see if I could track it when I looked through Hanley's personal papers.

The rest of the files seemed pretty straightforward. There were receipts, most of them for plumbing repairs, some electrical work—most of it in the upstairs apartments—and something that made me smile: an invoice from Hanley himself for modifications done to the attic space to make it into a "potential residential area."

Instead, he had used it to store things.

Had Earl Hathaway known that? Approved it? Or lost interest in the Queen Anne?

The files didn't tell me.

I continued to look through them, but found nothing else. Until I reached to the back of the file and found some phone-message slips, held together by an old, rusted paperclip.

I pulled the clip off, and read.

At first, they were nothing special. Written up in a flowery hand, all they contained were the day of the week, no date, a time, and Hanley's name, followed by a phone number. As the days went by, the secretary started adding "Urgent!" to the messages, but it became clear that whoever these went to wasn't responding.

Finally, the last message had a slip attached to the back, also in the secretary's hand:

Marshall—

Mr. Hanley says you must meet him tomorrow. He has items that could embarrass Sturdy. Perhaps you would like to collect them? If not, he will donate them to anyone who seems interested.

If you choose not to meet him or return his calls, please let me know how to deal with him.

—B.

I wasn't sure if Laura had seen this or, if she had, if she understood the implications. Even though there was no date, I was pretty sure that Marshall was Marshall Cronk, Earl Hathaway's right-hand man, the person who ended up controlling the team that ran Sturdy from Hathaway's death in 1960 to Laura's takeover eight years later.

I also found it odd that the messages had found their way into the file. It led me to believe that the secretary, whoever she was, believed she needed a paper trail to prove—what? That she had given the messages to Cronk? That Hanley had called? That she had acted professionally?

I couldn't imagine why Cronk would want to keep these, except perhaps as evidence that Hanley was not always reasonable. Even though the messages were calmly written, it was clear from the secretary's bland prose that the conversations with Hanley had become more and more heated.

He remained employed at the Queen Anne through those phone calls and beyond. Even though the ledgers disappeared—they became corporate ledgers rather than hand-scrawled things, and Laura couldn't take those—Laura had managed to find the year-end documents pertaining to the building, one that cited revenue in, expenses, and any net income.

The Queen Anne earned substantially from 1952 on, even without the cash payment. It seemed to have a good occupancy rate throughout the first ten years of the corporation, dropping off only after 1962. Then, it seemed, when a tenant vacated, no one made an attempt to rent the apartment again.

Was the Queen Anne slated for remodel? Demolition? Nothing in this file told me that.

Or was Cronk responding in his own passive-aggressive way to the blackmail that Hanley had obviously used to keep his job? It would make sense; why pay someone to manage an apartment building if there were no tenants?

I checked the files. The last two tenants moved out this year, six months after Cronk had been fired. His plan had taken time, but it worked.

Of course, I was just guessing, and I would have to continue guessing. I wouldn't ask Cronk what happened. The old Sturdy team was still looking for leverage against Laura, and I wasn't about to give them any.

Although it was beginning to look like Earl Hathaway had given them more than enough.

THIRTY-THREE

I went through the same routine Tuesday morning to lose the tail, although this time I dumped him near Jimmy's school, just for variety's sake.

Eventually, the tail would figure out that I was losing him on purpose, rather than through bad traffic and poor driving. I only hoped he wouldn't be assigned to me long enough to figure out the pattern.

I spent my morning in a basement work area that I'd set up in the storage room away from the boiler. Minton had asked for a few days to work on the skeletons and to see if he could rearrange his schedule so that he could come during the daytime.

LeDoux was working on the next opening, the one farthest from the original site. We now had pasted little cards on top of each one. That one was unoriginally called Site B.

The grocery bag was a small gold mine of information. It contained torn letters, a well-worn pocketknife, coins, and tobacco tins. In addition, there were matches, some paper money, and some tags that I didn't recognize.

LeDoux had told me that all the paper, except for one letter, came from the leather wallet, which somehow protected the paper from disintegration. The other letter had been found in the breast pocket of one of the shirts—it had fallen away from the body, and hadn't been subject to the worst of the decay.

He had bagged the wallet. It was longer than any wallet I'd seen and looked like it would fit into a breast pocket or a jacket pocket instead of the back pocket of someone's pants. It was covered with a long, greenish-grayish stain that looked foul.

I was happy the entire thing was bagged, so I wouldn't have to smell it.

I set it aside. LeDoux had already pulled the pertinent items, so I didn't have to do much with it. I would want to look inside to see if there were maker's marks or if someone had written a name or initials in it, small things that LeDoux might not think to look for.

Then I turned my attention to the matchboxes. One had a paper label that was half worn away. It had been blue or green or some similar color, and the letters KITC were visible. I assumed the box contained kitchen matches, but I would check. Nonetheless, I wrote everything down.

The other matchbox had *The Four Deuces* written on it, with cards with deuces of each suit sketched under the name. The drawing was crude, as if it were done by an amateur.

The penknife had no real markings on the outside. But a lot of knife owners carved their names on the blade. I had promised I wouldn't open the evidence bag, and I didn't, but I was tempted.

I started a second page in the legal pad I'd been using for my notes. This page was directed at LeDoux, asking him to look for certain things on the evidence when he examined it. The first thing I wanted him to do was see if someone had scratched a name on the blade of that knife.

I also added the wallet to the list, asking LeDoux to check for maker's marks or a hidden name.

Then I looked at the coins. They were old. I hadn't seen most of them since I was a boy. One was a Morgan dollar, with a woman's face on one side. I seemed to recall that nowadays the Morgan dollar had value to coin collectors, but how much I didn't know.

The rest of the coins were American—they had United States and their denomination engraved on them—but I had never seen them in circulation. That they had been in circulation, I had no doubt. They were worn from use. Even the dirt from the years in the tomb hadn't hidden that.

But the most interesting thing in my searches so far was the currency. The wallet had held one-dollar bills—three of them—and a single five-dollar bill.

I had never seen anything like them. They were bigger than any money I'd ever seen before. The dollar bills had Washington's portrait stamped on the left side and a bluish mark on the right. They were marked with the phrase *Federal Reserve Note* and they had the words *New York* prominently displayed on one side. One note had a reddish mark instead of the blue one.

The blues were dated 1918, the red 1914.

The five-dollar bill was the same size and general design, only it had Lincoln instead of Washington. It also carried the 1918 date.

I marked the dates down and set the money aside to examine later. There were coin shops in Bronzeville that might help me with the money, should I need it.

I had saved the other paper for last. The first item I picked up was a cocktail napkin. It had been folded, but it seemed remarkably intact.

The notation LeDoux had made on the evidence bag said that the napkin had been hidden in a flap in the long leather wallet, underneath other pieces of paper, most of which were unreadable. LeDoux had even made a small drawing of where the napkin had been located and stapled it to the bag.

The napkin itself had a small gold logo in the corner. All it said was *Calumet-412*. In ink, someone had written:

Sorry.
Love forever
V.

I stared at it, unable to make much sense of it. Yet it looked distinctive enough to be important.

A tattered business card had been in the same wallet. The card came from a place called Colosimo's, which claimed to be "The Best Italian Restaurant in Chicago." It also had "refined cabaret and good music" as well as "public dancing" between four and one. The address, listed in small print below the name, was 2128 South Wabash Avenue, right in the heart of Bronzeville.

Finally, there were the letters. The first one had pieces torn out of the center, probably by the mice as they ate their way to the bodies.

That letter had a date—May 1, 1917—and a salutation, *Dearest Lawrence.*

The rest I had to piece together. It seemed that Lawrence's younger sister was either writing the letter or had had something bad happen to her. "Ma" insisted on sending him a package. And Edwina had died. Her death was "a mercy" so Lawrence "shouldn't be sad."

The only other intact area read:

> *Ma thanks you for the money. She's moving in with Aunt Lula, so if you want to write, do so care of Lulabelle at the Dickerson's.*

The other letter was intact. It had also been folded up in that long wallet. The letter was written in ink again, only this ink was smudged, not by time, but by the writer. Dabs of ink marked the beginning of some of the phrases, as if the person hadn't been used to using a pen.

> *Zeke*
> *Coming 6 Nov morning*
> *train*
> *Miss you*
> *Darcy*

I didn't have a lot to go on—no addresses, and only a few dates—but it was more than I'd had before.

For the first time, I felt like I had a place to start.

THIRTY-FOUR

Colosimo's was not listed in the phone book. Neither was The Four Deuces. The missing listings were not a surprise. Nothing about this investigation was going to be easy.

I left the Queen Anne just before lunch and ate at home again, for the benefit of my tail. Then I called Franklin Grimshaw to see if he remembered a business named Colosimo's on South Wabash Avenue. He didn't. And he didn't recognize Calumet-412 either, although he did say that it made him think of a phone number.

"You know," he said, "like when we were kids."

"But there aren't enough digits," I said.

"It depends on how old the number is," Franklin said. "The phone company kept adding numbers as more and more people got phones."

Of course. I'd been thinking so hard about the other items I'd found that I hadn't put this together. How old did a phone number have to be to only use three digits?

"Would you mind asking around about both things? See if anyone knows what they are?"

"Sure," he said. "Can you tell me why?"

"Investigation," I said.

He knew better than to ask for more, and I didn't offer anything. I hung up, packed up the ledgers from Laura as well as the other items, retaped the envelope, and set it in my briefcase.

I called Laura and told her I was returning the documents. She sounded strained. She said, "I've been getting hang-ups at home."

"Any idea who it is?" I asked.

"None," she said. "It might not even be related to this. For all I know, it's a wrong number."

My stomach clenched. She was right, but I worried that this had something to do with our case. "Be careful," I said.

"I always am," she said, which wasn't exactly true. But I didn't argue with her. She was in a hurry, and so was I. She asked me to leave the papers with Judith, since she would be out of the office again.

Then I got back into the van and headed uptown. The tail followed me. I wished Jimmy was in the van, so he could tell me if the driver was the same man. I had no way of knowing.

I headed to Twenty-first and Wabash. It was a desolate part of town, near the Coliseum where, in June, the SDS had held their convention. The Coliseum was a decaying wreck, obviously built in the previous century and not maintained.

Most of the buildings in that area hadn't been maintained either, not even the one at 2128 South Wabash, the address on the business card. That building was relatively new—built or remodeled in the forties or fifties, I would have guessed—but not touched since. It looked like it was about to tumble down.

Nothing on the building read Colosimo's. Not a faded sign, not paint on the corner. The building did house a restaurant, but it had been closed for a long time. The windows were soaped and covered with dirt, and the door had been padlocked shut.

A dead end, which was not a surprise, given the age of the money, the age of the letter, and the age of the bodies. So far, the indications that I had were that the skeletons had been in that tomb longer than forty years. They'd been put inside in the teens, not the twenties.

I drove over to Michigan and went back to the library. I had a hunch that I would spend a lot of time here over the next few days as I worked the identification part of this case. I wished I was still in Memphis or even Atlanta. I knew the history of those cities as well as I knew my own.

Chicago, pre-1950 or so, was a true mystery to me.

Once again I parked near a meter rather than go to the parking garage under the Conrad Hilton like I would have done had someone not been tailing me. I grabbed the briefcase and headed into the library.

I had planned to go through the same routine as I had the day before, but the library's information desk actually had someone staffing it and no one stood in line to talk with her. I decided to take advantage of that small bit of luck.

The librarian behind the desk was about my age, white, and slender, with graying hair pulled away from her face. Her entire body tensed as I approached and she bent over the desk itself, moving papers, as if she were pretending to work.

I set the briefcase down, gently, then waited patiently until she couldn't avoid me any longer.

As she looked up, her gaze went to that scar on the left side of my face. Her lower lip actually trembled before she forced herself to smile.

"Help you?" To her credit, her voice didn't shake.

"Thank you." I made sure I spoke softly, trying to seem as gentle as I could. "I have a few questions, if you don't mind."

She steeled her shoulders. She minded, but she was going to act like she didn't.

"First, have you ever heard of a place called Colosimo's? It was at—"

"Twenty-second and South Wabash, I know. You doing work on Al Capone?"

I was startled. I had thought, initially, there might be a Prohibition connection to that room in the basement, but once we found the bodies I had dismissed that.

"Capone?"

"Rumor has it that he invested in Colosimo's with The Greek after Big Jim's death."

"Big Jim?" I sounded like my Jimmy, repeating answers that startled me and made no sense.

"Colosimo." She had apparently forgotten her fear of me. "He was the first Chicago gangster, you know—or at least that's what the historians say. In his day he was bigger than Capone. He was gunned down in the restaurant in 1920."

"And then it closed?" I asked, wondering if I had just found the end of the timeline for those bodies to have been dumped—sometime between 1918 and 1920.

"Oh, no. That's when The Greek stepped in. You know, Mike

Potson? He wasn't as well known, but he should've been. The word was he fronted a lot of things for Capone."

"Capone," I said again.

Finally her eyes widened a little. They were a bright blue, and quite intelligent, something I hadn't noticed before. "You're surprised by all this."

"I am," I said. "I found this business card in a friend's basement. It was for Colosimo's, which we'd never heard of, and I told him I'd ask about it. I didn't expect this kind of history."

"There's quite a bit of it in that period," she said.

"Prohibition," I said, almost to myself.

"No," she said. "Even though Prohibition started earlier in Illinois than many other places in the country, that's not what Big Jim was about. He was all about vice. He was the king of the Levee."

"The Levee?"

She smiled and it softened her. She was actually pretty. "Chicago's red-light district—the scourge of the early twentieth century. Everyone's heard of Capone and the gun-runners and the speakeasies and the gangs battling for control of Chicago's streets, but no one seems to realize that the fights were just as bloody twenty years before."

"The Levee was around Wabash?" I asked.

"The city finally won when it put the Dan Ryan right through the heart of the Levee," she said. "But until then, people used to visit all those sites. They'd start with Capone—he had a suite in the Metropole—and they'd work their way back. I think the Levee is infinitely more interesting."

I was beginning to find her interesting, mostly because of her enthusiasm for this topic.

"Why?" I asked.

"Because of the women involved." Then she waved a hand. "I mean, it was tragic. It was the source of white slavery—"

She hesitated just a bit. White slavery always had a worse connotation than other kinds of slavery, and it was all racial. Slavery was bad, the culture said, but white slavery was worse.

"—and prostitution and gambling, but many of the people who got rich were the women."

"Madams?" I asked.

"Much more than that. Have you heard of the Everleigh sisters?" She paused as if she expected me to answer the question, then an-

198

swered it herself. "Of course you haven't, if you haven't heard of Big Jim."

I was beginning to feel as if not knowing who Big Jim Colosimo was had been a flaw in my education.

"The Everleigh sisters ran the most famous bordello in the United States. It was called the Everleigh Club, and it was on Twenty-first and Dearborn, not too far from Colosimo's."

"I don't understand." I spoke with my usual forcefulness and the librarian jumped. So I softened my tone. "I thought you said these rich women weren't all madams."

"To call the Everleighs madams is to raise other madams up. The Everleighs came into Chicago with a small inheritance and set up their house. They'd never worked in the trade, as it's called, and they never wanted to. They made Everleigh Club a show palace, and advertised it worldwide. It was said that it outclassed the bawdy houses in Paris."

She, apparently, was impressed by that, probably because she'd never been in a house of prostitution. I had, and I had tried to help more than one woman escape the life. I had no romantic illusions about it at all.

"The Everleighs became so famous that the mayor finally issued a special order to shut their house—and theirs only—down. He got re-elected because he did that."

"And this is a good thing?"

"For the sisters, yes." The librarian grinned. It was a saucy look that I hadn't believed her capable of. "They retired after twelve years of running the bordello, moved to New York, and lived there until they were a ripe old age. The last one died nine years ago. They made millions."

"Off the exploitation of other women," I said, feeling shocked at her attitude.

"I'm not so sure about that," she said. "They paid their girls more than any other house by double—a prostitute in the Everleigh house could easily keep a hundred dollars a week, not counting what she earned—and the Everleigh sisters never charged overhead or any of the other prices that took away a working girl's wages. These girls kept fifty percent of what they earned, where most others kept less than ten percent. I don't think that's exploitation."

"But—"

She held up a finger. "And it was said that the girls would often convince their clients to gamble rather than spend an hour in bed. The girls would get paid more if their clients stayed the night and sat at the card tables than they did if clients went upstairs for a quickie."

I stared at her, as shocked as I'd ever been by another person. She was not at all what I expected. "You're fascinated by this."

"I hope to write a book about the Levee someday. I think it's much more interesting than Prohibition. Vice is always going to be with us, Mr.—?"

"Grimshaw," I said.

"Mr. Grimshaw. It's unrealistic to pretend that we can rid ourselves of it. So I like the Everleigh sisters' approach. I think if prostitution is going to be with us, let's stop exploiting those poor girls, give them some personal power, and pay them a decent wage."

She had been speaking so fast, she was almost breathless. Then she caught herself, smiled at me, and flushed.

"I'm sorry," she said. "You stepped right into my corner and found me a soapbox."

"It's all right." I was smiling too. "I'm fascinated. What happened to the Levee?"

"It was subject to raids all through the teens, and by the early twenties very few businesses were left—at least of the original ones. Some were taken over by Capone's gang, others by Johnny Torrio—you know Johnny Torrio—?"

I shook my head.

"Oh, I could talk with you all day. He was one of the Big Four Gangster Chieftains of the early twenties. He—"

"I don't have all day," I said awkwardly.

"And you haven't even gotten to your other two questions." She smoothed her hair with one hand, as if catching herself. As the hand moved, she reclaimed her librarian persona. "You probably want to look at some books. I'd recommend that you start with Herbert Asbury's *Gem of the Prairie*. It's a history of the Chicago underworld written for the layperson. There are better histories, more recent ones, but his is the best written."

She wrote that down as she spoke, no longer looking at me.

"Thank you," I said.

"It covers the Levee and Big Jim and the Everleigh sisters. It ends with Capone's arrest in 1931. It was written in 1940, so it still has a contemporary feel, which I think is a good thing."

I nodded.

She looked up as she handed me the paper with the citation. The librarian persona was now completely in place. The woman who waxed enthusiastic about brothels had vanished.

"You had two other questions?" she asked.

"I assume that The Four Deuces is part of the Levee?" I asked.

"It was the first place Capone ever worked before he became a known gangster," she said. "He murdered 'Ragtime' Joe Howard there in 1924. It was as famous as Colosimo's, just not as nice."

"Nice as in fancy," I said.

"In all ways," she said. "It opened in 1914. It was Joe Torrio's place, funded, they say, by his uncle Big Jim Colosimo."

It seemed to come back around to Colosimo's. I wondered what the connection was to my case.

"But The Four Deuces became famous—in a seedy and corrupt way—in the twenties. It was raided, oh, probably two dozen times in the Dever administration."

"I assume Dever was a mayor?"

"You need to read some Chicago history." She smiled at me, then caught herself, and returned to the librarian again. "Yes. He was a mayor in the twenties. Did you find something with the Four Deuces as well?"

"A matchbox," I said. "With just the name and some cards on the front."

"Oh, a classic!" she said, clasping her hands together. "I'd love to see it."

"I'll try to remember to bring it in," I said, even though I wouldn't. No sense in telling her it was all part of a grisly investigation.

She grinned again, that librarian mask lost forever. "You said your name was Grimshaw? I'm Serena Wexler."

I extended my hand. "Bill Grimshaw."

She took it without hesitation, as if she'd forgotten her initial fear of me. Maybe she had.

"I'll be sure to ask for you when I remember that matchbox," I said.

Her grin widened. "And any time you have questions about that period. I'm not an expert, but I'm trying to be."

"You sound like an expert," I said.

"I'd love to give tours," she said softly. "You know, old murder sites—where Dillinger was shot by the police, the site of the St. Valentine's Day Massacre—but those neighborhoods are so bad, some of them, and I doubt anyone but me would be interested."

"You never know," I said. I had a hunch a lot of people would be interested. "Thank you for all your help."

"You said you had three questions," she said, amazing me again with her memory.

"Oh, yes," I said. "I found a napkin with the other items. It had only *Calumet-412* written on it, but the writing was in gold."

"It's a phone number," she said. "Odd that it would be on a napkin. Written in gold? As if with a gold pen?"

"Printed," I said, "as if someone made a lot of them."

"Hmm. I would wager it's a phone number for either a speakeasy or a vice house. Something no one wanted to advertise."

I hadn't thought of that. But all I said, in keeping with my pose as a man helping a friend, was, "Wow."

"I can tell you a few things about the number, though," she said. "The Calumet region was the Levee. If I remember right, Capone's number at the Lexington was a Calumet number."

"How would you know that?"

"Trivia," she said. "My husband always teased me about that. He said if anyone wanted to know useless things, they should ask me."

Then she flushed again.

"I think it's fascinating, all that you know," I said.

"Well, he never saw me reach my calling. I got this job after he died."

"I'm sorry," I said.

She nodded, then shrugged. "Life never takes you where you expect, does it?"

No, it didn't. I never expected to be in Chicago, let alone working on a case that had such deep Chicago roots.

Which made me think of something. In the South, the red-light district was often segregated. Black women did not work in the same houses as white women.

I had no idea if the North was that way, so I asked.

She frowned.

"You mentioned white slavery, so I assume most of the prostitutes were white, and I know that Capone was."

"So was Big Jim. Everyone I mentioned," she said, her flush growing. "But the Levee was at the edge of what we call Bronzeville. I even think the Everleigh became a boarding house for blacks, but I don't know for sure."

"Would the women who worked in these places be black?" I asked.

She shrugged. "But this is Chicago. And even if blacks weren't patrons, they would have some work. Maids, porters, drivers—unobtrusive work, you know."

Then she shot me an apologetic look.

"I do know," I said. "It's all right. It's past."

"Is it?" she asked, and she fixed that non-librarian gaze on me.

I smiled. "Sometimes."

She smiled back. "That phone number. It's early. Real early. If you can find a phone book from before 1920, it would help you."

"Is there one here?"

She shook her head. "No one saw those as important. No one realized what kind of history they have."

I sighed. I hadn't worked on a case this old. I found it ironic that one of my favorite methods—using a phone book—would be as important to an old case as it was to a modern one.

"You know," she said, "I have some resource books I can look in. Can you give me that number again?"

I did, and she wrote it down.

"If they used it as advertising," she said, "and they clearly did, some of the records should tell me. I'll check in the next few days. I'm in the stacks for the next two days, but then I have the information desk again on Friday."

"I'll make a point of being here," I said.

THIRTY-FIVE

I left Serena Wexler, my head spinning. I had assumed most of those bodies were black. Now, it seemed, there was a good possibility that many belonged to whites. And, oddly enough, that made me uncomfortable.

I knew that the original owners of the house had been white and so had Hanley. I had just assumed—probably because we were using techniques pioneered by civil-rights advocates—that the bodies we found scattered through the basement were black.

It made more sense for them to be white, given Sturdy's involvement. Given that the neighborhood had always been mixed, because of the University of Chicago. Given the ties, however tenuous at the moment, to the Levee, which specialized in white graft, not black.

My assumption had been false, and I hadn't even realized I held it. I wondered how many other assumptions I held about this case that I hadn't even realized I had.

I went out a side door, feeling a little uncomfortable. In my zeal to talk with the librarian at the information desk, I hadn't noticed if someone had followed me inside. Then Wexler's tales were so absorbing that I hadn't looked around to see if someone suspicious lurked nearby.

I had no idea if I was being followed on foot or if, like yesterday, the tail waited in his sedan. There was no way to find out either, without constantly checking over my shoulder, which would only show the tail that I knew I was being followed.

Since my contact with Sturdy was common knowledge, I suppose I shouldn't have been worried that someone followed me to their building.

The clouds had grown dark since I had gone inside the library, and as I walked the few blocks to Sturdy's offices, lightning flared against the blackness. No thunder yet, so the storm was still miles away.

But I hated late-fall storms. They felt wrong, like something left over from the summer, as if the weather gods couldn't remember what season they were easing us into.

I hurried as the sky grew darker, noting that there were more protestors today outside the City Hall-County Building, where the trial was taking place. The same signs made the rounds with a few new ones, including *Support the Moratorium!* and *Send Hayden to Vietnam!*

I wasn't sure if that last was a joke or a lone voice of dissent in those protestors. The moratorium was a nationwide march against the war in Vietnam. Jimmy had already asked me if he could skip school and attend Chicago's version.

Even though I didn't want him to go, I didn't say no. Instead, I asked him how our friend Malcolm Reyner would feel, knowing that Jimmy was protesting the war Malcolm had chosen to fight.

Jimmy hadn't answered me, but he hadn't asked to attend anymore either. I wasn't sure if the issue was done; we'd see about that tonight.

Laura wasn't in when I arrived, so I left the package with Judith, giving her strict instructions to hand it to Laura the moment she entered. Judith nodded and promised she would.

Then I hurried back to the main doors, only to be greeted by a downpour.

Four other people huddled in the antechamber between the revolving door and the emergency doors, waiting for the rain to stop. As the rain continued, more people joined us.

A man wearing a suit sidled up beside me. His suit was dark and cheap, his shoes lacking a shine. He had a crew cut, and I remembered Jimmy's description of our tail.

"You Grimshaw?" the man asked softly.

A few people looked over at him, but most of them turned away when they saw who he was talking to. Outside, thunder boomed so loud it shook the stone building.

"What's it to you?" I asked.

"Just wondering."

I didn't respond to that. I watched the rain grow heavier. The water could no longer be called raindrops—there wasn't enough space between the wetness.

"How come Fred Hampton visited you Sunday morning?"

So he was the tail, and he was beginning to think what I'd wanted him to think—that I was just a family man with an unusual job, trying to make ends meet.

I had to play this right to keep him away from me.

I looked over my shoulder at him, making sure I showed surprise.

"We keep an eye on Hampton," the man said quietly. Two other people stood close to us, both of them men. I wondered if they were FBI or police as well. I couldn't tell just from a simple glance.

I made myself swallow hard, so that it looked like I was nervous. "You know what I do?"

"I heard odd jobs. Don't know exactly what that means."

I shrugged one shoulder. "Painting for one client. Helping someone move. You know, whatever needs to be done."

"Some investigating?" Another man, older, heavyset, asked that question. He was one of the two standing near Crew Cut.

"I look into things. For friends. That's all."

"Heard Hampton wanted you to investigate a murder."

The hair on the back of my neck rose. Fred Hampton had promised me no one else would know about this. I had believed him. But he hadn't been the only person at my apartment that day. His bodyguard knew why he was there, and I hadn't asked the bodyguard to make any confidentiality promises at all.

Rather than deny what Hampton wanted, which would automatically make me suspicious to these men, I lied. "I don't investigate murders."

"How come Hampton thought you would?"

I shrugged.

Thunder boomed again, just as loud, with lightning right on top of it. The lights inside the building flickered. The rain was still coming down heavily. I couldn't even see the protestors across the street.

"So he didn't hire you?" Crew Cut asked.

"There was no reason to. I didn't have the expertise he needed."

"Odd he would talk to you if you didn't have the skills, don't you think?" Older Guy asked.

"Not really," I said. "I get recommended for jobs I can't do all the time. Usually I refer those people to someone else."

"Who'd you refer Hampton to?"

"I told him there were some good detective agencies in the Black Belt. He didn't ask who they were and I didn't volunteer."

"You think he's going to hire them?"

"You're the ones following him. You probably know better than me."

Crew Cut gave me half a smile. Older Guy looked annoyed.

"You know what murder he wanted looked into?" Crew Cut asked.

"Sato? Soto? Kid killed over a traffic light. Hampton said no one would investigate."

The two men looked at each other. I wondered if I should have played that dumb. Would they think everyone knew about the Soto brothers?

"You said no."

"And asked him to leave before my son got home," I said. "I didn't want my boy to see the Black Panthers at my house."

That got a lot of people's attention. I had spoken too loudly. I hadn't planned to, but it didn't matter. They eased away from me and the three FBI/cops, and let us finish the conversation.

"You scared of the Panthers?" Crew Cut asked.

"I don't want my son involved with gangs," I said, which was a true answer. It also covered my ass in case these were Chicago PD officers. Since I had acquaintances in the police department, these men might have heard about my encounters with the Blackstone Rangers and how I convinced them—at least in the short term—to stay away from Jimmy.

"So you avoid gangs too," Crew Cut said. I didn't like his flat tone. It implied that he already knew the answers.

"I try to. Every now and then I have to remind them that they don't have automatic rights to the kids in the neighborhood."

"How do you do that?" Older Guy asked. He actually looked interested.

I smiled. I made sure the smile was slow and cruel. "I did some street fighting in my day. I know how to hurt a boy and impress him.

I did that once to a Ranger, told him that going after my son was like he was walking on my turf, and I told him I'd defend my turf just like he defended his. I suggested a truce, and they agreed."

"Why would they?" Crew Cut crossed his arms. The story made me guilty of something, in his mind.

"They like things easy," I said. "I made it clear that taking my son would be hard. It's that simple."

"And you know this how?" Crew Cut asked.

"I do some volunteer work with my cousin Franklin. It includes some gang reclamation. I've been told by former members what works and what doesn't."

"You believed them?" Crew Cut asked.

"It's worked so far," I said.

"Gang reclamation," Older Guy said. "Idealistic stuff. You know, a minister was just murdered on the North Side for doing that kind of work."

Franklin had told me. He knew the minister, Bruce Johnson, and his wife, who'd been murdered in their home while their children slept. The crime was, so far, unsolved.

"Yeah, I know," I said. "It's risky. That's why I don't want these people anywhere near my house. If Hampton hadn't been armed, I would have taught him the same lesson I taught the Rangers. But I don't mess with people who carry guns."

"You know we've been watching you," Crew Cut said.

"You have?" I made my body tense, just the way a normal person would if he suddenly found out he'd been tailed. "Why?"

"To see what you were doing. What's so important at the library?"

I smiled, and this time I made the smile warm and a bit lecherous. "There's a librarian there I got my eye on."

"Who's that?" Older Guy asked.

The thunder was farther away now, and the rain was starting to let up.

"Why do you need to know?" I asked.

"Just curious," Crew Cut said.

I sighed, shifted as if I were nervous, then said, "If I tell you, you'll just follow her around and harass her too. You haven't gone after my son, have you?"

My topic shift worked. Crew Cut actually looked a little uncomfortable, as if the idea of me threatening him unnerved him.

"Of course not," he said.

"See that you don't," I said. "You can follow me all you want, but my boy deserves the best, you know? He doesn't need to be treated like a criminal."

"We wouldn't dream of it, Mr. Grimshaw," Older Guy said. He was smoother than Crew Cut. "Listen, if Hampton approaches you again, you contact the local branch of the FBI."

So they were FBI. I had thought so.

"We won't let him harass you any more."

"I appreciate that," I said. "Does that mean you won't harass me any more?"

"I don't believe we have been," Crew Cut said.

"You just said you've been following me," I said.

"But you didn't notice," Crew Cut said.

"I'll notice now," I said, deciding I could use that as leverage.

"We won't bother you again, Mr. Grimshaw," Older Guy said. He nodded to Crew Cut, who gave me a small smile as if in acknowledgement.

Then they went out the emergency door into the rain. The third guy, who had remained quiet through the entire conversation, followed a half second later.

I waited until the downpour stopped. I had to catch my breath anyway. I hadn't expected them to approach me, although on reflection it made sense.

My ruse had worked. They had no idea who I really was. They thought I was an ordinary guy who had been visited by the wrong people. They worried that they were wasting manpower on me, and I had proven to them that they were right.

I hoped.

Because now that they had revealed themselves to me, they would be more circumspect if they followed me again. I had to assume that this was a little game they were playing, a game designed to see if I was deliberately leading them around (like I had been) or if I was as naive as I had seemed.

I'd have to continue to be vigilant, even though I didn't want to be. Even though I wanted to believe that they were gone for good.

THIRTY-SIX

When the rain ended, I had to hurry out of the Loop. I had nearly forgotten that I promised Jimmy a reprieve from his after-school lessons. Game Three of the World Series was being televised that afternoon, and I told him he could watch.

Mrs. Armitage hadn't approved when I told her my plans, but I promised her that he would do a paper on baseball and statistics, and she looked mollified. Whether Jim was capable of such a paper, I had no idea, but since I'd gotten him into it, the least I could do was help him finish it.

The game wasn't worth the trouble. The Mets won—and Jim loved that—but as baseball went, it was agonizingly slow. Five-nothing Mets in Shea, the lead so big that the game ended after the Orioles' dismal at-bat in the top of the ninth.

I hoped the next few games were more of a contest. I'd had trouble concentrating while I watched, my mind wandering to Colosimo's and matchbook covers and Serena Wexler's enthusiasm for madams of the past.

Interesting that one of my first assumptions made before I found the bodies was probably right after all, that all this had to do with Chicagoland vice. That the vice predated Prohibition surprised me, and its location surprised me as well: How come bodies associated with the Levee were entombed nearly thirty blocks south of it?

The problem was that I couldn't look at any of that until Jim and I finished our game, our dinner, and our evening together.

I had just convinced Jim to prepare for bed when the phone rang. It was Minton. I asked him to hold for a moment, then gave Jim another reprieve, allowing him to read in his room until I finished the conversation.

My office was right near Jim's bedroom, so I took the call in the living room and used that morning's *Defender* as a notepad.

"Got something for you," Minton said.

"Already?" I asked. "I figured you'd be at this for days."

"The skeletons were pretty much intact," he said. "I'll have to make sure some of the smaller bones were in the right place, but the longer ones were easier."

"So what did you find?" I asked. "More gunshot wounds?"

"Better," he said. "I found a name."

I sat down at the kitchen table and tapped my pen against the *Defender*. "A name?"

"Sewn into the remains of one of the shirts—you know, like your mom used to do for your school clothes?"

My mother never did anything like that, figuring if I lost my clothing it was my fault, and I'd have to use my allowance to buy something new. But I wasn't raised poor—not in either household, my real parents' or my adopted parents'. I was middle-class.

Sewing names into clothing, especially adult clothing, showed how poor someone actually was. Nothing dared get lost because it often couldn't be replaced.

"Actually," Minton was saying, "I'm not sure if it was a shirt or a jacket—you know, one of those heavy cloth jobs. Maybe you can tell from the piece, but—"

"What is it?" I asked, still tapping my pen.

"The name?" Minton said. "Junius Pruitt."

"Junius?" I said. "You sure it's not Julius?"

"Oh, I'm sure," Minton said. "In fact I'm positive. I went to school with a Junius Pruitt."

"But you said this body is over forty years old. You're not even thirty."

"It's not him. Junius is off at Stanford or Berkeley or someplace like that, getting too much education. But his mom is still here."

"And she named him after someone," I said, finally catching on.

"You got it. You want me to call her or should you?"

Minton had worked with death a lot, and with grieving families, but he'd never done anything like this, at least that I knew of.

"Let me," I said. "But be prepared for visitors."

"Oh, I will," Minton said. "She's been in the same house forever."

He gave me the address. It was in the heart of Bronzeville, in a residential neighborhood that was still intact.

"So Junius Pruitt is black," I said.

"Darker than either one of us, maybe than both of us combined," Minton said. "Why?"

I told him about what I'd found, and how my expectations had changed. I thought now that these victims were white.

"Well, at least one of them's black. Unless he stole that coat before he died."

Which was possible. Anything was.

"Did you find anything else?" I asked.

"Not yet. Can't even tell how two of these poor souls died. There's nothing on the bones, and most of the clothing that I brought with me is too decayed."

"Yet you saw the name," I said.

"You can see it tomorrow if you want. The shirt was underneath the last skeleton, the one that got shot in the head. It was attached to the wristbone, so I brought it with me to separate it. I think its position protected it from some of the worst of the body's putrefaction."

"Was that near the wallet?" I asked.

"That was on the other side, closer to the younger body. LeDoux made a diagram."

"I'll take a look before I visit Mrs. Pruitt," I said.

"What do you think this is?" Minton asked.

"I don't know yet," I said, "but I think we're about to find out."

THIRTY-SEVEN

The Pruitt house sat in the middle of its block. It was a decaying, single-story starter, built after the war. Apparently that marked, in Minton terms, forever as longer than twenty years.

I arrived shortly after ten. I had gone through what had now become my morning routine—driving like a madman through the Loop to lose any potential tail.

The traffic was horrendous, in part because it was National Vietnam Moratorium Day. Marches, rallies, and speeches were going on all over the country, coordinated to draw the Nixon administration's attention to the growing dissatisfaction with the war.

Chicago's main rally would happen after five, when Jimmy and I would be happily ensconced at home, watching the World Series, but there were some preliminary speeches and rallies already happening all over the city.

I used them to make sure I wasn't being followed. I hadn't seen anyone, just like I expected, but I was paranoid enough to believe the tail could still be there.

When I picked up LeDoux, he was happy to hear the news; happy too, I think, to have me out of the house again so that he could work in peace. He found it odd that I had thought the bodies were black. Until he heard about Junius Pruitt, he'd thought they were mostly white.

Amazing the conclusions we came to, based on ourselves and our views of the world.

LeDoux figured he'd be done with the first row of tombs by the end of the week. Then he'd need me again to see what was behind them.

We both hoped that there would be a single large room filled with liquor. We both doubted that would be the case.

I parked a block away from the Pruitt house and waited for nearly fifteen minutes, to see if anyone had followed me. The streets were quiet here; this was an old Bronzeville neighborhood, one of the few that hadn't been destroyed by the city's quest for housing projects that would "benefit" the poor.

Most of the homes were stately or had once been impressive. This house looked like an afterthought, which seemed strange. Maybe it had been built on a parcel of land sold off for the money.

I hurried up the cracked sidewalk, doubting anyone would be home at this time of the morning. I figured I'd have to come back three or four times before I found Mrs. Pruitt.

Minton had told me that her husband was long dead—a heart attack in his forties, just after his eldest son, the Junius that Minton knew, had graduated from high school. Mrs. Pruitt had raised two more boys and a daughter, getting them through school on her own. The daughter stayed home to help her mother. The boys had all gone to college, a remarkable feat that I was beginning to realize was less unusual in this part of Chicago than it had been in my adopted hometown of Memphis.

The stairs up to the front porch were also cracked, but the iron railing was new. I rang the doorbell and listened to the chimes echo through the house.

Then, to my surprise, a woman yelled, "Hang on. I gotta get to you."

There was some banging, as if drawers or doors closed, a curse, and then a small woman, barely bigger than Jimmy, pulled the door open.

She peered around it as if she expected trouble. Her hair was cut short, and her features were delicate, making her small face seem even smaller. She wore gold eyeshadow that accented the brown of her eyes, but no other makeup. One eye appeared to have eyeliner, while the other didn't.

Apparently I had interrupted her morning routine.

"Now what is it?" she snapped. "I paid off the stupid loan."

She thought I was some kind of enforcer.

"I'm not here to collect a debt, ma'am," I said, using the same soft voice I'd initially used with Serena Wexler. "My name is Bill Grimshaw. People hire me to investigate things, and I'd like to ask you some questions if I could."

"Sorry," she said, starting to close the door.

I grabbed it, knowing that would scare her, but I had no other choice. "Your son's name is Junius, right?"

She froze, and I saw fear in her eyes. "So?"

"Was he named for someone?"

She tilted her head slightly. I had her attention.

"Why?" she asked.

"Because I came across a shirt with the name sewn in, and I have reason to believe that shirt had been hidden for a long time. More than forty years."

She stared at me as if I had just told her that President Lincoln was alive.

"Who did you say you are?"

"Bill Grimshaw, ma'am."

"You're a detective?"

"I do that work sometimes, yes," I said.

"Where did you find that shirt?"

"That I can't tell you," I said. "But I can answer some other questions, if you would like to answer a few for me."

She opened the door wide, then stepped away from it. She wore a gold waitress uniform with white piping and nylon stockings, but no shoes. I clearly had interrupted her routine.

As she walked across the worn gray carpet, she said, "I let you in, you hurt me, and my son-in-law'll make sure you never hurt anybody again, you understand?"

"I do," I said. "I promise I won't touch you."

She looked at me over her shoulder, grabbed a pair of white nurse's shoes off a nearby wooden chair, and sat on the edge of an afghan-covered armchair. "Junius was named for his grandfather."

"Same last name?" I asked. "Pruitt?"

"Oh, yeah," she said. "Both names were in the shirt?"

"They were," I said.

"How come you're investigating this? An old shirt doesn't seem like much." She was clutching the shoes as if she would throw them at me if I came near her.

I had thought all the way over here how much I would tell her and how much I would keep to myself. "It's not a lot by itself," I said. "But I found it in a bricked-up area, along with the skeletons of three men."

"My God." She leaned back and nearly tumbled into the armchair, her hand over her breastbone. "You think that one of those skeletons might be Grandpa Junius?"

"I don't know, ma'am," I said. "Until you asked that question, I wasn't even sure he was dead."

She took a deep breath and got her balance again, setting the shoes on the seat of the armchair. "We didn't either. We just guessed."

"Mind telling me what happened?" I asked.

"I don't know," she said. "It was before my time. He disappeared when my husband was a little boy."

"Disappeared?" I asked.

She nodded. "That's all I know. I mean, there's a family story, but it's been years since I heard it. You're probably better off talking to Minnie."

"Minnie?"

"His wife."

THIRTY-EIGHT

Minnie Pruitt lived with her eldest son, Jasper, but she spent her days at the South Side Senior Center. The Center wasn't too far from Poehler's Funeral Home. The neighborhood had deteriorated—gang graffiti decorated the door of a nearby building, and the dry cleaner's next door had clearly gone out of business.

But the Senior Center seemed to have an attitude that carried it through the decay. A sign on the door said *Anyone Under Sixty Enter at Own Risk.* Through the large, plate-glass window of what had once been a storefront I could see twenty or so elderly people at various tables, cards in hand. The group at the table closest to me seemed to be playing for money.

I knocked on the door and pushed it open, stepping inside as I did so. The place smelled of coffee and old age. A refreshment bar stood just behind the door, with coffeepots sitting on warmers. A window opened to a back room with a kitchen. More coffee percolated on a stove back there.

"Kid, can't you read?"

The voice startled me because it came from directly behind me. An elderly man with rheumy eyes stood as close to me as anyone had gotten in years without my knowing it. He held a cane in one hand and a brownie in the other.

His face was as scarred as mine.

"No one's called me kid in a long time," I said.

"You're a baby," he said. "And I don't care how hungry you are, you aren't getting our snacks. Danine made them special, and baking is something she can do, unlike playing cards."

"Sit down," said an elderly lady with a voice deeper than mine, "and I'll show you who can play cards."

She had to be Danine.

"I'm looking for Minnie Pruitt," I said.

Half the room whooped at me. The other half laughed, and looked at a woman who stood near the kitchen door.

"Told ya you still had it," one of the men said to the woman.

She was statuesque, with a long face and dark, dark eyes. Her hair had gone white, but that was the only sign of her age—that, and the orthopedic shoes she wore. She wore a blue dress that accented her still-impressive figure, and a single gold band on her left hand. Unlike her daughter-in-law, she wore no make up at all.

"Do I know you?" she asked, her voice a vibrato-filled tenor that suggested either a lifetime spent in music or standing in front of a pulpit.

"No, ma'am," I said. "My name is Bill Grimshaw. Your daughter-in-law sent me to you."

She made a sound like an elongated pshaw. "What's that no-good girl done and got herself into now?"

"Junius's mother," I said, just in case she misunderstood and thought I meant the other daughter-in-law, the one she lived with.

"I know who you're talking about. Jasper's wife knows I like my privacy and wouldn't send nobody here."

"I'm sorry, ma'am," I said. "She didn't explain that to me. But she thought what I had to say was important enough to tell me where you were."

Minnie Pruitt crossed her arms beneath her ample chest. "She thinks everything's important."

The games around the room had stopped. The level of conversation had been high enough that I hadn't realized a radio played in the background. WHO's noontime news program thrummed across the room, too softly for me to pick out much more than the anchors' voices.

"Well, she may have been right this time," I said. "Is there some-place we can talk?"

"Right here's fine," Minnie Pruitt said.

"This's rather personal. You might want—"

"These are my friends," she said. "They can hear this."

I glanced at them, feeling trapped. The more people who heard about this, the more the risk I took in getting the word out. "Ma'am, please. We can stand outside in full view. I just think—"

"Heavens, young man," she said. "You're a caution. You don't look it, but you are. Grab me a chair, Hector. I'm taking the young man to the woodshed."

Everyone laughed, and I felt my face flush. That phrase brought back old memories, memories that predated my parents' death, and made me feel like I was six years old again.

One of the younger men—he had to be about seventy—picked up a folding chair and carried it into the kitchen. "You asked for it, son."

"It's not every day that Minnie takes a man to the woodshed," said one of the nearby women, her eyes sparkling.

"Thank you," I said to Mrs. Pruitt, and followed her through the kitchen, ignoring the comments and the catcalls.

The woodshed, apparently, was the back office. Hector flipped the light switch and fluorescents flickered, then caught. A desk was al-ready inside, with a dirty coffee cup on top and a half-eaten donut still sitting on a plate. Papers sat off to one side. I glanced at them as I walked in. They were registration forms for a bridge tournament that was going to be held on Halloween.

"This isn't the woodshed that I remember," I said, and Mrs. Pruitt laughed. It was a deep, throaty sound, the sound of a woman who knew how to enjoy herself.

"It's all we have." She sat behind the desk and looked pointedly at Hector. "You mind waiting in the kitchen?"

"I'm winning penny-a-point," he said.

"Bring the game in there."

Hector sighed, then glared at me. "You be nice to her, you hear?"

"Yes, sir," I said.

He backed out of the room, keeping his eye on me, pulling the door closed behind him. Mrs. Pruitt and I watched as he made his way to the kitchen serving window and beckoned the other players inside.

"Your daughter-in-law sounds like she's in some trouble," I said.

"She told me after my son died that her kids were going to get the education he promised them come hell or high water." Minnie Pruitt stacked the papers, thumped them on the desk to even the edges, and then set them aside. "It's been hell. I expect the high water any day now."

I sat on the folding chair. It creaked beneath my weight. "I'm not it. I'm here because I found something in the course of an investigation."

Her eyes brightened. I had caught her attention.

"I do odd jobs," I said. "Sometimes that includes finding things out for people."

She nodded her head once, indicating that she understood.

"Recently I found a shirt hidden in an enclosed area. It might have been a jacket, it's hard to tell. But it had the name Junius Pruitt stitched inside."

Her expression didn't change, but she threaded her hands together, clasping them so tightly that her unpainted nails reddened. "Probably belonged to my grandson. Didn't Irene tell you that?"

Irene, apparently, was the other Mrs. Pruitt.

"No, ma'am," I said. "We're both sure it didn't belong to her son."

Minnie Pruitt's eyes narrowed. Her lower lip trembled. "Are you having fun with me? Because if you are—"

"Ma'am, I'm sorry," I said. "But I found it in a wall, along with three skeletons. One had been shot in the head."

"Oh, my God." She ran a hand over her mouth. "Oh, my God."

"The shirt wasn't on one of the skeletons that we could tell. But it was there with one. It might've been stolen, or it might've been someone's clothing. We don't know. Your daughter-in-law told me your husband disappeared when your son was just a baby."

"When Wayne was just a baby, yeah. Jasper was five or so, and Jolene, she was three." Her eyes were lined with tears. "Only Junius, he wouldn't run from us. He loved those babies. He loved them."

"I'm sorry to bring up old pain, ma'am." I waited.

She blinked hard, forcing the tears back by sheer will. "You think that's him you found?"

"I don't know," I said. "I didn't even know he'd been missing until I spoke to your daughter-in-law a little while ago."

"How'd you track her down?" Mrs. Pruitt asked, suddenly suspicious.

"Your grandson went to school with a friend of mine," I said. "He remembered the unusual name. I thought I'd check to see if it was a family name."

"You knew that body didn't belong to my grandson?" she asked.

I nodded. "It's too old, ma'am. It's been there a long time."

She pursed her lips. The tears appeared again, and then faded back. Then she nodded. "I'm tired of the *ma'am*. They'll all tease me out there when I get back, so we'd best be on a first-name basis. I'm Minnie."

"Bill," I said.

"You don't look like a Bill," she said. "You got trouble in your eyes."

I smiled and decided to take a risk. "My friends call me Smokey."

"Now, that's a man's name." She leaned back in her chair. "You have to understand. Juni left me with three little children. It was 1919, and I didn't have a pot to piss in. The only money we had was from Juni's work, and that went away the minute he did."

I nodded.

"He wouldn'ta done that. I told folks he wouldn'ta done that, not with the babies. He didn't even want to enlist and leave his children. He certainly wouldn'ta run out one day and never come back. Something happened to him, I said, and everyone nodded, but no one did nothing."

I felt on shaky historical ground. World War One was not my specialty. I knew it had ended in 1918, but that was about all I knew.

"Did you go to the police?" I asked.

She gaped at me, revealing a mouthful of gold teeth which made me think, uncomfortably, of those gold teeth in that attic room. "Lord, son, you're not from here, are you?"

"No," I said. "I came here almost two years ago now."

"Well, in 1919 the police was trying to slaughter anyone with skin as dark as ours. We spent our nights that August on rooftops, with rifles and field glasses, hoping they wouldn't come into the neighborhood."

I frowned. Fred Hampton had mentioned something about this. I had ignored it as Black Panther rhetoric. It surprised me to hear similar words come out of this elderly woman's mouth.

"You were on a roof?" I asked, mostly because I couldn't picture it.

"When I had to be," she said. "I tried to stay with the babies, but the nights was hot, and I liked to be near Juni. He was always up there, protecting us, him and the vets, the good shots. They killed a lot of police from up there. Our block was considered the safest."

"Where was that?" I asked.

"Ah, honey," she said softly. "That neighborhood's gone. They done tore it down so they could put up projects and a damn freeway. That's how they still treat us."

"I know," I said.

"And you ask how I could be on a roof with a shotgun," she said.

"I don't know what provoked it."

Her brown eyes flashed, and I saw in that moment the strong young woman she had once been. "It wasn't just me and Juni. It was all of us. They were trying to massacre us that summer, and we held them back."

"The police?" I asked.

"The whites." She hissed the word, and I heard hatred in it. Deep, powerful hatred. "You don't know the history, so lemme give you some, then you can understand a little."

I nodded.

"It started with the Great Migration. I hear the South in your voice. I know you know about it. You probably got relatives who come up here, relatives who vanished into the terrifying north."

I smiled. "I have a few."

"The Migration started in the early teens. I was already here. I had family here and so did Juni. We were born here. Our people came after the War—"

And by that I knew she meant the Civil War, which was, to our people, the Great War, not World War One.

"—and established themselves south of the stockyards. The Irish in Bridgeport, they hated us more than anyone else because they were the next ones on the rung up the ladder. You know how that works. If you're getting spit on, spit on the people lower than you so you feel better."

I nodded again.

"The population doubled, tripled, year after year, till finally we was busting out of the ghetto they'd let us live in." Her language got coarser the farther back she seemed to go. She wasn't really seeing me any more. She was staring into her own past. "We tried to move to new neighborhoods, but they bombed us out, burned our houses, and murdered our children. Does that sound familiar?"

Then she did look at me.

"It sounds like the North wasn't much better than where we came from."

"Ah," she said softly. "But it was better. We got jobs. Real jobs with real wages. That's why the Irish hated us so much. They had to work side by side with us, get paid the same amount, live in the same kinds of houses. Why, if they weren't careful, they'd become just like us, and white folks just couldn't stomach that, now could they?"

"I take it this all came to a head," I said.

"Summer of 1919. Hottest summer I remember. We were sleeping on the roof with other families by May. By June we thought we was gonna die of the heat. Juni, he was spending half his salary on ice, just so I could put it on the children, cool them down."

She shook her head, looked down, and finally seemed to give in. She rubbed her eyes.

"That summer, things were worse for a lot of reasons. Prohibition started July 1—no more alcohol, and businesses were going under."

I frowned. Now I had to show my ignorance. "I thought prohibition started in 1920."

"Illinois went dry by state referendum. That's how we got all our gangsters. They were up and running already when the entire country went dry. They had systems and men in place, ways of running the liquor, and Chicago, being the center of the country and a major transportation hub, could act as a supplier. I know lots of men who could only get jobs working that, and there was no shame in it, I thought. Craziness, it was, taking one of people's only pleasures."

She glanced at me, as if taking a measure of me.

"So we have no alcohol, and our men've just come back from the war. It ended in 1918, you know."

"I know," I said, feeling some relief that I had that right at least.

"And the soldiers were decommissioned, coming home to parades and such in January, February. They had pride, those men did. They went to Europe, learned that not everyone saw them as inferior. They thought they'd served and they come home and they were just the same niggers they'd been before." She crossed her arms and leaned against the desktop. "Only this time, they weren't gonna take it. White man calls them a name, they answer back. It was worse in our neighborhood, because we were full of Black Devils."

I opened my mouth to ask for clarification of that term, and she spoke before I had a chance to.

"Black Devils. The Eighth Illinois. They were such a fierce group, the Germans nicknamed them Black Devils. Most of them got the Croix de Guerre from the French—"

And she pronounced it as if she spoke fluent French.

"—and twenty-one of them got the Distinguished Service Cross from our government. Most of those men came home to my neighborhood. Juni was ashamed he hadn't gone with them. He didn't say much, but his eyes did. He would always hug his babies, though, when I'd ask about it, and tell me it was worth it. I wasn't ever sure he really believed it."

I frowned, trying to put all of this together.

"It was the Black Devils that taught us sniping," she said. "They'd show us how to lie flat, keep our eyes partly closed and the lights off, how to use the rifles . . . but I'm ahead of myself."

Hector peered into the window, startling me. She didn't even see him. He stared for a minute, saw that she was talking, and then moved back into the kitchen proper. A small group of men had moved a card table into the middle of the room and seemed to be playing a heated game of gin rummy.

"Lots of things happened that July, most never hitting the papers, and I could keep you for three days telling you all about it." She gave me a tired smile. "But you got work and you didn't come here for no history lesson. So I'll cut to it. On July twenty-seventh, four boys decided to go swimming."

I felt a shiver run down my back. So many Southern stories started like this, and they all ended badly.

"They weren't little little. They were fourteen, fifteen, thirteen, somewhere in there. Not quite bright enough to realize they could get into trouble sure as they were breathing."

Just a little older than Jimmy. I felt my entire body stiffen.

"The beaches was segregated—not by law, like in the South, but by custom. The same custom that was keeping us out of new neighborhoods, the custom that gets reinforced with fists and bombs and guns."

Her voice got stronger as she spoke of this, but her gaze seemed farther and farther away.

"Those boys took a raft out deep, and they drifted on the current, away from the black beaches and into a white area. And you know what happened then, right?"

"They got killed," I said.

"Only one of them, but that was enough. He was stoned, if you can believe it. Rocks thrown at him till he got hit on the head and drowned. The other boys went back to our beach for help, got the lifeguard and a black policeman to arrest the man who threw the rocks. Only a white policeman wouldn't let the arrest happen. It got ugly from there. Fighting and riots and accusations. Someone started shooting, and there you had it. A race riot, they called it. It went on for nearly a week, and at the end, they say, sixteen people died and more than 500 was injured."

"They say?" I asked.

"They. The official whites, the counters. I heard it was closer to a hundred dead and a thousand injured, but who counts us anyway, right?"

"That was when you went on the roofs?" I asked.

"Better to die nobly, fighting those that would kill you, than like a hog in a pen with mad dogs circling outside." She shook her head, smiled faintly, and cursed. "I used to be able to quote that for real. And now I can't remember a line, just the gist. You know it?"

I shook my head.

"Claude McKay's poem. They didn't teach it to you in school?"

"We learned James Weldon Johnson, ma'am."

"Minnie," she snapped.

"Sorry," I said. She was so like a school teacher at the moment that calling her by her first name felt wrong.

"You go look it up. McKay was living here. He published it in *The Liberator* that summer. It caught how we was all feeling. If they were going to slaughter us and burn our neighborhoods, then we'd go down fighting. It was better than just letting them kill us."

"Your husband disappeared then?" I asked.

"Lord, no," she said. "We got through that. The city calmed, as much as it could. The whites got afraid. The Bridgeport gangs, they invaded us first, and then we went after them. In the sixteen dead—the ones they counted were mostly Bridgeport boys."

She seemed proud of that. Then her gaze met mine and she was back in the present.

"That's why Mayor Daley leveled our neighborhoods, you know," she said. "Retaliation."

"He remembers that?" I asked.

"Remembers, hell," she said. "He was in the gang that started the murders. He says he wasn't in the riot, but you go look it up. He became head of that gang right after. How does that happen to a boy who won't get involved? He hates us. He'd kill us all if he could."

She spat those last words. She hated the mayor as well.

"You look it up," she said. "They call it the Chicago Race Riot, like it was our fault. Race. That's always a code word for Negro."

"But your husband didn't disappear then."

She shook her head. "The city was afraid, afraid it would get worse and we'd burn them out of their homes or something, I don't know. But things calmed, more or less. And in September the weather eased. By October, things wasn't exactly back to normal, but they were better. That feeling—you know that feeling, that tenterhooks feeling?—"

I nodded.

"It was gone by then. The mothers in the neighborhood, I remember us talking, saying maybe it would be safe to take our babies out of the Black Belt now and again. Maybe by Christmas, we thought. Maybe then."

Her voice faded. She looked at the wall. I realized she was fighting tears again.

"He went to work," she said, so softly I could barely hear her. "He went to work on Wednesday and he never come back. And no one knew what happened. No one would tell me."

"Where did he work?" I asked, even though I had a hunch, a hunch I wasn't sure I wanted to have.

She blinked, seemed to gather herself, and then straightened, looking at me with a mixture of sadness and shame.

"He was the piano player to a coon shouter," she said.

A coon shouter. I hadn't heard that expression since I was a boy. A coon shouter was a white person, usually male, who sang Negro-inspired songs while dressed in blackface. Al Jolson was probably the most famous coon shouter of them all.

"So he worked in a white speakeasy," I said.

She nodded tightly, as if she expected me to say more, say something judgmental. No wonder she had trouble finding help. She had been right about people looking down on each other, and the only thing worse than a coon shouter from a black point of view were the blacks who helped him get rich off our music.

"Was that speakeasy Colosimo's?" I asked.

She closed her eyes. "You found him, didn't you?"

"Yeah," I said softly. "I think we probably did."

THIRTY-NINE

The idea that her husband's body might have been found broke through Minnie Pruitt's tough facade. She didn't cry—she'd been living with this too long to cry—but she was silent for a moment.

I didn't press her. I waited until she was ready to talk again.

"Skeleton," she finally said. "That means there's not much to identify."

"Yes, ma'am."

She didn't yell at me for calling her ma'am. She probably didn't even notice.

"So you need something else to go on, maybe things he was carrying, things he wore."

"Yes, ma'am."

She nodded, then sighed. "I can't help much. I sewed his name into everything he owned because he had a little uniform he was supposed to wear at work—his trained-monkey uniform, he called it—and because he was colored, he wasn't allowed to take it out of the building. He had to change there."

"Can you describe it?" I asked.

"I never saw it. I wasn't supposed to go to the Levee." The way she said that implied that she had.

"But you did."

She nodded. "After he . . . disappeared . . . died, I did. I went two

228

nights later, found someone to watch my children and took the trolley up. They wouldn't let me in."

"Colosimo's wouldn't let you in?" I asked.

"Yes." Her gaze met mine. The sadness and humiliation were back. That moment was as alive for her as this current one was. "I couldn't go in the front door, and no one would let me in the back, so I sat there, in the alley, watching people come and go, and asking about my husband."

I could just imagine her, frightened and alone, in the worst section of town, trying to get information on her husband. Clutching at people's arms, asking them for help.

"Finally, one of the busboys—who wasn't a boy, he had to be older than you are now—he come out and pulled me aside. They probably sent him because he was colored, as dark-skinned as my Juni. He said he ain't seen Juni for two days, and when someone don't show up for work, he got fired."

It sounded like she was quoting now, but she was staring at me.

"He didn't expect my Juni back ever. So I asked if anyone seen him leave that night, and no one did. At least no one I talked to. No one seen him after the last show, no one knew what happened."

"What about his clothes?" I asked.

She shook her head. "I wasn't thinking clear. I never did ask. I was thinking he walked home, got beat, and was lying in a ditch somewhere, dying. I got folks looking for him, but they never did find him. No one did, and people started looking at me funny. They started thinking maybe he had enough of me and the children and had gone off. It wouldn'ta been hard. The train stations weren't far from the Levee. That's one of the reasons it opened where it did. And the more people said that . . ."

"The more you thought it," I finished for her.

She closed her eyes and buried her face in her hands. "Fifty years," she whispered. "For fifty years I thought he'd left me, I *hoped* he'd left me, and at the same time I hoped he was dead, because then he hadn't left at all."

Hector peered in again. He seemed overly concerned for a mere friend. I held up a hand, mouthed "It's okay," and then nodded toward her. He grimaced at me, but backed away from the window.

Finally, she lifted her head. Still no tears, but she looked ragged. She looked old.

"He wore a ring," she said, extending her left hand. "It isn't much, but it was what we could afford back in those days. He never took it off. He always carried a jacket because you never knew when the wind would come off the lake. His was flannel, heavy. And he had a knit cap I made for him."

"No identification?" I asked.

She let out a small ironic chuckle. "We didn't have driver's licenses then. No one thought of carrying something that said where they lived or who they were."

Minton hadn't said anything about a ring, but I would ask. "Was the ring engraved?"

She shook her head.

And then, because I couldn't help it, I looked at hers again. "You never remarried."

She teared up, and this time the tears threatened to spill over. "I never knew if he was dead or not. I kept thinking maybe he would come home. . . ."

She swallowed hard, then wiped angrily at her face, looking away from me as if the tears embarrassed her. Then she extended her hand.

"It's not that distinctive," she said. "But it's what we got."

I touched her ring. The metal was thicker than I expected—my adopted parents had rings they got during the Depression, and the gold was so thin it felt like it would snap with the slightest pressure.

Her ring was scratched and worn with time. Would his be? I didn't know.

"Did he know a family named Baird?" I asked. "Maybe a Gavin Baird?"

She shook her head.

"How about a man named Mortimer Hanley?"

"I don't think so," she said. "I don't know for sure."

So as far as his wife knew, over a distance of fifty years, Junius Pruitt hadn't had a run-in with anyone connected to the Queen Anne.

"Did he walk home alone?" I asked.

She shrugged. "He said he didn't. Said he always had friends from work go with him, but I couldn't find them either."

"Couldn't find the friends or couldn't find anyone who walked with him?"

"He wouldn't let me meet the Colosimo's people. He was happy to have a job doing what he loved—that piano was something, he said—

but the people weren't. He said I didn't need to know them, and I agreed with him. Foolish of me, I know."

I shook my head. "It's not foolish to protect your family."

She gave me a half-smile. "When the protection backfires, it is."

I stirred, making it clear we were nearly done. "By chance did he mention anyone named Lawrence?"

She frowned. "I don't recall the name."

"How about Zeke?"

"Zeke Ellis." She said the name like a prayer. "I haven't thought of him in a hundred years."

"Where is he now?"

She shook her head. "He run off. He got word that his woman was coming up from Alabama, and he took off out of here like she was the devil herself."

I frowned, remembering the intact letter that had been found in the wallet. "Was her name Darcy?"

"Oh, yeah. Sweet thing. Cried buckets when she found that he'd left her again."

"Where's she?" I asked.

"The Negro section of Oaklawn cemetery."

Another closed door. "Is there anyone who might remember Zeke? Anyone you can think of?"

"He had a woman here. Her name was—Vivienne? Viola? Vita?— something like that."

"Do you know where she is?" I asked, doubting that she would when she didn't even know the woman's name.

"No, I don't," Minnie Pruitt said. "But Felix out front, he would."

We left the woodshed and went back to the main room. Hector tried to pull Minnie aside, but she wouldn't let him. Instead, she took me to Felix.

Felix turned out to be a grizzled, bent-over man of about ninety. He had a hearing aid twice the size of one ear on his left side, and an old-fashioned hearing horn that he stuck in his right. He sat on a wide rocking chair in the back of the main room as if he'd been placed there eons ago and abandoned.

Our conversation consisted of my shouted questions and his shouted responses. No one played cards during that, and a number of people helped interpret for me and for him.

Apparently Felix, whose last name was Cayton, wasn't the marrying kind, and everyone knew it. Still, Vivienne Bontemps had gotten involved with him. She had given him two children before deciding he wouldn't make an honest woman of her, even though he'd already told her that.

He continued to support the children until they reached fifteen—he was a good man after all, a lot better than they were, the ungrateful bastards, never visiting their old man now that he had only a few good years left.

I could see why they didn't, and half the people listening rolled their eyes midway through the question-and-answer session. I learned nothing of Zeke, except that he had vanished—and good riddance too!—and that, not Felix, had broken Vivienne's heart.

Vivienne Bontemps sounded like a stage name to me or a very sad joke. Bontemps, unless I missed my guess, was badly pronounced French for "good time," and I had a hunch, although I couldn't ask it at the top of my lungs and I doubted Felix would answer me at the top of his, that he had met her at one of the whorehouses near the Levee, maybe one of the Bronzeville houses that took colored women.

I thanked Felix for his time, and as I made my way to the door, the man who had greeted me when I came in, the man with the scarred face, pulled me aside.

"Vivienne Bontemps lives on Cottage Grove Avenue," he said. "She has a nice little house there, and she's not near so bad as Felix makes her out to be. She knew what she was getting into. So did Felix. He was forty years old when he met her, and took care of her when that Darcy showed up."

"Darcy, Zeke's old girlfriend."

The older man nodded. "Zeke aired right out when he saw she was coming. And I don't blame him. That was one gator-faced woman."

"Ugly?" I asked.

"Inside. When she heard he'd beat it, she took to blaming everyone, not the least Vivienne. I don't think Vivienne knew a thing about it, and the thing was—" he lowered his voice—"that first baby of old Felix's there, t'weren't his. 'Twas Zeke's and everyone knew it. Even Felix. He just pretended he didn't. He talks a mean game, but he ain't a bad man, even if those kids don't realize it."

I glanced at Felix, who had set down his ear trumpet and closed his eyes. Apparently I had tired him out.

"Will Vivienne talk to me about this?" I asked.

"I'm sure she will if you don't treat her like a good-time girl." He winked at me. I smiled.

"What was her real name?" I asked.

"Ain't nobody knows, 'cept Vivienne, of course. And she won't tell you that." He kept his voice low. "How come all the questions 'bout ancient history?"

"I'm helping out a friend," I said.

"Mighty old friend," the man said.

"Not that old. Family things." I nodded to him and waved at the room. Hector hadn't come out of the back yet, and Minnie had disappeared into the kitchen as well. I had told her, before I left the back room, to check with Tim Minton at Poehler's Funeral Home in a few days. I figured we'd have more information for her then.

People watched as I left, almost like I was a vice cop who would arrest them for playing cards. I stepped into the chilly afternoon air, which felt chillier after the warmth of the Senior Center, and gathered my coat around me.

Old secrets, old friends, old hurts. I was walking into things I didn't entirely understand, from a world that was quite alien to mine, even though I'd been born at the tail end of the 1920s.

I felt bad for stirring up Minnie Pruitt's life. But at the same time, I might have just given her answers to fifty years' worth of questions.

I only hoped they were answers she wanted.

FORTY

The World Series again interfered with my day, and although I wanted to resent it, I couldn't. Not entirely. Jimmy was getting such joy from the games that I vowed to get baseball tickets next spring. He needed something to focus on besides his schoolwork, me, the Grimshaw family, and staying out of trouble.

The Mets won again, but this one was a squeaker, and as the game went into extra innings, I found myself forgetting about the Queen Anne. An error in the tenth gave the Mets a 2-1 victory, made Jimmy's day, and made me smile as well.

We spent the rest of the evening together. I didn't look at work once, even though I felt guilty about it. After Jimmy went to sleep, I planned the next day. I had some driving to do, and as I went through my notes, I realized that the mailman who had discovered Hanley's body worked only four blocks away from Vivienne Bontemps.

Maybe, if I timed things right, I could show up at the post office just as he ended his rounds.

The next morning, LeDoux and I both went into the Queen Anne as if we had weeks of work ahead. I had donned my coveralls and carried more paint inside, affecting a world-weary look as I hurried past the neighbors' windows.

I had asked LeDoux about the ring and he hadn't seen it, but that didn't mean Minton hadn't found it. And, LeDoux reminded me, given the amount of gold in that attic room upstairs, there was no guarantee it wasn't up there either.

The very thought of digging through that room still made my skin crawl.

I went back to my worktable past the boiler room. LeDoux hadn't taken the evidence bag away yet—he'd just plain forgotten during the past two days, as I'd hustled him out of the building so that I could pick up Jim.

I was pleased: there was one piece of evidence I wanted to look at before I visited Vivienne Bontemps. It took a minute of digging, but I found it.

The cocktail napkin with the phone number. And the spidery handwriting:

Sorry.
Love forever
V.

I carefully put the bagged napkin into a folder, then carried it out of the building. On the way, I reminded LeDoux that I would be leaving early again, and he sighed heavily.

"At some point I have to get back to New York, you know," he said.

"I know." I managed to sound patient, even though my leaving early had little to do with the amount of time it would take him to finish working this basement.

I got into the van, put the folder in my briefcase, then headed to South Cottage Grove. On the way there, I pulled over and took off the cap and coveralls. No one followed me.

I was beginning to relax my vigilance just a little.

Vivienne Bontemps's neighborhood in South Cottage Grove was nicer than I expected. The houses were all 1920s bungalows, most of them freshly painted over the summer, and all with well-trimmed lawns. Most of them even had leaf piles near the large trees that arched over the street.

I hadn't expected an oasis like this. Most of the neighborhoods I went into on the South Side might have looked like this once, but didn't any longer. Here, it seemed, people still cared about their homes and the way they appeared. Here, people had some pride in the way that they lived.

The address the folks at the Senior Center had given me was right in the middle of the block. This house was painted white. Someone had added a front porch that would have looked better on a Victorian than on the little bungalow.

A white wicker armchair with green cushions sat in front of the picture window. A matching table sat in front of the chair. Beside it a smaller wicker chair, not as expensive, sat as if waiting for a supplicant to talk to the owner of the lawn chair. The smaller chair had no cushion at all.

All around the porch's floor and on its railings pots stood. Some had dark, trailing leaves, turning brown as the fall hit its full force. Others were simply filled with dirt, probably awaiting their spring blooms now. A few still had green plants, but what they were I couldn't tell.

Someone had placed a leaf arrangement—a kind of orange-and-brown, fall-themed wreath—on the front door, and in the window hand-drawn jack o'lanterns glared out of white school paper in vivid blacks and oranges.

I had a moment of concern: I hadn't even thought of Halloween. Last year, Jimmy and I had partnered with the Grimshaws because I hadn't done Halloween with a child before and, it turned out, Jimmy hadn't celebrated the holiday either.

He later told me he thought trick or treating was lame. It felt too much like begging, which had, apparently, reminded him of his old life. So I had promised something else this year, although I hadn't given any thought to what that something else might be.

Time to investigate it, I guessed.

I sighed and walked up the porch steps, briefcase in hand. I felt like an encyclopedia salesman approaching a quiet house in the middle of a workday.

Someone moved behind the picture window—a flash of vivid blues—but I couldn't catch the face. I was being watched, though, and the movement let me know it.

I didn't mind. My behavior was probably unusual in such a nice neighborhood on a drizzly fall day.

The door opened almost before I finished my first knock. A woman in a satin, blue day dress stared at me, her straight black hair pulled back in a bun. Her skin was that white-tinged chocolate color that pale blacks sometimes got when they aged, and her eyes were as blue as her dress.

I would have wagered that at times in her past this woman passed between the color lines.

"Help you?" she asked.

"My name is Bill Grimshaw," I said. "I'm looking for Vivienne Bontemps."

"You're looking at her," she said. "What'd you want?"

I had a feeling she already knew, that someone from the Senior Center had called her and told her a man with a scar was asking about her. I explained my purpose anyway, telling the same story I'd told at the Senior Center, and this time asking about Zeke Ellis.

Her lips thinned, and she looked at me with great disapproval. "I don't like discussing Zeke."

"I can understand that," I said, "but there's a chance that he might not have skipped town. I have some evidence that indicates he might have died the week he disappeared, right here in Chicago."

Her mouth opened slightly, as if she'd never considered it, and color rose in her cheeks. Then I saw, through the fine lines that time had left, what her appeal had been.

"You sure about that?" she asked.

"No," I said. "That's why I want to talk with you."

She nodded, bit her lower lip, and considered. She was clearly alone in the house. Then she shrugged. "Ah, what the hell. You only live once. Come on in."

She stepped away from the door, opening it wide. A blast of perfume hit me, heavy and cloying. I wasn't sure I wanted to follow her, but I smiled at her, nodded, and walked inside.

The room was cluttered with knickknacks and pillows, but it was clean. A white carpet covered the floor, thick and obviously new.

She led me into the dining room, just off the living room. A large, oval-shaped, oak table dominated the space, with fake fruit sitting in a bowl on top of a hand-made doily. She took the captain's chair at the head of the table. I sat in a more modest chair to the side.

"Okay," she said. "You tell me what you got that makes you think Zeke didn't take a flyer."

Rather than answer her, I opened my briefcase and removed the folder. Then I took the evidence bag out and slid it across the table's polished surface.

"Please don't open the bag," I said. "It's evidence."

"Evidence." She raised her plucked eyebrows, then slid the bag closer to her. She reached into the pocket of her dress and removed a pair of half glasses, which she placed on the end of her nose. Then she peered at the napkin.

And went gray.

"Where did you get this?" she whispered.

"It was folded into the back corner of a wallet," I said.

She looked up at me over the glasses. "A wallet."

I nodded.

"Where was that wallet?"

"We found it near three skeletons," I said as gently as I could.

"Where?"

"In a house on the South Side."

Her lips thinned.

"You recognize that?" I asked.

She ran her finger over the front of the bag. "Yeah."

"What is it?"

"The note I left Zeke," she said. "The morning I told him I didn't want to see him again."

Her head was bent, her expression pained.

"When was that?" I asked.

"October 28th 1919," she said, with such a firmness that I knew she had regretted doing it.

"Why'd you end the relationship?" I asked.

She was still staring at the note. "Because I found a letter from his old girlfriend from Alabama, saying she was moving here."

"It didn't say she was going to move here," I said. "It said she was coming here on the train. All it did was give the date and time."

She raised her head, and her eyes were filled with such anger I almost leaned back. "Darcy was moving here. That's what that letter meant."

Vivienne hadn't yet realized that I had seen the letter too. It would come to her.

"How do you know that's what the letter meant?" I asked. "It didn't say anything like that. Did Zeke tell you?"

"He didn't have to. It's not like now, when people just travel on a whim. If Darcy was taking the train to Chicago, she was going to stay here. And Darcy could barely read and write. She wasn't going to pour herself onto the page. Me and Zeke, we both knew she was coming up here to live."

"You talked with him about it," I said.

"More like shouted at him," she said. "He said he didn't ask her. He said he didn't want to see her, but I didn't believe him. Then when he run off, I figured it was to prove to me that he didn't want anything to do with Darcy. I kept expecting him back in a year or two, and I was going to show him."

"That's when you met Felix."

"I already knew Felix," she said. "Felix took care of me. Someone had to."

Then the color left her cheeks. She had been more honest with me than she had intended to be.

"Felix managed you, didn't he?" I asked gently.

Her gaze was wary. "That's a nice word. *Managed.*"

I waited.

She sighed and shook her head. "He took care of me. Someone told Big Jim that I was passing not two weeks after Zeke left. Big Jim threw me out of Colosimo's and told most of them on the Levee that I was a colored girl. I lost my place to live, I lost my man, I lost everything, and to make it worse, I was pregnant. So Felix, he offered to help me out . . ."

She frowned, closed her eyes as if she couldn't believe what she was saying, and opened them very slowly.

"My children don't know this," she whispered.

"I'm not going to tell anyone," I said.

"I haven't said anything about this in forty years." She put a hand to her forehead. "It must've been Zeke. You mentioning Zeke."

I nodded, but didn't add to it. She was still in a confessional mood. I was going to let her talk.

Then she tilted her head. "You saw the letter."

She finally realized what my comments meant. "Yeah," I said.

"It was in the wallet too?"

I nodded.

"Son of a bitch," she said, then put her hand over her lips. "And a fin? Did it have a fin?"

"A fin?"

"A five-dollar Treasury note. The large size, you know? Old money. Zeke always kept a fin, said you never knew when you'd need a bit of grease."

"He bribed people?"

She rolled her eyes. "He lived on the Levee. Of course he bribed people."

"And he visited you in your rooms, even though no one knew you were black?" I asked.

"I visited him," she said. "No one other than employees could come into Colosimo's."

"You lived there?"

"Near there. There was a network of buildings we all used." She leaned toward me. "You didn't tell me. Did you find a fin?"

"Yes," I said.

"God." She stood up and walked to the small window that overlooked the hedge between her house and the neighbors'. "All these years I thought he took a flyer."

"I don't think so," I said. "I think he was with Junius Pruitt and maybe someone named Lawrence."

"Lawrence Talgart, the fucking bastard," she said. "Yeah, it would make sense those three were together."

Then she turned, and she looked perplexed.

"But you said you found them on the South Side. Not in the Levee?"

"No," I said. "Closer to Hyde Park."

"That makes no sense." She sat back down. "Zeke wouldn't go through Bridgeport for nothing, not after the riots."

"Maybe he and Lawrence walked Junius home?" I asked.

"Walked." She snorted. "They always drove Junius home, dropped him half a block away so that wife of his wouldn't know what he was doing."

"What was he doing?" I asked.

"Anything that paid him," she said.

"Minnie Pruitt said he was a piano player."

"And he was, for about two hours a night."

"What did he do for the rest of the night?" I asked.

She took a deep breath. "He enforced."

"He was—what? A bouncer? A muscle man for Colosimo?"

She smiled and adjusted her sleeves over surprisingly thin arms. "We didn't call them bouncers then, but that's sort of what the job was. He made sure the girls didn't get hurt, and no one trashed up the club. He wasn't muscle. Colosimo used Italians for muscle. He was scary brawn."

"I thought he wasn't very big."

"He was big enough," she said. "And he was black. Black-black, the kind white folks find terrifying."

"Why didn't he tell his wife what he did?"

"Protecting white ladies of ill repute?" Vivienne said that with just a touch of a fake English accent. "Minnie couldn't handle the fact that he played piano for a white man doing 'race music.' Imagine how she'd've reacted when her husband's real job was keeping an eye on ladies of loose morals and even looser clothes."

That sense I'd had the day before, a sense of history still living for these women, came back strongly. And I felt like I was digging into a pool of anger and misunderstandings that was so deep there was no real way to get to the bottom of it all.

"Do you think he enforced against the wrong person?"

"And got my Zeke killed?" She shook her head. "Big Jim made sure you knew right up front which customer could beat a girl to death if he wanted to. In fact, Big Jim had a room off to the side just for those men. So no one could hear the screaming."

She shivered. I clenched my fists, pushing back anger at something that happened decades ago, something that was so long past many people didn't even know who Big Jim Colosimo was.

"If you say those three were together," she said, "then something happened after work. They didn't work near each other."

"So Zeke didn't work for Colosimo," I said, remembering a remark she'd made earlier about only employees going into the building.

"Zeke worked for Zeke," she said.

"And who did Lawrence Talgart work for?"

"Whoever'd hire him." She shivered again.

"Why didn't you like him?"

Her entire body seemed to collapse in on itself. "He knew."

She paused. I waited, and when it became clear she wasn't going to say any more, I said, "He knew you were passing?"

"And that I loved Zeke. He knew, and he told me I could buy his silence, and I did. Once a week." She shivered a third time.

He was dead, I reminded myself. And if he wasn't dead, he was so old that it no longer mattered.

"Did Zeke know about this?"

"You think he'd let Lawrence drive him around the city if he knew?"

I didn't know. But she didn't think so, and that was all that mattered.

"What did they do together?"

"Found people to con."

"Do you know what the con was?" I asked.

"Usually something simple. Renting a ride in Lawrence's Model T—which was still pretty rare, especially for a black man to have—or making change. They loved that one. Asked some sucker for change, then passed bills and coins around so fast that person never knew they got shorted till a lot later."

Variations of that scam survived even now. I'd seen a lot of drug addicts use it in Memphis.

"But they ran a floating card game, usually set up by Lawrence, with Zeke in it as the dealer. He was good at pocketing money and chips and at getting folks to win more than they should so that they'd bet more than they should, and then some ringer'd take them for all they were worth. They made a lot doing that."

"Could they have scammed the wrong guy?"

"They were always scamming the wrong guy," she said. "The question is, did that guy figure it out?"

It was a good question, and one that might be difficult to discover the answer to after fifty years. So I tried another tack.

"Did Zeke know anyone named Baird?"

"He didn't," she said. "I did. Name was Gavin. A little white mama's boy, determined to spend every dime of the family fortune. He'd run through most of it by the end of the war."

My fists relaxed. Finally, a connection, even though it was a tentative one. "He visited you?"

"Till that summer. Heard he ran out of money, might even have to get a job."

"Did he?"

She shrugged. "I know that Felix asked me later if I'd consider a few nights with Gavin Baird, because he'd been asking about me. I said I'd rather walk the street."

"Was he mean to you?"

She shook her head. "He had mean friends, though. And without Junius or someone like him, I just didn't feel safe. Specially if Gavin wanted to share."

No wonder she hadn't told her children any of this. I was a little amazed she was telling me.

"Did he share before he ran out of money?" I asked.

"Not with me," she said. "Some of the other girls. They hated it. They hated him. He watched. They said it was like he was storing up secrets."

He'd stored up quite a few, but not the kind she was thinking of.

"Was one of his friends Mortimer Hanley?" I asked.

She shook her head. "I'd remember that name. No."

"Any other names come to mind?" I asked.

"No." She answered a little too fast. A few names clearly did come to mind, but she wasn't willing to share them.

"These were all white men?" I asked.

"Yeah," she said softly.

"Men it was worth holding secrets about?" I asked.

"Oh, yeah," she said.

"Some of them still around?"

She looked at me. "I said I don't remember. I mean I don't remember. You understand?"

I did. They were around, and she was afraid of them.

"Do you think any of them could have hurt Zeke?" I asked.

"They didn't even know Zeke," she said.

"But say they did. Say Zeke interrupted them with one of the girls or cheated them in a card game. Would they have hurt him?"

"They'd've hired someone else to hurt him."

"Do you know who that someone else might've been?"

She gave me a half smile. "You know, it doesn't matter. They're all gone. Lost in the gang wars. The life of one of those white boys who went with Big Jim, and later Johnny Torrio or The Greek, was pretty damn short."

"You think they're all dead?" I asked.

"The ones that worked the Levee?" she said. "I know they're all dead. The ones that worked later, mostly for Capone, there's still some of them. But Zeke disappeared before anyone heard of Capone or any of those bums."

"What about Lawrence? Would any of them hurt him?"

"Hell if I know," she said. "I tried not to pay attention to him."

"Is there anyone who did pay attention to him? Anyone I can talk with about him?"

She stared at me for a long minute, as if she suddenly realized she was talking to a crazy man. "You trying to *solve* this thing?"

"If I find out what happened to them, it might help on another case I'm working on," I said.

"You think their deaths are tied to something now?" she asked. "I thought you wasn't even sure you had the right people."

I pulled the plastic evidence bag back toward me. "Do you think I have the right people?"

She looked at it, ran her finger over the words again. "Somebody could've stole his wallet," she said without conviction. "Everybody knew he carried cash."

"The cash was still in it," I said.

"They didn't get a chance to spend it."

"So that somebody, he'd end up dead with a guy who had Junius Pruitt's name sewn into his clothes and a letter addressed to Lawrence?"

She looked chagrinned. It was becoming clear how easily, and how often, she had lied about those years.

"Can I . . . see him?" she asked quietly.

"I'm afraid there's not much to see," I said.

"Oh," she said, as if she hadn't realized that entirely, and looked down.

"You can do one thing for me, though," I said.

"What's that?"

I pushed the evidence bag toward her again. "That logo on the napkin, it's a phone number, right?"

"Yes," she said.

"Do you know what for?"

To my surprise, she smiled. "The Everleigh Club, the gold standard."

"I thought that was closed in 1919," I said.

"It closed in 1911," she said. "I missed the good years. I was too young."

She sounded regretful, although her expression was carefully neutral.

"Where'd you get the napkin then?" I asked.

She laughed. "Zeke lived in the Everleigh Club."

"Before it closed?" I asked.

"After. It was his boarding house, and even all run down, it was something. The Everleigh sisters, they just left a lot of the stuff. Some of the things in here—" she swept her hand toward the living room "—came from there. That gold ashtray, and a few of the antimacassars, some of the vases."

"And the napkins," I said.

"They were in a drawer in the hallway. We used them for notes between us. People saw them and thought they came from before." She touched the bag one final time, as if she were touching Zeke himself. "I'd forgotten all about those."

The words hung between us for a moment. Then I pulled the bag back.

"Do you know anyone I can talk to who might've known Larry Talgart?" I asked.

"I know a lot of people," she said.

"People who might have an idea what happened to him? People who knew him well?"

She wrapped her arms around her waist, as if just thinking of Talgart made her nervous. Then she shrugged.

"Guess the only person who fits that description is his brother, Irving."

"Do you know where I can find him?" I asked.

"Nope," she said. "But the police probably do."

"Why?" I asked. "What'd he do?"

She gave me a sly smile. "He didn't do nothing, Mr. Grimshaw. He just went to work every single day like a good citizen."

"Irving Talgart was a cop?" I asked.

"One of Chicago's finest," she said.

FORTY-ONE

The meeting with Vivienne Bontemps was a lot more profitable than I had imagined it would be. Not only did she give me Lawrence's full name, but she also gave me another lead to follow.

But she also confused matters, in such a way that I was beginning to despair of ever figuring out what happened in the Queen Anne.

I hadn't expected the tie to Gavin Baird. I had somehow expected Mortimer Hanley to have some kind of link to the house, even back then. That staircase leading to the attic room still confused me.

Had Hanley found it and reveled in it? Or was there some other explanation, one I hadn't found yet?

I drove away from her house, checking the time before I checked my mirrors. I would be glad when the World Series was over. I didn't like cutting my afternoon short, even though I was enjoying the time spent with Jimmy.

I had one more stop before I went back to pick up LeDoux: the post office where Carter Doyle worked. I hoped I would be able to catch him as he ended his shift.

This postal branch was a large stone building like so many other official Chicago buildings. But unlike the ones downtown, this one didn't look like it had been built by the Founding Fathers. It was a mixture of stone and brick and looked worn from the weather and time.

I parked around back, where the postal delivery trucks parked.

Someone tried to wave me away, but I ignored him. It was close to quitting time for the mailmen—nearly a dozen trucks were parked there, some with mailmen still carrying mail bags from the trucks to the post office itself.

As I got out of my van, I ignored two of the white carriers who were staring at me. I walked to the nearest black carrier.

"I'm looking for Carter Doyle," I said.

The carrier pointed to a man dumping contents of postal tubs into a large canvas bin. I thanked the carrier and walked toward Doyle like I visited the back of the post office every single day.

"Carter Doyle?" I asked, as I climbed the stairs to the bin area. A sign hanging beside a post warned me that only official postal personnel were permitted beyond that point.

Doyle raised his head. He was younger than I was, and tall. His shoulders were broad, and his arms corded with muscle. He looked like an aging football player, one who hadn't gone to fat.

"I'm Bill Grimshaw," I said. "I'm investigating the death of Mortimer Hanley."

"Yeah?" Doyle set down the tub he'd been holding and pointedly crossed his arms. "What's that got to do with me?"

"I understand you found him."

"Huh?"

"The body. I was told you were the person who found his body."

He blinked and his arms fell to his sides. "I don't know who told you that, but they got it all wrong."

I started in surprise. Laura had told me that. "You didn't find him?"

"Nope." Doyle frowned at me, no longer as hostile as he was at the beginning. "Why're you asking?"

"Because there were some discrepancies," I said. "I was told you saw him through the window of his living room and then called for an ambulance. But it was clear that he died in his bed, which isn't visible from the living-room window. So I was going to ask you what really happened."

Doyle lifted his cap and scratched his head. Then he kicked aside one of the tubs, and walked toward me. "You a cop?"

"No," I said.

"Some kind of private detective?"

"Some kind," I said.

"You work for Hanley's family?"

"I don't believe he has any," I said, "at least that I can find. I'm working for the owner of the building."

Doyle tilted his head slightly, as if I had surprised him. "I thought Hanley owned the building, the way he acted."

"No," I said. "He just managed the place for more than twenty years."

"Wow," Doyle said. "I never had any idea that someone else owned it."

I could feel the clock ticking. Jimmy would be struggling through his last subject of the day right now, counting the minutes until the bell rang and we could go home for the final game.

"So you really didn't find him?" I asked.

"Nope."

"Know who did?"

"Nope."

I sighed. This case was getting stranger and stranger.

"Thanks," I said to Doyle, and started down the stairs.

"You know, this Hanley guy," Doyle said, "he was one mean piece of work."

I stopped and turned. Doyle was coming down the stairs beside me. He glanced over his shoulder as if he didn't want to be seen.

We hit the parking lot together and he led me to one of the mail trucks. We stood beside it, hidden from the back door.

"You didn't like him?" I asked.

"Hell, if I *had* found him, I woulda left him there to rot," Doyle said. "And my friends would not call me a particularly vindictive guy."

"What'd he do?" I asked.

"What didn't he do?" Doyle said. "When I got the route, he called and complained. He'd throw crap at me, stuff I couldn't identify, and he said he wouldn't touch any mail that I touched, demanded I wear gloves. Called that in too."

"What'd your boss do?" I asked.

"Nothing." Doyle's mouth thinned. "That's just part of my job. I got a crossover neighborhood."

No wonder he looked so strong. He probably kept himself in shape just in case something did happen in one of those neighborhoods he had to walk into alone every day.

"I'll wager you didn't wear gloves," I said.

"I didn't," Doyle said. "And they didn't put me on a different route. They told him he could sign up on the waiting list for a post office box or he could deal with it. He told me one morning that he disinfected the jigaboo germs off the letters before he opened them."

I shook my head. Stories like this made me glad that I worked for myself. I wouldn't have taken such abuse day after day. I would have had to respond to it or avoid it. I couldn't have walked the route every single morning knowing that Hanley and his foul mouth waited for me.

"Did he ever harm you?" I asked.

"No one gets that close to me," Doyle said.

"Did he try?"

Doyle shook his head. "He was one of those all-talk bigots. I was glad too. Last thing I wanted was him aiming a gun at me."

"You don't think he was violent?" I asked.

"Maybe if he had someone weaker living with him, a woman or a kid, he mighta been violent. But he wasn't going to go after—what'd he call me that time?—a big strapping spade like me."

"Every day he'd say something like that?" I asked.

"Every day for ten years," Doyle said.

"You didn't report him?"

Doyle gave me a cold smile. "To who? I got my job to do, and part of that is interacting with the customers, good and bad. And you know about the cops around here."

I nodded. "But there are blacks on the force."

"Sure there are," he said, with great sarcasm.

I almost corrected him, and then I understood what he meant. He felt that the blacks on the force were more interested in keeping their jobs than helping their people.

"Not every cop is bad," I said.

"Maybe not, but none of them would've helped me. Besides, they were visiting that house enough."

I frowned. I hadn't heard this. "Domestic disputes?"

"I don't know what it was, but it seemed like every coupla weeks I saw some cops there."

"Doing anything special?" I asked.

Doyle shook his head. "We'd just get there around the same time, is all. I don't know if they were responding to something or bringing donuts, and I didn't want to know. I got outta there as fast as I could."

"Was that around noon?" I asked, remembering the police car I'd seen driving by.

He shrugged. "Early afternoons, usually. That's when I got to that house."

I frowned, wondering what that meant. Surely the police had known that Hanley was dead by the time I'd seen them. Or had there been a lot of visible trouble at the house, trouble that made them stop on their regular sweep of the neighborhood?

"When did you find out that Hanley was dead?" I asked.

"I don't know," he said. "End of September, maybe? Around the first time I saw your van there."

I turned and looked at it. I hadn't even thought of parking a block away from the post office. I hadn't thought he'd recognize the van.

"You investigating something in that house?" he asked. "Because until today, I thought the van belonged to some painters."

"Not in the house," I lied. "We're trying to find out more about Hanley. Can you tell me the names of anyone who wrote to him?"

"Besides Commonwealth Edison and Illinois Bell? Nope, and even if I could, it wouldn't be legal. I'm not supposed to notice." Then his features softened a little. "But I'll tell you this. He never got a lot of mail, and I was happy for that."

In other words, not many people wrote to him at all.

"Did you ever hear why there weren't any tenants toward the end?" I asked.

"No one said, but I think old Hanley scared them away. I had saw a couple of prospectives last summer, and they were paler than pale coming out of that house."

"White kids, then," I said.

"With what I told you, you think he would've rented to us?"

"Just checking," I said. "He didn't work for himself, so maybe he had a mandate."

"Like one of those quotas?" Doyle grinned at me. "Thank God he didn't. Could you imagine having to live near that guy?"

I couldn't, but not for the reasons Doyle mentioned. I couldn't imagine living near anyone who kept those mementos in that attic room.

"Thanks," I said, extending my hand. "I appreciate your time."

He took my hand, shook, and then said, "You have any idea why someone would say I found him?"

"I don't," I said. "But I'm going to find out."

FORTY-TWO

Despite what I'd said to Doyle, I couldn't find out who had lied about him right away. I was running late. I picked up Jimmy first. I hoped that no one was still tailing me—I wasn't being as cautious as I had been earlier in the week—but I had Jimmy keep an eye out the back windows, and he didn't see anything.

Jimmy complained about the change in plans all the way to the Queen Anne, and by the time I'd come out with LeDoux, Jimmy had found the game on the radio. The three of us rode in silence to LeDoux's apartment on the north side, listening to the game instead of talking.

We got home in time for the third inning. Jimmy parked himself in front of the television while I made some popcorn on the stove. As I rubbed the covered pan against the burner, I mentally listed all the things I had to do the following day.

A few of them I could do as soon as the game ended. I could call Laura and ask about that mailman story, and I could call Jack Sinkovich for two pieces of information—Hanley's death report and the whereabouts of Irving Talgart.

The last game was a game, and for a while I forgot about the case. The Mets won 5-3, which gave them the entire series, and the crowd—including the two in our household—went wild. While Jimmy danced around the living room, I decided to hell with it. We needed a real celebration. So we went out for pizza and soda and one long round of pinball. By the time we got back, it was nearly nine.

Jim went to bed soon after. I brought my notepads to the living room and placed my two calls from there. I had expected to reach Laura and hear the phone ring at Sinkovich's. Instead, Laura didn't answer and Sinkovich did.

"I been meaning to talk with you," he said. "I got an idea, but it's gotta be in person."

"All right," I said, wondering what he could want. He probably figured I still owed him for past favors. I figured he owed me for the time he stayed in my apartment after his wife threw him out.

"I got your message," he said. "I ain't been in the precinct lately, and it took a while for someone to tell me you called."

"It's all right," I said.

"It's not all right. They got me on stupid duty. I'd tell you about it, but I'm not supposed to talk, and I ain't gonna do it on the phone. But I gotta say they're pushing hard enough that I might take them up on it. They want me out, but they want me deciding, maybe so I don't get no pension or something. I gotta check that."

"Do you want out?" I knew the last year had been hard on him. As he followed his instincts instead of the culture of the police department, he lost friends and eventually got relegated to a desk job. His wife left him and took his child with her because, she said, she didn't know him anymore.

"I dunno. I gotta keep the job so I got some leverage with the wife, you know. The divorce's nearly done, but they tell me we can 'revisit' custody any time. She's already got most of the stuff she wanted and alimony too, and she's talking about moving to Wisconsin. She does that, I'll never see my kid."

"You can fight it," I said.

"Yeah, I know. I just gotta question what it's doing to the kid, you know? All he hears about is how much we fight, how we don't get along, and probably what a shmuck I am, and what's that gonna do to him? How's that raising him good?"

"I don't know," I said. I had my own problems raising Jimmy.

"So the job, it's good because it's money. It's bad for a million other reasons, most of them got nothing to do with nothing except they want the old Jack Sinkovich back, and they ain't getting him. I actually almost bitched about that Panther raid last week."

"Almost," I said.

"Listen, if I could tell you what I been sitting through, you'd understand the almost. If I don't quit, they're gonna have me on mudhole duty by next year."

"Mudhole duty?"

"Guarding manhole covers so nobody steals them. It don't exist as a job, not yet, but everyone says it will someday, and the lowest of the low'll get it. That'd be me. Which, I suppose, sounds like self-pity to you, and it does to me, so let's get to it. What do you need?"

I felt odd asking him to help me when he was having so much trouble helping himself. Maybe I did like Sinkovich more than I wanted to admit.

"I have two things," I said. "First, I need to see a copy of the report filed on the death of Mortimer Hanley."

"You sure there was a report? Because you can just ask for the death certificate from the county."

"I was sure this morning," I said. "Then I talked with the man who supposedly called the police, and he had nothing to do with this. So I need to see this report more than ever."

"You gotta date?"

"Not an exact one. The middle of September sometime."

"I'll see what I can find. What else?"

"Do you know a black cop—I'm sure he's retired by now—named Irving Talgart?"

"Nope."

"Can you look him up for me? I need to talk to him."

"How soon you need it?"

"Tomorrow, if you can get it to me."

Sinkovich sighed. "I gotta be at the courthouse by nine. If I got stuff for you, it's gotta be before that. I'm sure I can't find that report that early."

"Talgart would be good enough for a start," I said.

"Expect a call about seven."

"I appreciate it."

"I'd say don't mention it, but you will. It's gonna take some to get that report, but when I get it, I'm bringing it to your place. We need to have a conversation."

"Deal," I said, and wondered what I was getting myself into.

FORTY-THREE

The following morning, the phone rang before seven, but it wasn't Sinkovich. It was Laura. She wanted to catch me before we both headed off to work. She knew I would be away from the phone, and she felt this was important.

She had had no idea that I was trying to reach her.

"Someone asked me what we're doing at the Queen Anne," she said.

"Who?" I asked.

"A man by the name of Kaztauskis. They call him A. A. because, I'm told, his first name is Lithuanian and nearly unpronounceable."

"A. A. Kaztauskis?" I asked. "Have I met him?"

"I doubt it," she said. "I barely know him except to nod at him in the hallways. He nodded hi yesterday, then nearly walked by before he called my name. I stopped, feeling a little confused, and he said, 'Sorry to bother you, Mrs. Hathaway—'"

"He called you Mrs.?" I asked.

"A lot of people do. They don't know what to label me now that I'm back to my maiden name. Especially the old-timers."

"He's one of them?" I asked.

"Yeah." She sighed, and in her voice I heard her frustration. "He said he lived near the house, and some of the neighbors were asking why it was taking so long to paint the place."

My breath caught. "What did you say?"

"I told him that you weren't just painting. That Hanley's body had been in there long enough to permeate everything with the smell. So you were cleaning and disinfecting, and restaining some of the wood. I almost told him that you were tearing off plasterboard, but then I realized that was the wrong thing to tell anybody."

She was right about that. We had no idea who had been involved with that house, if anyone, and we had to be cautious.

"Did he buy it?" I asked.

"I think so," but she didn't sound as sure as she could have. "He said, 'I hope you're not paying them by the hour,' and walked away. What should I do, Smokey?"

"Nothing yet, at least about the house," I said. "But if you can surreptitiously check his files, maybe ask someone you trust about him, that might be worth your time."

"Do you think he was putting me on notice, or do you think he was actively curious?"

"I don't know," I said. "But either way it worries me. Because if he isn't involved, then the neighbors are wondering, and if he is, then someone else is noticing and put him up to asking you. Did you check his home address? Does he live nearby?"

"I did think to do that," she said, "and yes, he does."

I didn't like any of this, and not just for the reasons I told Laura. The mailman had claimed he didn't know Sturdy owned the house. If Kaztauskis wasn't lying, some of the neighbors did know who owned it. If he was lying, then we had a whole other problem.

"We're going to be there weeks longer," I said.

"I know," she said.

"We're going to have to come up with something other than painting to explain our presence. And you're going to have to come up with a reason to keep such a valuable property under wraps. Let's give it some thought and try to have a plan by Monday."

"All right," she said.

"We also need that secondary storage area."

"I have it," she said. "It's—"

"Why don't you drop off the key, and we'll talk about it then."

"How about after work today?" she said. "Bring Jim. We'll have dinner."

"Sounds like a plan." I almost hung up, and then I remembered I had wanted to talk with her as well. "Laura, who told you what happened to the manager?"

"I don't know," she said. "Someone at the rental agency. Why?"

I told her about the discrepancy between what she'd heard and what the mailman had told me.

"I'm positive that he was there," she said.

Then I told her how the body couldn't have been seen from the window, not if he had died in the bedroom.

"I don't like this," she said. "What's going on there?"

"I don't know," I said, "but I'll need your help to find out."

We hung up after making plans to meet at her office around six. Then the phone rang again. It was Sinkovich, complaining about my busy phone line. When I finally got him calmed down, he told me Irving Talgart's current address.

"I did a little digging," Sinkovich said. "He's got a good record. Lotsa collars, most of them clean. Nothing bad in his file. No commendations, neither, but then you said he's Neg—bla—ah, hell, Grimshaw, what do I call you people now?"

And that was the problem he had with sensitivity. He tried, and usually failed.

"People is good," I said.

"I'm doing you a favor," he snapped.

"I know," I said. "I appreciate it too."

"So you know, the department ain't in the habit of—or at least wasn't in the habit of—recognizing the work of *people,* not until the last few years, and even then the rumor is that they only get the commendations when they're being run out or getting too much media attention."

"Yeah," I said drily.

"Didn't know if you knew that," he said. "What it means is that I can't tell from his record how good a cop he was, but he looks okay—at least on paper."

"That's good to know," I said, and meant it.

"Wasn't able to look up the other thing for you, though. Tried, but half the crap isn't filed yet or in the right place. So I'll get back on it soon's I can."

"Thanks," I said.

"Yeah, well, I'd rather be chasing your paperwork than putting on this monkey suit," he said, and hung up.

Since he wore a suit every day to the precinct, I didn't know quite what he meant. But I did know that some of the detectives had their suits for work and their suits for court. And Sinkovich had mentioned that he was going to the courthouse today.

I just hoped it wasn't more hassle with the divorce.

I rousted Jim, took him and the Grimshaw children to school, and then picked up LeDoux. No one followed me—or at least the tail wasn't obvious. When we got to the Queen Anne, LeDoux pressed me into service for the first few hours of the morning.

I hadn't been in the secret room for nearly two days. I was surprised at how much he'd gotten done. He'd pulled down some of the bricks himself in front of the B, C, D, and E sites, but he was having trouble with F, G, and H. Whoever had done the brickwork there had been a master craftsman compared with the earlier sites.

So I labored at pulling down brick to enable LeDoux to go inside the tombs. I tried to ignore the bodies facing me in each site, wondering who they were and who they had left behind.

Wondering what their connection was to Pruitt, Ellis, and Talgart, and to Baird or Hanley.

After LeDoux finished with the F, G, and H sites, he would need Minton. He would also need me to see what was on the back walls of those tombs—or perhaps better stated, what was behind them.

Neither of us really discussed much more than that. I couldn't imagine working down here, alone like he had the last few days, with only the dead for company.

He told me he was used to it, but I wasn't sure how anyone got used to that kind of work.

I certainly knew I couldn't.

FORTY-FOUR

After I finished helping LeDoux, I went to Poehler's. The basement work area was filled with bodies, most of them elderly, most of them, Minton told me, part of the weekend funeral schedule. He was buried—quite literally—in work.

But he promised me he'd come to the Queen Anne the following morning. He'd gotten permission to spend his afternoons and evenings at Poehler's, so long as he arrived around two.

He also told me that Minnie Pruitt had come in, demanding to see her husband. Minton hadn't let her, nor had he told her where the body was found. But he did show her the wedding ring he'd found near the fingerbones.

"I think from the way she cried," he said, "that we have a positive identification."

I nodded, thanked him for keeping the location quiet, and promised to pick him up in the morning. Then I drove to the address Sinkovich had given me.

Irving Talgart lived in a rundown part of the West Side, not too far from some of Sturdy's other buildings and the Black Panther offices. He had a one-bedroom apartment in a converted house and it looked like he hadn't left it in a long time.

"Neighborhood's not safe anymore," he told me as he led me inside the overheated apartment. The weather had turned cold the last couple of days, but not that cold. The steamy temperature of the apartment made me feel like I'd entered a sauna.

A smelly sauna. Two cats draped over newspaper piles like they'd been the ones who'd read every single word. I assumed the smell came from their untended litter box.

Talgart pointed to an empty space on the cluttered couch. I gave it a quick once-over, hoping to avoid any cat accidents before I sat down.

He sat in an armchair positioned in front of the television set. He pulled a blanket across his legs, and one of the cats leaped from the newspaper pile to the armchair and made its way to Talgart's lap.

I said, "I've come about your brother Lawrence."

Talgart started as if I'd used a forbidden word. "What do you know about Lawrence? You wasn't even born when he died."

The word "died" surprised me. The women had thought the other two men had run off. I wondered why Talgart knew what happened to his brother.

"When did he die?" I asked.

Talgart put one bony hand on the cat's back, gently pushing the animal down onto the blanket. "October, 1919. What a hell of a year that was."

"Because of the race riot," I said.

"And the bombings and going dry. Then Lawrence finally gets what's coming to him." Talgart shook his head. "I was happy when 1920 rolled in."

"What do you mean, he got what was coming to him?" I asked.

"My brother wasn't a nice man, Mr. Grimshaw," Talgart said. "He was the reason I became what I did. I saw him hurt our ma, hurt us kids, hurt everyone who came in touch with him just because he was out to make a buck, and I vowed I wasn't going to be a thing like him. I hope to God I wasn't."

"But 'what was coming to him.' That's harsh language."

"You don't anger the kind of people my brother angered without payback," Talgart said. "He got his."

"I was led to believe no one knew what happened to him."

Talgart rolled his eyes. "We all knew. They found that car of his in Orchard Place. What they call O'Hare now. It was just a field back then, but north of the city. Folks like us didn't go up there much. We wasn't welcome."

"Like now," I said.

"Not like now," he snapped. "You won't get lynched if you go to the north suburbs. There's no way Lawrence drove up there. No way. Someone drove him."

"Do you know who?"

"Yeah," he said. "Can't prove it. Never could."

This was not the conversation I'd expected to have with him. I'd expected it to be similar to the other conversations, filled with guesses and misinformation.

"Why can't you prove it?" I asked.

"Need a body, son. Or don't they teach that to you in investigating school these days?"

I'd told him that I wasn't a cop, that my investigation was private. I'd worried about that too, because a lot of police officers didn't respect private detectives. But Talgart had had no problem letting me in, and I had a hunch that dig would have remained the same whether I was a private detective or a police officer.

"I didn't realize you hadn't seen the body," I said.

"Don't play games with me," he said. "There's only one reason you'd be here. You found Lawrence, didn't you?"

"I don't know," I said. "We might have, but it might be someone else. The body has no identification, and there's not a lot to go on."

"Body? After all this time?" He gave me a sideways stare. His eyes were clear, shining with intelligence. I wouldn't have wanted to face him in an interrogation room. He would have seen right through me.

"That's what I mean. There's nothing recognizable left." I didn't want to give him much more than that. I was here to find out what he knew, not to give him information.

"So what makes you think it's Lawrence?" he asked.

"Some anecdotal evidence," I said, "and this."

I opened my briefcase and removed the damaged letter. It was still in its plastic evidence bag. I handed it to him.

He took it with two fingers. "I thought you wasn't police."

"I'm working with a forensic team," I said.

"One of those off-the-book nightmares who thinks he's knows what he's doing?"

"A highly credentialed man who occasionally runs independent investigations," I said.

"On crimes no one cares about." He hadn't looked at the letter yet. Instead, he was watching me. "He's out-of-state, is he?"

"He's from out of state," I said.

"Good thing." Talgart brought the bag closer to his face. As he reached for the side with his other hand, I moved forward to tell him not to open the bag.

He saw the movement and smiled.

"I know, I know. Don't contaminate it. Wasn't planning to. That paper looks too fragile to touch."

He stared at it, as if he didn't want to understand it, then his eyes moved as he read.

"Edwina," he said softly. Then a moment later he added, "And Lulabelle. I haven't thought of her for forty years. Hated the Dickersons. And Ma. . . ."

He shook his head, then leaned forward, nearly knocking the cat from his lap, and handed the letter back to me.

"It's not conclusive identification," he said.

"I know that."

"But judging from content, my sister Karla wrote it to Lawrence. She would be the only one who'd call him dearest. The rest of us hated him."

Those last two words had a vehemence that added to their veracity.

"Edwina was my momma's cousin. They were close as sisters. She died of some kind of female complaint—I suspect we'd call it a cancer of the female parts these days—and Momma insisted on staying with her until she was gone. Then Momma came up here, along with the rest of the family. I forgot she lived with Aunt Lula for a while. We was saving up money to bring her. Or I should say *I* was saving up money. Lawrence was spending it as fast as he got it. Then he got all the credit when the money arrived. Ain't it always like that?"

Apparently, in Talgart's life it had been, and he hadn't let go of it, even though the other players were long dead.

"Which is," he said, "a long way of saying if you found that letter on his body, and I'm thinking from the stains you did, then you found my brother. Where'd they put him? A ditch somewhere?"

I shook my head. "I'm afraid I can't tell you."

He narrowed his eyes. "Something else going on?"

"I can't tell you that either. But I can ask you some leading questions."

He inclined his head toward me, a regal movement that acknowledged I was giving him more information than perhaps he deserved.

"Did you or your brother know a Mortimer Hanley?"

"Can't answer for my brother on most things. We had pretty separate lives, and he died fifty years ago. But I never heard of this Hanley."

"What about Gavin Baird?"

To my surprise, Talgart smiled. "Yeah, I knew him. Everyone working the South Side knew him. My brother routinely bilked him of the fortune he inherited."

"I thought you didn't know about your brother's business."

"This one was hard to avoid. Baird came into the precinct one night demanding to see me. Now, if you knew Baird, you'd know he didn't normally associate with anyone with dark skin."

"Except your brother."

"I can't vouch for what Baird did on the Levee. There folks went to be something they weren't. He slummed a lot, and men like him often dipped into the things they professed to hate."

I'd seen that. I never completely understood it either.

"But to come into the precinct, and ask for a colored patrolman—no, demand to see him—and in a public place, well that was nigh unheard of."

"What'd he want?" I asked.

"He wanted me to give him his money back. He said, and I got no reason to doubt him, that my brother pulled the last of his savings—about five grand—off him in one night."

"That was a lot of money then," I said.

"It's a lot of money now," Talgart said. "I'd love a piece of that."

"Then too?"

His smile faded. His eyes became hard and his jaw rigid. Even though he had shrunken with age, his expression gave him a power that suggested he could take me in a fair fight.

"I'm not dirty. I've never been dirty. I've had plenty of opportunity, starting with my brother, and right up until the day I retired I never once took a bribe, never once hit someone who didn't deserve it, never once lied to get a righteous conviction. So don't you come into my home and accuse me of stealing."

My cheeks were warm. I hadn't quite accused him of that. But I had implied it.

"My mistake," I said.

"That's not an apology," he snapped.

"I'm sorry," I said. "I was out of line."

"Damn right you were."

I took a deep breath, waiting for him to toss me out. But he didn't. We stared at each other for a moment, and since I was the one who had offended him, I was the one to break the eye contact first.

"I guess what I was trying to ask you is if you told your brother you envied him that kind of money," I said.

"Now why in holy hell would I do that?"

I shrugged. "You said you were supporting your mother. Wouldn't there be some resentment—"

"You asking me if *I* killed my brother?" That flinty look was back.

"No," I said. "I'm trying to gauge your relationship with your brother and how you reacted to Baird that night."

"How I reacted to Baird was I told him to solve his own damn problems. Another colored officer was there with me, and he asked Baird if the money changed hands in an illegal vice game. Baird took issue, a scuffle ensued, and that was the last I saw of him that night."

"A scuffle?"

"He lunged at the officer—I can't recall his name now—and some of the others in the precinct broke it up. They hauled Baird off, and that was the end of that."

"That other officer, was he—"

"He was just trying to help the idiot. If it'd been an illegal game, which it was, we might've been able to arrest Lawrence and get Baird's money back. But by the time we got confirmation the game was illegal, there was no game to be seen, no one to arrest. Not that I would've gone up to the Levee anyway. Black police officers didn't end up so good up there."

I nodded. "When did all this happen?"

"About a week before Lawrence and his expensive automobile disappeared."

"And that was the end of it?" I asked.

"The incident? Sure," he said. "No one was gonna tell me how they got Baird's money back. My captain talked to me, to see if I was in on the fleecing. When he realized I wasn't, he sent me back onto the streets, warned me to stay away from Baird and the Levee and Lawrence, and I did."

"So you didn't see your brother at all before he died."

Talgart sighed and handed me the letter. "I didn't even know he got that, which would've been nice, because I spent three months writing letters to my mother before one of them actually got to her. I had no idea where she was."

"You finally had enough money to bring her up here?" I asked.

"Her and my sister. I sold Lawrence's car to do it too."

"Wasn't it evidence?" I asked.

"In what? The death of a colored man? A colored man who stole from white people? Who was going to investigate that?"

"His policeman brother?"

He petted the cat, then leaned back in his armchair. The springs squeaked.

"You're that type, aren't you?" he said. "The type that rushes in, feels each death's got to be examined, each killer's got to be brought to justice."

"I didn't know it was a type," I said.

"It's a type, and it's a dangerous one. Because not every killer should be brought to justice. You pick up those rocks, and you find dirty little secrets that cost even more lives. And sometimes the life lost should've been lost."

"Are you saying your brother should've died?" I asked.

"I said he got what he deserved and I meant it."

"You weren't curious? Or worried that the same people might come after you?"

"Curious? No. My brother was so deep in Chicago's cesspool that I figured he finally crossed the wrong person. I wasn't about to make that same mistake. Worried that they'd come after me? Not really. I had enough to worry about just walking around in my uniform."

"Being a policeman made you a target?" I asked.

"It was 1919, son. I was a colored policeman. I was in trouble from the Irish gangs who hated me in a patrolman's uniform, and I was in trouble from the coloreds who thought they owned the South Side. I had 'betrayed my race,' sided with the white man. I couldn't hardly walk out of the precinct without worrying about being beat up or shot. So why worry that my brother's killer was coming after me? I figured it was just one more name on the Get-Talgart list."

"Why didn't you leave Chicago?" I asked. "Family?"

"If you mean a wife and kids, I never got that lucky. Had two wives, both left me because I seemed too taken up with my work. I always wondered what they expected, marrying a policeman. That I wouldn't be involved with my work?"

He placed both hands on the cat's back. The cat licked his fingers, then bit one. Talgart didn't seem to notice. The cat's ears went back and it jumped down.

Talgart adjusted the blanket. "I stayed because I had a good job. A *professional* job, one I couldn't get back in Mississippi. I stayed because I knew it was worse other places. East St. Louis rioted for weeks—*weeks*—that year. You read about 1919, son. You'll learn that all the upsets we've been having about the war, about the racist stuff, about the bombings, barely compares to fifty years ago. Back then, coloreds weren't just taking to the streets, they were getting shot, fire-bombed, lynched, and not just in the Deep South. In places like Iowa and Illinois and Missoura. And not just us, neither. Germans was worse. You were a German or had a German last name, and you could be lynched same as a colored man. I never thought anyone'd make it out of that year alive."

"Your brother didn't," I said.

"Nope, he didn't," Talgart said.

"You ever have proof of that besides the car?" I asked.

"And that paper you just handed me?" Talgart said. "Not proof. But words."

"Words?" I said.

"About a week after the car got found, some of the Levee boys came to me and told me that I had to give them what was in Lawrence's apartment or else."

"Or else what?"

"You just dumb or do you like asking dumb questions?" He gripped the arms of that chair. "Or else I'd end up just like him. It was implied, but the implication was clear, just like yours was earlier."

I nodded. "Who were those Levee people?"

"Boys," he said. "That's what we called them. And they wasn't colored. They were whiter than white. They worked the area."

"For Colosimo?"

"Not on paper." Talgart shook his head. "Do I have to spell it out for you?"

"I'm afraid so," I said. "I know very little about that period in Chicago history."

"It ain't that different from now. Pay the right person and he'll look the other way. The city's corrupt down to its core, and what's interesting about that is this city don't try to hide it." He smiled. "I kinda like that."

"You're saying these 'boys' worked for the city?"

"I'm saying that if you think you're gonna solve my brother's murder from this distance and with your lack of understanding, you're not going to get nowhere." He pounded the flat of his hand against the upholstery. Dust and cat hair rose. "I'm saying the Levee boys was police officers, hired by the city, and paid by Colosimo and his ilk to look the other way."

I felt cold. I wasn't sure if his news upset me more because the corruption went back so far or because he did nothing about it in all his years on the force.

"Your brother was killed by policemen?"

He shrugged. "I don't know if they killed him or just pretended not to notice. Same thing, right?"

I guessed it was. And by not doing anything, he'd looked the other way too.

"Who were they?" I asked.

"A coupla losers named Rice and Dawley," he said. "But we always called them Friends of Gavin Baird."

My breath caught. Talgart looked pleased with himself. He watched me put all the pieces together.

"I didn't surprise you, then, when I mentioned Baird," I said.

"Nope," he said.

"You think Rice and Dawley killed your brother for Baird?" I asked.

"Dunno if it was intentional. Don't even really know if it was for Baird. Always thought that they probably roughed him up a little, trying to get the money, and he died along the way, but no one told me that. No one even implied it. Like I said, what I do know is that Rice and Dawley were Baird's personal security team. They were there when my brother died. They told me how he cried and begged them not to let him die."

Talgart said all of this in a flat voice.

"But what they did, what they saw, who did what to whom, I don't know. I don't care. Rice and Dawley ain't here no more and neither is Baird. I made it through forty-three years on the force and got threatened maybe four thousand times, and I decided it wasn't going to touch me. It never did."

It did touch him, whether he admitted it or not. He was one of the coldest men I'd ever seen.

"You never asked them about it?" I asked.

"Never wanted to," he said. "That little conversation was enough for me."

I let out a small sigh. I was never going to get past that statement. I didn't even know how to ask a question that would take me beyond that statement. Maybe Talgart didn't allow himself to think more about his own motivations than that.

"Did you give them the contents of the apartment?" I asked.

"I figured, what could it hurt? I didn't want none of that stuff. Most of it was either stolen or came from stolen money. I sure didn't want my ma to know about it."

"But you could've used the proceeds to bring her here sooner."

He eyed me as if he really couldn't figure out how the younger generation had gotten so stupid. "I didn't want her here, not till the whole thing with Lawrence blew over. And I told you. That stuff was stolen."

"So you have qualms about stolen goods, but you don't have qualms about working with the men who murdered your brother."

His face grew bright red. I'd never seen a transition like that; one moment his skin was grayish brown, and the next so red I thought he might have a heart attack.

"I didn't know if they murdered my brother. I told you that."

"But you suspected it. And they told you they were there. That makes them accessories."

"I know the goddamn law."

"Then why didn't you enforce it?"

He held out his hands. They were bent, the knuckles swollen with arthritis. "Do I look white to you?"

"You were a police officer. It was your job."

"It was theirs too, Mr. Morality."

"And they should've been taken off the force."

"It was 1919, you moron. Things only got worse in Chicago. And you think they take dirty cops off the force now? Hmmm?"

"That's your excuse?" I asked.

"Who's gonna listen to me? Especially then."

"How about the *Defender*? It was being read all over the country."

"And what woulda happened? Everyone woulda said tough luck.

Some stupid Nigra got himself caught skimming a rich white boy. What did he expect? And what can we do about it? Next page."

I stood up. I still had questions for him, but I couldn't sit with him any longer. He disgusted me, and he knew it.

"Besides," he said, his voice trembling with rage, "he wasn't worth it."

I looked at him. He was halfway out of that armchair, the blanket in a jumble on the floor. He hadn't talked about this in a long time, and he clearly felt the need to justify himself to me, somehow.

"Your brother wasn't worth the fight?" I asked.

"Maybe if he'd been some upstanding citizen, but he wasn't. He was a low skunk who hurt women and stole from people he shouldn't've. I tried to get him out of there. I tried to talk to him. He didn't listen. He laughed at me. He said it was rubes like me what got the short end, not a B.T.O. like him. He told me to crawl back in my hole and not bother him again, and I did it. I didn't want nothing to do with him, and if he was going to kill himself using a police-issue, it wasn't my problem."

I threaded my way through the slang, still standing. I hadn't heard a lot of it since I was a boy. "B.T.O.," I said finally. "A Big-Time Operator."

"You may be slow, but you ain't stupid." He lowered himself back into the chair. Either his anger was easing or he was getting tired.

"You expected him to suicide by cop?" I asked.

"I don't think it was that calculated, but yeah. I expected him to die in one of them shoot-outs that was becoming more and more popular. I didn't expect a quiet beating on a back road."

"You're sure that's what happened?" I sat down again as well.

"No, I'm not sure. I told you. I'm guessing. You don't think that's what happened, and you ain't revealing why."

"He was found with two other bodies," I said.

"You're admitting it's him now, not just using me as a means of identification."

"You said——"

"I know what I said," he snapped. "And you don't think he was beat to death."

"One of them had been shot in the head." I didn't know which one yet. I hadn't even thought to ask Minton if he knew.

"Shot." He leaned back, tilted his head away from me and looked at the empty television screen. I could see our reflections in it, distorted by the bubble-shape of the glass. I looked round with a small head and he looked thinner, as if he were being pulled in a thousand different directions.

"We think the other two were Zeke Ellis and Junius Pruitt."

He closed his eyes. "That explains it," he said in a small voice.

"Explains what?"

He opened his eyes, reached down, and pulled the blanket back over his legs. Then he smoothed it long after the wrinkles were gone.

"Explains why he begged for his life," Talgart said. "I always thought Lawrence woulda laughed when someone threatened to kill him. I knew he would've. I saw it once. So I couldn't understand why he begged."

"He would've begged for his friends?" That didn't sound like a hopeless case to me.

Something of that must have come through my voice because Talgart glared at me. "You're mighty judgmental, son."

"And you picked up some neat verbal tricks from your white colleagues," I said. "I'm not your son."

He tugged at the blanket, not looking at me any longer. "Those three were trouble together. Don't know why I hadn't thought of it, because Ellis disappeared right at the same time, and so did Pruitt. But their families had reasons for believing them gone. Never put it together."

"You think Rice and Dawley threatened the others, trying to get Lawrence to give them the money?"

He shrugged. "Or maybe give them some information, or maybe they were just playing. I don't know."

"But they didn't get the money," I said. "Did they find it in the search of the apartment?"

"I dunno," he said. "Didn't ask. But they laid offa me."

"I heard that Baird lost his fortune by then."

He grinned. The grin was a mean one. "Just cause his trained watchdogs found the money don't mean they gave it to him."

"They weren't well trained, then, were they?" I said.

"They were just like everyone else back then. Out for themselves."

Like you, I thought, but didn't say. I'd antagonized him enough.

"You said Rice and Dawley are dead," I said. "Is there anyone else still around who might know what happened?"

"Not that I know of." He gave me a superior little smile. It made my skin crawl. "You're such a hero. You got long-dead victims and long-dead perpetrators. It's ancient history, hero. No one cares."

"I care," I said as I stood and headed for the door. "Which is more than anyone could ever say about you."

FORTY-FIVE

I left, feeling very unsettled. I had driven nearly five blocks from Talgart's apartment before I realized that I hadn't asked him for Rice and Dawley's first names.

Talgart had gotten to me. He had intended to upset me, but he had upset me in ways that he hadn't even realized. He was the kind of man who had irritated me all my life: the grateful black man who had his job and his minimal acceptance in the white world, a man who was willing to bow and scrape and ignore to keep that relatively meaningless position.

He was a house nigger—which was exactly what Fred Hampton had called me when I had refused to take the Soto case. And *that* was what had upset me—a nagging feeling that I finally understood where Hampton had been coming from.

Talgart and I both knew the risks of getting involved in these cases, and we both knew there wouldn't be any rewards except the satisfaction of a job well done. And maybe not even that. Maybe the only satisfaction would be knowing what had happened, knowing down to the minute detail, rather than in broad strokes.

But Talgart had been trying to protect his work and himself. I had been trying to protect Jimmy. I would have argued with anyone that my reasons for staying away from the Soto case were better than Talgart's were for staying away from his brother's.

But were they? Hampton probably wouldn't agree. Hampton, who had a baby on the way and presumably a wife somewhere. He had already given up a scholarship to college to work for black people in his own way.

From his point of view, I hadn't given up anything.

He didn't know that I was living in Chicago under an assumed name, having abandoned my own family—my adopted parents, my friends, and my home in Memphis—to take care of a boy who wasn't even my blood child. That's why Jimmy came first. Because if our identities got revealed, he would die.

I didn't see anything similar in Talgart's life, but I was judging from fifty years distant. Fifty years distant and based only on an afternoon's conversation. A conversation that did reveal a family side to him as well.

He'd wanted to bring his mother and sisters here, and he hadn't done so until his brother's death. Talgart had said that Lawrence wouldn't beg for his own life, but he would beg for his friends. Given that, he might have begged for his family's too. And the only thing that had saved his brother Irving from the same fate that Junius Pruitt and Zeke Ellis had suffered was the fact that Irving Talgart had been a cop.

My hands were shaking on the wheel. I didn't remember the last few blocks I'd driven. There was no way to know other people, not deep down, not their motivations, not their rationalizations.

Talgart had been right. I was being judgmental, based on very little evidence. Just like Hampton had been with me.

There was an element of truth to Hampton's assumptions, and there was an element of truth to mine.

Just not the whole story.

About six blocks away from the Queen Anne, I finally remembered to look for a tail. I didn't see one, but that didn't mean a thing. I hadn't been watching, so I wouldn't know if the same car had been behind me for the last mile.

I went around two separate blocks, narrowly avoiding college students on bicycles hurrying toward their late-afternoon classes. Still no one. So I made my way to the Queen Anne, put on the coveralls inside the van—in the back, away from the windows—and hurried inside.

When I reached the secret room, I announced myself by saying, "Give me some good news."

LeDoux popped his head around a corner to my left. He was covered in brick dust that made his pinkish skin a deep red.

"We actually have some," he said. "With the exception of the body in B, all the others come with identification."

I blinked, not expecting that at all. I had feared that I would be spending weeks of my life following bread crumbs, just like I had the last few days.

Minton peeked out of E. He was covered in dust too, but he didn't look quite as sloppy.

"These guys were just tossed in here, wallets and all," he said.

"The last time the wallet didn't have any identification," I said.

"Driver's licenses," Minton said, as if they were the holy grail. "Sometime between Suite B and Suite C the state started requiring driver's licenses, and men started sticking them in their wallets."

"You're calling these things suites now?" I asked.

"It's better than using the word tomb. We could slip up in outside conversation, and then we'd all be in trouble."

"It looks like you got pretty far," I said. "I thought this would take you days."

"I left the skeletons for later," Minton said. "I photographed everything so far, but as for packing up, I'm doing the intact guys first."

I winced at the thought of those bloated, decaying corpses being considered "intact."

"Figure out yet how come some of these guys aren't as decayed as the others?" I asked. "Or is it a mystery like the way the decay worked with the letters?"

"The letters aren't a mystery," LeDoux said. "At least one was in that wallet, which protected it. The other one wasn't really close to the third body. It got protected by the wall and some other fiber, something I haven't identified yet."

How typical that he would answer the second question, which I had only meant as rhetorical, and ignore the first.

Minton waited until LeDoux was through, throwing me a private grin as he did. Then he said, "It's no mystery why these bodies are in different conditions. It's the same reason the walls were built differently."

I waited.

He smiled, a young, proud-of-himself smile. "C'mon, Bill. It's obvious if you think about it. They died at different times."

"I knew that. I know they weren't all killed together, because if they had been they'd've been buried together."

"No," Minton said. "Different times, meaning different decades. I figure the span between Suite A and Suite E over here has got to be at least thirty years, maybe more."

I felt slightly dizzy, as if I couldn't catch my breath. "What?"

"The guys in Suite E died ten to twenty years ago. The guys in Suite A died forty to fifty years ago."

"In 1919," I said. "They died in October of 1919."

"See how good you are without ID? Imagine how quickly you'll find out information when you actually have the victims' names."

Minton was still smiling, but I wasn't. I looked at all of those tombs and felt the dizziness increase.

I had thought I was actually onto something. I thought that Gavin Baird had worked his own scam or got his own revenge through his personal security team, Rice and Dawley, and for his own reasons, reasons we would never understand, buried them down here.

But Gavin Baird had died in the 1938. Thirty-one years ago.

"I thought this would please you," Minton said, apparently reading my reaction on my face.

"At first, I thought Hanley had done this. Then we figured out who was in A, and I realized that Baird had done it. Now you tell me that the guys in E died a minimum of eleven years after Baird." I glanced at LeDoux. "Could the skeletons we found in A have been moved?"

LeDoux shook his head. "Not in the last ten to twenty years. They died somewhere else and were moved to Suite A, but they decayed right there. And they were probably placed in there shortly after they died."

I didn't like the direction my mind was going in. Someone had known about this place—several someones, in fact. Maybe street gangs, maybe the Levee thugs, maybe Capone's boys. Certainly Baird's "security team" had known about it, but those corrupt police officers had died—if Talgart was to be believed—before Baird.

Vivienne Bontemps had said that Baird had lost his fortune. Talgart had said that he had lost five grand, which would have been a fortune to a prostitute in 1919, but would have explained how he kept his house.

I knew little about Baird and I hadn't tried to look. What I did know was pretty minuscule—he had remained single his entire life, he

274

loved to gamble, and he had been important enough to have police officers do his bidding. He had enemies, he was intemperate with money, and he professed to hate blacks. He also misused Vivienne Bontemps, which may have reflected his attitude toward women or, given that he might have known she was passing, his attitude toward blacks.

He had managed to keep his house after the "loss" of his fortune through the 1920s and into the Great Depression. He sounded like a young man in 1919 from the descriptions I heard, but I had no idea if that was the case. He died in 1938, not quite twenty years later, and I had no idea what he died of.

But I knew who could help me. A woman who loved this sort of research. A woman who specialized in the Levee. She might even know something about Baird, something she had come across in her various readings.

Serena Wexler.

FORTY-SIX

I had forgotten that I had told Serena Wexler I would return to the library that afternoon. So many things had happened since we first spoke, and my question—what was Calumet-214?—no longer mattered. I had gotten the answer.

But I felt relieved nonetheless that I would be able to see her. I had liked her. I wouldn't be able to bring her the matchbox like I'd promised, but I would show up just the same.

First, I had to help Minton remove some of the bodies. They were intact enough that he had put them in body bags. We draped the bags in a tarp and carried them out as if they were stacks of wood that we were trying to protect from the impending rain.

I hoped no one was watching too closely. Our behavior bordered on suspicious, and if Laura's employee had been right, the neighbors already worried about what we were doing.

Even though the following day was Saturday, Minton and LeDoux wanted to come back to the house. I promised to drive them—I only wanted the van here while they worked—but I wouldn't stay. I had promised the weekends to Jim, and I was going to keep that promise as much as I could.

We dropped off Minton and the bodies at Poehler's. Then LeDoux and I picked up Jimmy. Jim was excited about having dinner with Laura, and I had to admit that I was too. For the first time in a long time, it felt like we were going on an actual date, even though we weren't. Perhaps it was because it was Friday night, or maybe it was just wishful thinking on my part.

LeDoux wanted to talk to Laura as well, but I told him to call her. I had other stops before we went to her offices. I let him out near his apartment building, then backtracked to the library, parking in the same old spot.

I had an odd sense that I was still being followed, but not by someone as obvious as the FBI had been. Even though I hadn't seen cars for the last two days, I had that creepy, eyes-on-the-back-of-my-neck feeling that you sometimes got when people stared at you too long.

"How come we're parked here?" Jim asked as he plugged pennies in the meter for me.

"I've been doing it ever since those guys started to follow us," I said.

"I haven't seen them," he said. "They're not even at the school any more."

That made me look at him. "They were at the school?"

"Yeah. Every day somebody'd wait there and then follow us to the church for after-school. I thought you knew that."

I hadn't, even though it made sense. Two black sedans—one for the apartment because they knew I'd return to it eventually, and one for Jimmy because I'd return for him too.

"We all took turns watching them," Jim said as we walked to the library. "Keith wanted to go knock on their window and scare them, but I told him to stay away. Told him we didn't know who they were and they might hurt us if we got too close."

"Good thinking." I was taking slow, deep breaths, trying to force back my anger. If I had known those clowns had gotten that close to my son the day they spoke to me, I'd've taken them apart.

"It's okay, Smoke," Jimmy said, looking up at me. He could sense my change in mood. "They're not going to do nothing now."

"We don't know that," I said. "We're going to keep an eye out anyway."

We went up the stone steps into the library. Jimmy did what he always did in this place—looked up at the ceiling three stories above us. He loved the feeling of space and had told me, after we returned from Yale, that his favorite part of the campus had been the spectacular buildings. That was when I started to point out Chicago's spectacular buildings as well.

He wanted to go to the children's section, and I let him, promising to get him within the hour. Then I walked across the large lobby to the information desk, and Serena Wexler.

She was there, just like she'd promised she'd be. Her hair wasn't pulled back as tightly today, and she wore more makeup. Her dress was a pale peach, which was a better color for her skin tone. At first glance, she no longer seemed severe.

I hoped that she hadn't changed her look for me, and then I grinned at my own egotism.

"I was afraid you would be gone already," I said.

She smiled at me, and took her glasses off her nose. They hung on a pearl-studded chain that fell around her neck like a piece of jewelry. She did look amazingly good this afternoon.

"Was that your son I saw come in with you?" she asked.

"Yeah," I said. "I had to pick him up from school today, so I didn't have time to go home and get the matchbox."

Her smile faded just a little. She had been looking forward to my return, but to see a bit of history, not me.

"Well, that just gives you an excuse to come back," she said.

I nodded. I would have to figure out a way around that evidence bag.

"I guess we're even then," she said, "since I wasn't able to find that phone number."

"I did find it." I rested my hands against the polished marble surface of the information desk. She had a stack of books behind it, all of which looked older than both of us. "It was for the Everleigh Club."

"How did you find that?"

"I ran into an old woman who wanted to work there," I said.

Serena's eyes sparkled. "Now, why would she tell you that?"

I shrugged. "Why would you tell me about your fascination with the Levee?"

"You're just that kind of man, huh?" she asked.

"I guess," I said. "I still have some research I'm doing for my friend. Since you'd been so knowledgeable about the Levee before, I thought maybe you'd know this."

She rested a hand on those books. "Let's give it a try."

"You ever hear of a man named Gavin Baird?" I asked.

She thought for a moment, then shook her head. "Not once. He's not in the materials I read, that I know of. I'll look for him, though."

"Look for some friends of his too. Two policemen, one named Rice and the other named Dawley."

Her face lit up. "I don't have to look for them. That's Stanton Rice and Alfred Dawley. They're notorious."

She said the word "notorious" like it was a good thing.

"For what?" I asked, surprised that they were better known than Gavin Baird. Had I misjudged the relationship? Had the police officers been the ones in charge?

"They were so crooked, they outdid the crooks. They took payoffs from the entire Levee, said it was protection money. And they did protect. Their favorite method was to extort money from big winners of various card games—gin, poker, bridge. I heard they sometimes took as much as two thousand dollars a week off unsuspecting types, which was a lot of money in those days."

"I'd heard five thousand," I said.

"From your lady of the night?" Serena asked, that sparkle still in her eyes.

"*Ex*-lady of the night," I said. "She's a grandmother now."

Serena shook her head. "That's what I love about history. People become such different things as they get older. All those secrets."

"What were Dawley and Rice's secrets?" I asked.

"They were big rough-'em-up men. They didn't have a lot of secrets. Even the other cops knew to stay away from them and knew why." She frowned, then thumbed through her pile of books. A few titles caught my eye, but I didn't recognize the subjects. Then I saw *Gem of the Prairie* go by. That had been the book she'd recommended to me.

She stopped near the middle of the pile, looked in a battered old book with yellowing pages.

"Here it is," she said. "In the early twenties a reformer named Stuart Breen caught wind that Rice and Dawley had a dump site for the people they'd killed. Until then, everyone who crossed them just disappeared and people believed they had given them concrete boots and tossed them in Lake Michigan."

"Concrete boots?" I said.

She raised her head and grinned at me. "You're lucky I'm paraphrasing. This is a self-published book, a memoir of the gangster period, as the author called it, and I just love it. But to call the language colorful is a bit of an understatement."

I stood very still, trying not to let my curiosity overwhelm her. A dump site.

"Breen claimed it was on the South Side, that he'd actually seen them carry bodies to it in the middle of the night. He promised the *Chicago Evening Post* an exclusive story, but the day they were supposed to run it, they ran a retraction instead. Apparently Stuart Breen vanished a few days before. His family said he was murdered, but other witnesses say he ran off, afraid of Rice and Dawley."

"What does your author say?"

"My author coyly avoids the entire issue of what happened to Breen. My author knew Rice and Dawley, and occasionally acted—at least in this book—as if they're still alive."

"They're dead?" I asked, even though I knew they were.

"Oh, yeah," she said. "Theoretically, they died in a shoot-out with some of Capone's boys when they tried to confiscate some moonshine out of one of his South Side warehouses."

"Why do you say theoretically?" I asked.

"Because Capone always denied involvement."

I shrugged. "Why would he admit to the murder of two police officers, even corrupt ones?"

"Because a flat-out denial wasn't Capone's style," she said. "He was good at sideways stuff. He let people know when he did something he thought was in their best interest. And he could have made shooting two corrupt police officers sound like it was in people's best interests."

A body dump on the South Side. Rice and Dawley were friends of Baird's. I wondered if my scenario was right: they had helped Baird by killing Ellis, Talgart, and Pruitt, and they had taken the five grand as payment for doing so. Baird had made the tactical error of suggesting his basement as a dump site—or had Rice and Dawley suggested it so that Baird would get in trouble if the bodies were found? And then, somehow, Rice and Dawley had continued using the basement for their site through the twenties.

"Does your self-published author have a name?" I asked.

Serena flipped to the front of the book. "Twombly," she said. "Lloyd Twombly."

"Is he still around?" I asked.

"Oh, yes," she said. "That's how I got interested in the Levee in the first place. I couldn't believe the stories this little old man used to tell me when he'd come in here. I thought he was trying to shock me. Then he told me to read his book. He'd donated a copy to the library, and the head librarian took it because she considered it history of a period we didn't have a lot of first-person accounts for. I read it, and then I went to the other books and realized, if anything, Mr. Twombly was holding back."

"How do I find him?" I asked.

"He spends Sunday mornings in the newspaper room," she said. "He claims it's better than church."

FORTY-SEVEN

Laura met us in the lobby of the Sturdy building. She wore her rabbit-fur coat, which I hadn't seen since last winter, and her blond hair was piled high on top of her head. Her skirt was too short, her boots too high, and her makeup too pale. It looked like a rebellion outfit instead of something a woman who was trying to be taken seriously would wear.

"No more Model Cities people, huh?" I asked.

"I *hated* those people," she said, and grinned. "They were convinced I was some kind of front for the organization, as if Sturdy thought it could hide something behind a dumb female executive."

"I'm sure you set them straight," I said.

"I did." She put her arm around Jim and pulled him close. "I missed you, kiddo."

"Me, too," he said, his face so red I thought it was going to explode.

She handed me a key on its own ring and a number-ten envelope. "The address is inside," she said.

I pocketed the envelope and put the key ring on mine. Then we walked to dinner, which surprised me. I would've thought that we would go away from the downtown.

Until we went into the restaurant—a diner not too far from the Chicago Theater. It was filled with young people in blue jeans, longhairs, and mixed race couples.

"Thank the Conspiracy Trial," Laura said as we waited for a table. "You wouldn't believe the kind of people who've been hanging out downtown."

"Is it safe?" Jimmy asked me. Anyone else would have thought he meant being around hippies. I knew he meant being downtown, so close to the police and the FBI.

"No one important comes in here anymore," Laura said to Jim. She nodded at a balding man in a blue shirt and black pants. "See the manager? He wishes it were still as dead at night as it used to be."

The manager stood behind the cash register, which was next to a counter filled with people of indeterminate gender. The tables that went all the way around the counter were full too.

A waitress saw us, grimaced, and grabbed some menus. She led us all the way to the back, near the kitchen door, not because she disapproved (which she clearly did), but because that was the only available table.

Still, I looked around to make sure I didn't recognize any faces.

"Is this gonna be business, or can we talk about cool stuff?" Jimmy asked.

"How about both?" Laura said. "You first."

"No," he said. "You guys first. I gotta figure out what to order."

In a low voice, I told Laura the good and bad news—that our discovery predated her father's purchase of the building, but that the basement was being used illegally for years afterwards.

"You think he knew?" she asked.

"I don't know how he couldn't," I said.

She chewed the lipstick off her bottom lip.

"But I'm only guessing at this point," I said. "We may never know for certain."

"You keep saying that, and then we get more and more certain." Her gaze flicked to Jimmy, who seemed preoccupied with the menu. "My father couldn't have used that basement himself, could he?"

"I don't know." That thought had crossed my mind, and then I had ruled it out. Initially, it didn't seem like something Earl Hathaway would have done. Now, though, it made an odd kind of sense. If he had decided to become a thug, he had the perfect storage space.

"This is a mess no matter what," she said.

"Yeah," I said, "and it was a mess all the way back. I'll give you a fuller update later."

"When the kid's not here," Jimmy said. "Because, you know, it's all confidential."

"It is," I said. "There are some things you're better off not knowing."

"Then you shouldn't talk about them in front of me," he said, a little earlier than I expected. The waitress hadn't even taken our order yet.

I ignored that last comment. "Did you find out about Kaztauskis?"

"Loyal soldier to Cronk," she said. "He'd been doing yeoman's work for a long time. Nothing really identifiable. Mostly overseeing projects that existed only on paper. Needless to say, he's going to be one of the first to go in the next round of layoffs."

"Why not ask him to retire early?" I said.

"And give him a pension?" she said. "With all that I suspect he's done?"

"It might be better for the company," I said.

She grimaced. "I hate it when you think like a corporate man."

I grinned. "I'm practical."

The waitress hurried past us, setting three waters on the table as she whooshed by. Jimmy tried to catch her—he wanted to order so that he could eventually take over the conversation—but she didn't seem to notice.

"I don't think he's speaking for the neighbors," she said. "I think someone's noticed what you're doing. Someone who shouldn't."

I was afraid that would happen. I was amazed we'd had this much grace time.

"What are you doing?" Jim asked.

"Helping Laura," I said in my best imitation of my adopted father. That tone meant children-should-not-ask-questions-in-an-adult-conversation.

Jimmy flounced back in his chair.

"Do you think anyone is going to do anything about it?" I asked Laura.

Her lips thinned. "I got a personal phone call from Cronk just the other day."

"At the office?" I asked.

"At home," she said. "I think he's the one who's been hanging up on me."

My stomach clenched. "What did he say?"

"He asked if I had any questions for him." Two spots of color decorated her cheeks. "When I said no, as innocently as I could, he said I'd been in charge for nearly a year now and people would think that I knew more than I did. I asked him what that meant, and he laughed. He said I would know soon enough."

"He was threatening you."

Jimmy stopped fidgeting. "You gonna be okay?"

Laura smiled at him. "He threatened my reputation. He's too much of a coward to hurt me."

"Do you think he'll act?" I asked.

"Not until he's sure we have something," she said. "At least I hope so. I have a hunch he'll sic Kaztauskis on me before he does anything else."

"I hope you're right," I said. "But we'd better take precautions."

She laughed. "Smokey, we're taking all the precautions we can. If something comes out, I'll go after the messenger first. He's giving me some time to think about it."

Jimmy seemed reassured by her tone, but I wasn't. I knew this frightened her. It worried me.

"What about the mailman story?" I asked.

"So far as all my records go, it's accurate. I don't think it came from within the company."

"Where do you think it came from?" I asked.

"According to the records, we got a call from the local precinct asking if Hanley had listed next of kin with us."

"Had he?"

"He doesn't seem to have any. Our rental agency actually looked. The office manager over there is really quite a nice woman, unlike so many other Sturdy employees."

"This guy die?" Jimmy asked.

"Alone and unloved," I said. "It's a recommendation against living life as a mean SOB."

"Smokey!" Laura said with a smile.

I shrugged. "It's true. Everyone I talked to hated him. Even his mailman."

"I thought mailmen were supposed to be nice to everybody," Jim said.

"Me too," I said, thinking about what Laura had told me. The police station told them the mailman had found the body. Which meant I needed that death report from Sinkovich more than ever.

This was more police involvement. It was a pattern, one I didn't like.

FORTY-EIGHT

My Saturday started out good. Marvella watched Jim for an hour while I delivered LeDoux and Minton to the Queen Anne. Then Jim and I spent the morning and the early part of the afternoon running errands and living what I liked to call a Normal Life.

That normal life changed when I left Jim with Marvella for a second hour, and returned to the Queen Anne.

The lights were out and the basement door was locked. Neither man answered when I called for them. The hair on the back of my neck rose.

I walked around to the front of the building. The main door was open about a foot. My heart started pounding hard.

I didn't like this.

I went up the steps. The sharp odor of paint caught me, followed by voices. I pushed the door open.

Tarps covered the scuffed wood floor. LeDoux and Minton stood near the far wall. LeDoux was pouring paint into a tray, and Minton was rolling paint on the plaster, doing an adequate job. It would've looked better if the paint I'd bought, on sale, hadn't been a robin's egg blue.

"What the hell's going on?" I asked.

They both jumped as if I'd shouted at the top of my lungs. LeDoux set the can of paint down, wiped his hands on his coveralls, and came toward me, one blue-stained finger to his lips.

"He still out there?" he asked.

My stomach knotted. "Who?"

"There was a guy, claimed he wanted to buy the place," LeDoux said. He peered out the front door. "I don't see him."

I hadn't noticed anything, and I had been looking.

Minton balanced the roller on the edge of the tray, then joined us. He stepped outside, stretched on the porch as if he'd been working all day, and then came back in.

"Car's gone," he said.

LeDoux visibly relaxed. He walked over to the stairs, sat down, and covered his face with his hands. "I've never been so scared in my life."

"What happened?" I asked.

Minton pulled the front door closed. The paint smell grew sharper. "We were having lunch out back. We'd decided to go outside because that last body was whew!"

He raised his eyebrows and flapped his hand in front of his nose to accompany that descriptive non-description.

"This guy comes around the side of the building." LeDoux rested his arms on his thighs. He looked tired and pale, as if the strain had been too much for him. "He's big—"

"White," Minton said.

"Crew cut," LeDoux said.

"Mean-looking," Minton added. "Little piggy eyes."

"Strapping shoulders," LeDoux said. "Like he'd been in a lot of fights."

I nodded.

"He comes up," Minton said.

"Talks to me and completely ignores Tim, like he's not even here." LeDoux's mouth tightened in disgust.

"Like I'm the ignorant help," Minton said.

"And he asks when Sturdy's putting the building up for sale."

"Sturdy?" I asked. "Not even the mailman knew who owned the building."

"I remembered that," LeDoux said, "and before I could answer, Tim said—"

"I told him we were just painters and we didn't know nothing."

288

"He said it that way too, as if he'd never opened a book in his life," LeDoux said.

"The guy still ignored me," Minton said. "He looked right at Wayne here, and said in this tone of utter contempt—"

" 'You haven't spent these last few weeks painting, have you? No one takes that long to paint a house.' " LeDoux managed to catch both the contempt and a bit of a South Side Chicago accent.

"I said it does when you gotta sand and spackle. The house's been settling for a hundred years. And he still didn't look at me. He said to Wayne, 'You let this boy do all the talking?'

"And I said, 'I work for him. You have a problem with that?' " LeDoux's face was even paler. I could see how much this cost him. "And he said to me, 'I wouldn't work for him.' And I said, 'Your loss.' "

"He wasn't interested in the building, that was for sure," Minton said. "He was interested in us."

"Thank God we were covered in dust from the mortar. I'd had Tim helping me remove some bricks this morning. We wanted to see what was behind Suite B."

"What was?" I asked.

LeDoux shook his head slightly. "Just what we were afraid of. More."

"I figure the tombs go all the way back. There're probably a bunch of bodies underneath us right here. It'll take weeks to get to them," Minton said.

I sighed. It didn't sound like we had weeks. "So how did you get rid of the guy?"

"I asked him for a business card," Minton said. "I told him that we'd have someone call him."

"He clearly didn't have a business card," LeDoux said. "He ignored Tim and told me he'd come back when we were done. Then he asked when I thought that would be."

"That's when I shrugged," Minton said, "and told him we got paid by the hour."

In spite of myself, I laughed. Minton let this intruder think that they were working slowly and unsupervised so that they could make as much money as possible.

"The thing was," Minton said, "when we finally got rid of him, he just walked across the street and sat down on the curb. So we decided we had to make it look like we were painting."

"The only place I could think of that wasn't connected to the crime scenes was out here," LeDoux said.

"So there I am, carrying tarps and paint buckets through that stinky manager apartment, up that horrible staircase, and down the front. That was something. I don't envy you going through everything in there."

"See why I've been putting it off?" I asked.

Minton nodded.

"Did you have any idea who he was?" I asked.

"Not a clue," LeDoux said. "I'd never seen him before."

I looked at Minton. "I hadn't seen him before either. But he didn't look like a guy who wanted to buy an apartment building. And once he started into the questions, it was clear he wanted us out of here."

"Was he older?" I asked, thinking of Kaztauskis.

"Hell, no," Minton said. "He was my age."

"There was something menacing about him," LeDoux said, "and if you ask me to describe it, I couldn't. It was the way he stood, the way he looked at us, the way he treated Tim—"

"He wanted to scare us," Minton said.

"It worked," LeDoux said.

"You think he'll be back?" I asked.

Minton glanced at the door, as if he were considering. "He wanted us to know he's keeping an eye on this place. I think if he wanted to hurt us, he would've done it."

"He wants us out of here, that much was clear," LeDoux said. "But what he'll do to get rid of us, I can't say."

"Since he knows about Sturdy," Minton said, "I think he'll go through channels—back channels—and put some pressure there."

"He doesn't think we found anything," LeDoux said. "That was also clear. He almost relaxed when Tim mentioned being paid by the hour."

I smiled at Minton. "Good thinking."

"You warned me people might ask questions. I just figured I'd better have some answers."

I nodded. "They've officially put us on notice. Someone's watching us. I wondered if that was going to happen."

"Doesn't it worry you?" LeDoux asked.

"Yeah," I said. "But I have a hunch the threat won't be to us."

Minton frowned, but LeDoux tilted his head as if he were considering.

"You're worried about Miss Hathaway."

I nodded.

"You think someone'll hurt her?" He sounded almost like Jimmy.

"Not physically," I said.

LeDoux waited. Then, when I didn't elaborate, he said, "You're not going to tell me any more, are you?"

"It's better if you don't know," I said.

He let out a small, humorless laugh. "Last week, I would have agreed with you. Now I want to know everything."

"Someday," I said, making a promise I wasn't sure I could fulfill. "I'll tell you as soon as I can."

FORTY-NINE

LeDoux stayed up front and painted while Minton and I loaded the day's bodies into the van. We had three in body bags and five more boxes of carefully packed skeletal remains.

"I think it's best if I do as much here as I can," Minton said. "Get this done as fast as possible."

"You think they'll be back," I said.

"I do," he said. "and I think the longer we take, the more hostile they'll become."

"You were worried he was going to hurt you?" I asked.

Minton nodded. That surprised me, even though he had said the man was menacing. I still didn't expect a physical threat here.

"I can take care of myself," Minton said. "But Wayne can't."

I nodded. "We might need a new cover story."

"You might need to get that from your lady boss at Sturdy. She might have to head them off, give us a little more time."

"I'll talk to her," I said. Maybe she could make a comment to that Kaztauskis, after we come up with something. We didn't discuss a new cover story last night, and we had planned to, but Jim ended up dominating the conversation, and Laura and I didn't mind. I liked being more relaxed with her. I liked the comfortable feeling we were returning to.

We locked up the van, got LeDoux and his two boxes of evidence, then drove to the new building. It wasn't far from Poehler's. It was at the end of a row of warehouses, not too far from the steel mills on the South Side.

We went inside and found three rooms and the rest warehouse space. LeDoux was pleased, Minton less so. They had suggestions, which I was to pass along to Laura. The warehouse was set up for a refrigeration unit—a large one, the kind restaurants used—but didn't have one. We'd have to get one installed for Minton, and he also needed a walled-off work area.

We decided not to store any evidence here until the workers finished redoing the interior.

LeDoux said he'd keep the evidence he brought in his apartment. After the interaction with the stranger that afternoon, both LeDoux and Minton wanted as much removed from the building as possible.

I had a hunch my next few days would be a combination of interviews and work at the Queen Anne, probably in Hanley's disgusting apartment. I mentally braced myself for the task.

I was glad the baseball games were over. I would probably have to spend more time working on this case than I wanted to. We had a time pressure that I hadn't felt before.

My journey around Chicago had taken an hour and a half longer than I had expected. When I got back to the apartment, Marvella was sitting at my kitchen table with Jimmy and Jack Sinkovich. Sinkovich clutched a can of beer, Marvella was drinking hers from one of the jelly glasses I'd saved, and Jimmy was drinking from a can of Coke.

The apartment smelled of pizza and Sinkovich's disgusting after-shave.

"Took you long enough," Sinkovich said, tilting his chair back on two legs. He wasn't a small man, and the movement put a lot of strain on my cheap furniture. "I'm saying it because the lady's been wondering about it and she's too much of a lady to say something to you."

Marvella gave him a fond grin. They'd met in passing before, but so far as I knew had never had an interaction, I wouldn't have thought they would get along—in the past, Marvella had gone out of her way to make any whites who showed up at my apartment uncomfortable.

"Jack was telling me and Marvella about the trial," Jimmy said. He sounded excited.

Sinkovich's pale cheeks turned a light pink. "I only been saying what's in the papers."

"What trial?" I asked.

"There is only one trial in Chicago right now, Bill," Marvella said. "Haven't you been paying attention?"

"The Conspiracy Trial?" I said. "I've been trying not to."

I pushed the door to my apartment closed, hung up my coat, and walked into the kitchen to wash my hands. I would have liked a shower after all that body removal, but since I suddenly found myself to be entertaining guests, I figured I'd be somewhat social. The need for a shower was more psychological than physical anyway.

"How come my kitchen smells like pizza?" I asked.

"Because Jack brought three pizzas," Marvella said, "and I went to my place, got us some pizza trays, and we've been keeping them warm."

"Which is why she's been worrying," Sinkovich said. "She's afraid the pizza's getting dried out."

"Pizza's good no matter how it is," Jimmy said loyally. He and Sinkovich had words last year, and since then they'd been sort-of friends.

"You run into trouble?" Marvella asked me, and her question seemed pointed. Was she thinking of the Panthers? If so, it was good of her to keep that part of things quiet.

"No," I said. "I just had to make one more stop than I'd planned on and it was clear across town."

"You coulda called," Jimmy said, and the inflection was such a perfect imitation of Sinkovich that I knew where Jimmy had gotten the idea.

"I could have," I said. "Finding a pay phone would've added another fifteen minutes on my arrival time."

I took some plates out of the cupboard, then ripped up some paper towels as napkins. Marvella got up and took one of the pizzas out of the oven. It was pepperoni and sausage, and it looked like it hadn't dried out yet. Sinkovich had gone out of his way to get the pizza too—the pepperoni and sausage looked homemade, not like the mass-manufactured kind most pizza places bought.

"Three pizzas're a little excessive, don't you think?" I asked Sinkovich.

He shrugged. "Jim's a growing boy. I could pack away an entire pizza by myself at his age."

"Don't give him ideas," I said, and then grinned at Jimmy, who had already taken three pieces in the time it had taken me to grab a can of beer out of the refrigerator.

"Beer?" Sinkovich said. "The world must be ending. I thought nothing so crass would touch your lips."

"It sounded good," I said, thinking crass was appropriate right now. I sat down, took two large pieces, and tucked in. This was perfect, better than I could've expected. Jim and I hadn't been eating well lately, and for once I didn't care. Food was food, and pizza was even better.

For the first hour, we talked and laughed and gossiped. Sinkovich had dozens of stories about the Conspiracy Trial, some quite funny.

"I ain't supposed to talk about it," he said, "but screw them. They're not following the rules, so I'm not gonna either."

"Is that right?" Jimmy asked me. "Can you break the rules when other people do?"

"Jim hasn't read Emerson yet, has he?" Marvella said, surprising me.

"I think it's Thoreau," I said, "and no, I don't think teaching budding teenagers about civil disobedience is always a good idea."

"Bull pucky." Sinkovich took the last piece of pizza, then took the tray and, without standing up, set it in my sink. "Kid, sometimes there're rules you follow and sometimes there aren't. Your dad knows this. He knows about Dr. King. And the good doctor, he broke a lotta laws. Went to jail a few times for it too."

"You're saying that telling us about the Conspiracy Trial is the equivalent of breaking segregation laws?" I asked.

Sinkovich's grin faded. "Guess I am. Those bastards—pardon my French—think they own the world."

"I'm pretty sure coming to court under guard has changed their minds about that," I said.

"I don't mean the defendants, Grimshaw. I mean the prosecutor, the goddamn judge, and the assholes lying on the stand." He bowed at Marvella. "Excuse the language."

"Why?" she said. "Mine's worse."

"But Jim's isn't yet," I said. "Let's be careful, shall we?"

"It doesn't matter to me," Jimmy said with a grin. "I like French."

Sinkovich got up and took the second pizza out of the oven. He set the tray on the nest of hotpads Marvella had built, then gave us each another piece, before adding to his own pile.

"They got me and four others sitting in there day after day, undercover, you know why?"

I shook my head. I couldn't imagine why they would want five undercover cops in the courtroom.

"They say it's because they need help when those kids get out of hand. They say they're expecting riots inside the courtroom."

I had seen a shooting inside a courtroom. I would've expected something like that in the trial of the Chicago Eight.

"You don't?" I asked.

"Hell, half those kids think it's theater, and two of them are just plain confused. Only one of the white kids seems real serious about it—and he's not a kid. He's the old guy, what's his name? Dillinger?"

"Dellinger," Marvella said quietly. Obviously she'd been following the trial too.

"But that black kid, Seale. Man, he's the only one who's been respectful, standing every day when the judge comes in, yessir and nossirring him, and the judge is treating him like dirt. Worse than dirt, not letting him have a lawyer or speak up for himself. Which ain't legal, by the way. I asked some lawyer friends of mine. They're part of that national group of lawyers that's been calling for a mistrial."

"Jack told us how they tried to talk to the court yesterday," Jimmy said, his mouth full of pizza.

The sense of relaxation had left the room. Sinkovich was unhappy about all of this, and the feeling radiated. Jimmy didn't seem to notice, but he was the only one.

I didn't need any more tension in my day, and I was about to ask him to change the subject when Marvella said, "Tell Bill why you think you're there, Jack."

Sinkovich nodded, then ran a hand through his thinning blond hair. "I don't think it's coincidence that the five of us who gotta wear a suit and tie every day and scatter ourselves around that room were the five who wouldn'ta lied on the stand if we were called."

The tension increased. "Lied about what?" I asked.

"What you yelled at me about after the Democratic National Convention. What got me thinking about what I was doing in the first place. Birdshot in our gloves, going out there to beat up the kids and start the riots ourselves, the speeches the bosses gave before the cops headed out to Grant Park those days. All the stuff the defense claims happened, which did happen, which half the cops on the stand and more than half the officials've been lying about, saying none of it happened."

He was getting red. We had had a fight back then. I'd told him exactly what I thought of a cop who would beat up an unarmed student. Sinkovich actually listened to me, which was the beginning of his transformation from a guy who went along with department policy, whatever it was, to a guy who stood up for what he believed was right, no matter what the cost.

"Thing is," he said, "we got the assignment before we know what it is, before we can say no. I'm hearing undercover, which after being at a desk for almost a year is like a blessing. *Then* when we show up, in our suits and stupid neckties, we get told where to sit. First day of testimony—because you know what? If we hear the testimony, we ain't gonna be considered good witnesses. They deliberately contaminated us. Deliberately."

I wasn't sure he took a breath throughout the entire speech. Jimmy finished two more pieces of pizza while he listened, but Marvella watched, spellbound. I wasn't even appalled any more. On the scheme of what I was dealing with, this seemed relatively minor.

"Which brings me to what I gotta talk to you about," he said to me. "Can we go to your office?"

"Sure." I got up. Marvella picked up her dishes. I waved her away. "Leave them. You've done enough. You're welcome to stay. I don't think this'll take long."

She smiled at me. "If you don't mind."

"I don't mind," I said, "and I'm not sure Jim's done with his entire pizza yet."

"I get hungry," he said.

"It's not a competition. Just because Sinkovich could eat an entire pizza at your age doesn't mean you have to."

And with that I went to my office. It was the smallest bedroom in the apartment. I had crammed a desk, credenza, and some filing cabinets in there. They were the nicest furniture we owned, all thick, polished, blond wood. I sank in my heavy metal desk chair. Sinkovich took the wooden table chair across from me.

"Before I forget, I got your report." He had been carrying his coat. He slipped his hand underneath it and pulled out a manila file.

"You brought the actual report?" I asked.

He shrugged. "No one else's using it. Give it to me next week."

He set it on the desk.

"That's not what you wanted to talk to me about?" I asked.

He shook his head. "I got issues," he said. "I got the divorce—my wife, she found some guy who's convinced her he's in love with her, and he wants to take her and my kid to Northern Minnesota, if you can believe it."

"I thought you said Wisconsin."

He frowned at me. "What's the difference? It ain't Chicago. My attorney says I don't got much to fight with. My job's hanging by a string, and if I lose it, I can kiss any chance of taking the kid bye-bye. Then there's the issue of me. I wasn't the best father in the first place, and I ain't sure I can do it alone."

"You want me to advise you on how to raise a child alone?" I asked. "Jim was a lot older when he moved in with me than your son is."

"No," Sinkovich said. "I know my limitations. I don't even got family close."

"You're gonna give in," I said.

"I'm gonna make the right decision for my son. If he can have a real family and me, y'know, summers or something, then that's maybe the best. She ain't staying here. That much I know. It's either her family in Wisconsin or Northern Minnesota, and if I follow her, I got nothing."

"Except your family," I said.

"Not even that. She says she'll make it real hard on me if I do that. She wants out. She means to get it however. That can't be good for my kid." He was shaking. This was hard for him, and he clearly had been thinking about it. "My lawyer says I can split Christmas and Easter with her fifty-fifty, then get all the other holidays and summer too, if I just play ball. That's like half the year in little chunks."

I nodded, wondering how this concerned me.

"If I do that," Sinkovich said, "I don't need this cocksucking job no more. I can resign and tell these motherfuckers what I think of their games and their lies and the way they treat the people they're supposed to protect."

He had obviously been doing a lot of thinking. He had lines on the sides of his face that hadn't been there before. His hair was nearly gone and he looked older—as if the past year had been harder on him than any other in his life.

"What would you do?" I asked.

"That's where you come in." He rubbed the side of his nose nervously, then looked out my window as if there was no more interesting view than the side of the neighboring apartment building.

"Me?" I asked.

He nodded, still not looking at me. Then he took a deep breath. "I'm wondering if maybe we can join up, you know, two detectives. Rent an office not far from here, work together. You need help. You got the kid most of the time, and you can't be everywhere all the time. Then when my kid comes, I got back-up, you know? We trade off."

The pizza I ate turned into a lead ball in my stomach. "I've never worked with anyone."

"I been a cop my whole life," he said. "My dad was a cop. My grandpa too. We'd be learning how to do this business thing together."

"It takes money management," I said. "Some months you don't get paid at all. And an ability to keep a secret."

He flushed. "Which I wasn't doing out there because I was pissed off."

"Yeah," I said. "That worries me."

I didn't want to say no outright. This man had been trying very hard this past year and everyone had rejected him for doing the right thing. I didn't want to, but I didn't want to work with him either.

"I got department contacts, like a million of them, guys who'd be willing to give me information even if I'm not on the force. There're a lot of disgruntled guys out there who need an outlet, maybe someone to take a few cases the police ignore, you know? We'd get those. I know the city better than most. I grew up here. My grandparents grew up here. I went to school with half the mayor's office. I'd be willing to be the junior guy, the trainee, you know? And if you need an investment up-front, I got some savings. I could rent the office."

He said all that in a rush. I stared at him. He fidgeted in the chair, knowing that I was as uncomfortable as he was.

But he had some points. I had trouble working alone. In the past I'd hired Malcolm Reyner to help me on some cases, but Malcolm got drafted this summer and wouldn't be back from his tour for more than a year. I didn't know a lot of people in the city, and I certainly didn't know a lot of white people.

Sinkovich was the extent of my police-department contacts these days, and as he said, he was on the outs. With his attitude, he might get fired before he quit.

But there were a lot of disadvantages, including his volatility, his family situation, and the fact that he had never lived without a paycheck. Not to mention his inadvertent racism and my inability to trust someone one hundred percent.

"Why do you want to work with me?" I asked. "Why not do it on your own? Or go with one of the big white firms in town? They'd be happy to have an ex-cop on their force, and they could pay you a salary."

"I'd be lying if I said I didn't think about both those things," he said. "But most of those firms, they do shadier stuff than the cops do. And I don't like them. Hell, I busted half of them."

"I do shady things," I said, hoping I wasn't saying too much. "It's part of the job."

"You do shady things for the right reasons," Sinkovich said. "You're a stand-up guy, and you been showing me there's other ways to be, you know? You got an open mind. And you can't be bought. I don't want to be bought neither."

"You think you would be if you worked for the other detective agencies?"

"Hell, half of them are owned already."

"What about working for yourself?"

He took a deep breath. "I'll be honest. Working for myself scares the crap outta me. Maybe we could say I'm training, huh, and then I could see if I like this."

"And if you don't? You've already resigned, you've lost your pension, you won't be a cop any more. You'd have to do something else."

"Yeah, like nighttime security at the steel mills or something. I can do that. But I want to try this first."

It would be a crime to let Sinkovich work a security job at a steel mill. He did have a good investigative mind.

"Don't say no right away," he said. "Think about it, okay? I mean, give it a chance."

I could do that. "How much time do I have?"

"As much as you need," he said. "I can stay with the force if I gotta. I'm gonna decide the family thing no matter what. But if I'm gonna be the kinda guy who can make my kid proud, I'm not sure it can be as a Chicago cop no more."

"That's a sad statement," I said.

"But it's true," he said. "It's fucking true."

FIFTY

After Marvella and Sinkovich left, I assigned Jimmy kitchen clean-up and went back to my office to read the death report. The file folder held three standard pieces of paper, just like I expected—the incident report, the coroner's report, and a death certificate.

Before he left my office, Sinkovich tapped the file on my desk and said, "One thing you need to know. The guy who answered the call? I'd call him one of Them."

Meaning Sinkovich didn't trust him and thought the cop could be bought off. It was a good thing to know, because it affected the reliability of the report.

The death certificate was on top. It was a carbon of a carbon, so faint that it was almost impossible to read. But it did certify that Mortimer Hanley had passed from this world on September 15, 1969. The coroner's report was less precise, claiming Hanley died in the weeks before September fifteenth, the exact date impossible to determine, given the condition of the apartment where he was found and the excessive heat of the last few days before his body was discovered.

There was no autopsy. The coroner guessed that Hanley died of natural causes, and then checked off the box that said no autopsy had been requested.

The incident report was a lot more interesting. It said that the mailman had gone into Hanley's bedroom to drop off the mail, and found the man dead. Then the mailman used the apartment's phone to call an ambulance.

There was no interview or incident report with the ambulance drivers, which made sense, since everyone thought Hanley had died of natural causes.

But the report made me wonder.

There were a lot of errors, inconsistencies, and missing information for a page-long typewritten report. First of all, the mailman's name wasn't listed. Not anywhere in the document. It wasn't in the coroner's report nor anywhere in the file.

Secondly, anyone who smelled that empty apartment wouldn't have casually walked into that bedroom when the body was still inside. The stench had to have been infinitely worse. Add to that the fact that the heat was on full blast in the middle of a fall heat wave, and the stink had to be unbearable.

Anyone with half a nostril would have opened that door, smelled what was inside, and fled, using a phone in a neighboring building or down the street.

Thirdly, if it was the mailman's custom to walk into the apartment and drop off the mail in the bedroom, how come he hadn't done it the previous eight to ten days that Hanley's body had lain on that bed? How come he'd only done it the once?

And finally, if this was a substitute mailman, where had he come from? I'd spoken to the post office, and the person on the other end of that phone had had no reason to lie to me. Carter Doyle had worked every single day in September, and wouldn't ever have entered Hanley's apartment, not to deliver mail, and certainly not in that stench.

Sinkovich had said the cop who completed the report—presumably the cop who had arrived on scene when "the mailman" had called the police—wasn't trustworthy. In fact, Sinkovich's comment assumed that the cop would lie.

So the question was, who was he lying for? Himself? Or someone else who found the body? Someone who paid him to keep his mouth quiet?

I looked at the name typed beneath the illegible signature. Herman Faulds. I'd never heard of him, but that meant nothing. Chicago had over five thousand police officers on the payroll.

I wondered if I could talk to him without revealing what my mission was about.

This was where Sinkovich would actually come in handy. He could ask questions about this case without raising suspicions at all, maybe even after he had retired.

I sighed, unable to believe I was actually considering his proposal.

I was also unable to believe what I saw on the report in front of me.

The death certificate had a firm date on it. The coroner was more circumspect, but he too had used the same date.

September fifteenth.

I looked at my notes from Laura's accounting books.

Back in the 1940s, that extra rent payment came into Sturdy's accounts on the fifteenth of every month.

The person who had found Hanley was the same one who'd been paying him off.

And that person was important enough—or rich enough—to get Herman Faulds to falsify his police report.

I was one step closer, but I wasn't quite sure what I was closer to.

FIFTY-ONE

I spent most of the following morning ferrying people all over Chicago. Jimmy and I were running late, so I called the Grimshaws and told them to meet him at church. Then I took Jimmy, in his Sunday best, to Poehler's with me, where we picked up Minton on the way to Sunday services.

While Minton put on his coveralls, I dropped Jimmy at the church's back door. Then Minton and I went uptown to get LeDoux, who was waiting for us outside his favorite restaurant. The three of us went back south to the Queen Anne.

I dropped them off, promising to return after my interview with Twombly, the self-published writer. I figured that wouldn't take very long, no matter what he had on Gavin Baird, and then I would be back.

I would finally do the task I was dreading: I would go through the files in Hanley's odor-filled apartment. I warned LeDoux about that and told him to get what evidence he could off those file drawers.

He shot me a contemptuous look and told me to wear gloves.

I knew then that it was going to be a long day.

By the time I got to the library, a conventional white Sunday service would have been half over. Thank heavens Althea Grimshaw believed in good, old-fashioned preaching. Lately, Althea had said she felt the need for a lot of the Lord's word.

Jimmy would be hallelujahing and praising Jesus for hours. Then he'd go to the Grimshaws for dinner, which might even give me time for a shower before I picked him up.

I was already looking forward to that shower as I walked into the library. That told me just how much I was dreading my time in Hanley's apartment.

Serena Wexler wasn't at the information desk, but Lloyd Twombly was exactly where she'd said he would be: in the leather, overstuffed chair near the arched windows of the newspaper room, the week's newspapers from the *New York Times* to the San Francisco *Examiner* in a pile around him.

He was a small white man with snow-white hair. He wore spats and a brown suit that was older than I was. A bowler sat on the edge of the marble table that held his week's worth of newspapers. When I sat down near him, I caught the faint scent of mothballs.

He looked up from last Sunday's *Los Angeles Times* and frowned at me. "This table's taken."

His face seemed slightly deformed and it took me a moment to realize why. His right ear had cauliflowered. Someone had once beaten him so badly that the ear was destroyed. Several smaller scars disappeared under his collar, some of them looking like the work of an intent person with a knife or a straight razor.

"Mr. Twombly?" I extended my hand. "I'm Bill Grimshaw. Serena Wexler told me I could find you here. I found some items that date back to 1919, and she told me you can give me the history of the people involved."

His expression softened just a little, but his blue eyes remained cold. He touched the left side of his face.

"Knife fight?" he asked, referring to my scar.

I nodded, then touched the right side of my neck. "Looks like you were in one too."

He grinned. It was an impish grin, a boyish grin that made me understand why the library had taken a self-published book, and why Serena Wexler had known where to find him.

"We must be great fighters," he said. "We both survived."

A woman three tables down rose slightly out of her seat and shushed us. Twombly glared at her, and she sat back down.

"Guess we can't talk here. You buy me breakfast, I'll tell you everything you want to know about Big Jim, Al Brown, and the rest of them."

"Al Brown?" I asked.

"Capone back in the day. Before he got so famous."

Another woman rose from a seat farther back—I hadn't even seen her—and shushed as well.

"Breakfast it is," I said.

He closed the L.A. *Times* and slid it back on the dowel. Then he shoved the other papers to the edge of the table and said to me in a conspiratorial whisper, "Hardly any staff today. I doubt anyone'll have touched the papers when I get back."

He grabbed his bowler and led me out of the library and down the Loop to a restaurant I hadn't even noticed before. It was hidden between two of the larger department stores, and looked like it had been there since the Chicago Fire.

I had to struggle to keep up with him. He walked very fast, and as he opened the door to the restaurant, he gave the man behind the counter a two-finger salute.

"Usual, Manny. And whatever my friend wants too."

The man behind the counter nodded, then turned and shouted something in a language I didn't recognize. From the kitchen came the sizzling sound of meat slapping on a grill.

"If you don't know what to get," Twombly said, as he slid into a booth toward the back, "get the potato pancakes. Me, I'm having them after my hamburger steak. Since you're buying."

I nodded and wondered how much this would cost me. I also wondered if it would be any good. We were the only two customers on a Sunday morning, which didn't seem like a recommendation.

He slid a greasy menu at me. The owner came by with two cloudy glasses of water and some good, strong coffee. I ordered a fried-egg sandwich, figuring no one could ruin eggs fried hard.

"So who're you trying to find out about?" he asked.

I decided to ease my way into the information. "Serena told me about Big Jim and the Everleigh sisters. The Levee sounded like an interesting place."

"It was," he said. "I only caught the end of it, and I was a bit young for the Everleigh Club, but I reaped the benefits anyway, if you know what I mean."

Then he winked at me, and I had to sit through fifteen minutes of stories about famous ladies of the night and how well trained they were. Halfway through that long speech, I realized he thought I was as interested in the female side of vice as Serena Wexler had been.

I let him think so.

Then, after we'd spent some time comparing vice in the Levee to vice in the bootleg era, I said, "I've been hearing some stories about a man named Gavin Baird."

Twombly used the arrival of our meals to cover his reaction, but I still saw his features twitch with surprise. "How'd you hear about Baird?"

"Apparently he hung out with two cops, men named Rice and Dawley. I was actually looking into them when I learned that Baird lost five grand in a single night, and yet somehow remained flush. That caught my attention."

The smile had left Twombly's face. "There're some things I didn't put in my book, you know? Things that echo through the generations."

I added ketchup to my fried-egg sandwich, pretending that I didn't see his reaction. "Well, Baird's been dead over thirty years. I doubt he echoes."

Twombly set his fork down. "What do you really want?"

He saw through me. Not many people did.

"I need someone to level with me," I said, dropping my pretense at innocence as well. "I need to know what Baird was into."

"Because?"

"Because if it's what I think it is, it might echo through the generations and hurt a friend of mine."

He pulled his plate closer, as if protecting it from me. "In my day, we wouldn'ta done nothing for a nigra."

My cheeks warmed, and I had to remind myself he hadn't been bothered by my skin color when we met. He was obviously trying to bait me, and he had done it because he didn't want to talk about Gavin Baird.

"This isn't your day," I said. "It's mine, and I'm buying your meal."

He clung to the plate. He might have known a lot of things, but he clearly didn't have a lot of money. This meal mattered to him.

"There's no one here but us," I said. "You can tell me and it won't go any further."

"Sure it will," he said.

"If it does," I said, "I can promise that I won't mention your name."

"You want to know about Baird?"

"Yeah," I said.

"And Dawley and Rice?"

"Yeah."

"And what come after?"

"Yeah."

He nodded. "Then you buy me a week's worth of meals."

He had done this before—not over meals, but over information. How strange it must have seemed to him now to sell information for food.

"Today's lunch and tonight's dinner," I said.

"A week's worth of dinners," he said.

"Today's lunch, tonight's dinner, and tomorrow's lunch," I said.

"A week's worth of lunches. That's twenty dollars if you pay Manny here ahead."

"He wouldn't just pocket the money?" I asked.

"He's okay like that," Twombly said.

I leaned forward, grabbed my wallet, and pulled out a twenty. I'd been planning to use that for new clothes for Jim.

I slid the twenty across the table but kept my fingers on it. "You can decide where you go to lunch."

He reached for the twenty and I pulled it back.

"After you tell me about Gavin Baird, Rice and Dawley, and what came after."

He looked down at the cash, then sighed a little and picked up his fork as if the money didn't matter to him. "Gavin Baird. Only surviving son of the Kenwood-Hyde Park Bairds, a family that got most of its money in the upscale rebuilds after the Great Fire."

I nodded. Upscale rebuilds meant they rebuilt homes for the wealthy at a huge price.

"There were daughters, but they only got a portion of the fortune, more if they married well. I don't know what happened to them. Gavin got the house, the business, which he promptly sold, and all the rest of the inheritance. He spent most of it gambling at Everleigh, and when that closed, he went to private games."

None of this surprised me.

"You was right, he lost big one night in 1919, lost big, claimed he was cheated, and happened to be playing against a nigra dealer and his nigra partner."

"You can stop using the word now," I said. "I get your point."

308

"I can use any damn word I want," he snapped. "You're the one who's here for information."

"You're the one who needs lunch," I said.

His eyes narrowed, and he sucked in air as if he were preparing to launch himself across the table at me. Then he flattened his hands on the Formica surface. They were big hands, as scarred as his neck, and they still had strength in them. Those were the kind of hands that could choke a man and not even feel sore afterwards.

"Gavin Baird," he said slowly, "told Rice and Dawley what happened, asked them to take care of it and bring his money back. They took care of it, but claimed they couldn't get the money. Even though they were living high off the hog in those days before Big Jim Colosimo died."

"When was that?"

"May 11, 1920, the end of an era. Those in the know mark that—and not July 1, 1919—as the start of Prohibition in Chicago." He recited that as if he had said it often.

"You think they got the money from Baird," I said.

"I *know* they got the money from Baird through that . . . colored boy what stole it from him. Baird noticed too. He was pretty hungry the fall of 1919, selling off some of his momma's lovely lamps and his daddy's gold cuff links. Then he realized Rice and Dawley was spending the last of his money."

"What did he do?" I asked.

"He threatened to go to the papers. Seems they stored something in his basement."

A surge of excitement ran through me.

"And I think you know what that something is." Twombly met my gaze.

I didn't confirm or deny. "What good would going to the papers do?"

"Big reform movement going on at that point. Mayors got elected on the platform of cleaning up the Levee—that meant the madams, the white slavers, and the dirty cops. It'd shut Rice and Dawley down, having their names in the papers, and it'd probably've shut down a bunch of others as well."

"But he didn't go to the papers," I said.

"They made a deal with him." Twombly finished his meal, sopping up the last of the salt on the side of his plate with the last of the pancakes.

I couldn't swallow the last of my egg sandwich. "What was it?"

"I think you know that too."

"I think I'm paying you to tell me."

He sighed, and looked around. "They got to use his basement to get rid of things that no one should ever see again. For that they paid him regular every month, like rent, for the usage. He wasn't to ask questions, and he wasn't to bump the rent up, though he got the next guys to give him what he called a 'cost of living raise,' and he got them to bump it even more every few years. He didn't die rich, but he lived comfortable."

I was cold. "Rice and Dawley weren't the only cops who used this house?"

Twombly pushed his plate aside. "They died in twenty-five. He died in thirty-eight. You figure it out."

"How'd the others know about it?" I asked.

"Dirt runs in packs," Twombly said. "Rice and Dawley used the place, but they had a trainee, who was the contact with Baird. That way they wouldn't get their hands dirtier than they already were. The trainee lived to twenty-nine, shot by a woman, if you can believe that, and by then he was the Big Palooka and he had his own little trainees. It's like a secret, passed down through generations."

"How did you know about it?" I asked.

He leaned back in the booth. "The stink was something awful by December 1919. They needed someone that could do good, lasting ceiling brickwork."

The egg sandwich rolled in my stomach. I wanted to pick up my twenty and leave the place. But I needed to know.

"You didn't do it forever," I said.

"I had other work. I trained a guy and moved on. It was dumb. I didn't realize the yahoo that bought the house outta probate was amenable to keeping up the basement."

The yahoo was Earl Hathaway.

"By then, how many people knew about this?" I asked, trying not to let my disgust show.

"Rice and Dawley and the trainee was dead. The new guys, they worked it with the others like this: they'd handle a problem someone got himself into for a fee, but they wouldn't tell him what they done with the physical remains of that problem, if you get my meaning."

I nodded, not entirely trusting my voice.

"So there was two of them, the second trainee and his partner. They set up new with the yahoo and the sad sack he hired."

Hanley.

"Those men are still connected with the house?" I asked.

"Nope. Moved on to two new guys long about '49. The trainee's the only one I met. Mean SOB name of . . . Fault? Fold?"

"Faulds?" I felt cold. No wonder the police had cruised the neighborhood. They were keeping an eye on the house.

"That's him. Told me in no uncertain terms he didn't need some old fart down there laying brick. That was after I'd retired, asked for some work. He's a little thick too. Don't think he understood I knew what was going on down there."

"Why didn't you do anything to stop it?" I asked.

His eyebrows rose almost to his hairline. "Ain't you listened to nothing, boy? These're cops we're talking about, and I don't got the cleanest reputation even now. I do what I do, or at least I used to. Not much use for what I know any more. That's why I wrote the book. Promised a few guys I'd only have it in the library, unless they crossed me. Then I'm sending it to some real publisher. Those places in New York, they like shoot-'em-ups about dirty Chicago in Prohibition. I've got some interest."

I actually believed him, and I believed his reasons for not doing it.

I kept my hand on that twenty. "How much are you going to make off me?"

"Telling Faulds some colored boy's found his little hidey-hole?" Twombly shrugged. "Should be worth a hundred or more. You got an extra hundred in there to keep my yap shut?"

I grabbed my wallet and slid out of the booth. Then I slowly and ostentatiously opened the wallet and stuffed the twenty back in it.

"We hadda deal," Twombly said.

"We did," I said. "And this colored boy is proving himself as trustworthy as you are."

"The twenty'll hold me," he said.

"Nothing will hold you," I said. "Get your money from Faulds."

And then I hurried out of the diner. I had to get to the Queen Anne before Twombly reached Faulds on the phone.

FIFTY-TWO

Every city had dumping grounds. The cops used them, the gangs used them, and in some places, organized crime used them. I had known this.

I guess I never figured the cops were still using the Queen Anne because on the South Side they didn't bother hiding the bodies anymore. They left them on the street after shooting them in broad daylight, like they had done with the Soto brothers.

Which explained why business had dropped off at the Queen Anne. As black and Puerto Rican gangs grew in stature and number from the late 1950s on, the police stopped feeling the need to hide the "accidental" deaths of people in custody, and the outright murders of people they didn't want to bring to trial.

And why not? The police knew Chicago's white population wouldn't object.

Even white bodies could be tossed into gangland territory, and the gangs would get blamed, not the police.

The dumping areas had moved aboveground.

And because of that, because my history with Chicago was relatively new, I never once considered the modern police force among my suspects. As collaborators, yes. But not instigators.

Of course, Faulds wrote the report on Hanley, and of course, Faulds listed someone else finding the body. If Faulds hadn't been so detailed in his report, I wouldn't have thought anything was wrong.

Faulds had discovered Hanley. Faulds, who had a key to the building. Faulds, who had probably come in to give Hanley his monthly payoff.

I was nearly at the Queen Anne. I didn't remember most of the drive. I knew I was probably going too fast, but I hoped no cops were watching, not this early on a Sunday.

Because Twombly would find the nearest pay phone—maybe he'd even use the diner's phone—and he'd tell Faulds we were investigating his old dumping ground.

Then he'd tell Faulds that I had shown disgust when I learned Twombly's connection to the Queen Anne, and that I had refused to pay the bribe.

Faulds would know what that meant, just like Twombly had. Faulds would know that he couldn't buy me off. He would come after all of us—me, Minton, and LeDoux. He might even go after Laura, if he thought she knew too much about that house.

I pulled into the neighborhood and saw nothing out of the ordinary— no people on the streets, which I was getting used to around here, no unusual cars parked along the curb. I started to turn into the driveway beside the Queen Anne when I saw the nose end of a squad car.

My chest constricted. He was already here. He must have been on duty and close by, and he'd come.

He'd come.

The squad was too close to the building, the kind of close you got when you were hiding something.

I parked him in, then got out. Halfway to the front of the van, I stopped. The position of that squad car bothered me.

It was too close. It prevented anyone from getting out of the house too fast—they'd have to run past that squad first, or run over it, or squeeze by. It also prevented anyone from getting in too quickly.

Something was happening in there.

Something I hadn't anticipated.

I hurried to the passenger side of my van, unlocked the door, opened it, and took out my gun. I made myself move slowly, made sure the safety was off, made sure the gun was loaded, then grabbed my coveralls and tossed them over my arm, hiding the gun.

I didn't want any neighbors panicking because a black man with a gun was on the streets. I didn't want anyone to call more police.

My breath sounded raspy to my own ears. I made myself walk around the building, checking as I went by to make sure the front door was closed. I didn't see any movement through the stained glass. I doubted Minton and LeDoux had gone back to painting up front.

In fact, I was gambling on that. I hoped they were hiding behind the secret door in the basement, and no one had found them yet. I hoped Faulds was off-duty, and had simply requested a squad to check out what was going on in the house.

I doubted I would be that lucky.

I barely made it around the squad. The radio was on, crackling, words lost to the static. I climbed up the back stairs, breathing shallowly.

The main door was open but the screen was closed. Through it I thought I heard voices, faint as the radio voices. A cry reverberated, then stopped mid-thrum.

A shiver ran down my back. I opened the screen, went in, and then closed it, keeping my hand on it until the latch caught. The last thing I wanted was a thud that might alert people to my presence.

Something banged—slapped—pounded. I couldn't quite identify the sound. I walked along the edge of the floorboards, cursing myself for not paying attention all these weeks to see where the creaks in the floor were.

I guess I never thought I would need it.

The place smelled of fresh paint overlaying that sour odor of death, and there was a new smell—the lingering cigarette odor that trailed a smoker like a cloud.

I opened the basement door, doing it slowly and carefully so that there wouldn't be any excessive noise. I wedged my coveralls against the jamb, preventing the door from closing all the way.

More voices, louder now. Male. I didn't recognize them. Still faint enough that the words were lost.

Then that sound again, and this time I recognized it. The thwack of something solid—a bat, a stick, a piece of wood—against bone.

I drew my gun, elbow tight against my ribs, and eased down the stairs sideways so that my back was to the wall. I didn't want any surprises—didn't want someone to join me from above, didn't want someone to shoot me from the side.

My breathing was still ragged and I struggled to control it. Even my heartbeat sounded too loud.

Another scream, this one bone-joltingly loud. A man's scream, the sound of someone beyond pain, beyond any thought at all. And more thwacks. Half a dozen of them. Then a voice, "Fuck! He passed out."

I had reached the bottom of the stairs. The door to the boiler room stood open. I swept the area, gun ahead of me like a shield, one hand supporting my wrist, the other holding the gun itself. I wanted to run into the back—I knew they were in the back, the sound told me that—but I couldn't.

I had to make sure they hadn't left a guard in the boiler room.

The search seemed to take forever. From the secret room: grunts, closed-mouth cries, someone trying to be tough. And no questions, just that thwacking noise, as if the hitting were more important than anything else.

The rooms checked out. No one had been inside. Even my bag of evidence remained on its table, untouched, as if it interested no one.

The boiler room was my next challenge. I had to get past that god-awful machine to the cabinet and into the back before the cops knew I was there.

My plan ended at that: I didn't know what I would do when I got inside.

Surprise was all I had.

I hoped it would be all I needed.

Going around the boiler was no problem. Getting my bulk through the cabinet quietly was the issue. I reached the area near the secret door, was relieved to see that someone—in a fury?—had yanked the cabinet aside.

The secret door was revealed in all its depravity, a narrow opening carved out of a wall.

A thwack, the sickening crunch of breaking bone, a whimpering cry filled with shame.

I swallowed, my breathing finally under control. I made sure my grip on my gun was firm, my body as calm as it could be, my mind clear.

I stepped into that doorway, saw four men, two sitting on chairs that hadn't been there this morning, one body leaning over, held in place by ropes only, blood dripping on the floor. Someone standing behind him, and someone—Minton!—in the middle on another chair.

A man, standing, took a swing at Minton's head with a nightstick, and as he followed through, like a baseball player happy to connect with the game-winning homer, he saw me and shouted.

His partner whirled, gun already in hand, and fired, the sound an explosion in the tiny space. The bullet pinged the brick above me, sending mortar and chunks at me—tiny bits of shrapnel, shredding my skin, narrowly missing my eye.

I fired at the shooter—another explosion—then at his partner, who had dropped the nightstick for a gun. Clouds of mortar dust and smoke from my weapon's discharge rose around me, but I fired in the same two places again, hoping I hit the cops.

Hoping I hadn't hit Minton or LeDoux.

Wondering if LeDoux was even alive.

The shots reverberated in my ears, but nothing pinged around me. No more shrapnel. No movement. Nothing.

My breathing echoed in my own head, too loud, the only sound I could hear except the memory of those shots. The air smelled like gunpowder. Then sulfur, then blood.

My eyes teared, cleaning out the smoke and the dust. I stepped closer, knowing I could die doing that, knowing that I would already be dead if those cops could shoot me again.

Shapes rose in the dust-filled half-light from those bulbs we'd put in a week ago. LeDoux, still hunched in his chair, his torso held in place with ropes—dead? Unconscious?

Fuck! someone had said. *He passed out.*

A body on the floor beside him, face gone. Another body in front of Minton, still moving, clutching at a blood-covered chest, gun at his side. Not going to shoot, not yet, anyway.

Minton's left cheekbone had caved in, but his jaw was so swollen that it looked like he'd swallowed that baseball. He said, "Untie me," and I didn't understand his words so much as divine them.

My ears weren't working because of the noise.

I doubted his were either.

I shoved the gun away from the man still clutching at what remained of his chest, hoping that son of a bitch would die soon, because I didn't know what I would do with him if he lived. My whole life would get real complicated then, and I couldn't handle complicated, not at the moment, not when blood was dripping into my own eyes, and I was shaking from adrenaline, and I needed to see if LeDoux was bleeding to death.

I looked at the other guy as I crouched behind Minton's chair. I'd been right: no face. Not breathing.

I'd killed him, but with the first shot or the second, I couldn't tell.

I didn't really care.

It took three tries to wrap my shaking fingers around the ropes that these cops had used to tie Minton in place. Two more tries to get the knot loosened.

Finally it all came apart, the ropes falling away like unraveling fabric. Minton leaned forward—how painful that must have been, all the blood rushing to his battered face—and untied his own ankles.

Then he came up, the second cop's gun in hand.

Before I could stop him, he shot the clutcher in the face—once, twice, three times—then kicked him, and burst into tears, his entire body shaking.

My ears were numb. I hadn't really heard those last three shots: I'd felt them. The room had shaken. I thanked whatever god was listening that we were in a brick-enclosed basement.

Even though it sounded like bombs going off to me, to the neighbors those shots had probably sounded like faraway car backfires, if they'd sounded like anything at all.

I took the gun from Minton, emptied the clip, stuck it in my pants. Put the safety on my own gun and headed to LeDoux, who seemed impossibly far away.

His mouth was bleeding. He was missing teeth along the top. The right side of his face was covered with large, purple blood-blisters—he hadn't been hit as hard as Minton, but he'd been hit hard enough.

He was breathing, though. In and out. In. Out.

I touched my own face, pulled out three chips of brick the size of fingernail clippings—all chunked just north of my eye—and understood the blood. I wasn't badly hurt. The shaking and unsettled feeling, the disorientation—that was all from the adrenaline, just like I thought.

For the moment I left LeDoux tied. I didn't want to lay him out on the floor next to two bodies. Chicago cops. Chicago cops who'd been the active guardians of this morgue for twenty years.

"Is there more?" Minton asked, and I heard him, faint and reedy, like a radio on a hot summer night playing several houses over.

"Don't think so," I said.

"This is the guy from yesterday." He kicked the body again. The cop might also have been the one I'd seen drive by. I would never be able to say for certain. "They got here about an hour after you left, wanting to know who else knew about this place."

"Tortured you for the information," I said.

"Not at first. At first they just waved their guns. LeDoux told them to leave, told them they didn't belong. They'd've gone after me first, but he made them mad. He's a good man, Bill."

I nodded. "We have to get him to a hospital."

"What do we do with these guys?" Minton asked.

"I'll take care of it," I said.

He looked at me. "You'll need my help."

I shook my head. "The less you know, the better."

"I shot the motherfucker. I'm not talking to anyone."

"I know," I said. "I just don't want anyone finding them either."

Minton and I looked at each other as the implications of what I'd just said reached both of us. Guaranteed, the men who'd entombed everyone here—the men over all those decades who, for some reason, had murdered civilians and lost them down here—had said those same words.

I just don't want anyone finding them.

I shivered, and got down to work.

FIFTY-THREE

First, I had to take care of Minton and LeDoux. They both needed medical attention, but Minton convinced me he was well enough to drive.

So I gave him the keys to the van. We carried LeDoux out to it, not caring what the neighbors thought, even though I knew they were probably panicked over two black guys limping a clearly unconscious and beaten-up white guy to the side of the van.

We laid him in back, and I told Minton to get the hell out of there before he passed out.

He wouldn't. Not until he helped me with the two cops.

The first cop was Faulds. I knew that. But I had to look up the other man's name. I couldn't leave someone I'd killed—even if it was in self-defense—a nameless corpse in my memory.

His driver's license identified him as Kirk Strom. He was in his late forties, and fortunately there were no photographs of children or a pretty wife in his wallet.

He had the keys to the cop car in his pocket.

Minton and I wrapped him in one of the painter's tarps. We did the same to Faulds.

"We're never going to be able to clean this up," Minton said to me as we stood back. I could barely understand him, the way he mashed the words against his damaged mouth. "LeDoux comes back here, he'll know it's a fucking crime scene. He'll know exactly what we did."

"You're not cleaning this up," I said. "I am. You've got to get him to a hospital. You don't know whether he's bleeding inside. You don't know if you are."

That got him. He insisted on helping me carry, but I told him no farther than the top of the stairs. We left the tarp-covered bodies on the floor outside Hanley's apartment.

Then I walked Minton to the van. It had started to rain—a cold, heavy rain, the kind that made it clear snow was coming, and coming soon. My fingers ached with the sudden chill, and I realized I had to get one more thing.

As Minton adjusted the driver's seat, I reached inside the glove box one final time and removed my leather gloves. I slapped them against my hand, then nodded to Minton.

"I'll meet you at the hospital."

"How'll you get there?" he asked.

"I just will. You wait there with LeDoux. Make sure you get checked."

Minton nodded. He was looking gray. The adrenaline that had been keeping him upright was wearing thin.

I looked at LeDoux—still breathing, still unconscious—and then closed the passenger door. Minton shoved the van into gear so hard the entire vehicle shook.

Then he drove off, leaving me there with two dead cops and one police car.

My stomach turned. The rain had become a downpour, gluing my clothes to my body, but clearing the blood away from my eyes. I ran back to the cop car.

I hadn't even tested the keys. I hoped they worked.

The door was unlocked. The keys went into the ignition and the car started, a welcome sound. I set my gloves on the floor, then shut off the car and went around back.

I opened the trunk. Inside was a spare, a tire iron, blankets, candy bars, and a jug of water—a blizzard kit. I left the lid open, and realized just how well these men had parked.

Unless someone was standing right next to the house, no one would be able to see what I was doing.

Then I went inside, grabbed the first tarp-covered body, and dragged. The tarp was already turning black with blood. A stain smeared itself along the floor—something I would have to clean up.

The body thumped halfway down the back-porch stairs. Then I stopped and levered the head and shoulders into the trunk. I grabbed the legs, twisted the body, and tossed it in.

I did the same with the second body.

Then I closed the trunk and leaned on it for a moment. I had to get rid of them somehow.

I knew the right place would come to me. I just hoped it would come to me fast enough.

I went back inside. I cleaned the back area and the stairs, using bleach I found in the laundry room. I moved the cabinet back in place, cleaned out the boiler room, and, after I scrubbed them, carried the blood-stained chairs to a long-emptied storage locker.

I didn't clean up the floor in the secret room. There was so much blood spatter that I wouldn't be able to get rid of all of it. I wasn't even going to try.

Instead, I grabbed the nightsticks and the police caps, and carried them to the police car. At the last minute, I decided not to put them in the trunk. I set them on the floor alongside my gloves.

Then, God help me, I learned what that horrible fourth-floor bathroom was for. I almost washed my face and hands in Hanley's bathroom—figuring after the afternoon I'd had, I could deal with the stink—then I remembered the supplies on the top floor.

Phisohex, butterfly bandages, cotton balls.

How many cops had used this bathroom to clean up after a fight? How many times had Hanley used it after he robbed the bodies the cops had placed in the basement? How many times had he scrubbed his hands here after adding to his grotesque collection?

I went up there with a flashlight, since I had a hunch I still didn't want to see the condition that room was in, washed my face, my hands, and used hydrogen peroxide to clean out my cuts.

The stuff stung, so I knew it was working. I pulled the cuts tight, used small butterfly bandages to hold them in place, and prayed I wouldn't need stitches again. If I did, that would be the third time in less than a year.

Which, I knew, was the least of my problems.

I swiped the bottom of my shoes with bleach, tried to see if there was more blood on my rain-soaked clothes but couldn't, and almost put on the painter's coveralls until I remembered that the white would show neon on an overcast day.

After I finished in the bathroom, I went back down, tossed the coveralls down the stairs, shut everything, locked it with Strom's keys—son of a bitch, he *was* the other one—and took a deep breath.

Now for the tough part.

The part that could get me life in prison.

The part that could get me killed.

I left the Queen Anne, went down the back stairs, got into the cop car, and grabbed one of the police hats, placing it on my head like it belonged there. Then I slipped on my gloves, put the car in gear, and drove away, hoping I looked one whole hell of a lot more confident than I felt.

FIFTY-FOUR

Alone in a cop car. A dead man's hat on my head, a bloody night-stick on the seat, bodies in the trunk. Driving through neighborhood after neighborhood on a Sunday afternoon, through quiet streets, rain falling lightly, face after face staring through their windows at the slow-moving cop car, wondering at the black cop going through their neighborhood.

At first I was okay, as okay as I could be. Once I was outside the University of Chicago area—the Kenwood-Hyde Park neighborhoods—I drove through black communities. Poor ones, where the police presence was frightening, even with a black officer—old neighborhoods, where Minnie Pruitt said she had lain on a roof and shot at cops fifty years ago.

Then middle-class black neighborhoods, then the neighborhoods in transition, Sinkovich's neighborhood, where last year the white families wanted to burn out the encroaching blacks. He'd stopped that.

He'd stopped it, lost his wife in the process because she didn't know him anymore. He didn't share her values.

There were some good cops.

Who wanted to quit.

I gripped the wheel tightly. The radio spit at me, asking questions, using codes I didn't entirely understand.

I finally knew where I was heading: a half-built canal near 120th. I'd actually inspected it. Now that the Army Corps of Engineers was done dredging, Sturdy would help with the construction—the outbuildings, the walls, the locks themselves. Laura had had me inspect the work in August, even though I told her I knew nothing about canals.

She wanted to make sure there was nothing shady going on.

I didn't find anything, but that didn't mean there wasn't. Unlike buildings, with canals I didn't know what to look for.

Another cop car pulled up behind me at a stoplight. I sat through the red, looked at my rearview mirror, made a little "hello" signal with my right forefinger. The cop behind me—white, also alone—made the same gesture in return.

He didn't get out of his car. He didn't follow me. He turned west and disappeared into traffic.

My heart was pounding so hard I thought it would never recover.

I saw the lights of the Ford Plant first, stretching over several city blocks, a small city in itself. I went around it, hoping no one noticed a police car this late on a Sunday afternoon, grateful for the rain that kept everything in a gray twilight, even though proper twilight wasn't for another hour or more.

Then I turned left, and left again, finding myself on the narrow road that took me into trees, made it feel like I was in a forest instead of a city.

Just like I remembered. Only no one here to greet me, no one to hand me a yellow hardhat, remind me I was in a construction area, and tell me where to stand.

I was alone—although I scanned my mirrors to make sure.

Nothing.

No one.

Just me.

I parked along the dirt access road, then shut off my headlights. I'd been following all the rules of the road—including the one which required lights on during a gray, rainy day—just because I didn't want anyone noticing the police car that sped south late on October nineteenth.

It was dark here—nighttime dark. The rain stopped suddenly, but the trees around me continued to drip, the sound as irregular as footsteps.

A few blocks away, the Ford Motor Plant rumbled and clanged. The noise had to be loud there if I could hear it through my still-clogged ears. The air smelled of rotten eggs and sewage; the stink was so thick it made my eyes water.

For five long minutes I sat in the car, staring out the windows, checking the rearview mirror, hoping no one had followed me here. That feeling that I'd had all month, the feeling of being watched, hadn't left me. But now I assumed it was because I felt like a giant target, with a blazing neon arrow pointing to the trunk.

When I could wait no longer, I took off the hat and tossed it onto the floor, rubbing my hands through my hair to get the feeling of someone else's sweat from my skin. Slid the gloves on. Picked up my gun, made sure the safety was on, then shoved it through my belt and covered it with my shirt.

Finally I got out, closing the door carefully so that no one could hear it slam. I could see my breath. My head ached, and blood trickled down the side of my face. One of the wounds hadn't closed.

More stitches after all.

I swiped at it with my arm, staining the sleeve of my coat.

I walked down the dirt road to the construction site. The rain had made the dirt soft, masking my footsteps. Only the rustle of my clothing and the harshness of my breathing seemed out of place. Spindly trees rose up around me, their leaves scattered on the road.

Equipment sat along the edge of the canal, ghostly shapes against the darkness. I stopped short of the edge.

They had finished dredging this section, I recalled, because someone had deemed the canal deep enough.

I hoped that unnamed someone was right.

The water glinted, black and filthy, its depth impossible to see in the darkness. Some lights from the nearby industrial plants echoed thinly on the water's surface, revealing a gasoline slick and bits of wadded-up paper.

I let out a small breath, hating this moment, seeing no other choice.

This was my dumping ground.

I hoped I would only have to use it once.

I went back to the cop car and pushed on the trunk, making sure the latch held. Then I opened the back passenger door and rolled down the window. I did the same with the front passenger window. I saved the driver's window for last.

I crawled back inside the car just as the radio crackled, startling me. The thin voice coming across the static talked about a fight at the Kinetic Playground—a concert venue for modern bands, this weekend it was supposed to be—the Who? Led Zeppelin? I couldn't remember with all the strange names.

Not that it mattered to me. I was as far as a man could get from the Kinetic Playground and still be in Chicago.

I started the car. It rumbled to life, the powerful engine ready to go. I was shaking.

I kept the car in park, then I pushed the emergency brake. I reached across the seat and picked up the bloody nightstick.

I released the emergency brake, got out of the car, and leaned inside the door. Carefully, I wedged the nightstick against the accelerator, making sure that thing flattened against the floor.

The car's engine revved, sounding even louder in that grove of too-thin trees.

I prayed no one heard it.

I braced my left hand on the car seat, grabbed the automatic gearshift, and shoved the car into drive. Then I leapt back—I was knocked back, really—sprawling in the cold, wet dirt as the car zoomed down the road.

I pushed myself up, my fingers slipping in the mud. The car disappeared over the bank and I braced myself for a crash of metal against concrete—a crash that meant I had failed.

Instead, I heard a large splash. I ran to the edge of the road and stared down the embankment.

The car tipped, front end already lost to the canal. The brackish water flowed into the open windows, sinking it even faster.

The trunk went under last, disappearing in a riot of bubbles. I could almost imagine it popping open at the last moment, Faulds and Strom bobbing to the surface like a bad dream, revealing themselves much too soon.

But the bubbles eventually stopped, and the car vanished into the canal's depths. I tossed the gloves in after it.

If I couldn't see the car, I doubted anyone else would be able to either, even in broad daylight. The water in the Calumet industrial region was the filthiest in all of Chicago, which was saying something.

The cop car and its secrets would remain hidden.

Now I had to.

Somehow I had to get out of there—and I had to do it quickly, without getting caught.

FIFTY-FIVE

This was the part I hadn't thought through: the walk. More than seventy blocks on a rainy fall evening. Alone, through good neighborhoods and hostile.

I walked due north because that took me through the best neighborhoods, the safest neighborhoods. The riskiest section was near the Ford Plant. What would someone think of a black man walking alone here, away from the houses, away from stores, away from everything but the secrets of next year's model cars?

But no one bothered me. No one even noticed me. The darkness, which came on fast and made me realize I had been near the canal longer than I thought, hid me better than I could have planned.

My trouble came near a strip mall just south of Avalon Park. A car filled with white teenagers started to follow me, all of them shouting at me in broad Chicago accents, calling me names.

My fingers itched to go to the gun. I was still raw, still ready to defend myself, and I knew that revealing that gun was the worst thing I could do.

So I bowed my head like a defeated, overworked family man and kept going, ignoring the taunts and hoping the situation wouldn't get worse.

It didn't. The boys got bored. The car veered off and I was alone again, just as the rain returned.

I walked the remaining few miles in a downpour, heading to my apartment instead of the hospital. I couldn't show up looking like this, especially with the gun. Someone would notice. I was already exhausted. I would make a mistake.

It wasn't until I turned onto my own block that I remembered Jimmy. I was supposed to pick him up around five. It was much later than that and I hadn't even called.

A lump formed in my throat. I hoped that Faulds and Strom hadn't thought of going after families and friends like Rice and Dawley had. I hadn't even thought to check.

My keys were on the van's ring. When I got inside, I had to knock on Marvella's door and ask her for the spare I had given her for moments just like this.

She started to ask what happened, but caught something on my face.

"Can you give me a ride to the hospital in about fifteen minutes?" I asked.

"Car accident?" she asked. I must have looked worse than I thought.

I shook my head. "Loaned my van to a friend trying to save someone who got beaten up. I promised him I'd meet him there."

"What'd you do, finish the fight?" she asked.

"Yeah," I said, and went inside my own apartment.

I closed the door, leaned on it, and let out a small sigh. I took off my ruined shoes and my wet clothes, leaving them in a pile on the entry rug. When I was about to leave, I'd bag them and toss them into the trash.

Then I went to the phone and called the Grimshaws.

Althea answered. "You're late," she said, without even waiting to see who was calling.

"I know," I said. "Some trouble at my job. Can Jimmy stay the night?"

"Can you bring him clothes?"

"No," I said. "Let him borrow Keith's."

"Smokey, this's got to stop," she said.

"I agree," I said, and hung up. I stood there a moment, feeling every bruise, every ache.

Then I took a long, hot shower, wishing I could wash the memories of the entire day away as easily as I washed away the dirt and the blood.

FIFTY-SIX

What followed was the longest month of my life.

Laura met me at the hospital—apparently Marvella had called her (I wasn't sure if I liked them being friends)—and immediately took charge. LeDoux had a concussion, several broken ribs, a dislocated shoulder, and a cracked elbow. The blow to the head had knocked him out—a mercy, the doctors said, given the pain.

When I arrived, Minton was already in surgery. They were trying to repair his cheekbone—they were afraid the bone fragments would damage his eye.

Otherwise his injuries were superficial. Apparently I had arrived in time to prevent him from suffering the way LeDoux had.

Figuring our cover was already broken, Laura had hired security guards for the Queen Anne, forbidden them from going inside. She also called Cronk. She told him she knew what he'd been hiding. She told him that his secretary had left memos, implicating him in all of it. Then Laura told Cronk if he took her on, she'd destroy him.

Apparently he believed her.

I talked with Minton, and we decided we could handle the remaining work—there was no way, after finding out who ran the dumping ground, that we were going to bring any of this to trial any time soon.

We told LeDoux we had enough from him for a dozen trials and, when he was well enough, sent him home. Laura paid all his medical expenses and then some, because she felt so very guilty. He was relieved he didn't have to go back there, and so was I. We never did clean up that crime scene.

But we cleared it. Minton and I, with guards outside. We took body after body out of that basement, some skeletal, some still decaying, many as old as the first three, with just as little identification. The newer ones mostly had purses or wallets, although the identification wasn't always readable. After the late 1940s, the wallets and purses held no cash either.

Hanley again. The bastard stripped the corpses of any real worth they had.

During November, at least, my job was to clear that basement. Once we were done with that, we would be notifying relatives—and identifying the dead—for months to come.

My greatest fear was that Faulds and Strom weren't working alone—that their team included at least one more police member. I asked Sinkovich to check if Faulds and Strom were partners, and if they were ever seen in the company of someone else.

He did, and said they weren't—they never trusted anyone else—and added: odd thing, no one had seen them in days.

I told him that was why I needed him on the police force, to look these things up for me and ask no questions.

"Is that your decision?" he asked.

"Right now, yeah," I said. "Things are too complicated to make such a large change. But maybe in a few months we can talk about it again."

I hoped he would forget it, but doubted he would.

Still, even knowing that Faulds and Strom trusted no one else didn't make the work easier. Laura kept the guards on the house, but no other police showed up.

Twombly did, once, looking for money, but I made sure I was nowhere near him. The guards handled him, and that relieved me. It meant he had no one else to report to, no one else to offer our information as a payout.

Laura gave Kaztauskis a generous early retirement. She bitched about it throughout the entire process, and finally, at my suggestion, had Drew draw up an agreement. Kaztauskis would get to keep his pension, plus the bonuses she added, only if he agreed never to talk about Sturdy or any connected business ever again.

That shut him up for good. Laura stopped bitching and we tried to move on.

The world continued its insanity: Black Panther Bobby Seale insisted on his constitutional right to a lawyer of his own choosing, and because he kept interrupting court business, asking for something most folks took for granted, Judge Hoffman had Seale bound and gagged during each session.

Finally Hoffman decided that was too big a disruption, and severed Seale's trial from the others. The Chicago Eight became the Chicago Seven, and every white person in the area seemed to breathe a sigh of relief. No one seemed to notice that Seale was shipped off to New Haven to stand trial on federal charges for a murder he couldn't have committed, since he wasn't in town when it occurred.

The Weathermen, feeling persecuted, went underground. The local Panthers, who *were* persecuted, remained aboveground and suffered yet another raid to their offices.

The fighting in Vietnam continued, unabated. The Strategic Arms Limitation Talks got under way between the U.S. and the U.S.S.R, presumably to make the world safer, although I doubted it. Apollo 12 landed on the moon and the entire nation acted like it was an old hat already, only a few months after the first time.

Thanksgiving seemed outrageously late, even though it fell on the final Thursday, like it always did. That day I had a quiet dinner at my apartment with Laura and Jimmy. After he went to bed, she snuggled in my arms for the first time in months. She told me she'd been doing some thinking about things I used to say back when we first met.

"Like what?" I asked.

"A family has many different meanings," she said. "It's not just blood relatives. When you first said that, I thought you said that for Jim."

"I said it because it's true. The people who've loved me the longest have no blood ties to me at all, yet they're my parents in all the ways that count."

"I know," she said, and burrowed in closer. "I realized, in my pouty last few months, there are only two people who matter to me. You and Jim."

"Laura—"

She put a finger over my lips, stopping me. "We have a non-

traditional relationship. I don't want to be traditional. Do you understand that?"

I did. It solved a lot. It left a lot open, but it solved a lot.

And the rift between us closed—at least for a little while.

FIFTY-SEVEN

And now it's December, December seventh, to be exact—a day that shall live in infamy, Franklin Delano Roosevelt said twenty-eight years ago. That infamy was long gone, defeated, but new infamies have arisen, and I stand in line at one of them, trying not to freeze to death in the mid-morning cold.

Althea is angry at me: I've brought the oldest four children here instead of taking them to church. Jimmy stands beside me. Lacey is subdued for the first time in months. Jonathan shifts from foot to foot, his hands shoved in his pockets, and Keith leans against me, frightened by this strange new world.

We're on the 2300 block of West Monroe, only one street up from the Black Panther offices. We're in a line that stretches down this block, around the corner, back to West Madison, and down it as far as the eye can see.

About five houses away from me, Bobby Rush stands on the front porch of 2337 West Monroe, a blue building that I hadn't even noticed last year when I was inspecting some houses on this block. Bobby Rush is now the Illinois Black Panther Party Chairman, because on Thursday morning, December fourth, the police murdered Fred Hampton in his sleep.

The police have lied about it. Their story is what their story is. They raided his home at five in the morning, they say, because they heard he was storing weapons there. Hampton and his cohorts returned fire, and the police, in self-defense, fired back. Hampton and another Panther, Mark Clark, died. Four others were injured.

The surviving Panthers say the police showed up while everyone was asleep and came in shooting.

The Panthers have the evidence to back their claim up.

I've seen the evidence; it's grisly. The police failed to close off the crime scene, so the Panthers are giving tours of it. I went through the apartment yesterday.

Today I came back—this time with Jimmy, Jonathan, Lacey, and Keith. I wouldn't have brought them if it weren't for Tim Minton.

"They have to go, man," he said to me, with that lisp he's developed while his cheekbone is healing. "They have to know what they're up against."

"I'd like to see that they don't," I said.

But he was right. I knew that he was right.

So I'm taking two eleven-year-olds, a thirteen-year-old, and a fifteen-year-old on the tour of a massacre site. They'll walk in the front door and see hundreds of bullet holes. They'll go into the second bedroom—the one where Fred Hampton slept through the entire gun battle—and will see a mattress so blood-stained that even an untrained eye knows that the person who bled like that could not have lived.

His girlfriend did. She had been in bed with him, nine-months pregnant, so convinced she was going to die that she clung to him, and somehow the bullets missed her.

The police dragged her out of the room, and then someone said, "He's still breathing," and she heard two more shots.

Fred Hampton isn't breathing any longer.

I want to pull him aside. I want to take him back into my apartment on that day in October and explain to him the folly of what he was doing. It was custeristic, I said to him then, using his word, meaning: you're going to die.

And Hampton, barely twenty-one, didn't believe me. He didn't have the premonition of his own death the way Martin had. He didn't have the certainty, even though he knew it was a possibility.

The Panthers are saying he was drugged. His girlfriend says he fell asleep in the middle of a conversation with his mother the night before.

With his mother.

Such a dangerous revolutionary that he fell asleep talking to his mother, the mother of his own child beside him.

And I have a wager on who drugged him. That bodyguard he brought with him when he visited me. The only person who could have could tipped off the FBI to our meeting. O'Neal. He'd been in the apartment that night. He'd given Hampton a glass of Kool-Aid.

The police don't need dumping grounds anymore.

They're murdering children in their sleep.

And I'm taking my children through this death house. Because it's the only thing we can do. We have to bear witness.

For the past month I've taken bodies of people who died without witnesses, without anyone to acknowledge their murders, the injustice, the horrors. I still can't prosecute, but I can bring them back to their families.

Fourteen years ago, Emmett Till's mother opened her son's funeral to the public. She left the coffin lid up, showing how her beautiful boy's face had been destroyed, his eye nearly falling out of his head, his features unrecognizable—so badly beaten, so badly *tortured*, that the undertaker couldn't repair him.

I'm not even sure he tried.

That act of courage made Rosa Parks remain in her seat on a city bus only a short time later. Made Martin Luther King support the Montgomery Bus Boycott. The death of Emmett Till—and the witness people bore to it, seeing what had been done—was the beginning of the end of the Old South.

I've told Jimmy and Jonathan and Keith and Lacey that. I've told them that this, the death of a man with so much potential, a man who could've led us like Martin did if he'd only found his way, might have the same effect.

If they look at what's been done to him because he stood up for us.

If they look and understand.

If they remember.

And if they don't ever let it happen again.